HAVE NO DOUBT

Pushing our plates aside, Jackson and I clasped hands across the table.

"That's the beauty of the way I feel about you," I told him, my voice low. "I know you're imperfect, and I love you anyway. It's taken me ten years to build up the courage to tell you. So please believe me when I tell you I love you."

Jackson brought one of my hands up and gently ran the palm of it over his cheek, then he met my gaze. "And I love you, Cheyenne. I love you the way a man should love a woman; with every fiber of my being, I love you. I believe I've been in love with you since you were eighteen. But I never would have said anything. Never. That's just the way I am. When you told me you wanted me that day in the cemetery, I was in shock. Sure, we flirted outrageously. But that was harmless. When we kissed . . . I tried to stop it, but apparently some part of me wanted it more than anything else I've ever wanted before. So, you believe me when I tell *you:* I love you. I love you so much that I refuse to allow you to settle for a broken-down rancher when you can have anyone else in the world you desire."

He released my hands then and gave me a stern look. "Now eat your dinner."

I picked up my fork and started eating. However, I was so excited by his declaration of love, that I could barely swallow.

BOOK YOUR PLACE ON OUR WEBSITE AND MAKE THE ARABESQUE ROMANCE CONNECTION!

We've created a customized website just for our very special Arabesque readers, where you can get the inside scoop on everything that's going on with Arabesque romance novels.

When you come online, you'll have the exciting opportunity to:

- View covers of upcoming books

- Learn about our future publishing schedule (listed by publication month and author)

- Find out when your favorite authors will be visiting a city near you

- Search for and order backlist books

- Check out author bios and background information

- Send e-mail to your favorite authors

- Join us in weekly chats with authors, readers and other guests

- Get writing guidelines

- AND MUCH MORE!

Visit our website at
http://www.arabesquebooks.com

FOR KEEPS

JANICE SIMS

ARABESQUE
BET
BOOKS

BET Publications, LLC
www.msbet.com
www.arabesquebooks.com

ARABESQUE BOOKS are published by

BET Publications, LLC
C/o BET BOOKS
One BET Plaza
1900 W Place NE
Washington, D.C. 20018-1211

First Printing: September, 1999
10 9 8 7 6 5 4 3 2 1

Printed in the United States of America

"Today in America, black-owned farms are disappearing at three times the rate of farms generally. This has meant the loss not just of economic opportunity but a rich heritage, since, oftentimes, this land passed through several generations of a family dating back to Reconstruction."

—*U.S. Agriculture Secretary, Dan Glickman,*
at the NAACP convention, 1998

This book is for my husband, Curtis. For his inspiration, his dedication to our family and his unfailing adoration of yours truly. You're the reason why I revel in romance.

On you,
I could compose
the definitive how-to

How to make you smile
when you're sad
How to quell the anger in you
when you're Mr. Bad

I know the lines and planes
of your face
The way your muscles, beneath
dark, rich skin ripple with grace

The timbre of your voice
is music to my ears
And your hands on my body
banishes worrisome fears

The words, "I love you"
fail miserably
in the attempt to describe
the power you'll impart to me

When you finally recognize
the size, the scope
Of this thing living
between my breasts called . . .

hope

—The Book of Counted Joys

ONE

In 1875, my great-great-grandmother, Josie, then twenty, an ex-slave, was among a group of settlers seeking their fortunes in Kansas. What they found was poverty, prejudice and starvation.

Josie, an enterprising young woman, who, in slavery, had been sold away from the plantation of her birth at the age of ten, and hence from the only family she knew, recognized opportunity when she saw it.

In her case, opportunity came in the form of one, Jacob Roberts, a freed slave twice her age who was a mountain man of some renown. Jacob had been married before, but lost his wife to cholera. Passing through Kansas on the way to Wyoming, he'd heard of the influx of blacks and went looking for a young wife who would bear him strong children.

Josie was a healthy, strapping lass and had a face like an angel's. She suited Jacob fine. Jacob was equally robust, and by the time they reached Wyoming, Josie was heavy with child. She gave birth to a healthy boy in the middle of winter, and by summer, she was expecting again.

However, something happened after the birth of their second son, because Josie didn't bear Jacob another son for five years.

My grandfather Riley says this is what happened: Josie went to Jacob and said, "I've given you two sons; now, you give me something. A woman without a man to protect her is defenseless in this land. I want you to teach me everything you know about surviving out here. After that, I'll give you more sons."

Apparently, Jacob saw the wisdom in Josie's proposal because legend has it, Josie became as adept at riding, shooting, trapping game and surviving the harsh Wyoming winters as her husband had been.

Which was fortuitous, as it turned out, because shortly after the birth of their sixth child, a daughter, Cheyenne, Jacob was mauled by a bear. Josie wound up rearing the children on her own.

In the spring of 1889, Josie was the owner of one of the few way stations in northern Wyoming. That particular year, Josie and her family entertained an inordinate amount of trappers and the topic of conversation was gold. Someone had discovered gold in Montana.

Josie, always looking for a way to put food on the table for her children, packed several mules, put her small children in a wagon with provisions, then she and her older sons mounted their horses and she pointed the way north.

Josie figured that if her own gold-mining efforts didn't pan out, then she could always play hostess to the danged fools who kept coming to Montana with gold dust in their eyes.

Josie and her sons were highly successful at their gold-mining endeavors. They found enough of the shiny mineral to purchase five hundred acres of land. Texans had started bringing in long-horns from the southern state and Josie invested in thirty head.

By the time she died at age eighty-seven, the Roberts ranch was the most successful spread in southern Montana.

Josie Roberts was who I thought of whenever I was depressed.

And I was depressed as the 727 I was a passenger on left Chicago's O'Hare International Airport that morning in September.

I was flying into Billings, Montana, and then driving on to my hometown of Custer, because my grandfather Riley, the last surviving grandchild of Josie Roberts, was dying.

I was not unfamiliar with death. Seven years earlier, I'd been the first to get to my father, Cole, after he'd been thrown from his horse and trampled by cattle while on a drive into Wyoming. He died with his head in my lap and my tears on his face. I'll never forget the dread I felt at having to return my father's battered body to my mother. But my brother Chad, who was barely fourteen at the time, and I made the journey on horseback to do just that.

Now, even as I recalled the violence of my father's death, I knew he'd died doing what he loved and he would've preferred that death to a lingering one in a hospital, with tubes protruding from every orifice of his body. He was born a cowboy, and he'd died one.

The same was true of Riley, or Slim, as we call him.

Shortly after Daddy was killed, Slim made me promise that if he were ever laid up with machines maintaining his bodily functions, that I should pull the plug.

"Don't discuss it with anyone," he'd said at the time. "Just come visit me alone, say the Lord's prayer over me, and give it a good yank."

I'd stared at him as if he'd taken leave of his senses.

"I don't think I have it in me to be able to do that, Slim," I'd told him, actually sorry to disappoint him.

"You're a Roberts, ain't ya?" he'd gruffly replied. "Grandma Josie had to put Jacob out of his misery. Do you think she hesitated for one moment?"

That was a perfect example of Riley Roberts's reasoning. He figured that family was not only responsible for one another's lives, but equally responsible for putting one another out of pain and misery. It would've been a waste of my breath to explain to him that euthanasia was against the law in the state of Montana. In Slim's mind, the law was null and void when it came to personal, family concerns. Family first, the law second.

So there I was, tying to relax in coach class while I wondered if Slim had summoned me home just to be certain that, should the need arise, I'd be on hand to pull the plug.

"Cheyenne, over here!" my little sister's voice rang out across the terminal.

I turned in the direction of that strident sound, and smiled.

Clancy looked like a clone of me at that age. Slender, all legs and an attempt at the latest hairstyle framing her heart-shaped, chocolate-brown face.

I was sure, though, that I didn't have her curves at seventeen. She bounced as she walked.

My eyes searched the area around her. Had she come alone? Nearly sixty miles from Custer, and Momma had allowed her to come alone?

I dropped my bags and we hugged fiercely.

I placed a kiss on her cheek. "You're wearing Momma's perfume."

She laughed and bent to pick up one of the bags. "And you're wearing the ever-popular soap-and-water fragrance. But, I must admit, it works for you."

I swatted her behind through her navy pea coat. "Don't get sassy with me. I'm still ten years older than you. Who came with you?"

Clancy gave me an amused look with her big, brown eyes. "I'm legal. I've got my driver's license."

I stopped in my tracks and stared down at her. "Things must be pretty busy at the ranch if they couldn't spare anyone to come with you."

"No," Clancy insisted, pulling on the cuff of my faux-fur-lined jacket to hurry me up. "Everything's fine, Sis."

"Slim?"

"He has a case of the sniffles, but otherwise, he's the same cantankerous old coot."

"What?!"

We continued walking toward the exit. "He told me he was failing fast. I'm glad to know he isn't on his deathbed as he said he was, but wait until I get my hands on him!"

"Two hours ago, he was reading Uter Morrison the riot act over the phone," Clancy calmly informed me.

Uter Morrison was president of Custer National Bank. It didn't surprise me to learn Slim had been in an altercation with Mr. Morrison; there wasn't a rancher in the area who hadn't made Mr. Morrison's ears nearly bleed from the cutting words they used at one time or another.

The temperature outside felt like it was in the lower fifties, so

I removed my jacket. It was a warm day for September in Montana.

"I think he wanted you home because they're talking about taking the ranch," Clancy said as she pulled on her sunglasses and transferred the suitcase from her left hand to her right.

"Who's talking about taking the ranch, and why?"

"The bank. Because we're six months behind in the mortgage payments."

"Six months? The nearly thirty-six hundred acres is worth more than a million. They're not taking the ranch. And why didn't you pay the mortgage out of the bonds if you were low on funds?"

"Slim bought a new, bright-red John Deere with the bond money. Besides, beef prices are down, or haven't you noticed?"

"I told Slim never to pay cash for farm equipment. What was wrong with the old tractor, anyway? And I've been following commodities. You're right, it's been a bad year for ranchers. But not bad enough so that Momma and Slim would have to forego paying the mortgage."

"How would you know?" Clancy asked sharply, her dark eyes accusing. "You live in Chicago in a high-rise apartment."

The raw resentment in her voice hurt me.

"I work seventy hours a week at an accounting firm, telling professional athletes how to hang onto their newfound riches. I don't get home until after eight o'clock most nights. I'm not exactly living it up."

"Sorry," Clancy said softly, with a hangdog expression. "I'm just so sick of Montana, I don't know what to do. Why don't Momma and Slim take a hint from the thousands of other fleeing people who've left for warmer climes? It's bitterly cold in winter, some white folks hate us. And now that the ranch is in the red, what do you suppose they'll do? They'll dig their heels in and hang on for dear life, that's what they'll do," she ended with a tired sigh.

"You're too young to be so cynical," I told her, already forgetting her accusations. We Robertses are given to emotional outbursts. But we never hold a grudge.

"Unless *you* can talk them into selling." Clancy looked up at me with a hopeful expression.

"And risk hearing the Josie Roberts speech from Slim again?" I joked as we ran across the street to the waiting Ford 4x4.

I held out my hand for the keys. She reluctantly relinquished them and we placed my bags in the bed of the truck and climbed inside.

I turned to her before starting the engine. "Just so you'll know, for future reference: I would leave Chicago in a split second if I had a good enough reason to. I get paid well, but half the time, I'm homesick; and as for romance, the men I meet are all so busy climbing the corporate ladder, they usually mistake a sister for a step stool."

I turned the key in the ignition.

"Now who's being cynical?" Clancy asked mildly. She grinned and reached over to grasp my hand momentarily. "I'm glad you're back, Chey."

I smiled my thanks and pulled away from the curb.

"Where to?" I asked. "I know Momma gave you a list of things to pick up in town while you're here."

"I've got to get a few items from Big Fresh," Clancy replied.

Billings had three Big Fresh supermarkets, but we were closer to the one on Grand Avenue, so we went there.

When we got out to go into the market, I asked, "What is it with you and Montana, Clancy? Isn't there anything you like about the state?"

"Come on, Chey," Clancy began. We stopped at the automatic doors to allow an elderly woman to precede us.

"In the last few years, what have you heard about Montana on the national news? Just last year, that guy who shot up the Capitol in Washington, D.C., Weston . . . he wasn't even born in Montana, but apparently he lived here awhile. More bad publicity for us. Then there was the Unabomber, that Ted Kaczynski dude. You got the Freemen staging an armed standoff with the FBI, and the Kehoes wanting to begin an all-white nation."

We walked inside. The market was busy. It was a Saturday afternoon, so many farmers and ranchers were doing their weekly grocery shopping.

The smell of freshly baked bread permeated the air, and I realized I hadn't eaten anything in hours.

"Are you hungry?" I asked Clancy, looking around. "Don't they sell pizza in the food court?"

"I could eat a slice," she said amiably.

We began walking in the direction of the aroma.

"So there's nothing good about Montana, huh?" I said, prompting her.

Clancy stopped walking and stared straight ahead. People pushed their carts around us as I followed her line of sight.

Two men were engaged in an animated conversation while buying coffee at a counter in the food court.

I recognized one of them right away as Patrick Conley. Patrick was two grades ahead of me in school. He was a burly blond with slanting dark-blue eyes. Patrick was a rancher and lived outside of Billings with his wife, Cathy, and three small children. I knew all of that from gossip. I hadn't seen or spoken with Patrick since our school days. He'd always been kind to me. He hadn't picked on me like some of the other white kids had. It wasn't easy being the only black child in your class.

The man standing next to Patrick was black. He hadn't turned around, so I couldn't see his face. His profile was achingly familiar, though. I prayed my assumption was correct. Seeing the man whom I imagined the stranger to be, would be the best homecoming gift I could wish for.

"Now that," Clancy was saying in my ear, "is a reason to stay in Montana."

"Patrick Conley?" I croaked. "You've got a crush on Patrick Conley? He's married, and he's at least two years older than *I* am, let alone you."

"Not Patrick," Clancy said, her voice husky. "Jackson."

I held my breath, and it felt as though my heart had fallen to the pit of my stomach. Oh no! I thought. She's been bitten by the Jackson Kincaid bug, too.

I let out a long breath. I must have zoned out for a second, because when I refocused, Clancy was pulling me, inexorably closer to Jackson Kincaid and Patrick Conley.

"Come on, let's say hello," she suggested with that unique form of exuberance reserved for the very young.

"They look pretty engrossed in conversation," I offered, wondering how my hair had fared throughout the flight from Chicago. And could I have lipstick on my teeth? I ran my tongue across them, just in case.

Why I was so concerned about my looks, I couldn't fathom. It wasn't as if Jackson would pay any particular attention to me. In his eyes I was just Cole Roberts's little sister.

My older brother, Cole, and Jackson had been best friends since childhood. They were still close, even though Cole was married to Enid now, had a successful career as a veterinary surgeon in Helena, Montana, and was the father of two sons.

Jackson was a bachelor, although he'd come close to tying the knot on at least one occasion that I knew of. Her name was Marissa Claiborne. She'd been beautiful and smart, and he'd lost her to the lure of the "big city." Some folks can't live with the sometimes desolate life ranchers have to endure. You are either devoted to the land, or you're not. There is no straddling the fence.

I know her decision to leave him had hurt him deeply because he hadn't become serious about anyone else in more than three years. I knew all that from reports my mother gave me. For some reason, she thought I was interested in what went on in Jackson's life. A very perceptive woman, my mother.

Patrick looked in our direction and smiled warmly as we approached. He tapped Jackson on the shoulder.

Jackson turned slowly, then fixed me and Clancy with a surprised look. He grinned, strong white teeth flashing in his dark face.

"You know these two ladies, don't you, Patrick?" Jackson said with obvious delight.

My body reacted to his presence in its normal fashion. A warmth began in the center of my stomach and spread to the rest of me, until a barely audible, filled-with-longing sigh escaped from between my lips. I'd flunked the Jackson Kincaid test, again.

Each time I returned home for a visit, I told myself: *If you can bear to be in a room with Jackson without your body betraying you, then you're finally cured of that silly crush you've had on him since you were sixteen.*

After eleven years, I was still sighing over him.

That disconcerting thought must have registered on my features, because Clancy poked me in the side and said, "Smile, will you? You look like you just ate a lemon."

Her rush to be near Jackson was completely understandable. If sex appeal were sold in a bottle, his picture would be on the label. Of course, I would be the buxom model gazing rapturously up at him.

At six foot four Jackson was six inches taller than I was, and in splendid physical condition. It'd been a while since I'd seen him naked. (I'd had that honor when I spied on him and a bunch of other teens while they skinny-dipped at Tucker's Creek). He was seventeen then. I was nine, and it was my opinion that nude males resembled frogs; frogs being the more attractive of the two. So I didn't fully appreciate the experience; not as much as I would if it happened today.

He looked good in his denim shirt and Wrangler jeans though. The Wrangler's were just tight enough to show off his spectacular . . .

"Cheyenne, is that you?" Patrick interrupted my thoughts.

Patrick came forward and grasped me by the shoulders, looking into my eyes. "I never would have thought that tomboy-with-a-brain would turn into a looker like you."

I laughed. "Even tomboys grow up. How are you, Patrick? It's been a long time."

"At least ten years," he agreed, smiling. "I hear you're living in Chicago." He glanced down at my ring finger. "Not married yet, huh?"

It seemed only the people from home cared if I was married or not. Friends and acquaintances in Chicago never referred to my marital status. In Chicago, they wanted to know whom you worked for, how much you earned, and what your future capacity for earning more was.

At home, you couldn't whip out your American Express card and impress them; you had to produce a loving husband and a cherubic infant, or two. I was a loser all around.

"No," I answered. "I haven't had that pleasure."

"The men in Chicago must be gay or blind," Patrick said, hooking his thumb in a belt loop of his jeans.

"How long are you home for?" Jackson inquired, coming to my rescue.

"Two weeks," I replied, turning to face him.

The color had risen in Patrick's cheeks. I believe he was actually blushing. Had I caused that reaction? Too bad Jackson was immune to my charms.

"Patrick, you know Clancy, don't you?" I said, trying to lessen his discomfort.

"Of course I know this little girl. She attends school with my kid brother, Webb."

I could tell by the frown creasing Clancy's brow that she wasn't pleased with being called a little girl; not when she was hoping that Jackson would take one look at her, one *real* look, and fall in love with her. I sympathized with Clancy, because I knew it was a futile hope. Jackson considered the Roberts girls off-limits. We were his honorary sisters, and to look upon a Roberts girl as a sex object was tantamount to incest.

"How are you doin', Clancy?" Patrick asked politely.

"Fine, thanks," Clancy said, forcing a smile.

"Jackson and I were just going to have a cup of coffee, won't you ladies join us?"

Clancy brightened. "We'd love to," she said at once, her large brown eyes resting on Jackson.

He *has* to know she has a crush on him, I thought. Of course, he *had* known, for years now, that *I* was half in love with him, and he'd never done a darn thing about it. I breathed a sigh of relief.

"Coffee and Danish all right with you?" I asked Clancy.

"Apple," she said.

Patrick and Clancy went to claim one of the few remaining tables while I walked up to the counter to place our orders.

Jackson sidled up to me and said, "Is your career keeping you so busy, you can't make it home in a year?"

"It hasn't been a year," I denied, looking up at him.

"May I help you?" the freckle-faced kid behind the counter asked me.

"Two coffees and two Danish pastries, apple," I said briskly. The boy went to fill my order and I turned toward Jackson again.

"How has life been treating you, Jackson? You look as yummy as ever." We indulged in private repartee. I made shameless passes at him and he laughed in my face. It had started when I was eighteen. Jackson looked upon my behavior as acting-out. I was the chaste girl honing her mating skills on a safe male. No harm, no foul.

"Behave yourself," he warned, his voice husky. "It's been a while since I had a date; even *you're* starting to look good to me."

His deep brown eyes raked over me. I felt my cheeks grow hot from his intimate inspection. "I keep telling you," I murmured, "not to overlook the women in your own backyard."

"You aren't in my backyard anymore, you're in Chicago," he was quick to note. "Besides," he moved a bit closer. "You're much too young and ill-equipped to handle a man like me."

"You *need* a young woman to keep up with you, Jackson. Although, if the truth is to be known, you'd have a hard time keeping up with me." I leaned in, looking up into his gorgeous downward-sloping eyes. He reached up and playfully touched the tip of my nose.

"Is that a challenge?" he said in my ear.

"Here you go, miss." The boy had returned with my order. "Will there be anything else?"

At that moment, I could've used a good hosing down, but I didn't think that service was offered in the food court, so I said, "This will be all, thank you."

"I'll get that," Jackson offered, paying the boy.

He placed a hand at the small of my back as we strolled over to the table where Clancy and Patrick waited.

"And you haven't been home since Thanksgiving," Jackson told me in a low voice. "You'd just as well call it a year. It'll be turkey time again in under two months."

"Quit it, Jackson," I said. "Or I'll begin to think you actually *missed* me."

"Maybe I did," he returned.

I didn't have a chance to reply because we'd arrived at the table and from the impatient expression on Clancy's face, Jackson's, if not my company had been eagerly anticipated.

I went to sit next to her; but with a quick jerk of her head, she indicated that she'd been saving that particular seat for Jackson. I graciously relented, going to sit beside Patrick, who smiled rather dreamily in my direction. I smiled back and pointedly glanced down at the shiny gold band on his ring finger.

He wiped that grin off his face *tout de suite*.

I handed Clancy her coffee and Danish and watched as she daintily broke off a tiny piece of the sweet roll and nibbled on it, her soulful eyes caressing Jackson's face.

"Patrick and I were talking about that big drug bust that went down last night," Jackson said.

"Let me guess," I said, "methamphetamine, right?"

"Crank, yeah," Jackson replied. He took a sip of his coffee. "Two teen-aged boys: one fifteen, the other eighteen."

"Where is it all coming from?" Patrick asked.

"Do you remember last year, when that guy from the Netherlands got fifteen years for possession of more than two kilograms? The article I read said there was a California connection. But, undoubtedly, it's coming from all over," I said. "I was under the impression the authorities were making headway with the problem."

"Ha!" Clancy said, sniffing derisively. "I know several kids who're strung out on the stuff."

"You've never been offered any, have you?" I asked, horrified by the thought.

"It's been offered," Clancy replied nonchalantly. "But I know better than to touch it. Crank fries your brain."

"Smart kid," Jackson said, playfully swatting Clancy's cheek. Clancy punched him on the arm.

"And then there's talk about a new vein of coal being discovered in Custer," Patrick put in.

"Where?" I asked. I certainly didn't want strip-mining going on anywhere near my family's property. The noise disturbed the cattle, and no matter how much companies claimed to keep their operations environmentally friendly, water pollution was another thing to consider. We had two pristine meandering streams flowing through our land, and we wanted to keep them that way.

"Sid and Harriette Beechum's place for one," Jackson said.

"Are they selling?" I asked, concerned for two reasons: Sid and Harriette were long-time friends of my parents and their property was less than three miles from ours.

"They haven't made up their minds," Jackson said. "But Sid tells me that King Mining made them an offer almost impossible to turn down."

"I wish they'd make *us* an offer," Clancy said.

The three adults at the table stared at her.

"What'd I say?"

"Ranchers hate mining companies," Patrick informed her gently. "They rape the land, gouging out tons of it in search of some treasure buried deep inside her. It's sacrilegious."

My opinion of Patrick shot up ten points. He was a good ole boy, but he was passionate.

"No matter what the Beechums decide to do," Jackson said, "King Mining isn't going to go away. Not when there's money to be made."

"And I know of several families who're having a hard time making ends meet," I agreed. "It isn't easy staying in the black any longer, especially if you don't diversify."

Clancy playfully crossed her eyes at me. "Oh no, the account-ant has made an appearance."

"What rancher doesn't diversify?" Patrick asked. "We not only breed the cattle, we raise it. We grow the hay that it con-sumes; most of us have vegetable gardens for supplemental in-come, and to help feed our families. How else could we stretch ourselves?"

"It's obvious, isn't it?" I said lightly. "What does Montana have that outnumbers the cattle? It's not Montanans."

"Tourists?" Jackson said, sounding skeptical. "You want us to cater to tourists?"

"I'm not saying open a gift shop," I replied, smiling slowly. "But a bed-and-breakfast is a good idea. There are lots of city folks with disposable income who're dying to spend time in one of the most naturally beautiful states in the United States."

"Tourists on my ranch?" Jackson said, laughing. "I'd rather wrestle a grizzly in his den."

"It isn't for everyone," I allowed. "But some families can make it work for them."

"She's right," Patrick agreed with me. "The Bateses opened a lodge and they still have a working ranch. It's something to think about."

"You wouldn't have to be open year-round," I said logically. "You could run the lodge in the slow season. Believe me, I know people in Chicago who would pay an arm and a leg to get a taste of the so-called real West. They dream about being Butch Cassidy and the Sundance Kid. It's a workable idea."

"Sounds good to me," Clancy said. "We could import some new blood. God knows the males around here are tired."

Both Jackson and Patrick glared at her.

"What are we, cow chips?" Jackson joked.

"He's married," Clancy said, pointing at Patrick. "And you're still stuck on Marissa."

Out of the mouths of babes.

Jackson frowned, then laughed heartily.

"I'm sure Miss Peaches taught you that it isn't polite to remind someone of his faults, Clancy," he said in a gentle voice.

Clancy, sorry for her slip of the tongue, hung her head. Raising her eyes again, she said, "I'm sorry, Jackson. But you're much too fabulous a catch to be pining away for another woman, when there are others who would be much more suitable for you."

I tensed, hoping she wasn't about to put her foot in it, so to speak. I reached for my coffee and "accidentally" knocked the cup over, spilling the café au lait onto the tabletop.

Clancy, Jackson and Patrick jumped up from their chairs to avoid getting coffee stains on their clothing. I got up and grabbed a handful of napkins, sopping up the mess as best I could.

"Sorry," I said, chagrined.

"Don't worry about it," Patrick said. "I'd better be going anyway. I'm supposed to meet Cathy and the kids over at Rimrock Mall in an hour. See you, guys."

" 'Bye, Patrick. It was good seeing you again," I said truthfully.

"Yeah, don't be a stranger," he said, smiling warmly. "Clancy."

" 'Bye, Patrick," Clancy returned, her tone a bit too animated.

After Patrick turned to leave, Clancy looked up at me, embarrassment flooding her features. "I'll go get some more napkins."

"You were afraid she was going to tell me I should consider her big sister?" Jackson asked when we were alone.

I stopped wiping the table to meet his gaze. "Are you saying that wasn't an accident?"

"Answer the question."

I smiled at him. "You know how I feel about you, Jackson. I didn't want the whole state of Montana knowing. It's between me and you."

"And Clancy."

"I've never spoken to Clancy about my feelings for you, not even jokingly."

"Maybe she just guessed," Jackson ventured. He circled me. "You know, Clancy could be right. Perhaps I *should* consider her sister." He appeared all business, but his dark brown, downward-sloping eyes held an amused glint in them.

"One of these days, you're going to take me seriously, Jackson Kincaid," I prognosticated. "Just wait and see."

TWO

The majestic Rocky Mountains run through western Montana, where the rocky terrain separates it from the state of Idaho. If you go far enough north, you wind up in Canada. Wyoming and Idaho touch the state line in the south; and North and South Dakota lie on its eastern border.

My hometown of Custer is located in the south, only a few miles from Wyoming. Josie probably figured that if things didn't work out for them in Montana, then they wouldn't have such an arduous journey back to the log cabin she'd left behind in Wyoming.

The Robertses' homestead began with a log cabin on the first five hundred acres Josie purchased with the proceeds from her gold-mining endeavors.

Subsequent generations bought up the surrounding property and made improvements on it.

The bulk of the land today is used for grazing, as most ranch land generally is. The main house sits in the middle of the acreage. However, there were seven structures dotting the Robertses' land: the main house, an extremely large log cabin; four smaller cabins, which were used by the foreman and other ranch personnel over the years, but are empty now because the family who resides in the main house, does the majority of the work today; the barn, where all sorts of equipment and tools are stored, as well as hay and feed; and lastly, the stable, with an adjacent corral, where the horses are housed and where the spring branding takes place.

It seems like a lot of property to the layman, however, the

Roberts clan has gone through times of great prosperity and times of near deprivation. Slim calls it boom or bust. Boom when money is abundant and bust when your pockets are bare.

When Daddy was alive, I can recall a time when we had so many head of cattle, it required twenty good hands to help get them to market. Today we have around a thousand head of Black Angus and Hereford, or a cross of the two, on the property. That amount needs no more than a dozen or so men to help get them shipped off.

Custer is located in the plains, so we don't have the Rocky Mountains as a backdrop. What we do have is the Yellowstone River, where Momma loves to go trout fishing and spectacular meadows that abound with daffodils, lavender crocus, yellow bells and white cherry blossoms in springtime.

Slim cleared the land for the main house in the center of a pine forest, so the compound is surrounded by pine trees. There's also a smattering of aspen birch, which lend their vibrant colors of golds, bronzes and reds to my autumnal homecoming.

Clancy and I got home that afternoon at around four o'clock. The moment I drove into the yard, after covering two miles of private road that led to the house, Bear, our burly, black husky, came running from behind the house, barking happily.

"I think he missed you," Clancy said as she reached for the door's handle.

I bounded down out of the truck and Bear's muddy paws were on the front of my crisp, white blouse in a matter of seconds. I bent to hug him and he licked my face repeatedly.

"I'm happy to see you, too," I cooed.

"You two make me sick," Clancy said loudly as she walked around us, heading for the porch.

"You're just jealous because you don't have a handsome male slobbering all over you," Momma commented as she met Clancy on the porch and gave her a quick buss on the cheek.

Clancy grinned and continued inside.

I smiled at Momma. Seeing her sweet face was worth all the hassles I'd endured in order to get there.

I rose and we hugged.

I was five-ten to her five-four, but she hugged me so tightly, I winced.

"All of my children are back in the same state. I feel complete. How are you, Chey?"

"I'm good, Momma. You look well."

Dubbed Peaches by my lovesick father when they were dating, the appellation was appropriate. Momma had golden-brown skin that was tinged with red. Her eyes were a dark brown with golden specks in them. Both Clancy and I had the same color eyes. The boys took after Daddy in skin and eye color.

At fifty-five, she looked forty. When men complimented me on my looks, I often replied, "Me? You should see my mother."

Diana Rainwater Roberts was the true beauty in the family. Over the years, her inner beauty had shone through, as demonstrated by her strength and fortitude when faced with life's crises.

"I have no complaints," she said now. "Except that your grandpa is driving me nuts."

We turned to walk up the front steps.

"What is it this time?" I asked in my role as family mediator.

She didn't have time to reply, because my younger brothers Chad, twenty-one, and, Lucas, nineteen, came barreling out of the house and swept me off my feet one after the other.

They were both dark-skinned replicas of our mother. They had our father's shade of deep, dark, rich chocolate-colored skin and dark brown eyes, but the aquiline shape of their noses and almond-shaped eyes were reminiscent of our mother's features.

Being older than they were, I usually thought of them as children. Their sheer size, however, forced me to grudgingly concede that they were, indeed, fully grown men. They were both over six feet tall with bodies gridiron heroes would envy. There was no dearth of female companions when it came to the Roberts boys.

"Hey, girl," Chad said, grinning as he set me back down on the porch. "You just get uglier every time I see you."

"Yeah, and if your ears were any bigger, we wouldn't have to rely on a satellite dish in order to get TV reception," I joked.

His grin grew wider. "That was a good one."

He bent and kissed my cheek. "Welcome home, Chey."

Lucas, the poet of the family, simply hugged me generously.

"Never mind him, Chey," he said. "Next to Momma, you're the prettiest girl in Montana."

"Hey, what about me?" Clancy cried from behind us.

"What *about* you?" Chad said dismissively. "You're a pain in the butt."

Clancy stomped down the steps, "Come help get the groceries out of the truck, you useless cretins."

"A very *loud* pain in the butt," Lucas said as he and Chad turned to obey their feisty younger sibling.

Momma and I went on into the house.

"God, it's good to be home," I said with a laugh.

I paused to gaze up at the portrait of Daddy on the foyer wall.

Beneath the portrait, on a cherry-wood hall table, Momma had placed a vase of fresh red roses. She always kept fresh flowers on that table.

She stood next to me, her right hand on the small of my back. "How was your trip, honey?"

"Uneventful. I was surprised to see Clancy at the airport by herself, though."

"She said she could do it," Momma said as though that had been good enough for her. "When have I ever put limits on what my girls could do? She knows to be careful. And we keep the truck in excellent condition."

"I know," I said. "It's just hard for me to see Clancy as anything but a toddler in diapers."

Momma laughed. "Maybe it's time you had some of your own. Then you'd know what a miracle it is to watch your children grow up before your eyes. It's always way too fast for the parents. But, there's nothing we can do about it, so we wish for the best and hang on for the ride. I've been luckier than most."

We were still admiring Daddy's handsome image.

"He would've been proud of all of you," Momma said wistfully. Sighing, she added, "I'll never forgive him for leaving me."

I made no comment. It hadn't been the first time my mother had expressed anger at Daddy for dying. The twenty-nine years they'd been together, they'd had a loving, but adversarial relationship. No couple took as much pleasure in fighting and making up as they did. They'd rail at each other for days at a time, then the storm would break and they'd go off to one of the cabins, where we kids knew not to bother them, and stay for several days. Afterward, when they returned home, there would be a special glow about them.

The arguing didn't faze us kids in the least. We knew they had a deep, abiding love and nothing could ever sever them. The calm was what interested us. The private glances. Furtive smiles. We wondered what they'd been doing out at the cabin all alone, without us to pester them. Of course, I knew what those sabbaticals from family life were for today. I only wished I would be as lucky in love as they were. So far, I hadn't been.

Clancy came through with Chad and Lucas on her heels, all of them carrying bags.

"Where's Slim?" I asked, not having heard his voice or seen his lanky form since entering the house.

"He's in the barn cussing out the tractor," Momma answered, laughing deep in her throat. "He spent all that money on it, and now it needs a new starter. He's bent out of shape about it."

"No," I said as I followed her back to the kitchen where my three siblings were putting the groceries away. "What he's mad about is investing in a tractor, when the mortgage should have been paid instead. But he doesn't have to worry about the mortgage because I have enough to cover it for a while. . . ."

Momma turned to stare at me. "No, you're not. You are not going to bail us out of this one. That old man needs to learn that he can't gamble with the family's livelihood. The tractor's going back; I've already discussed it with Beau Bradley. He wasn't pleased by my decision, but he's benefitted a great deal from our patronage over the years, and he can just like it or lump it. He hasn't sold the old tractor yet. We're getting it back; it only needed minor repairs. Slim will survive without his shiny new toy."

"He isn't going to be happy," I said sagely. My grandpa knew how to stretch out a sulk until everyone around him either wished they were dead, or *he* was. I suppose it was because he was so used to getting his way.

Daddy took over the management of the ranch when Slim turned seventy, fifteen years ago. Before that, Riley Roberts ruled with an iron fist. He was tough and he pushed himself to the limit, so he expected the same from anyone who worked for him. Several men had quit over the years complaining that Slim, though he paid them well for their labors, wrung every ounce of blood, sweat and tears out of them in exchange for the generous paycheck.

Since Daddy was killed, Slim had assumed he would step back into his role as head of the family and boss. Momma had something to say about that, though. She'd learned a bit about ranch management from Daddy, and, even in the face of Slim's initial protestations that the house was her true domain, she let her opinions be heard loudly and vociferously. Slim had come to respect her, though he sometimes backslid and turned a deaf ear to her suggestions, as in the case of the new tractor. He'd coveted the machine. Now he undoubtedly regretted his precipitous actions.

I dropped the subject of my bailing them out, for the time being.

"I'll go and say hello," I said.

Momma moved over to the stove and opened a Dutch oven, revealing a succulent-looking beef roast simmering in a bed of onions. The aroma made my mouth water.

"Tell him supper's at five, as usual," she said, as she stuck a meat fork in the juicy roast. "On your way back in, grab a couple of heads of lettuce out of the garden."

Momma's vegetable garden was the envy of the other farmers in the area. When they asked how she got so much yield and such healthy, delicious vegetables, she told them, "I give it plenty of sweat and manure, an unbeatable combination."

People with green thumbs could rarely explain why plants grew so well for them. Momma's mother, Grandma Isabella, who was half Cheyenne, said the land simply liked some folks better than others.

I left the kitchen through the back door, stepped onto the porch and ran down the steps. The barn was about a hundred yards behind the house. I could see the white-washed double doors hanging open, so I knew Grandpa was still out there.

Halfway through my trek, Bear put in an appearance, looking

for more attention. I paused to scratch him behind his ear, and he grinned up at me, his purple tongue hanging out the corner of his mouth.

As we approached the door, I called out loudly, "Slim, what are you up to in there?"

Slim was hard of hearing. He would never admit it, and would die the death of a polecat and stink his way to Hades before he'd submit to wearing a hearing aid. We simply made accommodations by speaking louder when words were directed to him, and repeating what we'd said if he appeared not to have heard us.

The bonnet of the new, bright-red tractor was up, and Slim was leaning over it, both hands inside, tinkering with something.

I walked over and touched his shoulder.

Slim jumped, there was the clang of metal against metal. He'd dropped the tool he'd been using.

"Gawl durn, gal," he fussed. "Why don't you announce yourself when you come into a room?"

Laughing, I knelt and felt beneath the tractor until I'd located the tool, a wrench. Rising, I handed it to him.

"It's good to see you, too," I said.

I went and gave him a sloppy kiss on the cheek. Slim was embarrassed by the show of affection, so I laid it on thick, smacking my lips for emphasis.

"Now see you done gone and got that war paint all over me," he grumbled. "When did you get in?"

He laid the wrench inside the bonnet and looked into my eyes, awaiting my reply.

"A few minutes ago," I said. "You look pretty good for a dying man."

"You'd been away long enough, gal. You needed to come home," he said, the apology I'd expected not even detectable in his tone of voice.

His attitude got my back up. Slim and I were the same height, so he didn't have the advantage of size with which to intimidate me. He did have my love and respect though, so I held my tongue as much as a Roberts could.

"You didn't have to deceive me," I said calmly. "All you had to do was say you missed me and you wanted to see me. I would have come home as soon as I possibly could."

"As soon as you could have *made* time," he said derisively. His brown eyes held a humorous glint in them. "This way, though, you hauled butt to get here."

"You manipulated me!" I said, my voice rising slightly.

Sensing the static in the air, Bear whined and ran out of the barn.

"See, you scared the dog," Slim accused lightly.

Allowing an exasperated sigh to escape my lips, I said, "If only I could strike fear in *your* heart."

"Bigger men have tried and failed," Slim said, enjoying our altercation.

He stood there, attired in worn jeans and an old plaid shirt, a lean, dark-skinned man with a full head of solid-white natural hair, a nose grown big with age and sun damage, brown eyes still clear and bright and thin lips drawn back in a crooked-tooth grin.

"Although," he continued, "no man has ever gotten the better of me; it's always been the women. First your Grandma Penelope, God rest her soul. She could make me jump through hoops. Then, there's your momma. She's a mean little woman . . ."

"She is not," I immediately contradicted him.

"And then," he said, his eyes tender, "there's my first-born granddaughter. She reminds me so much of my only son, that I sometimes crave the sight of her face."

With those words, he'd taken my righteous anger and reduced it to pettiness.

"All right," I told him. "You're forgiven."

"Thank you," he replied, looking self-satisfied. "Now climb up in the cab and turn the key in the ignition. I think I've finally got her going."

Mealtime in the Robertses' household is a finely orchestrated production. We all have our roles, which we carry out with precision. Momma usually does the cooking, so we children take turns setting the table and cleaning up afterward.

Lucas and I are a team, and Clancy and Chad form the other

one. Today, Lucas and I were pegged to set the table, so we went about it in the same manner as we always did; never mind the fact that I hadn't been home in ten months.

First, we'd put the food in serving dishes. This done, the food would be arranged in the center of the table.

Lucas would then place a plate before each of the six chairs at the big, round table in the kitchen. I'd be right behind him with the napkins, spoons, knives and forks. He would go back to retrieve the iced-tea glasses, put one next to each plate and I'd fill the glasses with ice.

By the time I'd finished with that task, Lucas was bringing up the rear with a pitcher of iced tea with lemon slices swirling around in it.

"So Chey," Chad said after the prayer had been said and everyone was eager to dig in, "you haven't hooked yourself a city boy yet?"

"Do you see one?" I asked. I took a bite of the beef. It was so tender it practically melted in my mouth. "Delicious, Momma."

"Thank you, baby," Momma said, smiling.

"I mean," Chad continued, "wasn't that the reason you stayed in Chicago after college? You figured you'd have a better chance of getting married in Illinois than Montana, the situation being what it is here."

That had been on my list of reasons to stay in Chicago after I graduated from Illinois State University more than five years ago with a master's degree in accounting. I'd been somewhat of a math prodigy and had won a full academic scholarship to the university when I was seventeen.

I'd been offered a full academic scholarship at the University of Montana, too, but I wanted to go to school out of state, so I'd opted to go to the University of Illinois.

Somewhere, on the back burner, there'd been the wish that I would meet someone special while I pursued a career in accounting. Prince Charming hadn't materialized, although there had been a few contenders for the honor.

I'd even been proposed to a couple of times. Amazing in itself because I never let my guard down long enough to allow Cupid's arrows to penetrate my heart. I couldn't have given Ahmad or Tad much to hang their hopes on, yet they'd professed their love and asked me to spend the rest of my life with them. I turned them down nicely; however neither of them could bear to remain "just friends" with me, decisions that I was wholeheartedly grateful for.

In my opinion, a relationship in which only one of the partners is in love isn't worth having. There's always too much pain and silent recriminations to contend with. Sure, he might *say* he'd do anything to be with you, but, in the end, he'd resent you for your coldhearted inability to love him back.

"That Tad guy asked her to marry *him,*" Clancy offered, coming to my defense.

Chad's questions had made me wonder, though. Why hadn't I fallen in love with either Tad or Ahmad? They had both been sharp, successful, caring, attractive men.

I had a theory that concerned a certain rancher; all I needed was the opportunity to test it out. It involved a bit of privacy and the pressing together of lips. If Jackson would just kiss me, once, I'd know if my infatuation was more than a pipe dream. And if the emotions weren't real, then the next time I met a wonderful man who was brave enough to love me, I'd have better sense than to rebuff his generous offer of marriage and babies.

I was twenty-seven. It was time I got Jackson Kincaid out of my system, once and for all.

"Maybe Cheyenne hasn't met a Chicago boy who was man enough for a Big Sky woman," Lucas suggested.

"Would you all stop talking about me as if I'm not present," I said, a little irritated. "I'm too *young* to get married, anyway."

"Young?" Chad guffawed, nearly choking on his salad. "If you were a horse, we'd have to put you down."

"If she were a dog," Clancy said, getting into the game, "she'd be a hundred and eighty-nine."

"It's good to see you're paying attention in math class," I returned. I looked beseechingly at Slim. "Slim, help."

"Be quiet, all of you," Slim said with finality. "The subject of Cheyenne's state of matrimony is now closed. Besides, I've chosen the perfect man for her. He's right here in Custer. He's older than Cheyenne by a few years, but that's what she needs: stability and strength in a man."

Everyone at the table, with the exception of Slim, sat in stunned silence.

He cleared his throat and drank some of his tea. He had everyone's undivided attention when he decided to name the paragon he'd chosen as my intended.

"Ben Summerall."

Ben Summerall was a very rich rancher north of us who'd made his fortune in oil down in Texas, then, tired of what he termed "swimming with the barracudas," he'd purchased what used to be the Bennett ranch (Claude and Mary Bennett had retired to Bradenton, Florida).

I could see my grandfather's reasoning in the matter. There was a severe shortage of eligible African-American males in Montana. Ben did meet the cultural requirement, but, being in his forties, he was at least fifteen years older than me. I was attracted to older men, but that was pushing the envelope.

Besides, as far as I knew, Ben Summerall hadn't expressed any interest in me. I hardly knew him. We'd spoken, in passing, on two occasions. Last year, he was at the Juneteenth celebration. African-American communities from the surrounding counties get together and have a barbecue and dance each June. Many in the black community were from Texas, and, like all immigrants, they brought their observances with them to Montana.

Anyway, I was manning the beverage table: filling paper cups with ice and sodas for the kids and cold beer for those who partook.

Ben sauntered up to my table and requested a beer.

I looked up into the face of a handsome, brown-skinned man with a ready smile and twinkling black eyes.

"Hey, aren't you Riley Roberts's granddaughter?" he asked.

"Guilty, as charged," I joked.

He offered me his hand. I put the cup of beer down long enough to grasp it and shake it firmly.

"Benjamin Summerall. I bought the Bennett place a few months back."

"Yeah, I heard about that. Welcome to Custer, Mr. Summerall."

"Ouch," he said. "It always hurts when a pretty woman calls me mister."

"What *should* I call you?" I asked tactfully.

"Ben," he replied. He still held on to my hand. "And you are . . ."

"Cheyenne."

A couple of small children rushed up to the table then, and bumped into Ben's long legs. He bent to grab both of them by an arm and said, "Slow down, partners."

He picked up his beer then, looked at me, smiled again and said, "Good to meet you, Cheyenne."

He then left.

The second time we ran in to each other, I was at the hardware store in town, picking up a tool Slim had ordered.

Ben was at the counter when I walked up and there was a lovely Native American woman standing beside him.

"Hello, Ben," I greeted him.

An embarrassed expression clouded his features. I immediately regretted speaking to him so cheerily.

He forced a smile. "Cheyenne, isn't it?"

At that point, I figured if he wanted to pretend he couldn't recall meeting me, I was willing to forget him, too.

I looked up at Mr. Carter, behind the counter. Ben had already made his purchase and was preparing to leave.

"Slim says you have something for him, Mr. Carter," I said briskly. I kept my gaze straight ahead.

I didn't even notice when Ben and his companion left the store.

And now Slim was looking to marry me off to a man who'd snubbed me the last time I'd seen him? No way.

Momma laughed suddenly. The levity served to make me put things in perspective. So what if Slim wanted to play feudal lord and arrange a marriage between me and a man whom he believed was a suitable mate? It was 1999, and he didn't have a legal leg to stand on.

I laughed, too. Soon, everyone, save Slim, was laughing heartily.

Momma turned her regal head to regard Slim with an askance expression in her gold-speckled brown eyes. "And exactly how did you come to this particular decision?"

Slim cocked his head to look at me. "With schoolin' and all, Cheyenne has been away from home for ten years. She can't convince me that she's happy in Chicago. Her heart's here with us. The rest of her should be here, too. I spoke with Ben Summerall just last week." He gazed at Momma. "You remember, Peaches, he came out here to ask my opinion on what breed of cow fared best in this area. He don't know nothin' about ranching, but he's a good man. . . ."

"Stay on the subject," Momma insisted calmly. "What did he say that gave you this asinine notion?"

"He asked after Cheyenne. Said she was a handsome woman and wondered if she was married or not. I told him she wasn't and it didn't look like she had any prospects."

"Slim, you didn't!" I exclaimed.

"Wasn't going to build you up as if you had so many suitors calling, he wouldn't get a chance to ring the bell," Slim said logically.

"Go on. What did he say after you told him nobody would touch me with a ten-foot pole?"

"He said, 'then if it's all right with you, I'd like to pay a visit the next time she's home.' To that, I said, she'll be home next week, so mark it on your calendar."

"Then, you phoned me and told me you were feeling poorly, and if I wanted to see you one last time, I should come home as soon as possible."

He might be eighty-five, but he was as cagey as ever.

"That's about the size of it," Slim answered. He speared a big chunk of beef with his fork, put it into his mouth and chewed thoughtfully. He raised his eyes to mine. "What do you say? Would you at least go out with him when he calls for you?"

"What? You're asking my permission now?"

"He's healthy, got all his teeth, slightly less money than that computer fella, and he likes you. What more could you ask for in a husband?"

"Oh, I don't know . . . love?"

"Who's to say you won't fall in love if you date?" Clancy said, putting in her two cents' worth. I could tell by the mischievous twinkle in her eye that she was enjoying seeing me on the hot seat.

"It's ridiculous," Momma said, glaring at Slim. "If you were going to play matchmaker, why couldn't you have chosen someone closer to Chey's age, at least? Ben Summerall must be fifteen years older than Cheyenne. A woman has no use for an old man. He won't be her partner in life; she'll wind up waiting on him hand and foot when he's old and decrepit and she's in her prime."

Slim nodded as he continued chewing. "Ben's so rich, he can hire round-the-clock nurses to see after his needs if he gets down. And anyway, isn't it the wife's duty to look after her man?"

I rose and tossed my napkin onto the tabletop. "This has gone far enough. I'm not interested in dating Ben Summerall. I've only seen the man on two occasions and sparks didn't fly on either of them. I don't care if he's as rich as Croesus."

I eyed Slim with a mixture of outrage and disappointment.

"Sometimes your desire to control us makes you do truly crazy things. This definitely qualifies. Tell Ben Summerall you made a mistake; I *am* involved with someone. Tell him anything you wish. Just make certain he knows I would *not* be amenable to a visit from him, all right?"

"All right," Slim said reluctantly. I'm sure he was thinking I was passing on a good thing. When Slim was courting Grandma Penelope, the fact that the suitor owned property and had no mental illness in his immediate family was enough. Today, we spoiled women of the nineties wanted to be loved. Wasn't that selfish, and slightly greedy, of us? Slim probably thought so.

I sat back down and picked up my knife and fork. "Good. Now, could we eat in peace?"

"I was thinking Jackson Kincaid would be a better choice," Lucas commented, with a sly grin in my direction.

I threw my napkin at him; he ducked, and it hit Clancy dead in the face. She promptly scooped up a handful of mashed potatoes with the intention of rubbing it into Luke's face.

"Clarisse Nancy Roberts!" Momma called from across the table.

The imperious note in her voice made Clancy freeze.

"Eat it," Momma ordered.

Clancy sighed and brought the offending hand up to her mouth and started eating the potatoes.

"I'm sorry," I told Clancy.

She smiled at me, but she cut her eyes at Lucas, who squirmed in his chair. He shrugged. "Good reflexes."

That night, as I lay in bed, I tried to come up with a plan whereby I could convince my family that ranching wasn't enough to insure a financially secure future.

The fact that they were six months behind on the mortgage payments worried me desperately. As an accountant, I was paid to help my clients use their money wisely. I felt as though I was failing my own family. Changes had to be made.

I had two very stubborn souls to contend with though: Momma and Grandpa. Would they go for the proposal I had in mind?

I also had to take my personal life to task. Grandpa's attempt to find me a husband was telling as to the state of my love life. I didn't have one.

More than a year ago, after I'd turned down the second marriage proposal, I made up my mind that I wouldn't date anyone until I was prepared to let down my guard. In my heart, I knew I wouldn't be ready to do that until I defined my feelings for Jackson. Was it a childish schoolgirl crush? Was it merely lust? Or was it the ever-after kind of love Momma and Daddy shared? And what kind of test could I conceive of that would leave no doubt as to what the answer to my dilemma was?

I snuggled down into my comfy bed. I knew what I *wanted* to do to Jackson. But, would seduction be the answer?

I'd devoted the last ten years to fantasizing about him. I wanted more than a night of passion with him. Besides, I really didn't have much faith in a twenty-seven-year-old virgin being able to lure Jackson into a situation that ended with us in bed together.

Sure, I'd always told myself that I wanted him to be my first. But, I'd invariably imagined the culmination of my sexual fantasies would take place on our wedding night.

I *could* go to him and tell him I'd been saving myself for him all these years. That would probably freak the poor guy out good fashion. No, I couldn't do that.

My eyelids grew heavy. As I drifted off to sleep, I thought, *I might have a better chance with Ben Summerall. Jackson never even said I was a woman, let alone a handsome woman.*

THREE

Monday morning, I awakened a bit disoriented. I was so used to getting up and going into the offices of Streiber and Farrar, the accounting firm I worked for, that my hand automatically reached for the nonexistent alarm clock on the nightstand.

I sat on the side of the bed a few moments, gathering wool, until I heard Clancy scream, "Chad, get out of the bathroom. Other people need to get in there!"

"Use Momma's," Chad shouted back.

Yawning, but fully awake after that little scene, I rose and went to the closet to pick out a pair of jeans and a shirt. I packed lightly whenever I came home for a visit because much of my wardrobe was in my old bedroom's closet. Momma was one to maintain the status quo. Cole, Jr. had been married to Enid for more than seven years, and had lived in Helena for ten, and she'd just cleaned out his bedroom's closets last year.

I suppose if the house were smaller, she'd be more space-conscious. However, there were six bedrooms, plus Slim's apartment out back, so there was room enough for everyone.

Slim built the house with a big family in mind. He and Grandma Penelope had wanted to have at least ten children, but Grandma Penelope succumbed to pneumonia shortly after giving birth to their only child, our father, Cole.

Plus, I suppose the wide, open spaces of Montana inspired the imaginations of home builders back then. Grandpa was a prosperous rancher with a beautiful new bride, whom he wished to impress, so he had what was then, the biggest, most intricate house in the territory built for her.

It's still impressive in my estimation. The outside has exposed, weathered logs. In the dry, cold atmosphere of Montana, logs don't have a tendency to rot and decay. The house had stood, without bowing for nearly seventy years, and it would, undoubtedly, be around for another hundred years.

The second story has six dormers, all on the front of the house, and the eight-foot columns supporting the wraparound porch are logs that came from the pine forest surrounding the compound.

Inside, the floors are all solid pine and kept highly polished. Some of my earliest memories involve being on my hands and knees, polishing the floors with a chamois cloth.

Ranch wives have this constant war with dirt. They intend to make sure it stays outside. Momma was no exception.

The living room, what we call the "company room," is characterized by exposed beams on the twenty-foot ceiling. A large stone fireplace is used each winter, even though the house has central heat and air. Thinking the house needed more light, Momma had three consecutive picture windows put into the east wall shortly after she married Daddy. She'd been right because the morning sun streaming in through those windows illuminates the whole house, making it warm and inviting.

My bedroom is on the west side of the house. Most nights, when I was living at home, I'd watch the sun set from the balcony of my bedroom.

By the time I got downstairs, everyone was present. Slim who scoffed at our dire warnings about eating too many nitrates, had a plate with several slices of bacon on it.

He looked up at me as I entered the room.

"It's a woman's prerogative to change her mind." He never gave up.

I ignored him and spoke to everyone else.

Walking around to Momma's side of the table, I bent and kissed her silken cheek.

"Grits are still warm," Momma said.

I went to the stove and dished up a bowl of grits and a spoonful of soft-scrambled eggs, placing the eggs on top of the grits. Not much of a meat-eater, I left the bacon and sausages for the others.

There was a loaf of Momma's fresh bread on the stove, though, and I got one of the thick slices and slathered it with margarine.

Going to sit down on the only vacant chair, I poured coffee from the carafe on the table into the cup at my place setting.

"You're as stubborn as your momma," Slim said.

"Thank you," I said.

Momma laughed.

"I just want to see you married and happy before I go," Slim commented. Unable to sway me with his position and power, he was now going for the sympathy vote. I knew all of his tricks.

"You going somewhere?" I asked innocently.

"Sooner than you all think," Slim said, eyeing each of us in turn. "A man had just as well be dead, for all the use he is to his family."

Clancy was the only one of us still capable of being whipped into an emotional frenzy when Slim laid his guilt trip on us.

Her big brown eyes welled with tears. "You're important to this family, Slim! I hate it when you talk like that."

She got up and ran from the table.

I rose and looked down at Slim. "You ought to be ashamed of yourself." I went after Clancy.

I found her on the front porch, sitting on one of the swings, her left leg folded underneath her, and her right leg dangling. She pushed the floor with her right foot, setting the swing in motion. Tears rolled down her cheeks.

I leaned against one of the columns, looking up at the morning sky, which was a clear, cloudless blue.

"You have to get used to the way Slim talks about his death, Clancy. It's a threat he holds over us to keep us in line as best he can. I don't know why he does it. But he did lose his only son seven years ago, and now, maybe, he's afraid of losing us, too."

"Sometimes," Clancy said, her eyes on my face, "I can't remember things about Daddy."

Hearing the pain in her voice, I went to sit next to her and pulled her into my arms.

"What can't you remember about him?"

She began crying in earnest then. "The sound of his voice. His laughter. When I was little, did he used to read me to sleep?"

"Yes, he did," I told her. "You wouldn't go to sleep until he read you your favorite story. It was about Atalanta, the princess who wouldn't marry anyone who couldn't outrun her."

"The golden apples," Clancy said, her voice low and childlike.

"That's right," I said. "And as for Daddy's voice, he had a great baritone. That man could sing! Don't you remember his singing around the house all the time? He even sang on trail rides; kept us all entertained. His favorite song was, 'Stand by Me.' You know, that old Ben E. King song: When the night has come . . ." I sang.

"You didn't inherit his vocal cords," Clancy joked.

I laughed. "No," I agreed. "I got his tenaciousness."

"That's true. You don't seem to know the meaning of the words *give up*. What did I get from him?"

"You got his quick wit and more and more, I recognize his restlessness in you," I answered without hesitation. "Did anyone ever tell you how much traveling Daddy did before settling down?"

"No . . ."

"Well he did," I began, remembering the tales Daddy would relate to me when we were sitting by the campfire while on a cattle drive. "He was eighteen when he left the first time. He'd known nothing except this ranch all his life. One morning, he woke up and told himself, 'this would be a good day to leave,' and he took the money he'd saved and walked away from here. He hitchhiked all the way to California and back. He left Slim a note telling him what he was up to, of course. He said Slim punched him in the mouth when he returned six months later, but that was the first and only time Slim ever hit him."

"You said the first time," Clancy noted. "Where did he go next?"

"Vietnam."

"Daddy went to Vietnam? I don't remember his ever mentioning it."

"Many veterans don't like thinking about it, let alone talking about it, Clancy. But he went. He was over there for two and a half years. He married Momma soon after he returned, and he said he had the wanderlust out of his system. He never left the state after that."

I didn't tell her what Daddy had told me about Slim's reaction to his joining the Marines. As an only child, Daddy would have been exempt from the draft, but he'd gone to Helena and volunteered for service. Slim, thinking his son had decided to see more of the country, hadn't been unduly concerned the first couple of weeks when Daddy turned up missing.

But about a month and a half later, when he received Daddy's letter (a short note written en route to Vietnam), Slim was fit to be tied. He disinherited Daddy. He changed his mind after Momma and Daddy presented him with his first grandchild, though.

In some ways, I could sympathize with Slim. Life had taught him that hard work and living right didn't ensure happiness. He'd done everything to build an inheritance for his son and that son had been cruelly snatched from him. No wonder he was overly protective of us. I also thought, though, that we had to rebel against his tight constraints. He wouldn't respect us if we docilely obeyed his every command.

"What you've got to understand about Slim," I told Clancy, "is that it's the challenges of life that keep him going. If he were in some nursing home somewhere, he'd have been gone a long time ago. But here, with us, we keep him so discombobulated that he doesn't know whether he's coming or going. But, don't feel too sorry for him, because he gives as good as he gets."

"Don't I know it," Clancy said, laughing.

"So, the next time Slim starts talking about dying, what are you going to say?"

"Can I have your saddle, Grandpa? I've always had my eye on that soft, supple leather."

"Atta girl," I said approvingly.

We went back inside to finish eating breakfast.

When we returned to the table, Slim looked up at Clancy, then glanced in my direction. "She okay?"

Clancy walked over and removed all of the remaining bacon from Slim's plate. "A dying man shouldn't touch this stuff, it's poisonous."

Slim opened his mouth to protest, then clamped it shut. He grinned. "She's okay."

We all scattered after breakfast. Chad and Lucas both had classes to attend at the University of Montana-Billings. Chad was a senior, majoring in animal husbandry; Lucas was a premed student. He hadn't decided what kind of medicine he wanted to practice, but he was leaning toward pediatrics. He loved children.

I sometimes thought living at home and going to college in a neighboring city was too much of a hardship. You had to be extremely disciplined to get up each morning, drive sixty miles, pay attention in class, go home and study, then start all over again the next morning. They seemed to be handling it well though. Chad had a GPA of 3.8 and Lucas had a 4.0.

Chad told me recently that the University of Montana was considering the idea of school via computers. It would work like this: The students would not have to physically come to the university. Transcripts from lectures would be accessible at a Web site. Exams would also be given in that way. It sounded very convenient, especially since Montana's population was so spread out. I had only one misgiving about it though: How would the professors prevent cheating? Ah well, I'm sure they'd iron out any snags before implementing the program.

Clancy was a senior in high school. She caught the bus at the end of our two-mile driveway. She was running late that morning, so I drove her down to the bus stop.

"Now that you know you're home on false pretenses, are you heading back to Chicago soon?" she asked as we sat waiting for the school bus.

"No, I need a break. Besides, I want to try to convince Momma and Slim to open a lodge. That they're behind on the mortgage payments worries me. I mean, the whole idea of a second mortgage was to make improvements on the property. It's true the buildings are all in good shape, but they're running out of funds too soon. I'll have to go over the books and see what the problem is."

"Good luck," she said.

We spotted the bus coming around the curve.

Clancy climbed out of the truck and waved good-bye to me as she ran toward the open doors of the big yellow bus.

Back home, Slim wanted me to drive him out to the northern section to take a peek at the herds.

He and the boys did this at least three times a week. It entailed either riding out to the site on horseback, or hitching the trailer to the 4x4, loading a couple of mares onto it, and driving out to the desired location, unloading the horses and then making a circuit of the area where the cows were grazing.

Slim didn't have the stamina he used to have, so the boys usually hitched the trailer to the 4x4 whenever he insisted on accompanying them.

The cattle were grazing in the lowlands this time of the year. In fall, when precipitation was low, the lowlands provided the cattle with water, found pooled in man-made ponds all over the property.

Slim had a horror of the ponds, one day, drying up. That, he said, would be the end of the ranch. It hadn't happened in more than a hundred years, yet he still worried about it.

Some folks thought that was what distinguished a good rancher from a bad one. A good rancher thought ahead. He never wanted anything sneaking up on him, so he was prepared for every contingency, or tried to be.

A disastrous storm could still wipe him out. In the case of the rancher, disease was always a problem. You had to keep the herd healthy, so every few months, we doctored the cattle. That meant inoculations for the young ones, and, since Cole became the family's vet, certain vitamins added to the feed. Cole believed in prevention. And, subsequently, the healthier the cattle remained, the less it would cost to maintain them, in the long run. I agreed with him.

Ever since the mad-cow disease scare over in England, the cattle industry here in the United States has also been under intense scrutiny. I can't vouch for all ranchers, but my family, and other ranchers we have known for many years, make certain that when we send cattle to the market to be slaughtered, expressly for human consumption, that beef is of the highest quality.

Slim and I arrived at a meadow about a quarter-mile from where the cows were grazing.

I parked the truck and put on the parking brake, then got out and went to unlock the door of the trailer.

Slim stood on the opposite side of the trailer, waiting to help back the two quarter horses out.

We'd brought Pie and Susie because they were both suited to travel. Neither of them got skittish when you loaded them into the trailer, and they were also excellent trail horses.

Pie was seven years old, he'd been born on the ranch. Susie was three and had been purchased at an auction when she was a year old. Slim could take one look at a horse and tell you its history. Susie, he said, would live long and bear healthy foals. I just thought she was beautiful. She had a chestnut coat and a flaxen mane and tail, and a blaze—a large white patch—covering her face. And her brown eyes, bordered by long, thick black lashes, seemed to have intelligence and depth to them.

Slim and I road the fence—that is we checked the fence for any damage done to it in our absence.

From a distance, the lowlands looked like a picture postcard for the state of Montana. Rolling hills covered in pale green grass, that rose to meet the hillier country, which was dotted with deciduous trees.

Much of the herd was near the biggest pond. Aspens grew around the edges of the pond, their trunks leaning inward as if the roots of the trees sought the succor of the nutrient-ladened water beneath the ground.

Slim halted Pie and raised his binoculars to get a closer look at the herd.

He checked for the general condition of the cows: how their coats appeared. Was there any among them limping, or showing other signs of injury, such as blood on its coat; or was its movements sluggish? He searched for all these things, and, probably, more that I, in my ignorance, wasn't aware of.

Momentarily, he lowered his binoculars, and said, "I don't see anything out of the ordinary. You want to take a look?"

I did, and reached for the glasses.

He was right, of course. There was no sign of trouble today.

I gave him the binoculars back and he placed them in his saddlebag. We road on.

After a few more minutes, Slim agreed that it was time to turn back and we pointed the horses up the slope toward the spot where we'd left the truck and the trailer.

It was at that point that I saw the glint of metal in the distance. There was a vehicle coming toward us. I couldn't decipher its make or model from my vantage point. But I had only to wait a few minutes and it would be in plain view.

Whomever it was, they were on private property. Occasionally we got overzealous tourists combing our stream beds for agate, that's a colorful quartz with formations in it. It's plentiful in this area and our streams are full of it.

Folks use them for paperweights and all sorts of interesting things. I used to collect them when I was a girl; my collection sits on a shelf in my bedroom.

"Wonder who that could be?" I said to Slim.

He didn't hazard a guess, which made me slightly suspicious. Slim didn't cotton to trespassers in the first place, and, secondly, when had he ever *not* had an opinion on any given subject?

The vehicle was a late-model Range Rover, so white, it glared in the afternoon sun.

The driver was wearing dark glasses and sat tall in the seat. We stopped the horses and sat upon them, patting their strong necks to encourage them to remain calm as the machine approached.

I'd never seen the Range Rover before, but, apparently, Slim knew the owner because he smiled and waved at him.

Momentarily, the driver halted the Range Rover, opened his door, got out and stood beside it. Ben Summerall, looking relaxed in his country apparel of loose-fit jeans and a blue western shirt, the kind with silver points on the collar tips. Maybe they wore those in his part of Texas, but I'd never seen a Montanan in one. It was too ostentatious.

"Good morning," he called in a friendly voice.

"Morning," Slim said.

I said nothing.

"Be polite," Slim coaxed me in a low voice.

I flashed my teeth in Ben's direction. "Hello, Mr. Summerall." To Slim, I said, "I'll put the horses in the trailer while you chew the fat with Mr. Summerall."

We dismounted.

"I can do that," Slim offered reasonably. "He didn't come all the way out here to see me."

I knew I'd been had by my fox of a grandfather, yet again, but short of coming off like an idiot and embarrassing myself, there was nothing I could do about it for the time being.

I handed Slim Susie's reins and Ben and I met halfway between his Range Rover and the truck.

I brushed the dust off my well-worn Levi's and smoothed the strand of jet-black, curly, shoulder-length hair that had come loose from my braid, behind my ear. I wasn't wearing any makeup.

Actually, I didn't care. When a man surprised a woman with his unexpected presence, he was entitled to what he got.

I didn't mince words.

"Slim claims you came out here to see me."

Ben removed his glasses and his Stetson. His dark brown, wavy hair was cut close to his square, but well-shaped head.

I remembered he had nice eyes. Dark brown, almost black, and almond-shaped with the beginnings of worry lines growing from the corners of them.

"I wanted to apologize for the way I behaved the last time we saw each other," he began.

"Why would you need to apologize to me?"

"I was there with a woman I knew from Texas. When you walked in, I was nonplussed. I worried about what you must think of me."

"I'm sorry," I said, "but I don't quite understand what you're getting at."

"She was Native American. I'm black. You're a black woman. I'd been entertaining the notion of asking you out and you walked in and saw me with a woman of another race. I figured you'd think less of me because of it."

Hands on hips, I stared up at him. "Wait a minute now. You didn't even *know* me and you'd already labeled me a bigot?"

"Plus," he quickly added, "I hadn't been too attentive with Gaye, and I didn't want her to think that I had my eye on another woman."

"Which you just admitted, you did," I said.

He grinned sheepishly. "Yes, well, as it happened, we went back home and had a fight. She said I'd behaved strangely when you'd shown up, and wanted to know why. I was honest with her, and she went back to Texas the next day."

"It's the same old story, isn't it?" I said knowingly.

He looked confused.

"Did you love her, Ben?"

He frowned. "I thought I loved her."

"Did she love you?"

"She said she did."

I sighed wearily. "It amazes me what a man can screw up just because his penis swells when he meets someone who, momentarily, looks better to him than the present woman in his life."

His eyes stretched in amazement at my words. I knew I'd shocked him, but Momma had once told me that when you mortally wounded a dumb animal, it was your moral obligation to put it out of its misery. So I continued.

"I don't know you well, Ben. But you're reputed to be a very rich man. No doubt, you had to be pretty smart to acquire all you have in such a short time. What are you, forty-five?"

"Forty-four," he croaked.

"Been married before?"

"Twice."

"Mmm huh. Okay. The way I see it, you're never going to know what true love and commitment are until you actually practice them. I know, I'm a brash, young upstart. God knows I've tried to tone down my attitude over the years, but I've never gotten used to lying or pretending. I tend to call a duck a duck. And, Benjamin Summerall, you are a big, fat spoiled brat. Gaye may still love you and will take you back. But she's probably too good for you anyway, so leave the poor woman alone."

Ben swallowed hard, his Adam's apple working in his throat.

"What?" was all he could manage. He stared at me for a long time, then he said, "People warned me that you Montanans were a bunch of nuts."

I cocked my head toward Slim who was leaning against the trailer, out of earshot.

"Slim, Mr. Summerall has withdrawn his interest in your eldest granddaughter, shall we go?"

Slim pushed his wiry frame away from the trailer and began walking toward us.

"Is there something the matter?" he asked, concerned.

Ben turned toward Slim as though he were about to report the bad behavior of a recalcitrant child to the child's parent.

"She called me a spoiled brat," he said loudly.

"The man already had a woman when he was eyeballing me," I explained to Slim.

That was enough for Slim. He was a man who'd been loyal to one woman all his life. And, consequently, he had no patience for a man who couldn't control his gonads.

"What?" He squinted at Ben, his anger barely contained. "Is that true?"

Ben had obviously had enough of us and slapped his hat on his thigh in an exasperated gesture, turned and started walking back to his expensive British import.

"Nuts! All of you. Nuts!"

I went to Slim, placed an arm about his shoulder, and we strolled companionably, back to the truck. The Range Rover's tires spat dirt and grass as Ben wasted no time getting out of there.

"You can really pick 'em," I joked with Slim.

As I drove out of the lowlands, I analyzed my actions. Had I been too judgmental? Some might say that I had been. But, I saw it like this: when a man is truly interested in a woman, he goes to her, not her grandfather.

And another thing: Ben had made me the scapegoat in his broken relationship with Gaye, when the problem had been his roving eye and his inability to commit to any one woman. It angered me that my accidental presence in a hardware store had caused heartache for a fellow sister. I was loyal to the sisterhood, and I'd never gotten involved with a man who already had a wife or girlfriend at home. That's just the way I'd been brought up, and I made no apologies for it.

On the ride back home, Slim took a nap. Convenient, since he probably surmised I had a few questions about how Ben Summerall had known we'd be in the lowlands that morning.

At any rate, the Ben Summerall chapter had ended, and for that, I was truly grateful.

That night, after supper, I asked the whole family into the study, just off the company room.

When Slim and I had returned from riding the fence that afternoon, I'd gone into the study and made an exhaustive inspection of the financial logs, both household and business.

There was no perceptible rise in spending found in the household books. But the ranch's logs indicated that we'd been losing money, steadily, for the past year.

I realized things hadn't been the same since Daddy was killed in that stampede, but I suppose I'd assumed everything would continue as usual.

And, I admit, with my life in Chicago, I hadn't been vigilant enough about keeping an eye on my family's financial well-being. I felt guilty for allowing them to fall into such a sorry state.

Slim sat on the burgundy cowhide chair behind the desk while the others reclined on the matching couch along the wall. I stood in front of the desk.

"I've been going over the books," I said.

Slim drummed his fingers on the desktop. I couldn't tell if he was upset because I hadn't asked his permission before perusing the logs, or he was simply impatient.

Momma rose to sit on the arm of the couch. "Go ahead, give us the bad news."

"Well, it's not all bad," I said hesitantly.

"Good news first, then," she said encouragingly.

"The household books are nearly perfect."

"That's good to hear," Chad spoke up. "What of the ranch?"

"We've been going downhill for some time now," I said. "The return of the tractor will take care of the behind mortgage payments. But, because you cashed in the bonds to buy the tractor, if you should get into trouble in the future, you won't have the cushion of the bonds to fall back on. Therefore, you need to find a way to bring in more income. And, you're going to have to tighten your belts. That means, no new clothing for six months. No auctions, Slim."

Slim looked up at me, but he didn't say anything.

"Will we have to quit school?" Lucas asked. "We have scholarships, but they don't pay for incidentals like books, gas money for the one hundred twenty-mile trip there and back."

"No, we can't compromise on your educations," I assured him. "You have to stay in school."

The both of them were trying not to show it, perhaps feeling that their desire to stay in school at the expense of their family was selfish, but I could tell they were relieved.

"So, how do we earn more income?" Clancy asked. "Short of seeing beef prices skyrocket, that is?"

"First of all, we need to take stock of our assets. What do we own that others will pay to get their hands on?"

"Are you talking about the agate in our stream beds?" Lucas asked. "Because, really Chey, the stones aren't as popular with tourists as they used to be."

"No, she isn't talking about agate," Clancy said impatiently. "She's referring to the land, our way of life. The beautiful setting we wake up to every morning, but take for granted. This ranch. That's our asset, our one and only asset."

I smiled at my sister. "That's right. The land that our ancestors sweated for and died for."

Slim made a sound that was like a shrill squawk and rose from his chair, his bony index finger pointed at me.

"Not a thimbleful of the earth we stand on will be sold out from under us while I draw a breath!" he bellowed.

"Sit down, you old fool," Momma said, coming to my defense. "There hasn't been a Roberts yet who would part with a parcel of land."

"That's not what I was going to propose!" I said loudly to Slim. "Now sit down and be quiet!"

He sat, his finger still up in the air.

"I have some money saved, and what I was thinking is: If we renovated the four cabins, we could open a lodge . . ."

"You mean have guests on the ranch?" Momma asked incredulously.

I nodded affirmatively. "The cabins are in relatively good shape already. They have running water, plumbing. Each has one big room and a separate bedroom. Each has a fireplace. But, for greenhorns, we're going to need central heating. Momma, you, Clancy and I can redecorate them, and by next spring, we could be a working ranch with one noticeable difference: we'd also be a lodge for paying tourists. I've thought it out, it's a feasible plan if we all pull together."

"But your savings," Momma said, frowning. She never ceased looking out for her children's benefit. "We couldn't take the money you've worked so hard for all these years. No, Chey. That isn't acceptable."

"What if you give me ten percent of your profits until you've returned the money I've invested? Is that better?"

"I'll think about it," Momma said, sounding skeptical.

"I like the idea," Clancy said, my first convert.

"How do we get the tourists to come?" Chad asked. "Most of the people who visit Montana never see a black person. Let's face it, at 0.3 percent of the population, that means there are about twenty-five hundred of us in the entire state of more than 850,000 people. We're practically invisible."

"Yeah," I readily agreed, "and because of that, many African-Americans are hesitant about doing the tourist thing in this state. Lots of blacks I've met in Chicago laugh when I tell them I'm from Montana. 'Montana?' they say. 'Girl, there are no blacks in Montana.' They change their tone, though, when I tell them how pristine, how beautiful the land is. They *want* to visit. One of my best pals in Chicago works in promotions. I'm sure, that with a few well-placed ads in upscale black magazines, we could be booked solid for the spring season."

Slim sat shaking his head.

Momma was smiling, but she wasn't in my corner yet.

Chad and Lucas appeared to be contemplating the idea. The thought of attractive women being among the visitors to the new lodge, might have been rolling around in their hormone-driven minds.

"Oh come on," Clancy wheedled. "What have we got to lose?" She laughed. Looking at me, she added, "Except your money, of course." She looked serious. "You sure you can afford to back this project?" She *was* her mother's daughter, after all.

"Yes," I assured her. "I've been lucky in the stock market. I got out while the getting was good, *really* good."

She smiled slowly. "All right. I'm in."

Slim cleared his throat. "I don't even like company for dinner. Don't count on me to pretend to be the sweet grandfatherly type to a bunch of hardheaded younguns."

"I understand," I said placatingly. "The fact is, Slim, I plan to work up a schedule that totally leaves you out of the operation of the lodge. We don't want to scare them off, after all. We want them to recommend the place to friends."

The sides of his mouth turned up in a minuscule smile. "Okay. I reckon, you're just doing your part to find a solution for the mess we find ourselves in due to my own stupid choices. I won't begrudge you that. You're a Roberts through and through."

Even though he'd afforded me a small smile, I saw sadness in his eyes. He blamed himself for the family's financial difficulties, just as *I* blamed myself. I suppose guilt was also part of the legacy Josie left behind.

"It's a go then?" I asked everyone.

"I'm behind you," Momma said.

"Yeah!" Clancy exclaimed, grinning from ear to ear.

"Babes," Chad and Lucas said in unison.

FOUR

Tuesday morning, Beau Bradley sent a semitruck with an attached flatbed to collect the new tractor. Slim was out there, watching, as they chained his pretty baby down, locking it into place for the journey back to the Billings dealership.

I was looking down on the scene from my bedroom window. The men had brought the old tractor, a green and yellow John Deere, with them. Slim considered the John Deere a dinosaur, but I'd learned how to drive on it when I was thirteen.

Daddy had a theory that if you knew how to drive a tractor, especially an older model with all the gears, you, more than likely, could drive just about any other vehicle. He'd been right in my case because I was adept at driving anything with a stick.

The semi pulled out of the yard, and Slim walked, forlornly, toward the John Deere. He placed his hand on the bonnet and patted it as you would a faithful dog.

I turned away and went downstairs. Clancy and the boys had already departed for school, and Momma was in her garden trying to decide if her snow peas were going to be able to push themselves up through the black, rich soil by mid-October.

She weeded the garden every other day, claiming that the weeds sprouted overnight. Weeds needed no encouragement to proliferate. They got their nutrients from the plants they threatened to choke the life out of.

Momma's face was a mask of consternation as she knelt, her denim-clad knees padded, and her hands encased in work gloves. She grunted with the effort as she pulled, and a trickle of sweat flowed down the hollow between her eyes.

I knelt beside her and began pulling up the weeds by their roots.

She looked over at me and smiled.

"I thought you were going to visit your daddy's grave this morning."

She knew I'd do just about anything to avoid going out to the cemetery. The place gave me the willies. Even though I believed that the souls of departed ones did not remain earthbound; and the essence of who they'd been returned to the Creator, graveyards still made me feel as though I was being observed.

"I picked some flowers for you to take with you," Momma said.

For her, making sure her children visited their father's grave periodically had its origins not in any religious dogma, but in the mere act of remembering.

I grabbed another handful of weeds before rising.

"All right," I said.

"Tell him I'll bring him some pot liquor from the greens I'm cooking on Sunday," she joked.

Daddy used to like to pour the liquid off collard greens into a bowl and sop it up with chunks of Momma's corn bread.

"I'll be sure to give him the message," I said as I ran up the rear steps, heading back to my room in order to retrieve my coat and shoulder bag.

Because Chad and Lucas had taken the black, late-model Ford King Cab (my favorite family-owned vehicle), I had a choice between Momma's forest green 1996 Ford Taurus wagon, or Slim's red 1969 standard-shift pickup. I chose the pickup.

Slim was in the yard when I drove it out of the barn.

"Bring her back like you found her," he admonished as I pulled away. That wouldn't be difficult. Even if I dented her hide, you wouldn't be able to distinguish the new ding from the myriad of others already covering her. The motor purred like a kitten, though.

You turned onto the ranch road from Highway 94, and the cemetery was six miles north of us on 94. Traffic was light, and I arrived there in under ten minutes.

The entrance to the cemetery was a ten-foot-high wrought-iron gate with the image of angels in flowing robes, blowing trumpets: one angel on each side of the gate. When the gate's closed, it appeared as if the angels are shooting at each other with old-fashioned muskets.

Visitors parked outside the gate and walked in. I always did this with a feeling of trepidation. What if I had to get back out, fast, and my wheels were too far away? I fought the urge to drive through the gate each time I went there.

Mine was the only car parked out there that day, and I wasn't too thrilled by the fact.

The cold winds whipped about me, and I paused to sit Momma's flowers on the ground long enough for me to button my jacket.

The cemetery was located on the crest of a hill, and in the center sat a great oak tree, its gnarled boughs reaching heavenward.

Daddy's last resting place was beneath the oak tree, so that's where I headed.

Some folks said the cemetery had been used by locals since the late eighteen hundreds. In my eagerness not to linger, I had not stopped to read the headstones, like I'd seen others doing; so I'd never sought the proof that would bear out their claims.

My boots made crunching sounds on the leaf-covered ground, and the scent of pine was carried on the breezes, owing largely to the Ponderosa pines that edged the area.

The closer I got to my father's grave, the more lethargic my limbs felt. It wasn't a physical tiredness, but a malaise of the spirit.

When I wasn't faced with undeniable proof of Daddy's demise, namely, his grave, I could remember him as the vibrant, happy man who'd loved to sing. A man who adored his wife and children. A man who, in my opinion, stood, head and shoulders, above other men.

It wasn't as if I'd deified my father. No, I also recalled his faults. He was headstrong, for one. He was lousy with figures, and Momma had to pull his fat out of the fire concerning the budget on a number of occasions. He was like Slim in that respect: He was partial to new farm equipment. Beau Bradley used to see him coming and lick his chops. He knew that after Daddy left the dealership, he could close up for the day, and call it a good month.

But, when I visited his grave, all those thoughts of the human side of Daddy vanished, and I experienced violent flashbacks of the day he died.

I'd never confided in Momma about the problem. If I had, I was sure she wouldn't insist on my going to the cemetery. So, I suffered—quietly, and alone.

There were wrought-iron benches throughout the grounds. One leaned against the trunk of the oak tree and I sat down on it.

Daddy's headstone read: BELOVED SON, HUSBAND, FATHER. Cole and Enid hadn't had Cole, the third, or Cody yet, otherwise "grandfather" would've appeared on the headstone, too.

That's when the first image hit me.

I was back, seven years earlier, in the wilderness that was the plains. The thunderous sound of hundreds of hooves reverberated in my head and the air was thick with dust, unbreathable.

I had been riding a few hundred feet behind Daddy. I kept Chad with me. He was fourteen and it was his first cattle drive. Daddy made me his baby-sitter, saying that wherever I was, there Chad should be also.

So, I'd kept my promise and, when it happened, Chad was at my side. I wish, to this day, that he hadn't been.

Unbeknownst to me, up ahead, a cougar had attacked one of the cows, bringing it down. Daddy had rushed toward the fracas, possibly thinking that he could beat the cougar off with a stick or something; it would have been suicide to use the rifle in its holder on his saddle. Its report would've sent the cattle into a mad panic.

Apparently, though, the sound of the wildcat's growls, and, then the scent of the blood was enough to stampede the herd. They went crazy, running all out in every direction. Daddy's horse got speared with a horn and it threw him. Daddy didn't have a chance.

By the time I got to him, the herd was several hundred feet in advance of me and Chad. Daddy lay on the ground in a twisted heap, blood pouring from his mouth.

I leaped from my horse. I really don't recall pulling my feet from the stirrups. My mind had gone into a sort of fugue state, I suppose. It was as though I were outside of my body, watching the events unfold.

The girl dismounted from a still-moving horse and raced toward what was left of her father.

His eyes were open, but he wasn't seeing anything. The pain must have been excruciating, because he had a broken leg, a broken arm, his lungs had been punctured and his back was broken.

He had been six feet, three-inches tall, and two hundred and thirty pounds, but, as he lay there, he appeared half that size.

The girl stood looking from side to side as if she were expecting someone to come to their aid. Some miraculous person who could rewind time and prevent this scene from coming to pass.

No one came though, and she screamed, her voice a high-pitched keen that she felt to the marrow of her bones.

Dropping to her knees, she placed her father's head in her lap. His eyes focused on her face for a split second. "Sorry, Peaches," he said, his voice barely a whisper.

Her tears bathed his bloody face as he drew his last breath. She reached down and closed his eyes.

The breeze was cold on my sweat-covered face as I slowly came back to the present. All in all, though, it had been a mild trip to the past. After seven years, the anguish was gradually diminishing. Maybe one day, a visit to Daddy's grave wouldn't trigger the images at all. I would just remember the good times.

"Sorry, Peaches," were his last words. I suppose, even as he felt his life force slipping away, he knew that Momma would be furious at him for leaving her. But, there was nothing he could do about it.

I often thought that if Momma's face had been the one he was trying to focus on that day, she could have saved him. With just her sheer will, her indomitable spirit, she could have pulled him from Death's clutches.

I wondered if that thought had ever crossed her mind. I hoped not. One obsessive person in the family was enough.

"Well, Daddy, it's me, Cheyenne," I said aloud. "I know it's been a while since I've been here. I won't make any excuses. You know I don't like this place. When I think of you, it's usually with us out riding the fence, doing the spring branding or calving. Or, singing 'Stand by Me'."

Just as I imagined he could hear me when I talked to him, I also imagined his questions to me.

"What have I been doing the last ten months? Working, mostly. I'm bringing in some high-profile cases for the firm. Once word got around that I'm good at what I do, professional athletes started coming out of the woodwork it seemed. Stu Farrar and Garrett Streiber are hinting around about making me a partner. And I'm not twenty-eight yet. I don't think I'm ready for the responsibility, although *they* seem to think so."

At that point, he would've asked, "What do you *really* want for yourself, Chey?"

"More and more, I dream of coming back home. Whenever I think of that, I develop a huge guilt complex: Why did I spend all those years in school if I wasn't going to devote myself to a career? My sole redeeming thought, when I find myself in a funk, is that the family didn't have to pay for my education. I made it on scholarships, and working part-time. Still, Daddy, I wonder why I'm not satisfied with my present life. I crave something . . . something more. Something lasting. And I think it's love, Daddy. I want to be in love. Now, my problem is this: I believe Jackson could be the object of my affection. But, I don't know for sure, *can't* know for sure, until I know how he feels about me. So, what do I do about it?"

I rose and placed Momma's flowers in the vase near the headstone.

"You think about it and give me your answer next time. By the way, Momma told me to tell you she'll bring you some pot liquor from the collards she's cooking Sunday. Sorry, she didn't say anything about corn bread."

I turned to walk away. "I love you, Daddy."

I knew Daddy wasn't really there, but it had been cathartic for me. Isn't the *real* purpose of cemeteries, memorial services, all the ways we, as a people, remember our dead, to help the living cope with the absence of those they cherish?

"Leaving?" a deep male voice said from behind me.

I recognized it immediately and took my time turning to face the person from whom it'd issued.

"When did you get here?"

I wanted to know if he could've possibly heard what I'd said at Daddy's grave a few minutes before.

"Just arrived, I came in from the east side." He held up a bunch of posies. "My mother's favorite flowers. Today would've been her birthday."

My heart did a little somersault at the sight of him. He wasn't wearing anything special. Just his daily uniform of Wrangler's, a denim shirt, his old tan suede jacket and his well-worn brown leather boots. Oh, and his ever-present tan Stetson. He didn't go anywhere without that hat.

My emotions were already tender. So the mere act of his remembering his mother on her birthday, made me want to tear up.

"You in a hurry?" he asked. He glanced in the direction of his blue, late-model Ford Explorer. "I brought a thermos of coffee. Want to share a cup after I visit with Ma for a while?"

Of course I did; however, I didn't want to appear too eager to spend time with him, so I threw a lasso around my enthusiasm and tied it down. "I'd like that," I said calmly with a small smile.

We walked to his mother's grave in companionable silence, and I stood aside while he knelt and placed the flowers in the vase near Ginny Kincaid's headstone.

Jackson had lost both his parents in a car accident when he was twenty-two. He'd been out of college—with a bachelor's degree in animal husbandry—a year by then. My family had been as supportive as he would allow us to be. Jackson's parents were from that stock of stoic farm families whose goal in life was to be self-sustaining. Which meant they asked no one for help in difficult times, and they always held their emotions in check.

If Jackson had cried when his parents died, I hadn't been a witness to it. But, I had noticed a subtle change in his attitude toward fun and relaxation. Prior to his parents' deaths, he was as big a prankster as my older brother, Cole, Jr., had been, and still was. Though he was adept at trading barbs with anyone, Jackson's underlying goal today, seemed to be work, work and more work.

He got to his feet after a few minutes, without having uttered a word, and smiled at me.

That he'd held his entire conversation with his mother in his mind wasn't surprising to me in the least. He kept a lot of things close to his chest.

Maybe that was part of his appeal: He was an enigma. I'd always enjoyed puzzles, that's why I was so good with numbers. Give me a mystery and I would keep at it until I solved it. No matter how long it took.

"How is everyone at the Robertses' place?" he asked as we walked across the cemetery toward the exit.

"Everyone's fine," I answered. "We're talking about renovating the cabins and turning the place into a lodge at least one season of the year."

He laughed. "Mr. Riley'll never let it happen."

"Slim has already given his permission. He just doesn't want to be bothered by, and I quote: 'hardheaded younguns' running all over the place."

"Well all right then," Jackson said. "Let me know if there's anything I can do to help."

"You've got your hands full with your own place. How many head have you got this year, more than a thousand, right?"

"Fifteen hundred," he answered. "I've got a foreman who's a good man, though, and I'm concentrating on enjoying life more."

I stopped to look up at him in shock. "You?"

"Hey, I'm not getting any younger. It's time I did something other than work."

"Like what?"

His brown eyes met mine. "Like get married and have some kids."

Oh, God, I thought, *don't let him tell me he's met someone.*

"Do you have anyone special in mind?" My voice cracked a bit. I hoped he hadn't noticed.

The few seconds it took him to reply, I was praying to God so fervently for the answer to be in my favor, that I was squinting with the effort.

I held my breath.

"Not yet," he said after an eternity, it seemed.

I breathed a sigh of relief.

"Had you going there for a minute, didn't I?"

We continued walking, and I pretended I hadn't heard his last comment. He was so conceited. Did he actually believe my nose would be bent out of joint if I learned he'd met someone special?

I made him wait a full two minutes before I said, "Seems to me, you're overdue for a little happiness, Jackson."

"The same could be said of you," he replied, smiling. "Why haven't you gotten married yet, Chey? And don't give me that career spiel you lay on me whenever I ask."

"I've never been in love," I said simply.

"What's stopping you?"

"I don't know, really." Well, I did have a theory, but I wasn't ready to share it with *him*.

"You know, but you don't want to tell me. I understand. You think I'm going to tease you about it at some later date. But I wouldn't do that, Cheyenne. We're friends. Solid friends, and it concerns me when you aren't happy, and you don't seem happy to me."

We arrived at the Explorer, and he opened the door and retrieved the thermos. Twisting off the cap, he poured some of the black coffee into the thermos's lid, which doubled as a cup.

Handing it to me, he said, "If it wasn't for the fact that I've known you since you were born, and have considered you a kid sister ever since, I'd seriously be in behind you myself, so I know you've had offers."

"A couple of proposals," I replied. I sipped some of the coffee, which was sweet, the way Jackson liked it. Black and sweet.

"Good guys?"

I nodded. Our eyes met and, not wanting him to read my emotions, I lowered them. "Tad and Ahmad were both good men. And I truly cared about them but I wasn't in love either time, so I couldn't, in good faith, marry them."

"No, you couldn't," he agreed.

I raised my eyes to his once more. "What about you, Jackson? Is what Clancy said the other day true? Are you still in love with Marissa?"

He shifted his weight from one leg to the other and removed his Stetson. He ran a hand over his naturally wavy, jet-black hair.

"Sometimes I think I am, and sometimes I feel relieved that she left me. On the one hand, I loved her with all my heart and I wanted to spend the rest of my life with her. On the other hand, I wouldn't want a wife who didn't want to be here. I mean, fully here. She said she loved me and would try to be happy. But what is happiness if you have to work so hard in order to achieve it? I felt she'd come to resent me someday because I was such an immovable part of this land that she hated."

What he'd said was a sad reminder of why one should never listen to rumors. The rumor mill had it that Marissa had left Jackson, which, I suppose, had been easy to accept for anyone who'd known Marissa for any length of time. She was beautiful. Not just pretty, as I'd describe myself, if pressed. She had the kind of looks that made everyone look twice, then stare.

When she was a teenager, she did some modeling in the area department stores. But, because of her height, five-two, she was not tapped by a hungry talent agent for runway modeling. She did print ads, and tried her hand at acting, but she felt remaining in Montana was stifling her career, so, for about five years, she lived in New York City. She came back home a local celebrity, but with little real experience in acting under her belt: just largely ignored off-off-Broadway plays and one national soft drink commercial that we'd all seen and admired.

Her return to Montana confirmed what we die-hard Montanans always suspected: there's no better place on earth than where you already are. Of course, when she and Jackson busted up and she left, again, for the bright lights of New York City, we labeled her ungrateful and a glutton for punishment. Jackson, who was considered a golden boy among the blacks, and whites, of the community, was generally looked upon with sympathy and understanding.

Now I saw that their parting had been mutual. She hadn't left him high and dry. They'd both agreed that it would be best if they went their separate ways.

The danger in that though, I thought, as I gazed up at Jackson, was: What if they suddenly decided to reconcile? They'd left a window of opportunity open when they'd parted so amicably. That worried me. And hadn't Jackson just admitted that he still had feelings for Marissa?

"So you're looking for someone who loves your way of life," I said, hoping to get off the subject of Marissa.

"Definitely," he said, narrowing his eyes. "What are *you* looking for?"

"Coincidentally, I'm also looking for someone who loves this way of life."

I drank half of the coffee and returned the cup to him. He drank the rest, then placed the cap back on the thermos, dropping it onto the Explorer's front seat.

"What about your career?"

"I can work anywhere. Besides, I want children soon. I'm twenty-seven. By the time Momma was twenty-seven, she had already had Cole and was expecting me."

"Women in your mother's day didn't have all the options today's woman has. Do you really want to limit yourself to being a wife and mother?"

"Jackson, being a wife and mother is the most important job on this planet. The faint-hearted need not apply. Plus, if I really want to work, I'll open an office in Custer. I'm not going to put off getting married and having children simply because I want to be president of my firm. I don't want to come to the end of my life, and all I have to show for it is a huge bank account, a fabulous house and a Siamese cat. I need more."

"Have you decided upon a time frame within which you should have achieved your goals?" he asked, his eyebrows raised in interest.

"I'm giving myself a year," I answered confidently. "A year to fall in love, get a proposal and plan the wedding."

Jackson laughed and shook his head. "The hubris of youth," he intoned knowingly. "What makes you think you can do all that in three hundred and sixty-five days?"

I eyed him smugly. "Because I'm going to marry you, Jackson."

He reached over and placed his hand on my forehead. "Have you contracted some kind of exotic fever?"

I grasped his hand, turned the palm up and placed a kiss in it. Our eyes met, and I believe he then understood the seriousness of my statement.

He smiled slowly. "You're sweet, Chey, but I'd have to decline."

I moved closer to him. Our thighs touched as he found his back pressed against the door of the Explorer.

"Don't be hasty, you've got a year to think about it."

My hands were inside his coat, massaging his muscular chest through his denim shirt. I felt his heartbeat, at first a steady, slow rhythm, speed up and become more erratic.

"A year to get used to the fact that our innocent repartee has been leading up to this moment, Jackson. A year to admit that you're attracted to me. A year to decide that you love me, not as a kid sister, but as a woman."

I held his gaze. "A year should be long enough, because you're already halfway there."

We looked into each other's eyes for a long moment. His arms had gone around me and he'd pulled me closer. Then he bent his head and kissed me. Our lips were immobile and hesitant initially. We had years of conditioning to put aside. Within seconds though, he sighed and gave up the pretense. His mouth devoured mine and I wrapped my arms around his neck. Jackson nearly lifted me off the ground as our bodies writhed together beneath our coats.

He tasted sweet, and, faintly of coffee. His lips were soft and pliable and his tongue, exploring my mouth with sensual intensity, whipped me into a deep sexual arousal. It was everything I'd dreamed it would be. I was weak with satisfaction.

At last, we drew apart, both of us groaning with pleasure.

I was, no doubt, starry-eyed.

He appeared confused. His dark, downward-sloping eyes regarded me with a combination of lust and something else, some indefinable emotion. Fear?

"It can never be, Cheyenne," he said with finality and, I thought, regret. "What would people say? That I was robbing the cradle, taking advantage of you? We'd never hear the end of it. Cole . . . Cole would have my head. I'd break a guy's jaw if I were in his position . . ."

His words caught me unawares. I'd believed that if he kissed me, everything would be made clear to us. We'd know, for certain, that we belonged together, and everything else would fall into place. I realized then, however, that Jackson was the product of his environment, as was I. He could *want* me. Desire me. Wish to rip my clothes off and take me to bed. But, in his mind, it wasn't the honorable thing to do, therefore, for the sake of decorum, he would resist.

Was I fighting a losing battle?

Backing away from him, I said, "Remember that kiss, and call me when you no longer care what other people will say once you and I go public, Jackson. But don't wait too long, because I've been waiting long enough already."

I don't believe I'd ever seen Jackson conflicted. A man who always knew his own mind, he had been decisive about life up until that moment.

"Where are you going?" he asked. "We need to talk."

I paused and smiled at him. "I want you, Jackson. You think about that and everything it entails. Keep in mind that you may have considered me a younger sister all these years, but I'm not related to you by blood, so there's nothing incestuous about it. Further, and after that kiss, I believe you've noticed: I'm not a child any longer. I'm a woman, and you're a man. I've chosen you; and whether you're ready to admit it, or not, you've chosen me."

I turned then and left him standing there.

FIVE

We had a lot of work to do in order to have the cabins in shape for guests by the spring season. The day after I'd given Jackson a reason to avoid me for the rest of our lives, I threw myself into the project.

I hired a building inspector to come out and go over the four cabins to determine if there was any faulty wiring. All of them got a clean bill of health. The plumbing was another matter. The commodes, sinks and tubs dated back to the forties. We agreed that we'd need to replace them with new ones.

Next, a technician from a pest-control company checked the logs for termites. None were found, thank God.

A gangly redhead with pale blue eyes, he'd blown air between his lips as though we'd escaped disaster by the skin of our teeth. "If you'd had an infestation," he'd said gravely, "you'd just as well have torn these down and built new ones."

The cabins being termite-free meant our project was viable. If we'd had to build new cabins, there was no way we could've afforded the cost without getting a loan.

The second Sunday of my two weeks at home, Cole, Enid and my nephews, Cole III, and Cody came for a short visit.

Momma and I were in the kitchen putting the finishing touches on a meal featuring Cole's and Enid's favorite dishes: fried trout, corn fritters, coleslaw and home fries, with the pièce de résistance, Momma's peach cobbler.

I was standing at the counter, grating a purple cabbage (we used a combination of green and purple) for the coleslaw, when we heard their car pull up.

Clancy, who'd been sitting on the porch swing doing her homework, was the first to run out to meet them.

Momma and I walked through the house and out the front door, and by the time we got outside, Cole, Enid and the boys were spilling out of their station wagon.

The day was cool, around forty-two degrees, and Enid had the boys in hooded jackets: one red, one blue.

Clancy scooped little Cole, age four, up into her arms and hugged Cody to her. Cole ran up the four steps and swept Momma into his arms.

Seeing Cole was like looking at Daddy when he was in his thirties. He was six feet, four inches tall and healthy. Not overweight, but a little thick around the middle from Enid's good cooking. His smooth, dark skin had the vibrant glow of a man who got his exercise the natural way, by working hard. He kept his thick, black hair cut short and tapered at the nape of the neck.

After Momma had let him go, he grabbed me about the waist, pulled me to him and planted a kiss on my forehead, just the way he used to do when there were none of his friends around to rib him about loving his kid sister.

"Hey, sis, whatcha know good?"

"Quite a lot, actually," I told him, grinning. "I'll tell you all about it later."

Enid, his wife of seven years, was a registered nurse. She stood around five-six, was plump and had the most beautiful golden-brown skin. People told her she favored her mother-in-law. It's true, that when it came to skin color, Enid and Momma were of similar complexions; whereas Clancy and I were born with skin that was a cross between our mother's golden-brown and our father's darker brown.

"Let's get inside," Momma suggested, grasping her daughter-in-law's hand.

Momma and Enid went into the house, followed by Cole and I, with Clancy and the boys bringing up the rear.

"Slim's in his apartment. Clancy leave the boys here and run up and get him," Momma said once we were in the foyer.

"Don't bother him if he's sleeping," Cole said in his deep, rich baritone, so reminiscent of Daddy's.

Clancy reluctantly put Cole on the floor and let go of Cody. Enid and I made short work of getting the boys out of their jackets, then she and Cole removed theirs and we hung them on the brass hall tree in the foyer.

Enid told Momma the air smelled wonderful.

Momma, who was on her knees hugging her grandsons, smiled her thanks and said, "Not half as good as my babies."

What she was referring to was the sweet, clean, new smell of young skin. Babies have it, and toddlers, small children. It was heady, that aroma. It made you want to cuddle them, love them, protect them.

I gave both my nephews intense, warm hugs before we went back to the hub of the household: the kitchen.

A few minutes after Cole and his family arrived, we were sitting around the kitchen chatting when the doorbell rang. Clancy sprang up from the window seat, where she'd been playing Hungry, Hungry Hippo with the boys, and went to see who was there.

Two minutes later, she walked through the kitchen's entrance with Jackson. "Look who's here," she said. If her grin had been any wider, her mouth would've touched her ears.

I hadn't known he'd been invited, but it wasn't uncommon for him to pop up at any time. Cole had probably told him he'd be in town that day. Or Momma, who thought Jackson was too isolated on his ranch, had phoned him and suggested he drop by.

We hadn't spoken since our kiss in the cemetery. He'd tried to get me, but I'd been out on one errand or another when he'd phoned. I knew he was probably under the impression I was avoiding him; which was half true. I didn't want him trying to dissuade me.

He and Cole clasped hands and patted each other on the back. They never hugged. Jackson went over and gave Enid a peck on the cheek then rubbed each boy's head affectionately.

"Miss Peaches," he said to Momma, "you're as pretty as ever."

Momma beamed and gave him a hug. "You're just in time for dinner." At home, dinner was lunch, and supper was dinner.

When in Chicago, lunch was at noon, dinner after five and supper, a late meal that few bothered with anymore.

Jackson went over to the table and shook Slim's hand, leaning down to hear something Slim was saying. When he straightened back up, he glanced in my direction and smiled.

"How much longer on that coleslaw?" Momma asked close to my ear.

"Ten minutes, tops," I said. I still had to grate half a cabbage, then mix in the carrots, relish and dressing.

"Clancy," Momma said, "you, Chad and Lucas, set the table."

After issuing her orders, Momma stood next me and began pouring the already grated cabbage into a large mixing bowl. "I invited Jackson," she stated in an off handed manner. "He's been trying to talk to you all week. What do you suppose he wants?"

I don't lie to my mother, so I said, "Can I fill you in later?"

Her fine brows arched with interest as she smiled at me. "Well, all right then. I hope it's something juicy."

"It is."

"It's about time," she replied in that knowing way she has.

"I want to hear about your plans for the lodge," Cole said from across the room. "Are you really going to cater to the whims of spoiled city folks?"

"All city folks aren't spoiled," Enid said gently. She hailed from Philadelphia.

"I stand corrected," Cole said, grinning at his wife.

"What kind of activities are you going to offer the tourists?" he asked, taking another tack.

Momma and I had spent so much time in the kitchen together over the years that we instinctively knew each other's movements. She'd gone to the refrigerator to get the dressing, relish and carrots, while I'd poured the remaining grated cabbage into the mixing bowl.

She gingerly handed me the jars while she went to the sink to rinse the carrots, which she'd grate as I answered Cole's query, while simultaneously adding the ingredients from the jars to the cabbage.

"We haven't decided on activities yet," I said to Cole. I licked a drop of dressing off my finger and stirred the slaw. "I'd like to hear you all's ideas . . ."

"Horseback riding, definitely," Enid said. "You don't come to Montana without going on a trail ride."

"Yeah, and since you're so close to the Yellowstone, fishing," Cole said.

"Hot tubs," Chad put in.

"You just want to see scantily clad women," Clancy accused.

"We don't want to see scantily clad *men,*" Luke said with a laugh.

Clancy was standing near him as they placed plates on the table, and she bumped his hip with her own. "Horn dog."

"Infant," he returned. Nothing incensed Clancy more than being reminded of her age.

"Moron," she hissed.

"That's enough," Momma said. "Clancy, finish up there, then go down to the cellar and get that booster seat for little Cole."

Momma poured the grated carrots into the mixture and I stirred them in, then went to set the bowl on the table. Luke and Chad put the rest of the food on the table: a platter of crisply fried trout, the home fries and the corn fritters.

Clancy was back with the booster seat in a short while, and we all sat around the big kitchen table, which Momma had earlier asked Chad to add the middle extension to.

"Slim," Momma said, "would you ask for the blessing?"

We bowed our heads. "Dear Lord," Slim began, "thank you for the gathering together of family and friends. Thank you for the wonderful meal that Peaches and my still-single granddaughter Cheyenne, who's a great catch, if I've ever seen one, prepared. And, thank you, Lord, for allowing me to eat it with my own teeth. Amen."

Everyone laughed as I sat and shook my head. Slim reached for the platter of trout, oblivious, as always, of the implications of what he'd just said.

"At least he didn't mention Ben Summerall," Momma said.

"What about Ben Summerall?" Cole asked.

Slim passed the platter of trout to Cole.

"Slim tried to fix Chey up with Ben," Momma answered as she fed little Cole a piece of potato.

I glanced in Jackson's direction, hoping to see a flicker of jealousy cross his features. Not a glimmer.

I sighed.

"Ben Summerall," Enid said, sounding as though she was having trouble placing the name, "isn't he that oil guy who moved here from Oklahoma?"

"Texas," Cole corrected her.

"You went out with him?" Enid asked me.

"There was nothing to it, really," I said, eager to change the subject. "Something Slim cooked up and I threw out the back door."

Enid smiled at me. "You gotta love him," she said of Slim's interfering.

"That's what they tell me," I quipped.

Slim bit into the trout. "These some of the ones you caught last week?" he asked Momma.

"Yes they are," Momma answered.

"They're delicious, Miss Peaches," Jackson offered.

"Thank you, baby," Momma said affectionately.

"Jackson," Cole said, "what are you doing around the fifteenth of next month? I'm going to be taking Chad and Lucas hunting, and we'd like you to join us."

"Elk?"

"What else?"

"Sounds good. I'll have to get back to you on that, though. I might have to stay close to the ranch since I have several heifers getting ready to go down."

"You do that," Cole said.

"Auntie," Cody, who was sitting on my right, pulled on my shirt's sleeve, "I need to go to the bathroom."

Cody, at six, was perfectly capable of going to the bathroom by himself. However, he had a fear of the dark, and the hallway through which he'd have to pass on the way to the bathroom, wasn't adequately illuminated.

I pushed my chair back and rose.

"Excuse us while we visit the facilities," I said to the others.

Cody and I left the table.

Cody allowed me to precede him as we walked down the hallway to the nearest bathroom, which was just off the kitchen.

When we arrived at the bathroom, I reached inside and switched on the light for him.

He backed inside, looking up at me with his big brown eyes, then he closed the door.

I leaned against the wall and waited for him.

After a minute or so, I heard him washing up at the sink. The door creaked open and he turned the light off.

"Auntie, can I tell you something secret, and you won't tell anyone—'specially not Momma or Daddy?"

He looked so serious, I was hesitant to make him a promise I might not be able to keep. What if one of the kids at school was bullying him? Or an adult, someone he trusted, was inappropriately touching him? Being a parent was a huge responsibility.

I knelt to look him in the eyes. "What is it, sugar? Has someone hurt you in any way?"

He cocked his head to the side and gave me a confused look that was so like his father's, my heart felt as though it would break.

"No, Auntie. Nobody's hurt me. My momma would kill 'em."

That made me smile. Not his Daddy, but his Momma. It spoke to what a fierce protector of her children Enid was.

I realized he was waiting for me to promise to keep his secret.

I raised my right hand as though I was about to take a solemn oath. "I promise that no one will get this secret out of me. Not even if they put lit matches under my fingernails."

He giggled. The macabre sense of humor of a six-year-old boy.

"Momma's gonna have a baby," Cody said.

I hugged him to me. "That's great news, Cody."

He appeared ready to join the others then. He clasped my hand in his and we walked back down the hall to the kitchen.

Enid was expecting. She and Cole had always said they wanted at least four children.

I was happy for them. And, maybe, a bit envious. I wanted their kind of happiness and stability; the generous manner in which they nurtured each other, and offered support, when needed. Those were the hallmarks of a good marriage, I felt: the willingness of each partner to give what's needed . . . *when* it's needed.

". . . selling," Jackson said. I'd caught the tail end of his statement.

"Selling what?" I asked as I helped Cody with his chair, then sat down myself.

"Sid and Harriette Beechum are selling their place to King Mining," Jackson said, his eyes on my face. "Sid says they're getting too old to run the ranch by themselves; and, since they have no children to leave the land to, they'd just as well get something out of it while they can still enjoy the proceeds."

"Where're they going?" I asked.

"They are originally from Alabama. They both have family back there. With the money they'll earn from the sale of the property, they can live pretty well in Alabama," Momma spoke up.

Momma sighed sadly. Harriette Beechum was a good friend. No doubt, she and Harriette had discussed their decision at length. She hadn't said a word to me, though. Maybe because she was hoping Sid and Harriette would change their minds, and there wouldn't be anything to discuss.

"We have *good* news to counter the bad," Cole announced suddenly.

Momma perked up a bit; sitting up in her chair, and regarding Cole with a hopeful expression.

Cole reached for Enid's hand before continuing. "Enid and I are expecting a bundle of joy in the spring."

An explosion of whoops rose from the assembly. Momma flew out of her chair and grabbed both Cole and Enid around their necks.

We offered our congratulations all at once. The joy in that room was a palpable thing, a moving spirit that enveloped and caressed.

Amid it all, my eyes sought Jackson's. In that instance, from the time he turned his well-shaped head, and his dark eyes met mine across the dinner table, I knew he was in total and full possession of my heart.

His lips curled in an enigmatic smile, and I lowered my eyes because I didn't want the others guessing what had transpired between us.

From that minute onward, as far as I was concerned, our fates were sealed and etched in time. He would be mine.

Sometimes, though, fate has a way of throwing you for a loop, and giving you your comeuppance. I was cocksure, to the point of being obnoxious back then. They say the first step in recovery, is recognizing you have a problem.

Later that day, we got up a game of basketball on the court in the front yard. We divided up the teams into two girls, two boys, and a baby (Cole III and Cody) on each team; so they were as follows: Cody, Enid, Cole, Chad and myself were the blue team, as signified by Cody's blue jacket. And Lucas, Jackson, Clancy, Momma and Cole III were the red team.

In the first quarter, the blue team was leading by two points when Clancy stole the ball from Chad and evened the score.

I'd never seen her play better, and no one was more surprised than Chad, who stood looking at his empty hands with a stupefied expression on his face, as our sister dribbled down the court and spiked the ball through the hoop.

"Way to go, Clance," Jackson applauded.

Clancy had grinned and given the thumbs-up sign.

It was our ball then, and Cole took it out, only to be blocked by Jackson. It must have been like old times for them. They'd both been on the team while in high school. Cole, Jr., had played a little in college, but he'd had to quit in his junior year because of an injury to his left knee. Jackson had gone to college on a football scholarship and had had no interest, whatsoever, in pursuing it as a career. Being a rancher was all he'd ever wanted to be.

Cole tried to fake Jackson out, but it didn't work. Jackson got the ball and passed it to Luke who shot nearly from half court. The ball bounced off the rim and I got the rebound, didn't fully believe in my ability to make a long shot, and passed it to Enid, who was closer to the goal. Enid caught the ball and shot it immediately, scoring easily.

By the fourth quarter, our team was behind by six points. Slim, sitting on the sidelines offering commentary, yelled, "Give the ball to Cody, he's your only hope."

So, we allowed Cody to take the ball out. He dribbled the ball down the court as the adults "accidentally" tripped over their own feet, due to his prowess. He was almost at the goal, when his baby brother challenged him by standing directly in his path and reaching for the ball.

Cody paused. Cole III pleaded with him with his eyes. His lower lip trembled. Poor guy, he hadn't been able to get his hands on the ball the entire game.

Cody handed his brother the ball; Cole III's face broke into a wide grin and he kissed his older brother's cheek.

Jackson lifted Cole III up to the goal and the four-year-old dropped the ball through the hoop.

We screamed as fans do for Michael Jordan when he scores the winning goal in the final game of the play-offs.

"Red team wins," Slim cried, "with a score of fifty-two to forty-four."

The teams dispersed. Jackson pulled me aside.

"I'd like to get your advice on a financial matter," he said.

Various members of my family groaned in sympathy.

"Just don't let her drone on until your eyes glaze over," Chad joked.

I playfully shoved him as Jackson and I walked past, making our way across the slope of the front lawn toward the cabins, which were several hundred yards behind the main house.

It was one of those ideal days for late September in Montana. Unseasonably warm at forty-two degrees, a clear, cloudless sky, the absence of fierce breezes and the sun, warm on your face.

Jackson and I were attired similarly in jeans, cotton shirts, light jackets and athletic shoes.

"I know what you're going to say," I opened the conversation when we were out of earshot of the others.

"Oh?" Jackson glanced down at me.

"Yeah. You're here to tell me the kiss we shared was a huge mistake."

"I rather enjoyed it," he begged to differ.

I made myself continue walking, but my legs had grown weak at his admission.

"That's good, because I did, too. And I'm curious to know what the second kiss will feel like."

"I'm sure it will be as splendid as the first was," he said.

We were looking straight ahead, not wanting to draw unwanted attention to ourselves.

It took all the restraint I had in me in order to refrain from launching myself at him when he said that.

I impatiently awaited his next words.

"I'm here to make you an offer," he said.

We'd reached a copse of Ponderosa pines and I leaned against the trunk of one of them, smiling expectantly up at him.

An offer, I thought then. *Yes! The answer is yes, I'll marry you!*

What he said, though, was: "You got me to thinking, Cheyenne. I'm thirty-five. You're twenty-seven. Like you said, that isn't such a great age difference. My problem is: I've known you since you were in diapers. It's hard for me to get that fact out of my mind. But, I'll diligently work on it, if you'll agree to this suggestion . . ."

"What is it?" I asked, barely able to find my voice. I was sorely disappointed he hadn't proposed to me.

"You get to keep your deadline of one year. But, we have to see other people in the interim."

My heart was racing. It sounded like a retreat to me. A tactful way to let me down easy. But, what if I was wrong, and he was attracted to me, just afraid to express his feelings? I *had* sprung quite a lot on him the other day. His head must have been reeling.

"I know you think you want me. Whether it's a crush, or something more . . . well, only time will tell. But I do know this, Cheyenne. I love you. I've always loved you like a sister. Yes, I *am* physically drawn to you, too. You're a pretty woman. And that kiss brought home to me the fact that you're definitely an adult."

"At least I got you to admit that," I said in a low voice.

"I need to admit something else, too," he said, his eyes boring into mine.

He had my undivided attention.

"I'm listening."

"You scare me, Cheyenne."

"Illuminate me," I told him as I reached up to touch his face.

He grasped the offending hand by the wrist. "Our little flirtations have been fun, Chey. But do you really know me? Deep down, I'm this great grizzly bear of a soul, hiding in his cave after being trounced by love. I talk a good game, but I think you could break my heart, girl, and it can't stand much more abuse."

"I'd never hurt you, Jackson," I breathed. I took his hand in both of mine and brought it to my chest. I wanted to tell him I was in love with him. That I'd always loved him. I knew he wouldn't be convinced of my affection simply by my voicing the words though.

"All right," I agreed. "You have your year."

"You won't regret it," he promised.

You haven't experienced real silence until you've slept in the woods. At night, especially on cold nights, there is no sound except the thump of your own heart. Your mind reaches for, hopes for any noise that will rescue you from your own thoughts.

It was around 2:00 A.M., everyone else in the house had been asleep for some time.

I got out of bed, stepped into my fur-lined slippers then put on the heavy chenille robe kept at the foot of the bed.

There was only one reason for my insomnia. I invariably panicked when faced with change. No one liked upheavals in their lives, even if the change was a positive one. I would have to take a leave of absence from Streiber and Farrar.

If we were to make the lodge the best it possibly could be, I needed to be there, on hand, working alongside my family.

I hadn't figured out how I would broach the subject with my two bosses in Chicago yet, though. They had recruited me right out of college, and had devoted their time and effort into teaching me the business. I'd paid them back over the last five years with loyalty and hard work. The last two years, I'd brought in more business than any of the other sixteen accountants with the firm; so I had no cause to feel guilty for asking for time off. That never stopped me before.

Then, too, I thought, as I descended the stairs, heading to the kitchen to make a cup of cocoa, it wouldn't exactly be a leave of absence, would it? Not when I planned to marry Jackson within a year's time. I would have to quit the firm.

Surprisingly, the notion didn't raise knots in my stomach. Sure, I'd miss Chicago, my friends, especially Dotty, who was my best friend in the city. Dotty was a secretary at Streiber and Farrar. Four years ago, I'd talked her into going back to school and getting her degree in accounting. Blessed with numerical acumen, Dotty was a plodder, like me. Plodders were workhorses, the sort of people who patiently wade through masses of work to the very end, without tiring.

Dotty had recently graduated in the top ten percent of her class and was presently interviewing with accounting firms.

I switched on the kitchen light and went to the cabinet above the sink where Momma kept the instant cocoa. I'd spied the box and was reaching up to get it, when someone cleared his throat.

I turned. There, sitting at the kitchen table, was Slim.

"What are you doing sitting in the dark?" I asked irritably. "You scared me."

"I don't sleep much anymore," he said matter of factly. "Sometimes I come downstairs and listen to the rest of you sleep."

He looked so small, as if he'd shrunk into himself. His clear brown eyes were watching my face.

"Can I get you something?" I asked.

"A cup of whatever you were going to make would be fine." Slim had never been a finicky eater.

I put the kettle on to boil and went to sit across from Slim at the table. I'd never known a time when Slim wasn't elderly. He was fifty-eight when I was born, and by the time I became cognizant of the differences between people's ages, around age three or four, he was in his early sixties. He had white hair even back then, his face was unlined, though, and his back was strong and straight.

It seemed to me that Slim hadn't really started showing his age until after Daddy got killed. Then, the wear and tear of life began to manifest itself in his face, and the weight of living bent his back. He still walked without a cane, but his steps had become slow and measured.

I suddenly had a need to touch him, and I clasped his hands, the knuckles grown big with arthritis, in my own. "I miss you when I'm gone," I told him.

"You know," he said contemplatively, "you and Jackson would give me handsome great-grandchildren."

I laughed. "You're always thinking aren't you, Slim?"

He leaned in and raised one eyebrow. "But that idea has merit, don't it, girl?"

"You think all your ideas have merit," I hedged. "But I'll give you this much, at least this one isn't seventeen years older than I am."

I let go of his hands. "Don't get your hopes up about me and Jackson, Slim. There are more important things that you could turn your thoughts to, such as getting the herd to the south field before snowfall begins. When are you going to hire extra hands to do that?"

A frown creased Slim's brow. "Come to think of it, Curtis Wade told me he was hunting last week and saw a white ptarmigan . . ."

Ptarmigans, a kind of grouse, are native to mountainous, cold regions. In summer, their plumage is brown, but it turns white in winter. Slim believed that if the ptarmigan's plumage turned white before the first big snowfall, we were in for a harsh winter.

"The boys and I'd better see about getting the herd in within the next two weeks," Slim said. He smiled, "I still think Jackson would make you a fine husband, though."

Meaning, my ploy to distract him hadn't been successful.

The kettle whistled and I hurried to pull it from the fire, not wanting to awaken anyone else from their slumber.

I returned to the table with two steaming mugs of cocoa. I placed one in front of Slim.

"Don't we have any marshmallows?" he asked petulantly.

I humphed and went to search the pantry.

After a moment, I spotted a small bag of mini marshmallows and went to pour some into Slim's mug. He cupped his hands and held them out for more. I smiled to myself. In some ways he was like a spoiled child.

I blew on the cocoa as I watched Slim over the rim of my mug. He slurped his drink loudly, then held the warm mug between his hands. "You weren't even a twinkle in your daddy's eyes when your Grandma Penny passed away," he told me. "But you've got some of her in you."

"What qualities?"

"She always thought twice before doing anything, too."

"It pays to be cautious," I said in my defense.

"Life is supposed to be lived by the seat of your pants," Slim disagreed. His eyes met mine. "I hate the fact that you were the one to get to your daddy first that day. It should have been one of the hands. Not his child. I fought with God about that for years afterward. Why did it have to be you? I still don't have the answer to that one. I know this though: it aged you. It brought the meanness of life to your attention way too soon . . ."

A few minutes earlier, I'd been thinking the same of him, that Daddy's death had broken him, when, prior to that, life had only been able to bend him a little.

"Maybe you're coming out of it now," Slim continued in a low voice. "Because I saw the way Jackson looked at you and how you shone in his presence. I may be a little hard of hearing, and I need glasses to read small print, but I know love when I see it, girl. So stop trying to pull the wool over your granddaddy's eyes."

Elbow on the table and my chin resting in the palm of my hand, I sat and stared at Slim for a few minutes.

Sighing, I finally said, "Okay. I'm in love with him. But that doesn't get me anywhere, Slim. The man can't get past our past!"

Slim chuckled. "Then you know what you've got to do."

I was stumped. I shook my head. "I have no idea, short of

kidnapping him and refusing to let him go until he agrees to marry me."

"That's the Josie part of you talking," Slim said with a laugh. "You've convinced us that opening a lodge will solve our financial problems, or, at least, put something in the larder when the ranch's profits fall short. You can't oversee everything all the way down there in Chicago. It'll cost you a fortune to fly back and forth every weekend. You're going to have to throw caution out the door and grab life by the throat and hold on, girl. You willing to risk everything for love?"

I was silent for a long time. Slim sipped his drink and waited patiently.

I could attempt to juggle things. But the thought of not seeing Jackson again for months (especially after he'd admitted he was drawn to me) sent rivulets of ice-cold fear down my spine.

Slim *did* have a point: I'd have to be willing to risk my safe, secure position. No seventy-five-thousand-dollar-a-year job. No beautifully furnished apartment. No more Donna Karan suits.

I'd accomplished a lot in the ten years I'd been out in the world. On my way up, I'd despaired of women who'd made it and all they did was complain about the loneliness, or the lack of true happiness. Somehow, they were never capable of defining what they felt true happiness amounted to. It was something elusive, something just out of their grasps. In that respect, I was more fortunate. I knew what made me truly happy. It was being close to the people I loved. You could be the richest person in the world, but it was meaningless if you didn't have someone you loved to share it with. Jackson was my someone.

The choice was obvious.

"I'll resign from the firm when I get back to Chicago," I said aloud.

Slim fairly glowed with triumph.

"It's the right decision," he said, his brown eyes lit with joy.

"Now, Slim," I cautioned him. "You must not repeat what has been said here tonight. I don't want anyone to know that my moving back home has anything to do with Jackson, least of all, Jackson. Do you understand?"

Slim nodded in the affirmative. He had the aura of someone

with a juicy secret, and was almost bursting with the need to spill it. So I should have known he wouldn't be able to keep our discussion under wraps for long.

SIX

I experienced culture shock when I arrived in Chicago ten years ago. I was a seventeen-year-old innocent used to wide, open spaces and a much less dense population. When I walked the streets of Chicago, I felt closed in, like a sardine pushed against the wall of the tin.

By my sophomore year at the Chicago Circle campus of the University of Illinois, I could blend in with the best of them. I traveled the city via the El, Chicago's elevated train system, like a native Chicagoan.

Even at nineteen, I knew that there was no going back for me. I wouldn't return home an abject failure. So I toughed out the loneliness and forced myself to see the positive side of my situation. I was in the third largest city in the United States. A city known for doing things in a big way. There were dreams galore for the taking. All I had to do was work hard.

The day I walked into the offices of Streiber and Farrar on posh South Wacker Drive near the riverfront, I'd made up my mind to *take* the position I was there to interview for.

At twenty-two, I'd earned my master's degree in finance. I was a certified public accountant and I was eager to know where the next rung up the ladder would take me.

In a conservative navy-blue skirt suit, matching pumps and carrying the expensive leather briefcase my family had pooled their resources in order to afford to buy me, I made a formidable figure.

However, I'd taken one look at Stu Farrar, a short, intense

Italian with a receding hairline, hooked nose, a square chin and horn-rimmed glasses, and my confidence fled.

He'd indicated that I should sit on the chair in front of his desk. I sat. I'd expected him to take the chair behind his huge desk, but he moved around the desk and sat on the corner of it, directly in front of me, frowning so hard, his thick eyebrows formed one neat line above his hooded black eyes.

"So you think you've got what it takes to work for us?" he'd asked.

I believe it was the note of skepticism in his voice that awakened the will to fight in me.

I'd sat up straighter, my knees together, my hands folded on my lap. Then, with a frown as severe as his, I met his gaze straight-on, and said, "It would be a mistake for you not to hire me; and you don't look like a man who abides many mistakes."

Stu Farrar had thrown his head back and laughed. Then he'd subjected me to the toughest interview I'd ever undergone.

Years later, I was to learn that it was his standard practice to scare the bejesus out of job applicants. Those whom he intimidated, he felt wouldn't have the intestinal fortitude to work for him anyway.

Stu had become my primary mentor within the firm. I'd worked closely with him and counted him among the persons I respected most in my field.

That very day, as I was leaving the offices, my spirits lifted by the positive outcome of my interview, a shrill feminine voice stopped me in my tracks with, "Hey, Stretch!"

I turned, my eyes searching the office for the body who belonged to that irritating, vociferous instrument.

Coming toward me, holding my briefcase aloft, was a young, petite African-American woman with very dark brown skin and an hourglass figure. She was wearing a royal blue dress that cinched her twenty-two inch waist. She was buxom and her hips flared out, reminding me of the style of clothing Dorothy Dandridge wore in her role as the first black sex symbol in films back in the fifties.

"You must have plenty of these at home if you can walk off and leave it behind like you did," she said accusingly.

The fact was, I wasn't yet used to carrying a briefcase and, in my excitement, I'd forgotten I'd even brought one with me to the interview.

In that instance, all I saw was a sister. Another black woman. I hadn't seen any others in the office upon my arrival, and I'd been inwardly fretting that I might be the only black person working for Streiber and Farrar.

"I got the job!" I blurted out.

She smirked, handed me the briefcase and said in droll tones, "Hallelujah!" With that, she spun on her heels and walked off, her pert nose in the air.

I'd met Dotty Renfrow.

Five years later, when I told her I was leaving the firm, she'd dropped her salad fork and stared. We were having lunch at our favorite restaurant down the street from Streiber and Farrar. I'd been back at work two days following my trip to Custer.

"I knew something was wrong when I picked you up at the airport day before yesterday," she said, her brown eyes narrowed.

She lifted her fork from the tabletop and laid it on the salad plate. "What? Did you get an offer from another firm?"

I told her about my family's plans to open a lodge and of my desire to be there supervising the project.

"You don't need to be there," she said. "With phones, faxes and e-mail, you can supervise from here."

Dotty had been a secretary for nearly eight years and knew the ins and outs of communications like the back of her hand.

"And then there's Jackson," I said by way of an explanation that she'd comprehend.

She smiled, satisfied. "Mr. For Keeps. The one you've been saving the boo-tay for."

Shaking my head and smiling at her choice of words, I said, "The one and the only."

"Well all right, girlfriend. Tell all," Dotty said, leaning forward as though I were about to whisper the details in her ear.

"We kissed in the cemetery."

"At a memorial service?"

"No. I was visiting my daddy's grave. He brought some flowers for his mother's grave. I had no idea he'd be there."

"How did it happen? Did he just grab you and kiss you after years of ignoring your behind?"

"I don't know, really," I began animatedly. "We were talking about life. We found out that we've both arrived at the point in our lives where we want to get married and have a family. His description of the perfect woman for him fit me to a *T* and vice versa. It looks promising, Dotty."

"And then . . ." Dotty said impatiently.

"And then I told him I was going to get married within a year's time?"

"How are you going to manage that?"

"That's what *he* asked."

"Talking to you is like pulling teeth. Out with it, Cheyenne!"

"I told him I was going to marry *him*," I said, relishing the stunned expression on Dotty's pretty face.

Laughing uproariously, Dotty dabbed the tears at the corners of her eyes with her napkin. "I wondered when you were going to get tired of waiting on that man to make a move. Girl, this is priceless. Is it all right if I tell Pete about it?"

"I can use all the moral support I can get," I said, giving my permission. Besides, Pete Renfrow, Dotty's husband of five years, didn't know anyone from Montana, where I didn't want the news broadcasted.

"Now, Dotty, there's something I'd like to propose to you," I said.

She balled up her napkin in her fist, tried to compose herself, and failed. "You didn't tell me how the kiss was."

Closing my eyes, I sighed. "Dotty, it was the best kiss I've ever had, bar none. The feel of his body, pressed against mine, made me realize what I've been missing. I'm glad he didn't suggest we hop into the cab of his truck, because, I swear, I would have."

"You country Jezebel!" Dotty cried, laughing anew.

"He has the juiciest lips since Tyson Beckford," was my considered opinion. "Girl, if I'd known it was going to be like that, I would've jumped his bones years ago."

Dotty sniffed, wiped her eyes again and regarded me with a

more sober expression. "You're really in love, aren't you? You're leaving Chicago for good."

"I'm taking a chance on a dream, Dotty. If Jackson loves me, and I think he does, then no, I won't be back. But if, God forbid, something goes wrong, then, who knows, I could be back with my tail between my legs."

"You've got to think positively, Cheyenne. He would be nuts if he passed on a babe like you," Dotty said enthusiastically. "You've taken the first step, now you've got to see it through. No backtracking, all right?"

I reached across the small round table and placed my hand atop hers. "I'm going to miss you, Dotty."

"Planes still fly from here to Montana," Dotty said.

"Which reminds me," I said. "Dotty, I want you and Pete and the kids to be our first guests when we open the lodge. Everything will be complimentary. You'd be doing us a favor. Test the facilities for us and give us your honest opinions."

"You know me," Dotty replied, smiling at me. "If the bedsprings are poking me in the butt, and there's a moose in the bathroom, I'm going to complain about it."

"We'll keep the beasts out of your bathroom, I promise."

That afternoon, I got Stu Farrar alone in his office and told him of my plans.

Stu had been sitting behind his antique mahogany desk, but he rose and began pacing, as he invariably did when he had some hard thinking to do.

He didn't look at me for the next few minutes. I sat on the leather couch near the window that looked down on the waterfront. I appeared to be engrossed in the picturesque view, but I was attuned to his every movement.

I smoothed the skirt of the gray Donna Karan suit I was wearing and crossed my legs, getting comfortable. I suppressed a sigh.

Whatever Stu's reaction was going to be to my resignation, I had made up my mind. I'd give them the two weeks' notice. I'd even agree to train my replacement for up to a month afterward. But I was definitely leaving.

I hadn't told Stu about the lodge, or Jackson, of course. Those were personal matters. I'd simply told him I had decided to leave the firm and move back to Montana.

I was fiddling with the comb holding my hair up when Stu spoke, "You're going out on your own, right? Look, Cheyenne, Garrett and I have been talking about taking on a new partner. We'd both like more time to spend with our families, maybe have a life outside of these offices. So how does a partnership sound to you? We'll split the profits three ways. That's fair, isn't it? Your clients bring in more money than the rest of the clients put together. What if they pull out once they learn you've jumped ship? Come now, think about what you're giving up. Montana? What is there in Montana that could begin to compare with what you have here?"

I got to my feet and went to stand in front of the picture window. Because he'd made me an offer without consulting Garrett first, I knew they'd weighed the pros and cons of inviting me to become a partner and had decided it would be to their best interest to do so. My question was: When were they going to tell me? Perhaps they were going to allow me to work for them another year or two, at *one-fifth* their salaries, and, perhaps, if I continued to bring in the capital I'd been bringing in, they'd consider putting the offer on the table.

The fact that they were using me, didn't anger me. It happened in business all the time.

It was my belief in the supposed friendship between Stu and myself that rankled. He'd given me the impression that I counted as a person. To Stu, money was more important than my feelings.

That realization made my purpose all the clearer.

I was too shrewd to leave burned bridges in my wake, however.

"You're right, Stu, I am starting my own firm. It may never rival Streiber and Farrar, but it will be my own. And, like you've said, family is important. My entire family's in Montana. I'd like to be near them."

Coming from a woman, those sentiments were easily understood by Stu. He'd nodded sympathetically, but wasn't ready to give up yet. There was still the threat of my clients walking when *I* walked.

"I'll tell you what, Cheyenne," he said, a stubby finger pressed against his forehead. "Let us get someone else in here who can take over your accounts. You introduce them to your clients as a dynamo, someone who's really going to make their money grow for them. You train them, nurture them. Then in about six months, you can walk away with stock options and a huge bonus check."

"How huge?"

"Fifty thousand?"

"Make it one month, and one hundred thousand and it's a deal."

"That's outrageous!"

"That's my offer, take it or leave it."

I thought he'd poke a hole in his forehead with his finger, the way he was pounding on it.

"All right," he agreed, at last. "One month, one hundred thousand."

"I'll have the papers drawn up by Pat Cisneros and you and Garrett can sign them," I told him, looking down into his dark little eyes. Pat was an attorney friend of mine whom I'd known and trusted since our college days together.

It was peculiar how your opinion of someone could change in the blink of an eye. I'd gone into Stu's office with genuinely warm feelings for him. I'd even felt regret for having to give him my resignation. Now that I knew what a toad the man was, I couldn't stand the sight of him.

"Don't you trust us, Cheyenne?" he'd had the gall to ask.

"No, Stu, my mentor always told me never to trust anyone; get it in writing," I said as I walked from the room.

Contrary to Clancy's belief that I was living it up in a highrise apartment, I lived in a small flat just north of downtown in an area called the Near North Side. My building was one of those old apartment houses from another era that had been built to last. There was a long waiting list to get into the building, so when I dropped by the office of my landlord to see about getting out of

my lease, Mr. Bouchard was in the mood to make me a deal: if I could be out within five weeks, he wouldn't exact a penalty for my breaking the lease. I could forget about the deposit. I thought that was fair, so I agreed to it.

I lived on the third floor, and, as I quickly ascended the stairs after leaving Mr. Bouchard's office, I felt certain that my plans would come together gracefully.

Unlocking the door and going inside, I closed and locked it and slid the dead bolt into place.

Stepping onto the wool runner that traversed the length of the foyer, saving the wood floor from being scuffed, I went back to the kitchen.

The apartment had a large living room, accented by a working fireplace. The seating group, upholstered in off-white fabric, consisted of a couch, a love seat and two overstuffed chairs. The coffee table and the end tables were in a light oak. There were various original paintings on the walls done by local African-American artists. They were the only things in the apartment I had formed an attachment to.

Besides the living room, there were two bedrooms, the kitchen that was big enough for a dining-room set, and two and a half baths: one full bath in the hallway near the second bedroom, and the largest, in the master bedroom. The half bath was located in the kitchen near the laundry alcove where I kept a washer and dryer.

I'd lived there ever since I'd started work at Streiber and Farrar.

It was nearly six o'clock in the evening. I was hungry, but I didn't feel like cooking, so I took a Lean Cuisine, turkey tetrazzini, from the freezer and put it in the microwave to cook.

The red light on my answering machine was blinking. I sat down on one of the high stools at the breakfast nook and pressed the play button.

After kicking off my heels, I flexed my tired feet as I waited for the first message to begin.

"Guess who?" the male caller asked with laughter evident in his voice. He went on in a more serious tone. "I'm in town. I hope you are, too. If you are, I'll see you at around eight tonight. I started to surprise you, but I wanted to give you the opportunity to determine whether you wanted to see me or not. I know it's been months since we've seen each other, but you've been on my mind. So be there, okay?"

Tad Kelly, a pitcher with the New York Yankees, previously of the Chicago Cubs, and the last man to propose marriage to me.

The next message began. I didn't recognize the voice. I figured it was a telemarketer, so I pressed the off button. I had to think. Tad. Tad with the soft brown eyes and strong arms. Tad, who was always tender and compassionate. He'd been a great guy. And if I hadn't been born to be with Jackson, Tad would have claimed my heart, I was sure of it.

From his message and the timbre of his voice, I couldn't discern why he wanted to see me. When we'd parted, he'd told me, in no uncertain terms, that he could not pretend to be my friend. Either he would have all of me, or none of me. I understood perfectly. I'd been very fond of Tad and I didn't want to see the hurt, mirrored in his eyes, every time he looked at me. I didn't want us turning into enemies when we'd begun as two people who'd truly liked each other.

Respect for Tad prevented me from changing clothes, forgoing the turkey tetrazzini, and going out to dinner someplace so that I would not be there when he rang the bell.

I got up and tidied up a bit. Not much, just a newspaper left on the coffee table and a few breakfast dishes. After I'd done that, I went back to my bedroom to take a quick shower.

As I undressed, I caught my reflection in the full-length mirror mounted on the back of the closet door. I pinched the skin on my waist, still taut, but I'd recently been lax with my weight-lifting routine, and jogging. I loved to eat, so I made a mental note to go to the gym the next morning, before work.

Of course, a warm bed on a cold morning sometimes seemed a logical trade-off for a few extra pounds. I'd gained five pounds on my visit home. I'd done good. Over the Christmas holidays, I usually gained seven.

I assessed my image as I imagined Tad would upon seeing me again. I was the same tall, shapely, slightly muscular woman with warm brown skin, jet-black, shoulder-length naturally curly hair combed away from her heart-shaped face.

My large, almond-shaped eyes were the color of brandy. Genetically a cross between my parents' eyes, I suppose.

Thanks to my African and Native American ancestors, I had high cheekbones.

All these features, unremarkable as they were, when put together formed a pleasing visage.

I was always wary of men who raved about my looks. There was an ulterior motive behind the compliments, I thought. If a man wanted to flatter me, he had to speak to my mind, not of my appearance.

I believe Tad had the most powerful-looking, well-defined thigh muscles I'd ever seen, up close, on anyone.

My eyes drifted downward when I greeted him at the door that night. He was wearing a Gianni Versace suit in an elegant winter white. I recognized the suit because I'd helped him pick it out.

He grinned, showing straight, white teeth in his dark brown, clean-shaven face. "Cheyenne. Give me some sugar, girl."

He opened his arms, holding the bouquet of red roses aside to make sure they didn't get in the way of our embrace.

"Mmm," he said, kissing my cheek and sighing. "You smell good."

So did he, actually. We parted and he stepped inside. I closed the door and stood with my back against it, watching him.

He turned and presented me with the flowers.

"To say thanks for being here."

I smiled up at him. I'd noticed that he was wearing his natural hair in a one-inch fade, shaved close on the sides.

His square-chinned face had the sharply defined bone structure of an athlete. His hazel, deep-set eyes were what some women called bedroom eyes.

"Of course I would be here," I said as though it'd never entered my mind to vacate the premises after I'd received his message.

He shrugged out of his overcoat and hung it on the hall tree.

I felt his gaze on me as I turned and went back to the kitchen to get a vase for the flowers.

"Thanks for the flowers," I called, not realizing he was right behind me. When I saw him standing less than three feet away,

I laughed in embarrassment. Lowering my voice, I said, "Sorry for yelling in your ears."

He was silent as I ran water into a vase, lowered the roses, one at a time, into it and set the vase on the kitchen table.

"What can I get you to drink?" I asked after finishing my task.

"Nothing, thanks," he said, moving closer to me.

I wondered what he was up to as he pulled me into his arms once again and simply held me. "Cheyenne . . ." he said, his voice husky, "I had to see you in order to find out if I'm still in love with you. Or, if I ever was . . ."

I tilted my head up to meet his hazel eyes. "You've met someone," I said.

He was visibly relieved that I'd known intuitively what he was having difficulty saying.

"Yeah. She's a reporter with an ABC affiliate in New York City. We met when she interviewed me for a story, and I couldn't get her out of my mind."

I placed my hands on his with the intent to pry them from about my waist. "That's great, Tad. I'm happy for you."

He only tightened his hold. "You don't understand, Cheyenne. When I walked in and saw you, my heart started pounding in my chest. I had that feeling of breathlessness that I always got in your presence. I may still be in love with you."

"I'm in love with someone else, too, Tad," I blurted out, hoping to throw cold water on his heated emotions.

Tad's hazel eyes took on a sad aspect. "I knew it had to happen sometime," he said resignedly. "Who is he? One of the professional athletes you have as clients?"

"No," I replied, smiling. "He's a rancher from my hometown."

Tad laughed softly. "Isn't that something? All the rich, eligible bachelors you come in contact with, and you lose your heart to a man from your hometown."

"Love is strange," I commented. I reached up and gently touched his cheek. "That reporter is a lucky woman, Tad."

"You'll always inhabit a corner of my heart, Chey," he told me softly. "Could I have some sugar to go?"

My throat had grown tight and I felt that tears were imminent, so I nodded my acquiescence.

We kissed tenderly, our lips not parting. Tad peered down into my eyes afterward. "You're going back to Montana, huh?"

"Very soon," I confirmed.

"I hope you'll be happy," he said.

"I wish the same for you, Tad."

He grasped my hand and we walked back out to the foyer where I helped him on with his coat.

"Do you think the Yankees will win the pennant this year, too?" I asked playfully.

"Anything can happen," Tad said, his hazel eyes caressing my face. "I fell in love again."

His last words to me kept replaying over and over in my mind for a long time after he'd gone: I fell in love again. It reminded me of my situation with Jackson. Was he still in love with Marissa?

I'd made a conscious effort not to compare myself with Marissa. I couldn't subjectively visualize what qualities Jackson saw in her, that I would be lacking in. If you were to have us stand side by side, we'd be two, obviously disparate, women. I was tall; she was short. I was attractive; she was ravishing. She was five years older than I was; but, Jackson had made a point of telling me he believed I was too young for him, so the age difference didn't work to my advantage, either.

There I was turning my life upside down, on the off chance that Jackson had been harboring secret feelings for me, as I'd been for him, all these years. That's what I was doing, wasn't it? Hoping against hope. God knows, it didn't make sense.

But, by then, I was too far gone to turn back.

October blew in like a ferocious lion. Walking to the office from the train station became an act of faith. You never knew whether the next gust of wind would send you hurtling into the stratosphere, or not.

Stu and Garrett had hired my replacement, a twenty-six-year-old by the name of Monte Pepper. He'd graduated from Loyola

University of Chicago, one of the Catholic universities. Loyola was Stu's alma mater, and I think that had been the determining factor in the hiring of Monte.

Monte was around five-ten, stocky, had brown hair and eyes and was constantly tense. I couldn't tell if it was because he'd just started a new job, or if it was his normal disposition.

One day, into the third week of the transition, we were in his office chatting with a client, Dale Parsigian, a professional hockey player.

I'd known Dale for three years. He was thirty-five, his star was waning and he was a conservative investor, the type of person who didn't like taking chances with his hard-earned money. He was a Mormon and believed in the sanctity of marriage. He and his wife, Donna, had five children and one on the way. So he wasn't interested in long shots.

Dale talked about his career. He had two good years left in him, he thought; then, he was retiring and working full-time in the family business. He and Donna owned four McDonald's franchises in the city and outlying areas.

Toward the end of Dale's speech, Monte had cleared his throat and said, "Have you ever thought about starting your own theme restaurant? I mean, actors have Planet Hollywood. Tiger Woods and a couple of other sports figures opened a sports theme restaurant. Everyone loves hockey, especially the city of Chicago. You'd probably rack up!"

Dale, a six-foot-three-inch hulk, had sat looking at me, the muscles working in his jaw. I knew what he was thinking. Monte was my responsibility, therefore it was up to me to set him straight.

"Dale and Donna already own four restaurants, which are doing great business," I said. "A new venture, like a theme restaurant, which will depend upon the changing whims of hockey fans, wouldn't be wise at this juncture."

"It was just a thought," Monte said a bit peevishly.

Dale rose. "I have to be going."

"I'll see you out," I told him, rising, too.

As I walked Dale to the elevator, he said, "I want you to know I don't appreciate your leaving me in the lurch like this, Cheyenne. I've come to depend upon your sane advice. I don't know about Monte Pepper; he's too nervous. I don't think I want a man that jumpy handling my family's financial future."

What could I say? I couldn't reassure him that Monte would prove to be a competent accountant at some later date. I wouldn't be there to witness that miraculous transformation.

I paused at the reception desk and asked Janet, the receptionist, for a pad and a pen. I quickly scribbled Dotty's name and new business address and number on the pad and tore off the top sheet, handing it to Dale. "Do what you think is best," I said reasonably. "I know, for certain, this person is adept at her job and won't lead you astray with get-rich-quick schemes."

Dale took the slip of paper, folded it, put it in his jacket pocket, grabbed me and gave me a bear hug.

"Stay warm up there in Montana. I'm from Utah, so I know how high the snowdrifts can get," he said, smiling.

He let go of me. "Good-bye, Cheyenne, and good luck to you."

" 'Bye, Dale. Give my best to Donna and the kids."

Did I feel guilty about steering a client to another firm after getting Garrett's and Stu's signatures on the promissory papers Patricia Cisneros had drawn up? Not in the least. Over the last five years, I'd earned them ten times the measly one hundred thousand I'd bargained for.

Monte met me in the hallway. "Did I do something wrong?" he asked worriedly. We walked together back to his office, where I closed the door. I was in a peckish mood. It wasn't Monte I was irritated with. I knew what it was like to begin work at a successful firm. You were always doubting your abilities, wondering if someone would find you out, that you were just *pretending* to be the wunderkind. He would find his legs though; just as I had.

"I don't believe Dale Parsigian will be returning," I told him baldly.

Fear crossed his young features, then was replaced by anger.

"You were supposed to be guiding me," he said, his brown eyes filled with indignation. His olive skin darkened at his cheeks, and I knew, then, that he was using anger to mask his embarrassment.

I went to him and grasped him by the shoulders, making him turn around to look me in the face. "Monte, you're not going to survive here if you don't learn not to sweat the small stuff. This is a high-pressure business. It's always difficult managing other people's money. You've got to learn to read your clients. Get to know them personally. Don't look at them as a paycheck alone. They have families, they have dreams; and believe me, most of them already know what they want to do with their money. Your job is to tell them whether they'll lose or gain by their decisions."

He breathed deeply, then exhaled and some of his anxiety seemed to dissipate. "Unc . . . *Mr.* Farrar told me you were the best, Cheyenne."

I dropped my arms to my sides and just stared at him, shaking my head. "So you're Stu's nephew."

"He didn't want anyone to know," Monte said, chagrined. "You won't tell anyone, will you?"

"It's Stu's prerogative to hire a relative," I replied nonchalantly. I glanced at the clock on his desk. "It's after six. I think we've done enough for one day, don't you?"

He smiled. He was finally relaxed. "Telling you about it has taken a huge weight off my shoulders."

I walked over to the door and reached for the doorknob. Turning to glance at him over my shoulder, I said, "You'll do okay here, Monte."

At that point, I thought I was remarkably fortunate to be on my way out. Let Stu hire his relatives. He could take nepotism to new heights for all I cared. I wondered, though, if Garrett was aware of Stu's relationship with Monte. I could imagine the firm, two or three years down the line. Stu would push to make Monte a partner, then he would secretly control two-thirds of the firm.

Garrett and Stu had been best friends when they'd founded the firm fifteen years ago. In recent years, I'd noticed that they rarely socialized outside of the office. Their wives disliked each other. Sometimes success took precedence over friendship. Garrett had better watch his back.

I had to walk around packed boxes when I got home that night.

Every night, after work, I'd methodically packed up my belongings, labeling the boxes with a black permanent marker.

I'd given away quite a few things to Goodwill, and the newlyweds down the hall had bought my seating group. They'd blown much of their funds getting into the building, so I gave them a great deal on the furniture. I wouldn't be needing it in Montana. I'd be living in the main house, in my old bedroom.

The boxes held books and clothes mostly. Books were my passion. I had more than three hundred of them, and I wasn't prepared to part with one. Not my Jané Smileys, Toni Morrisons, Ernest J. Gaineses, Louisa May Alcotts, Dean Koontzes, Barbara Neelys or Barbara Kingsolvers, and, definitely, not my Dorothy Wests.

Chad would just have to build extra bookshelves in my bedroom.

I was peering into the refrigerator, the light bathing my face, when the phone rang. I closed the refrigerator door, having still not decided upon what I wanted for dinner.

"Hello . . ." I said, as I slouched onto a stool at the breakfast nook. I was bored, and my voice reflected my boredom.

"When are you coming home?" Jackson asked sans a greeting.

I sat straight up on that stool, and smoothed my hair, even though I didn't have an audience.

"You know," I said, "planes fly both ways."

"Do they? I didn't realize that. Perhaps I ought to get on one and come see you."

My heart pounded at the prospect.

I rose, the cordless phone in my hand, and walked over to the window in my living room. The golden-hued lights in the windows of the neighboring apartment buildings had a calming effect on me.

"Yeah, right," I told him skeptically. "You in Chicago. That'll be the day."

"Or night," he said cryptically, and hung up on me.

I listened to the dial tone for a second, then I went to place the phone back on its base. The nerve of the man. I picked up the phone again and quickly dialed his number in Montana.

He refused to pick up.

"Wait until I see you again," I said under my breath.

Replacing the receiver, I blew air between my lips and went back to the kitchen to get salad makings from the refrigerator. Jackson's childish antics had stolen my appetite for anything more filling.

I threw the lettuce into the sink, but stopped short of tossing the delicate tomatoes in after it. I couldn't fathom what had gotten into Jackson. Maybe I *didn't* know him. Maybe he'd knocked around alone in that huge ranch house of his way too long. Whatever his problem was, I would disabuse him of it the next time I laid eyes on him. You could bet on that. It was a sure thing.

After rinsing it thoroughly, I tore the lettuce apart in record time. The tomatoes, I had to slow down and slice carefully, as I didn't want to lose a finger.

I'd sat down at the kitchen table and was grating a little Cheddar over my salad when the doorbell rang. I automatically glanced at the clock on the wall. It was 8:13. On a Friday night. Everyone I knew was either out partying, or spending time with their families. Single, romantically unattached women spent quite a few Friday nights eating dinner alone. At least I had lately.

Going to check out the caller through the peephole, I took two ganders before it registered that I was, indeed, seeing Jackson's smiling face outside my door.

I screamed and flung the door open, or it could have been the other way around. Anyway, the door was opened, and Jackson was standing there, looking so fine in his city duds of a dark wool overcoat, shiny black boots and dress slacks, that I forgot my manners, threw my arms around his strong neck and kissed him *before* inviting him in.

SEVEN

A tactician in the war between the sexes would have known not to display too much enthusiasm at the birth of a relationship. I was just a woman in love, so my happiness at seeing Jackson at my door, was a palpable emotion. Tactile, too.

My body shivered with delight as we kissed. Jackson backed me into the apartment and kicked the door shut.

He turned his head to the side, laughter bubbling up, "Chey, don't I even get a hello?"

Our lips were still touching as I said, "Four weeks, Jackson. It's been four weeks since I've seen you."

He obliged me then, pulling me more fully into his arms, closer to his utterly male, hardened body.

Jackson's hands moved downward and rested on my hips as my own were inside his coat, massaging his back. I arched into him as the kiss deepened, his tongue warm, urgent, yet gentle against mine.

He withdrew and rained soft kisses along the curve of my neck and bosom. I felt his erection on my thigh and was fired up by the rush I got due to my newfound ability to arouse him.

Jackson looked into my eyes. I must have appeared intoxicated with pent-up sexual desire, because he abruptly set me away from him and held me at arm's length.

"Just hold on, Miss Cheyenne Josephine Roberts, I am not here to seduce you, or be seduced by you."

I smiled longingly at him, and sighed. "It would be the perfect time for it, though, wouldn't it? We're all alone. No family, no friends around to interrupt us . . ."

Jackson shook me. "Snap out of it!"

I laughed. "Oh come on, Jackson. What did you come here for, a business meeting?"

"Exactly," he said, releasing me and standing with his arms akimbo. "The Cattlemen's Association annual convention."

"It's here this year?"

"I've been there all day. This was the first opportunity I had to see you."

That revelation put a damper on my libido, I tell you.

"Why didn't you *tell* me you were here for a stinking ole convention before I made a fool of myself over you?"

"You didn't give me the chance."

"That's what the telephone is for. You could have phoned and said, 'Chey, hey, I'll be in Chicago for the Cattlemen's convention, and I was thinking of dropping by to see you.' Instead, you phone me and get me all upset . . ."

"I upset you? I'm sorry."

"I'm not finished. You phone me, get me all confused by your behavior, and then you show up at my door. *Of course* I'm going to think you're here because you've finally come to your senses and are ready to admit you love me!"

"I do love you, Chey."

I turned away in a huff. "I'm tired of beating a dead horse, Jackson Kincaid." I faced him. "All right. If you don't want me coming on to you, I won't. The next time we kiss, and there *will* be a next time, you're going to have to be the one to initiate it."

With that said, I felt better.

I walked over to him and smiled. "Welcome to my home, may I help you off with your coat?"

"Now don't be that way, Chey," Jackson said as he handed me his heavy coat. "Do you have to be so prickly? I said I was sorry for upsetting you."

"You didn't upset me."

"You said I upset you."

"Well I'm not giving you permission to play with my emotions anymore, so I take it back."

"You can't take it back."

I hung his coat up and walked around the boxes in the living room back to the kitchen. He followed, his boots making crisp sounds on the hardwood floor.

He was wearing a white, long-sleeved shirt and you could see the sleeveless undershirt beneath it. The muscles in his arms, chest and abdomen were clearly defined, and the light color of the shirt, against the darkness of his brown skin made a delightful contrast.

His slacks fit him just right, not too baggy, not too tight, with the buckle of his western belt flat against the plane of his washboard stomach.

He leaned against the counter, watching me.

"I was just going to have some dinner, can I get you anything?" I asked politely.

"Is that all you're having, that salad?" he asked, frowning. "A growing girl needs more nutrition than that."

"It's all I want," I said.

He walked over to the table, selected a chair and sat down.

"Your mother told me to tell you she loves you."

"I know she loves me, you didn't have to come all this way just to deliver the message."

Sighing, he placed his elbow on the table, resting his chin on his palm. "Tell me what I have to do to get you to forgive me, Cheyenne."

"Are you contrite?"

"Extremely sorry." His eyes were somber.

"Will you ever do it again?"

"Never, not as long as I live."

"Are you miserable?"

"Totally dejected."

"I feel better already."

He grinned. "Good. Let's go out somewhere."

Bailey's was hopping by the time we arrived. However, I knew the owner and I did Jimmy Street's (the maître d') taxes every year as a favor to Chuck Bailey. Chuck was a well-known ex-Chicago Cub, and had been a client of mine since my first year with Streiber and Farrar.

Bailey's featured a laid-back atmosphere with elegant surroundings, a house band that played jazz, excellent southern-style cuisine and a solicitous staff.

Jimmy rolled his eyes when he saw me coming and stepped from behind his podium to clasp my hand in his. "Well if it isn't the Montana Kid. Good evening, Miss Roberts, how has life been treating you?"

"Just fine, Jimmy. And how're you?"

Jimmy was sixty-five years old, short and stout and sported a gold tooth in front that he flashed continually. He liked to smile.

"My rheumatism's acting up, other than that I reckon I'll survive." Jimmy invariably told you how he was actually feeling when you inquired.

"You always do," I said, happy to see him again. "Do you think you could squeeze me and my friend, Mr. Kincaid, here in tonight?"

"It would be my pleasure," Jimmy immediately replied, going to check his book. He picked up a couple of menus, put them under his arm and motioned for Jackson and me to follow him.

He guided us through the crowded restaurant with ease, coming to a stop at a table for two in the center of the room, and not too far from the dance floor.

Jackson gave him a nice tip.

After Jimmy had gone back to his post, Jackson and I looked around us. The buzz of human voices was a welcome respite from my day at the firm. I enjoyed the feel of excitement and expectation in the room. Jackson seemed to be enjoying it, too.

"Nice place," he commented. "Black-owned?"

"Yeah, Chuck Bailey owns it."

"Chuck Bailey of the Cubs?" he asked, sounding impressed. "I idolized him when I was a kid."

"He's one of my clients. I'm going to miss working with him."

Jackson perused the menu. "Do you really believe Montana will be enough for you after the city?"

My eyes were on his face, admiring the curve of his strong jaw, marveling at the way his lips turned up at the corners whenever he smiled. I knew where that particular question had come from, however. It was Marissa again. She'd made him insecure by preferring the transitory lure of the city over him.

"I like Chicago," I told him, reaching over to place a hand atop the menu so that he'd raise his eyes to mine. "But I love Montana. It's the only place I'm completely happy."

"Did I tell you how pretty you look in that dress?" Jackson said, changing the subject.

He'd probably sensed that the conversation was about to take a too-personal turn. I didn't push it.

"Yes, you did, thank you."

The band was playing a jaunty tune. Several couples were up, swing dancing. I loved the fancy footwork, and the high energy of the movements.

Some of the couples were attired in retro clothing from the thirties and the forties. I knew swing dancing was making a comeback but I'd thought it was popular among teens and college students, not the twenty- to thirty-something crowd.

The waiter, a young African-American man with a thin moustache and a pleasant smile, leisurely strolled up to our table.

"Good evening, folks. The chef's special tonight is the shrimp etouffée."

"Do you have smothered chicken?" I asked. Bailey's chef, Miss Lillah, as everyone called her, did a mean smothered chicken. It was tender, savory and made you lick your fingers.

"Sure, Miss Lillah put her foot in the pot on that dish," the waiter said. "You want buttermilk biscuits with that?"

"What else?"

"Vegetable?"

"String beans and potatoes. Iced tea, and the dessert menu afterward."

"She's gonna break you tonight," the waiter joked with Jackson. Then, "What can I bring you, sir?"

Jackson laughed softly. "That chicken sounds good. I'd rather have the fried okra and corn bread with it though. And a beer."

"Do you have a preference?"

"Domestic. Don't bring me any foreign brews."

"All right," the waiter said. "Be back in two shakes of a lamb's tail."

When he'd gone, Jackson said, "Do they use that expression often here?"

"That was the first time I've ever heard it," I denied.

I drummed my fingers on the tabletop to the beat of the music.

"You want to dance, don't you?" Jackson said, smiling at me.

"I wouldn't *presume* to ask you, Jackson. I know your opinion of dancing: *real* men don't dance," I replied, returning his smile.

"You remembered that?"

"I remember everything you ever say to me," I said, before I'd had sufficient time to think. I'd done it again, revealed the depth of my devotion. If I kept that up, I was convinced I'd succeed in chasing Jackson away.

"But, then, I have a photographic memory." Lame save, but it would have to do.

"Okay," Jackson said, preparing to put my memory to the test. "How old was I, how old were you and where were we?"

"Oh, that's easy," I said confidently. "You were sixteen, I was eight and it was at a church dance. You remember when they used to hold dances for young people on Saturday nights? It was their effort to keep idle hands and minds, busy. Of course, the kids who were going to get into trouble, always found a way to do so."

"It was still fun," Jackson said.

"You didn't even dance."

"Sixteen-year-old boys didn't go to dances to dance. They went to scope the pretty girls. I had a good time."

"You broke my heart, you know."

"You weren't even supposed to be there," Jackson said. "It was Halloween night, and you were supposed to be with a group of other kids your age, but you stowed away in the back of Cole's truck. We didn't even know you were back there."

"I wanted to find out what the teen dances were like. And I did. A wall of girls facing a wall of boys, with a few brave souls dancing to all the songs. How did you meet girls, if you couldn't get up the nerve to ask them to dance?"

"We managed all right."

"You and Cole were pathetic."

Jackson laughed. "We were. You can't imagine the knots I felt in my stomach whenever I even *looked* at a pretty girl. I was in my last year of high school before I could talk to a girl without croaking."

"Yeah, yeah, yeah. The hormones were busting out all over, and you didn't know what to do about it. Poor baby. I bet you made up for lost time when you got to college."

"Oh no you don't," Jackson cautioned, waving a finger at me. "We are not going to compare conquests."

"So it was that many, huh?"

"I'm not going there, Cheyenne."

"Okay, don't. I can guess how many women threw themselves at you. You were a star on the football team. That face, that body. Your little black book was probably full by your sophomore year."

"How about *your* little black book?" Jackson challenged me, his brown eyes alight with mischief.

"I don't own one."

"No, you own two."

I humphed. "I don't need to record the names of the men I've loved and left, because I haven't loved any."

Jackson frowned. "You mean you're still . . ."

"That's none of your business."

"You brought it up."

"I did not," I stated emphatically.

"You most certainly did," he disagreed, just as emphatically.

Regarding him through narrowed eyelids, I said, "If you want to know if I'm a virgin or not, you're going to have to take me to bed, Jackson Kincaid."

The waiter arrived at that inopportune moment and set our plates before us. His mouth hung open in surprise, but he didn't say anything. After depositing our drinks on the table, he turned and walked away, still having not uttered a word.

"You rendered him speechless," Jackson said.

"I bet he finds his voice as soon as he gets to the kitchen," I said. Sighing, I added, "Jackson, you infuriate me sometimes. . . ."

"What's the big deal if you *are* a virgin, Cheyenne? You're definitely all woman. Making love to the wrong person can kill you nowadays. You have to be circumspect."

I picked up my fork and pierced a piece of the smothered chicken, put it into my mouth, chewed and swallowed.

Jackson did the same.

"I just don't want you under the misapprehension that, when the time comes, you're going to have to teach me everything about lovemaking, that's all," I explained myself.

"That could be enjoyable for both of us, Chey," Jackson assured me with a mock leer.

"Now see, that's what I'm talking about. You say things like that and then you expect me to hold my tongue."

"When have you ever held your tongue?"

"I've been doing it ever since we kissed. You think I don't know my own mind; therefore, you came up with the preposterous idea of our seeing others for at least a year before letting it be known that we want to date each other. Now if that isn't convoluted reasoning, I don't know what is. I have no desire to see anyone else, Jackson."

"Neither do I."

"Then, why do this to us?" I plaintively asked, my eyes searching his face.

"I told you why, Cheyenne. Because I want you to be certain it's me you want, and not who you *think* I am. You've got some pretty romantic notions about me. I'm not some handsome hero in a romance novel. I'm just a hardworking rancher, who's a little too set in his ways and who wakes himself up snoring when he goes to bed exhausted."

Pushing our plates aside, we clasped hands across the table.

"That's the beauty of the way I feel about you," I told him, my voice low and emotion-filled. "I know you're imperfect, and I love you anyway. It's taken me ten years to build up the courage to tell you. So please believe me when I tell you I love you."

Jackson brought one of my hands up and gently ran the palm of it over his cheek, then he met my gaze. "And I love you, Chey. I love you the way a man should love a woman; with every fiber of my being, I love you. I believe I've been in love with you since you were eighteen. But I never would have said anything. Never.

That's just the way I am. When you told me you wanted me that day in the cemetery, I was in shock. Sure, we flirted outrageously. But that was harmless. When we kissed . . . I tried to stop it, but apparently some part of me wanted it more than anything else I've ever wanted before. So, you believe me when I tell *you:* I love you. I love you so much that I refuse to allow you to settle for a broken-down rancher when you can have anyone else in the world you desire."

He released my hands then and gave me a stern look. "Now eat your dinner."

I picked up my fork and started eating. However, I was so excited by his declaration of love, that I could barely swallow.

The next day, Saturday, I attended the conference as his guest. More than twenty-thousand ranchers—men, women and children—roamed the convention center, going to various presentations pertaining to ranching, or simply networking.

We sat through a monotonous speaker who was extolling the virtues of feeding cattle hay instead of grain before slaughter, because the practice would slow the growth of E. coli in the cow's digestive system, thereby preventing the bacterium from spreading to the people who consumed the beef.

About a year ago, I'd read an article in the journal *Science,* which said that the practice appeared promising because it prevented the buildup of acids in a cow's colon, where E. coli is found. Grain fattens cows more rapidly, but, hay, when given several days before slaughter, apparently lessens the amount of acid in a cow's colon. So if contamination gets into beef via cattle feces, then the E. coli bacterium won't be present. Cooking beef thoroughly kills E. coli, but some people still consumed rare beef, even when warned not to.

Riveting, right? Jackson had to nudge me with his elbow a couple of times to keep me awake during the presentation.

When we broke for lunch, Jackson and I wandered outside to get some fresh air and to decide where we wanted to go eat.

It was cold and we were both wearing overcoats. As we

rounded the corner of the building, a gust of wind hit us in the face. Jackson drew me close to his side as we pressed forward.

"This wind is as bad as the winds on the plains," Jackson complained, holding me tightly about the waist.

We ducked inside an entryway, out of the wind. Jackson reached up and smoothed an errant lock of hair out of my face. Then he bent his head and kissed me full on the lips.

"Having you here is wreaking havoc with my attention span," he said when he raised his head to look into my eyes.

"You mean you weren't simply enthralled by that E. coli presentation?"

"Absolutely not," he disavowed. "I thought my eyes would permanently cross if he didn't wrap it up soon. And you. Any minute, I expected you to lay your head on my lap and your feet up on the guy next to us and get comfortable."

We continued walking toward the street. "Well I didn't get much sleep last night," I said by way of explanation.

"Oh? Why not?"

"I had these truly erotic series of dreams about us. You and me in my bed. You and me in the barn, up in the hay loft. You and me in the cab of your truck . . ."

"My truck?"

We ran down the steps to the street where Jackson hailed a passing taxi. We got inside and the driver sped away from the curb.

After we'd told the driver where we were going, Jackson said in a low voice, "What were you wearing in your dream?"

"Mmm," I said as I naturally cuddled into the crook of his arm, "white chiffon. Flowing, and see-through."

"And what was I wearing?"

"Me," I said, deadpan. "I was all over you, boy. Closer than any article of clothing ever could be."

Jackson laughed. "You made it all up, didn't you?"

"Yeah, but you can make it come true, Jackson. We can go back to my place now and act out every love scene I've ever imagined; and I have a fertile imagination."

He pulled me closer. He smelled, faintly, of soap and water and a woodsy aftershave. The warmth emanating from his body enticed me, compelled me to touch him. I lay my head on his chest, and his clean exhalations tickled my cheek.

I felt his hand in my hair, which I'd worn loose and combed away from my face, gently caressing me. He possessed an earthy sensuality that he was probably unaware of owning. It spoke to me, though. I breathed it in.

"I want to," he said, finally, of my invitation to spend the afternoon making love. "God help me, I want to."

I could have lived in that moment forever.

Life wasn't that idyllic, however; and, on Monday morning, Jackson returned to Montana and I returned to Streiber and Farrar without having consummated our relationship.

It was my last week at the firm, Monte was increasingly showing his appreciation for my keeping his secret by hanging on my every word, singing my praises to Stu and Garrett and bemoaning my imminent departure.

I'd begun to rue the day I'd refused to ignore his slip of the tongue and called him on his relationship with Stu.

Friday afternoon, I was in my office cleaning out my desk, when Monte knocked and entered before I could ask who was there.

He strode in carrying a large sheet cake. Behind him was Janet, our receptionist, and about thirty other office personnel, along with Stu and Garrett, who I'd assumed had left for the day by then.

I hadn't been expecting a farewell party, so I'd already said my good-byes to Janet, the other office staff and the colleagues with whom I'd formed a working relationship over the years.

Stu and Garrett came forward, both of them beaming. Garrett's smile I took as genuine, but Stu's appeared phony to me after everything that had been said between us. Plus, I'd developed sympathy for Garrett since I suspected Stu was planning to stick it to him somewhere down the line.

Janet and a couple of secretaries were busy pouring champagne into plastic wineglasses.

They handed them around. Monte gave me my glass, then

stood beside me as Stu cleared his throat, getting everyone's attention.

"Friends," he began, sounding as pompous as ever, "we're gathered here to say good-bye to the best accountant Garrett and I ever had the pleasure to work with."

"Absolutely," Garrett agreed, smiling down at me. He was in his early fifties, as Stu was, but he was tall and trim, had thick dark hair that was gray at the temples, and a ready smile for everyone. "We're going to miss you, Cheyenne. But you're young and eager to get out on your own, and I understand that because I was just like you twenty years ago."

"Although you weren't as pretty," Stu put in, to which everyone laughed.

"We got you a going-away present," Garrett continued. He reached into his coat pocket and produced a business-size envelope, handing it to me.

I lifted the flap, which hadn't been sealed. Inside was a cashier's check for $125,000.

I stared at Garrett.

"It's only fair," he said. "The last five years, you've brought in a lot of money for this firm. You deserve your share of the profits."

I was stunned. I sought Stu's eyes. He averted his, and I instinctively knew that he had probably been opposed to giving me the additional twenty-five grand.

I walked over and kissed Garrett on the cheek. "Thank you, Garrett. It feels good to be appreciated."

Laughing, Garrett said, "Cut the cake, and let's get this party started."

Stu left shortly after that, but the rest of us ate cake, drank champagne, laughed and reminisced for more than an hour.

Monte lingered after the debris had been cleared away and everyone else had filed out of my office.

I'd placed a box on the desktop and was putting the framed photos, diplomas and certificates from the wall into it, when he came over to me and grasped me by the wrist.

Surprised, I glanced up at him.

"I've been wanting to do this ever since we were introduced," he said softly. Then he took me into his arms and tried to kiss me.

I turned my face to the side and his lips connected with my cheek. "Monte, what's gotten into you?"

He held me firmly as I wriggled in his arms. "Cheyenne, have you ever heard of the theory that when you sleep with someone, you retain a part of their essence, who they are inside?"

He was looking at my mouth, not into my eyes, and I was thinking that if he tried to kiss me again, I was going to bite him. I had strong teeth, and they could leave one whopper of a bruise.

We were the same height, but he outweighed me by fifty pounds, at least. I didn't think I could break free of his hold without kneeing him where all men have nightmares about being kneed.

"Let go of me, Monte, or I'll scream," I warned him.

"Go ahead, everyone's probably gone by now."

He was right. Promptly at six o'clock, the personnel of Streiber and Farrar vacated the offices like rats abandoning a burning ship.

"I'm a good lover, Cheyenne. Italian men take their time. We make love with all our senses. Our one desire is to please our women. Come on, leave me with something to remember you by, some part of you to keep."

"Next, you'll be asking to suck my blood," I quipped.

His right hand had slid down my body to my skirt, where he hiked it up from my knee to mid-thigh.

He was breathing heavily, and he looked determined, which convinced me that he might not wait for my permission.

The offending hand moved up, molding itself to my body as it did so. Then he reached up and attempted to touch my breasts.

It was at that point that I leaned away from him, my right knee came up with all the strength I could muster, and found its mark.

He immediately released me and a sickening wheeze issued from his throat as he doubled over in pain. I backed away and went to the desk to collect my things. Picking up the box, my shoulder bag and briefcase, I slowly walked over to the door.

I turned back to see Monte writhing on the floor. He squinted up at me, his eyes watering, "What, what . . . ?"

"Your uncle contracted with me to train you in the business, Monte, not in the art of love, which you could use a few lessons in, by the way. Never, ever try to force yourself on another woman. We respond better to tenderness and respect. And that, Monte, is my final lesson to you. Free of charge."

I smiled at him and closed the door behind me.

Twenty-four hours later, I was on a plane to Montana. My apartment had been leased by a young African-American couple who'd moved to Chicago from Atlanta. I'd met them when Mr. Bouchard had brought them up to see the apartment.

All the boxes had been shipped two days earlier and would be delivered to the ranch within the week.

The only luggage I had with me was a carry-on bag with a change of clothing and a few toiletries in it. Traveling light had become old hat for me.

I sat back on my seat in coach (even though I was $125,000 richer, I still wouldn't spring for a first-class seat), and closed my eyes. I was going home. Perhaps to stay for good. I hoped I would be, but I also knew that if Jackson couldn't get past his insecurities and wholeheartedly embrace the thought of our being a couple, I would not be able to bear living near him; and, a year from then, I *could* be on a different plane, heading for another, as yet not decided upon, destination.

EIGHT

"That water is never going to boil if you don't turn the stove on," Momma said to me as she strolled into the kitchen.

I was leaning against the counter after having put the kettle on to boil for tea. Or so I'd thought.

I looked over at the gas stove. I hadn't switched on the flame under the kettle. I went and turned it on.

"What are you so preoccupied with?" Momma asked, looking at me with keen, knowing eyes.

It was on a Wednesday morning. Clancy and the boys had gotten off to school early, and Slim had driven to the south field, which was closer to the main house, to observe the herd.

Momma and I had been in one of the cabins cleaning the walls prior to treating the wood by staining it, when I'd suggested we take a break. I'd gone over to the main house to make us cups of tea and bring them back to the cabin.

"Or should I say with whom?"

I looked up into her golden-brown eyes and smiled. It's true, my mind had been on Jackson. Since my return home, he and I had made a routine of meeting between the Robertses' ranch and his place. We both jogged early in the morning, before chores. My route took me within three miles of his ranch. He ran the three miles, and when we met up, we behaved like clandestine lovers.

I felt a little like a teenager sneaking out of her bedroom window to meet her boyfriend. The thrill was going fast, though.

I was becoming impatient. So far, the temperatures hadn't been below freezing, and we hadn't had any significant snow flurries.

But if Jackson thought I was going to be jogging in snowdrifts through November and December, he had another think coming.

All through October, I'd tried to convince him that we should tell my folks about us and get it over with. I was beginning to wonder at my own sanity. I had agreed to wait, but how long did he expect me to play out the Romeo and Juliet (minus the death scenes) scenario with him?

"It's Jackson, Momma," I confessed, moving over to the kitchen table and pulling out a chair.

Momma joined me at the table, "Slim told me you told him you were in love with Jackson. It's about time you confided in me. What's going on, Chey?"

She'd removed her heavy jacket upon entering the house, hanging it on the hall tree near the back door. Now, the green of the turtleneck sweater she wore made her brown eyes look more golden than brown.

"It's difficult to explain," I said.

"Has he told you he loves you?"

"Yeah."

"Then what's the problem? Why hasn't he been over here courting you? This is strange, Chey."

"You don't know the half of it," I said resignedly.

"Then let's have it," Momma encouraged me, sitting back on her chair. "We've got a few hours before the kids return from school."

I hesitated for a moment. I didn't know if I wanted my mother to know what a fool I'd been over Jackson. Agreeing to wait a year before we told anyone of our relationship. Grasping at snippets of time together. Risking charley horses in order to see him each morning away from the curious eyes of others. It was, admittedly, slightly demeaning. Patience was one thing, but come on . . .

"Why the secrecy?" Momma asked point-blank.

"He told me he couldn't accept the fact that I love him and I want to be with him until I gave myself a year to see others and make certain it isn't infatuation I'm feeling for him."

"That's just like a man!" Momma said irritably. Shaking her head, she added, "They always assume they know what's best for everyone concerned. I can see now that you and Jackson are going to argue just about as much as your father and I used to."

Her eyes narrowed as she continued. "You can't jump through hoops in order to be with him, Chey. That sets a precedent. It tells him he has control. Your acquiescence does neither of you any good. You may be satisfied with the kisses now, but how long are you going to put up with his reticence?"

"Not long," I said, and meant it. I was already peevish. Soon, the irritation would transform into anger and then there would be no telling what I would do or say to make him pay for making me angry. It wasn't logical. But, that's how I felt.

" 'Course not," Momma said. "You're half Rainwater and half Roberts, and neither bloodline is known for patience. I say tell him to go jump in a lake. Plenty of 'em around here haven't frozen over yet. The nerve of that boy, making stipulations. I'd like a word with him myself."

"That's his point, Momma," I began in Jackson's defense. "He's been a part of this family for so long that he worries about your opinion of him. What if he and I began dating and something went wrong between us? He doesn't want to lose your love. He doesn't want to lose Cole as a friend. It's difficult for him. It's difficult for me."

I sighed. "Clancy revealed to me that she has a crush on Jackson. What is she going to think when I tell her I'm in love with him?"

"Clancy's a child. She'll get over it," Momma assured me, smiling. "Clancy develops a crush on a different male every few months. With you, though, it was always Jackson."

"You knew?" I asked, surprised. Not once, in ten years, had my mother ever let on that she knew of my feelings for Jackson.

"Why sure I knew. I noticed the hopeful way you looked at him when you thought no one was watching. You've been more discreet in the last few years. I suppose that comes with maturity. I've often wondered if anything would come of it. Now I know."

Her facial features took on a serious aspect. "Baby, you've got to let Jackson learn what it's like to be without you."

"What do you mean?" I'd felt panic at her words. Cut Jackson loose? Be denied even the pleasure of his morning kiss? Whom would it prove anything to? I, for one, would be miserable.

"Your fawning over him has got to stop. Men, instinctively, covet what they can't have. Your own Daddy had been in love with me for two years before he said anything to me. And you want to know what made him speak up? Another man, Ray Guidry, started coming to my house every Sunday afternoon to sit in our parlor and drink coffee with me and your granny. Your granddaddy had been dead a long time by then. Ray and I never got farther than the parlor, but Cole didn't know that. One day, Cole came to see me and I 'accidentally' let slip that Ray Guidry was coming by every Sunday afternoon. That made him sit up and take notice. He proposed to me shortly afterward. I accepted promptly because I loved him and I thought he had suffered enough. Now, the question is: If you had another man interested in you, do you believe Jackson would stick to his plan of waiting a year before publicly proclaiming his love?"

I humphed. "He *wants* me to have another suitor. He's got it into his thick head that I should see others before settling for him."

"And you're acting like a lovesick fool," Momma said, pointing out the obvious.

Our eyes met across the table, and I believe we had a meeting of the minds. The devious minds.

"You have to turn the tables on him, child," Momma said. "Give him what he wants, and then see how long it takes him to hop to."

What she was saying was that by my smitten behavior toward Jackson, I'd inadvertently lulled him into a complacent position. He had me and he didn't have to make an effort to keep me.

"To him, your love is assured," Momma went on. "He knows you love him. But is he satisfied with that? Does it compel him to shout it to the world? No, he holds back, feeling safe in that warm cocoon you've wrapped around him. No, Chey. You've got to shake his tree. Make him realize he has to take action if he truly loves you. Love ain't easy, but it's worth the risk. What risk is Jackson taking if he can't even express his love for you to the family who has loved him, like a member of it, all his natural life? Give that boy something to think about."

The kettle whistled and I got up to pour the hot water into the waiting mugs, the tea bags already in them.

Carrying the mugs back to the table, I said, "The problem with ultimatums is they usually have an adverse effect."

"You don't have to issue an ultimatum," Momma said reasonably. "All you have to do for the next few weeks, is tell him you're busy with the renovations. If he phones and wants to see you, you won't be available. Let him wonder. Let him rethink his decision. Let him feel what it's like to want someone and be denied that person's presence. That's all *I'm* saying."

"Wouldn't that be a form of punishment?" I naively asked.

"And what do you think his stipulations are doing to you?"

She had a point.

Two weeks later, on a Saturday afternoon, I was in Cabin A (we'd designated them cabins A, B, C and D, simply to distinguish one from the other) hanging the curtains in the bedroom, when I heard the door creak open.

Thinking it was Slim, since Momma and Clancy had gone to Billings to do the weekly grocery shopping, and Chad and Lucas were also in Billings, but at the University of Montana's main library studying for exams, I called out, "I'm in the bedroom, Slim."

I could hear the crisp sound of boots hitting the hardwood floor from the hallway. I didn't pause in my task of hanging the curtains. I was eager to finish because all the other repairs had been done in Cabin A. We'd cleaned it, polished the floors, the furnishings had been delivered, now all that needed doing was the decorating.

Momma, Clancy and I had chosen different color schemes for each cabin. Cabin A was the red cabin. Not an overpowering amount of red, mind you, but all the accents were in red. For example, the curtains were basically blue, however, they were trimmed in red.

Everything was tastefully done, reminding one of all the comforts of home.

"I see you *have* been busy," Jackson's voice said from behind me.

I turned and smiled at him.

He was wearing his favorite tan suede jacket, Wrangler's and a blue and tan striped western-style shirt. He held his tan Stetson in his right hand.

"Hello, Jackson," I said. Having finished with the first window, I climbed down from the step ladder and moved it over to the other window. The remaining set of curtains lay on one of the twin beds.

Jackson shrugged out of his coat, placing it on one of the beds, then he set his hat atop the coat.

Picking up one side of the last pair of curtains, he handed it to me. "I stopped by to see if you'd go to supper with me tonight."

I climbed the step ladder and began hanging the curtain. "You mean as in a real date?"

"In a restaurant. Just the two of us. Yes, I suppose as in a real date."

I quickly hung the first side while I pondered his question, then I reached for the second half of the pair without having answered him. Frowning, he handed me the curtain and backed up a bit.

"If you need time to think about it, I could leave and you can phone me with your reply," Jackson said, his voice tense.

He ran a hand over his short, wavy cap of hair, and sighed. "What's going on, Cheyenne?" he asked suddenly, looking up at me.

"Nothing's going on," I said calmly; however, my insides were quivering. I'd missed him so much, that the sight and sound of him, even the scent of his aftershave, worked to heighten my body's awareness of him.

He stepped forward and grasped me by the arm. I let go of the curtain, which was partially hung, and stepped off the ladder.

We faced each other and he allowed the hand he'd been holding my arm with to fall to his side.

"Don't play games with me, Cheyenne. Tell me why you've

been avoiding me." The note of pain in his voice wrenched at my heart.

I didn't believe I had the strength to carry on with my private campaign designed to subtly convince him to change his mind about making me wait until September to announce our intentions. I was weak for him. I longed to reach out and wrap him in my arms.

However, I'd made up my mind I was not going to relent.

"No games, Jackson. I've simply been trying to get the cabins in shape before the snow arrives. You know how difficult it is to get workmen out here in winter. This cabin is finished, but there are three others that still need carpentry and plumbing work done before we can get in them and do the minor repairs, cleaning and decorating." I sounded convincing, even to myself.

"I can help you," he offered as though it was the perfect solution to the problem. "I know some men who can get the other cabins repaired over a weekend. Just say the word, and I'll have them here in a matter of hours."

I was touched, and my face must have mirrored my emotions because Jackson smiled and pulled me into his arms with a great sigh of relief. "Thank God that's all it was. I thought that maybe you'd changed your mind about us."

He squeezed me and I melted, or so it seemed. The sixty degree temperature inside the cabin suddenly felt like a balmy eighty-five; and the pleasure points on my body ignited. My breasts swelled, their tips hardened.

My nose was buried in his chest, inhaling the male scent of him.

"I adore you, Jackson," I breathed. So much for strength.

I peered up into his sexy eyes. "Don't ever think that I will stop loving you, because I won't. But I'm having a hard time pretending that you and I are still just friends. Every night, I go to sleep wishing you were next to me."

He kissed me on the forehead and hugged me closer to him. "I swear to you, Chey, I'll always be there for you. And, when you're sure, really sure, that you want me, you'll wake up one day, and I *will* be there."

I raised my eyes to his. "My mind's made up, Jackson; so keep your end of the bargain. Marry me. Marry me soon because fifty years together isn't promised to us, and we've already been apart long enough. What are you waiting for? What do I have to do to prove to you that I love you, I'm committed to you and I'm prepared to spend the rest of my life making you happy? What?"

Jackson's eyes were on my lips, and I knew he hadn't been paying strict attention to me. He wanted to kiss me, badly. I knew that because I was also undergoing sexual-tension overload.

I licked my lips. "Jackson, are you listening to me?"

His mouth fell upon mine and I moaned deep in my throat. My lips parted and his tongue entered my mouth and I was lost. I could not recall what I'd been saying, all I wanted was to get closer to him. My hand moved up to his chest, where my fingers began unbuttoning his shirt. Four buttons down, I reached inside to caress his naked chest, only to discover he was wearing an undershirt.

Jackson reached down and pulled the shirt up out of the waist of his Wrangler's. My hands then came in contact with his bare skin and he moaned with pleasure.

Meanwhile, I threw my head back to allow him to trail kisses along the curve of my neck. I was wearing a crewneck pullover sweater, and Jackson ran his hands up underneath, exploring the warm, tender skin of my flat belly.

He stopped abruptly and looked into my eyes. We were both in the throes of passion and breathing heavily due to the effort of restraint.

"All right," he said. "Let's get married. I can't take this any-more."

It's perverse, but at that moment, his words were like a knife, plunged into my gut, twisted, then pulled out and thrust in again.

Did I have a gun to his head? Was I the type of woman who enticed a man into marriage with the promise of conjugal bliss? No, I was a woman who loved him; a woman he'd known for twenty-seven years. I deserved more than a proposal made in haste, in resignation and, perhaps, with sexual release in mind.

I pushed out of his embrace, which was easy because he never saw it coming.

"Don't do me any favors, Jackson Kincaid."

I backed away from him, straightening my sweater as I did so.

He regarded me with still-dreamy eyes. "I don't understand. Didn't you just ask me to marry you?"

"I did," I said in a low, hoarse voice. "But I don't want you resigning yourself to me, Jackson. Just like you stipulated that you didn't want me until I was certain, I also, don't want you until you've made a sober decision. My proposal was made in love; yours sounded like a capitulation. You surrendered to the heat of the moment. I don't want that."

Squeezing his forehead with the fingers of his right hand as though he had a migraine, Jackson said, "I should have known not to get involved with a woman who is still wet behind the ears. You have a lot of growing up to do, Cheyenne. Sure, I proposed to you in the heat of the moment. Every fool who ever proposed to a woman proposed in the heat of the moment; otherwise, he never would have gotten up the nerve to ask in the first place!"

Tears sat in my eyes.

Jackson drew back as if stung by the sight of them.

"Forget it, Cheyenne. I was wrong to kiss you that day in the cemetery. I knew I was playing with fire, but, God, I loved you so much, I thought that maybe, just maybe, it could work out if we took things slowly. But like most young people, you had no patience for taking things slowly. It's my fault. I'm sorry. I'm sorry I hurt you. I'm sorry you were ever infatuated with me. I'm just plain sorry. Good-bye, Cheyenne."

He collected his hat and coat and left.

Stubbornness kept me rooted to the spot.

I dared not move, because if I had, I would've flung myself on to his legs and begged him not to go.

The Bible says pride goes before a fall and nothing was truer that day. I was too ignorant to see it then, though.

The next day, Jackson phoned to give Momma the names and numbers of the reliable carpenters he'd mentioned to me the day before.

I'd been out riding when he phoned. The moment I got back

to the house, Momma followed me upstairs to my bedroom where I began getting out of my riding clothes to shower. I'd been all over the property, which took a good two hours. I was perspiring, my clothes were rumpled and I smelled of horse sweat.

I hadn't been able to ride off the nervous tension I felt though, and my emotions were at the surface. I felt like crying one minute, and laughing uproariously the next.

"Jackson phoned and left the numbers of some carpenters he said he told you about yesterday. He says he's already spoken to them, and they can be here next Friday morning, if you want them."

"That was good of him," I said.

Momma sat on the chair next to the window as I stripped down to my underwear. "He didn't ask to speak to you, Chey. Why is that?"

I turned to face her. "Because we aren't seeing each other anymore, Momma, secretly or otherwise." I'd tried to make my voice sound unemotional, but it had broken toward the end and Momma had noticed.

To her credit, she didn't run to me and try to console me. I would've really broken down then.

"I should have stayed out of it," Momma said self-reproachfully. "Haven't I learned anything in fifty-five years? What possessed me to tell you to avoid him?"

She held her head in her hands. Raising her eyes to mine, she said, "I just love you so much, Cheyenne. I love Jackson, too. I wanted you two together. I'm just as bad as Slim is, trying to manipulate other people's lives . . ."

"It isn't your fault, Momma," I told her, going to kneel beside her chair and clasp her hand in mine. "I was impatient. I tried to rush him into marriage. I was rash and pigheaded. It was all my fault."

Momma's eyes were hopeful when she raised them to mine. "Everyone's allowed to make one big mistake, Chey. Jackson loves you, he'll come around. Just give him space. You'll see."

I forced a smile, kissed her cheek and got to my feet. "Don't worry, Momma, I'm not despondent. I'm just licking my wounds and healing. I'll get back into the battle soon enough."

"Good girl," Momma said, rising, too. "You go on and shower, you smell awful."

She left the room and I walked back to the private bath in my bedroom and peeled off my bra and panties, depositing them in the clothes hamper. Stepping into the shower, I switched on the hot water and let it run over my head, down to the rest of my body, and while it ran, I wept until I was emotionally drained.

After the shower, I dried off, put on my chenille robe, lay down on the bed and promptly fell asleep.

When I awakened, it was dark outside. The room was dimly lit from the light I'd left on in the bathroom.

I sat up, getting my bearings.

I heard the doorbell ring downstairs and went to the bedroom door to crack it so I could find out who was calling. Then, I remembered the date of the month: October 31, Halloween.

The kids who lived on the neighboring ranches all knew Momma made caramel apples for them every Halloween. Because the houses were so widely spaced, parents drove their children to neighbors' homes and walked with them to the door.

Vibrant children's voices cried, "Trick or treat, trick or treat, we want something good to eat!"

Momma's and Clancy's laughter followed, and Momma said, "Come in, come in you little monsters. Harry Johnson, is that you behind that Frankenstein mask?"

Harry Johnson was Momma's age. By two of his three grown children, he had six grandchildren. It had been their voices I'd heard raised in greedy glee.

I closed the door and went to the closet to choose something to put on. There was no use brooding upstairs like a recluse. I would go downstairs and greet the trick-or-treaters along with Momma and Clancy.

When I got downstairs, Mr. Johnson was in the kitchen with Momma having a cup of coffee while Clancy entertained the kids in the family room with a *Casper Meets Wendy* video.

Halloween in ranch country was a leisurely business. Not like in neighborhoods where the houses were closer together, and the kids tried to hit as many houses as possible. In Custer, Halloween was an excuse to visit your neighbors and catch up on what had been going on in their lives.

Mr. Johnson looked up at me and smiled when I entered the room. He was a slightly built gentleman with salt-and-pepper hair and warm blue eyes. His wife, Annie, had passed away eight years ago. He had been a good friend to Daddy and since Daddy passed away, I believe he and Momma had also found some common ground. They talked easily and I often teased Momma that I thought he had a crush on her.

"Hello, Mr. Johnson," I said, smiling back. "How are you?"

"I'm good, Cheyenne, and you?"

"Great," I said. "Whom did you bring with you tonight?"

Looking pleased that I'd asked, he replied, "I brought the whole gang: Sean, Neal, Mary Jane, Sarah, Jacinta and the baby boy, Eddie." Harry's youngest daughter, Deana, was married to a Mexican-American. From what I'd heard, some folks in the family weren't too happy with her decision; but Momma told me Harry had supported Deana and Eduardo from the beginning. I admired that in Harry.

"I think I'll go say hello," I told him, preparing to leave.

"Won't you stay and chat a while first?" Harry asked, showing dimples in his tanned cheeks. He actually was quite good-looking. He was fit and trim, with healthy-looking muscle tone. If his hairline were farther back from his forehead, he'd look like the actor, Patrick Stewart, of *Star Trek* fame. He had that same patrician nose and a dimple in his chin. His twangy accent would be a dead giveaway to his origins, however.

People joked that after the Civil War, the Confederate army did not surrender, they just retreated to Montana. It's true that native Montanans have southern accents. Some of us sound as twangy as Texans. Some, more like Georgians. I really couldn't detect an accent in the manner in which my family, or Jackson spoke. However, friends and acquaintances I've known in Chicago swear I have a slight southern accent.

"Your mother was telling me that you're planning to stay home for a while," Harry Johnson was saying.

"Yeah," I said, pulling up a chair and sitting down.

Momma got a mug from the tray on the table and poured me a cup of coffee from the glass carafe.

"And everyone's talking about the lodge," Harry continued. "When do you expect to be up and running?"

"By April, I believe," I replied, stirring cream into my coffee.

Momma was watching me. I knew she was wondering how I was doing after sleeping my afternoon away.

"We'll be advertising in the April issues of several national magazines and see who bites," I explained. "We only have four cabins, to start with, so we're not hoping for an avalanche. But it would be nice to be fully booked all spring."

"Are you going to be comfortable having strangers at your supper table, Peaches?" Harry asked, his eyes on Momma.

"A stranger's just a friend you haven't met yet," Momma intoned. She was blushing. I never would have believed it if I hadn't seen it with my own eyes.

I drank my coffee quietly as Harry and Momma talked about their grandchildren and whether the upcoming winter would be as bad as last year's.

I rose after a few minutes of eavesdropping on their conversation. "I'll go see how Clancy and the kids are getting along."

In the family room, the children were all huddled around Clancy, eating caramel apples on the floor in front of the TV.

On the screen, three animated, transparent ghosts were plotting to make poor Casper's life miserable.

I sat down next to them, "Hi, you guys."

"Hi," each child said in turn. They ranged in age from three to seven. The baby, Eddie, had liquid-brown eyes, dusky skin and shiny, dark-brown straight hair, his bangs almost in his beautiful eyes.

Seeing them triggered baby hunger within me.

Eddie got up, came over to me and climbed into my lap. I grinned and hugged him. He smiled up at me, then we watched the movie in companionable silence, broken only by intermittent laughter.

All too soon, Harry came to collect the children and Momma, Clancy and I bid them farewell at the front door.

It was after eight by then, and I inquired after Chad and Lucas.

I knew Slim had already gone upstairs to his apartment, and, more than likely, had retired for the evening.

"They're both out in behind some girls," Momma said of my younger brothers. She laughed suddenly. "You will never guess what Harry Johnson just asked me."

"To go out with him?" Clancy said, her dark eyes dancing mischievously. "Mr. Johnson's sweet on you, Momma."

Frowning, Momma seemed to consider the idea. "I believe he's just lonely. Men don't fare as well as women do when they're widowed. No, I think he simply wants someone to talk to sometimes, maybe have a meal with . . ."

"What did he ask you?" I interrupted her. Sometimes Momma could go off on a tangent and completely lose sight of what the topic of conversation had been.

She appeared flustered as Clancy and I followed her into the kitchen. "The Spring Roundup Dance," she said. "Can you believe it?" She was still laughing as she went to the table and removed the tray with the cups and saucers and coffeepot on it, took it to the counter next to the sink, then began putting the dishes into the sink of warm, sudsy water. "I haven't been to that dance since your daddy got killed."

Clancy and I flanked her at the sink: Clancy on the left, I on the right. "That dance's six months away," Clancy said. "Isn't it a little early to be asking you?"

"When you get to be our age, you have to think ahead," Momma joked.

"What did you tell him?" I asked softly.

Momma reached for the sponge to begin washing the dishes, and I said, "Leave them, I'll get them later."

She dropped the sponge into the dishwater and smiled up at me.

"It was nice being asked, but I told him I don't date friends."

"You don't date anyone," Clancy put in.

"Shhh . . ." I said, glaring at Clancy.

"What did he say to that?" I asked Momma.

"He said then I should just consider him an enemy," Momma said with a wistful expression. "So I told him I'd think about it."

"You'll think about it?" Clancy asked incredulously. "But, Momma, he's white!"

"Actually, he's the color of lightly done toast," Momma said, meeting Clancy's gaze. "But that's beside the point. Your father and I raised you not to dislike anyone based on the color of his skin. You know this family's history: Our ancestors were slaves, so, undoubtedly, there's some white blood in us. Your grandmother's half Cheyenne, which makes me one-quarter and you, one-eighth. We are proud of our heritage, but we do not think of ourselves as better than anyone else, be he black, brown, red, yellow or white."

"I understand all that," Clancy said, not backing down. "But there are some kids at school who shout profanities at me every day because of the color of my skin. They hate me, and I hate them."

"Oh, baby," Momma said, cradling Clancy, who was four inches taller than she was, in her arms. "There are always going to be people who hate us. Cheyenne went through the same thing when she was in school. Cole, Chad, Lucas, you've all faced it. In my day, we weren't even allowed to go to school with whites. A group of white boys used to accost your uncle Sammy and me practically every morning on our way to school. We started fighting back and they stopped bothering us. Back then, Martin Luther King wasn't around to tell us to turn the other cheek. We dealt with them the way our parents had to deal with *their* parents in order to live here in peace: We stood our ground."

I put my arms about the both of them, making it a group hug.

"You have to be strong, Clarisse Nancy," Momma said firmly. "You have to have more endurance than they do. And you have to stubbornly refuse to lower yourself to their level."

"That's the hard part," Clancy admitted, looking lovingly into our mother's face. "But I'll try, Momma."

"That's all I'm asking, baby. The more you try, the easier it becomes to keep your eyes on your goals and not be deterred by the hateful actions of others."

The both of them had managed to get through that emotional interval without shedding a tear, but I was crying, for the second time in a matter of hours.

Clancy stared at me, but directed her question to Momma. "What's wrong with *her?*"

"Can't a sister commiserate with her sister?" I asked through my tears. "It pains me to see you experiencing the exact same thing I did when I was in school."

Clancy laughed. "Well dry your tears, Sis, because I'm going to be just fine."

"You promise?" I was becoming maudlin, but I couldn't help it.

"I promise," Clancy said unhesitatingly. "Now stop getting mushy on me, and concentrate on getting Jackson back."

"Did you tell her?" I asked Momma. She had never betrayed a confidence before.

"I did not!" Momma said sharply.

"It was Slim," Clancy confessed. "And I sorta overheard you tell Momma you and Jackson had argued, earlier, when I passed your bedroom door."

"You mean when you had your ear pressed to my bedroom door, you little snoop!" I accused her.

I grabbed her around the neck and pretended to choke her.

Clancy was sputtering with laughter. "You should be glad Momma only allows me access to the Internet half an hour a week, otherwise your business might be all over the United States by now."

I hugged her. I was relieved that she was, apparently, not upset with me for being in love with Jackson. "You're okay kid," I said.

The doorbell rang and Momma went to see who it was.

Clancy grinned at me. "I bet I know who that is."

Her tone of voice was that of someone with a secret, and I knew, from experience, that she was up to mischief.

"What have you done now, Clancy?" I asked.

"You remember when I got up to go to the bathroom when we were watching the video with Mr. Johnson's grandkids? I didn't really have to go."

A few seconds later, Momma walked through the kitchen's entrance-way with Jackson, his face a mask of concern, close behind her.

"See?" Momma said to him. "I told you she was just fine."

Frowning, visibly confused, Jackson looked me over. I hoped the effect of my last crying jag had worn off. Apparently, it hadn't because a pained expression crossed his features.

Momma grasped Clancy by the arm and pulled her along with her.

"Come on, child, you've got some explaining to do."

Jackson and I were left alone in the kitchen.

He stood still, his back rigid, his eyes never leaving my face. I was afraid to speak, but I was more afraid not to. "She was just trying to get us together so we can talk," I said in Clancy's defense.

He swallowed, his Adam's apple moving in his throat. "Could we take a walk?"

My heart thundered in my chest. "My coat's there by the door," I said, indicating the hall tree next to the back door.

After I'd bundled up, we went out the back door and began walking in the direction of the cabins.

The night was illuminated by a full moon, and our breath was visible in the cold air.

I waited for him to open the dialogue between us. I was not confident in my ability to say the right thing.

"Your family knows then," he said. There was no censure in his tone. Relief, perhaps. I wasn't certain.

"It seems that Momma has known I'm in love with you for years now. Slim guessed it the day of the basketball game, and *he* told Clancy."

Jackson laughed. "And we thought it was our little secret."

We stopped walking and faced each other.

"Jackson, about yesterday . . ."

"I don't want to talk about yesterday, Cheyenne. When Clancy phoned and said you'd been thrown from your horse and were in severe pain, it made me feel the full impact of the folly of confessing to you that I was in love with you. I've loved you from afar for years, and it gave me nothing but pleasure to be able to do so. But now, I find, the mere *thought* of losing you in an accident sends me into a panic. I can't handle that."

Up until that point, I'd held on to a thread of hope that my words of the previous day could be taken back. The anger I'd displayed. The impatience. The foolishness. All retrievable.

I had no remedy for lack of faith, however. Faith in the power of love was something Jackson would have to learn on his own.

I don't know why, but as I stood there looking up into his dearly loved face, I saw his father. I realized that growing up in a house where love wasn't demonstrated, where shouting, or showing any emotion whatsoever was taboo, had affected him greatly.

I felt weak as a numbing sense of finality clutched my heart in its icy fingers.

"We can't go back to the way it used to be, Jackson," I told him. "I won't be able to be in the same room with you without my love for you bouncing off the walls for all the world to see."

"You're young, Cheyenne. You'll meet someone else, and what we've shared will be just a pleasant memory," he said, his voice calm and so maddeningly reassuring that I wanted to sock him in the stomach so that he'd be familiar with the pain I was experiencing.

"You've just broken my heart, so I don't think the memory is going to be all that pleasant," I said as I spun on my heels and walked back to the house. "Good night, Jackson Kincaid. Have a good life."

NINE

Autumn is my favorite season in Montana. It's characterized by mellow, sunny days, which display the vibrant colors of fall: orange, yellow, red, russet. The nights are crisp, cool and the black, velvet sky above is splashed with glittering stars.

Throughout my life, with the coming of autumn, I've acquired an air of expectation, a sense of something wonderful happening in the near future.

Every morning that November, in spite of the fiasco with Jackson, I awakened filled with that happy feeling. I'd programmed myself to go forward, behave as if nothing untoward had occurred between me and Jackson.

I hired the workmen he'd recommended. I saw no plausible reason to cut off my nose to spite my face. They proved to be skilled carpenters and plumbers. They did, indeed, finish all the heavy work in record time. The roofs of all three cabins needed new shingles. The front porches had to be rebuilt because of rotting boards. They put new basins, tile, tubs, sinks and showerheads in the bathrooms. And, new cabinets were built for the kitchens.

We were required to have the county's building inspector come out and check the final result before we could open the lodge. He arrived, unexpectedly, on the last day the workmen were at the ranch.

I was out at Cabin C with John Littlewhirlwind, the foreman of the crew, discussing how I was to pay them (did they want one big check, or eight individual checks?), when Frank drove up.

John was Native American, a local Crow. He was five feet eleven, stocky, brown-skinned, with dark eyes and hair. He looked around thirty, and there was a vibrancy about him that I immediately liked.

Someone must have told Frank Long, the inspector, where I was because he strode into Cabin C and greeted me. He had pockmarked skin on his ruddy face, light brown, almost blond straight hair, a large nose, slate-gray eyes and a slash of a mouth. I don't believe he smiled once when he was there.

He never glanced at John as he grasped my hand and shook it. "Miss Roberts," he said with a grimace. "Are these men licensed? When I drove up, I don't believe I saw a company logo on any of the vehicles out there."

"Mr. Long," I said. "I'd like you to meet Mr. Littlewhirlwind. Mr. Littlewhirlwind is the foreman of the crew I've hired, and I can assure you they are licensed, and that they do superior work."

John held out his hand, which Frank ignored.

"I'll be the judge of that," Frank Long said with his huge nose in the air.

He turned away from John and me, his size twelve boots, which he hadn't knocked the mud off of before entering, making tracks on my newly buffed floor. "I'll start with the first cabin," he said, and walked out.

"I had no idea he was going to show up while you all were still here," I told John honestly. "According to state law, I have to have the cabins inspected before we can open the lodge."

"I know that, Cheyenne," John said soothingly. We were on a first-name basis by then. "It isn't the first time Frank Long has tried to make it difficult for us to make a living in this state."

I wasn't naive. I knew that some folks in the area hated Native Americans as much as they despised blacks. It was still jolting to witness the hatred firsthand, however.

"I'll tell him to come back some other time," I suggested.

"And risk his giving you a failing grade next time he grudgingly shows up?" John said, shaking his head. "No, let him stay. And I'll stay as well. I'd like him to try to claim that my men and I didn't do a good enough job."

I liked him even more when he said that.

When we got outside, Frank Long was laying a ladder against the side of Cabin A, preparing to climb it in order to inspect the roof.

John and I stood, watching him, as the other men gathered around us one by one.

"You don't reckon he'll fall and break his neck and put us all out of our misery?" one of the men asked hopefully.

"We should be so lucky," John joked.

Frank didn't fall. He painstakingly went over every cabin. I had to admire his thoroughness, even if I didn't agree with his attitude.

Around two hours after he'd arrived, Frank handed me a clipboard with his findings on it.

John, true to his word, had stayed behind, but his men had packed up their tools, loaded their pickups and had been gone an hour by then.

I read over Frank's report. He'd found one loose tile in the bathroom of Cabin B, a board that "sounded flimsy" on the porch of Cabin D. It was his opinion that the kitchen cabinets were made of an inferior material. They were solid wood, so I knew he was stretching the truth there. And he thought the water pressure in the bathrooms could use improvement.

We'd passed. All the problems he'd found didn't constitute enough of a reason to give the cabins a failing grade.

I looked into his eyes as I gave him back his clipboard. "We'll repair all that before your next inspection."

"Which will be in two weeks' time," he said in serious tones. He then turned his slate-gray eyes on John. "Fair work, Mr. Littlewhirlwind."

The muscles worked in John's jaw, and his dark eyes were hard.

"Same to you, Mr. Long."

Frank Long smirked but didn't say anything else as he tipped his hat in my direction, and walked away.

John insisted on staying to repair everything on Frank Long's list. I worked with him as we repaired the tile in Cabin B, which only needed more adhesive on the back of the tile. We never found the "flimsy sounding" board on the porch of Cabin D that Frank Long had heard.

The water pressure, we both agreed, was fine. And as for the cabinets, they were made so well, they'd probably be there for the next fifty years if properly cared for.

I walked John to his truck and handed him his check, with an added bonus for him and his men.

"Thank you, John," I said, smiling into his dark eyes. "You've done a great job."

"We always aim to please," he said, his smile widening. "Thank you for hiring us, Cheyenne. And tell Jackson he was right about you, you *were* heaven to work for."

I managed to smile at his compliment, but I'd felt a twinge of pain, in the pit of my stomach, at the mention of Jackson's name.

John waved good-bye, and I walked back to the house.

It was around four o'clock on a Monday afternoon. Chad and Lucas hadn't gotten home from Billings yet. Clancy's bus hadn't arrived, and Momma and Slim had gone into Custer for Slim's doctor's appointment. Just a routine checkup. Except for a touch of arthritis, Slim was in good health.

I entered the house through the back door and went to the kitchen sink to wash up. Thirsty, I took a glass from the cabinet and drank some water directly from the faucet. Our water came from a deep well beneath the property and was cool and refreshing year round.

With the bulk of the work on the cabins behind us, I felt some tension dissipate from my body. We were on our way.

I owed Jackson a debt of gratitude for recommending John Littlewhirlwind, but I had no idea how to express it to him. I hadn't seen or spoken with him since Halloween night; and that had been ten days ago.

I would ask Momma to do it, I decided. Why should I be subjected to the cadence, the timbre of his voice over the phone?

Then a thought occurred to me: I could send him a note. A written thank you was personal, but detached at the same time. I could fulfill my duty and protect my feelings simultaneously.

Upstairs in my bedroom I sat at the desk facing the window,

and tried to compose my thoughts. From my vantage point, the tips of the Ponderosa pines seemed to kiss the azure sky.

A bald eagle glided above them, and I abruptly got up to get a better look. It *was* an eagle, its head white, its body black, its tail feathers white, and its wingspan perhaps six feet across. A young specimen.

Sighing, I went back to the desk and sat down. What should I write? What should I write it on?

I rummaged in the desk drawer. There was a book of self-adhesive postage stamps, white linen stationery with envelopes to match, another set of stationery in a more romantic design. I couldn't use that; it might give him ideas. My hand touched a leather-bound book, and I picked it up. It was a three-hundred page blank book Momma had given me for my eighteenth birthday.

"You're an adult now," she'd said on the occasion. "It's time you started recording your thoughts for future generations."

She'd been joking, of course. What did I, at eighteen, have to say that would be interesting to future generations?

I placed the book on the desktop and reached for the linen stationery.

I closed my eyes for a moment, thinking. Then I wrote: *Jackson, thank you for recommending John Littlewhirlwind to me. He and his men did a wonderful job. I'm grateful to you, Cheyenne.*

Three sentences. He couldn't possibly read more into it than what it was meant to say. He wouldn't be able to discern that I missed him terribly; I was having trouble sleeping, wasn't eating properly and that the cheery pose I'd adopted was wearing thin.

If I'd phoned, however, he might have heard all of that in my tone of voice.

I folded and placed the letter in an envelope, addressed it and sealed it. After I'd done that, I held the letter between my fingers a few moments, imagining Jackson's reaction when he received it. Would he eagerly tear it open, thinking it was a long letter from me begging him to reconsider and come back to me? Or would he be reluctant to open it, *afraid* that I'd written a pleading missive imploring him to take me back?

Either way, I would've suffered a loss of dignity. He'd never get a letter like that from me.

I put a stamp on it and set it aside. Then my attention was brought back to the leather-bound book. *It's been nine years since Momma gave it to me,* I thought, *I should use it for something.*

Therapy. I'd never been to a therapist, and I didn't think I'd be going any time soon, but, perhaps, by writing down my thoughts, I'd be able to get over my disappointment and heartbreak with my sanity intact.

I picked up a pen, opened the front flap of the book, wrote the date and then I began to write about Jackson. I wrote about the first time I saw him. It seemed as if I'd always known him, but I could remember the moment I became cognizant of him.

Experts have debated, for generations, about how old a child is when they first become aware of the world around them. As infants, they may only know that when they cry, their mothers hold them or feed them or change them. They learn what to do in order to get a desired result. As toddlers, their world is limited to the boundaries of their parents' world. I can recall the day my world expanded. I was four. Jackson was having dinner with us. He sat next to Cole, Jr., at the table. To my child's eyes, he had a very friendly, pleasing face. At that age, I worshipped my big brother, Cole, and I'd follow him around like a puppy seeking affection.

Sometimes, Cole got frustrated and yelled at me to leave him alone, especially when he had friends over. I know I embarrassed him on a number of occasions.

One summer when I was five, and he was thirteen, we were at a church picnic when Momma looked away for a second and I took off in search of Cole, who'd long since gotten scarce with his pals. He liked it when Momma wanted me close to her side, which she did whenever we were at certain functions. Momma had waited years for a little girl and she enjoyed dressing me in frilly costumes and having people tell her how pretty her daughter was. I hated it, and the day would invariably end with me looking as if I'd wallowed in the mud with the pigs.

I figured if I destroyed enough dresses, she'd get the message and put me in jeans, like the boys wore. I wanted to be exactly like Cole, rough and ready to fight at the drop of a hat.

On that summer day, one of the ladies had come up and started a conversation with Momma. When Momma turned her back to me, I quietly slid from the bench we were sitting on, and crept away.

I walked through a forest of adult legs before I found Cole in a clearing, playing touch football with other boys his age. A group of girls stood on the sidelines, cheering and looking pretty in their pastel dresses.

One of them looked down at me and said irritably, "Don't you belong to somebody?"

I pointed at Cole, who was running down the field with the ball.

"Cole," I said, then I nervously twirled the hem of my dress around my finger until, ultimately, my lacy panties were showing.

The girls giggled at my behavior. The same one who'd earlier asked if I belonged to anyone shouted at Cole, "Hey, Cole Roberts, is this your baby sister? Tell her it isn't nice to show her bloomers in polite company!"

Cole was so flustered, he'd faltered, another boy tackled him from behind and they fell to the ground, rolling to a stop near the sidelines.

Cole looked up at me, his face thunderous, "Get back to Momma. You little pest! Get out of here."

His anger had confused and frightened me. I was about to dissolve into tears when a pair of jeans-clad legs appeared beside me, and a voice said, "Never mind him, Chey. Come on, I'll take you back to Miss Peaches."

It was the small acts of kindness over a period of twenty-seven years that endeared Jackson to me.

Up until I was seventeen, he was the object of my hero worship. I saw him as a gentler, kinder brother. Cole did eventually learn to tolerate my presence, but Jackson never yelled at me, or told me to get lost. I figured it was because he didn't have any brothers or sisters, therefore the attention I gave him was a welcome substitute for the affection he'd been deprived of.

Sometime after my seventeenth birthday, I developed a real

crush on him. I blamed it on my hormones. My love for Jackson, coupled with my newfound womanly desires was a heady combination.

At any rate, by that time, he was a man of twenty-five, had lost his parents in a car crash and was sole owner of a thousand-acre ranch, so he didn't have time for a starry-eyed twelfth grader.

I got to sigh over him at holiday dinners and the occasional funeral or wedding.

One December, when I was eighteen, I actually had the nerve to ask him for a kiss under the mistletoe. I'd finished high school early and had won a full-academic scholarship to the University of Chicago.

The months I'd spent away from home had emboldened me.

All day, I'd been going to the window whenever I heard a car pull up, to make certain that when Jackson arrived, I'd be the one to open the door.

I'd taken special care dressing. It had taken me months to save enough money to buy the forest-green velvet A-line dress with its white, crocheted Peter Pan collar. I'd put my black, wavy hair up, believing it made me appear more mature.

I was so young then, though, that I resembled a gazelle: a long, graceful neck and legs that went on forever.

When Jackson had finally arrived, I'd peered out the window and noted, with satisfaction, that he'd come alone. I lived in dread that he would get seriously involved with a woman, the way Cole had. He and Enid were dating at that time.

The timing was perfect, because everyone else was gathered in the kitchen and the coast was clear for my sprint to the door once Jackson rang the bell.

I waited impatiently as I listened to him walk onto the front porch.

I counted to ten before opening the door and smiling pleasantly.

It was snowing out, and Jackson brushed the flakes off his coat and stomped his boots on the welcome mat before entering.

I had gazed up at him, my heart beating about as fast as a hummingbird's, and said, "Hello, Jackson, how've you been?"

He'd grinned, showing strong white teeth in his handsome face.

"Hey, Chey. I'm good. How about you? How're you doing in school? Keeping your nose in the books, I hope."

I helped him with his coat as we talked. "School's tough, but I'm getting into the swing of things."

"What were your grades like last semester?"

"I got three *A*'s and a *B.*"

"What'd you get the *B* in?"

"Statistics."

His eyebrows had arched in surprise. "That's a brain drainer. I'm impressed."

"Don't be," I'd told him. "If it hadn't been a required course, I would've avoided it."

"But you like numbers."

"I like solving problems. Statistics is all about data. I swear, the whole point of the course was to twist your brain into knots. After the final exam, some of my friends and I went out and partied all night, we were so relieved to have it behind us."

Laughing, Jackson said, "Still, you applied yourself, and I'm proud of you, Cheyenne."

I'd hung his coat on the hall tree and observed that we were standing directly beneath the mistletoe Daddy had hung in the foyer.

I paused and purposefully looked up at the green and red twig. Jackson's eyes followed my line of sight.

Then our eyes met, and I said, "It'll be a merry Christmas for me if you'd kiss me, Jackson."

He bent his head to plant a chaste buss on my cheek, and I turned my head at the precise moment when his lips were to touch my face, and his mouth brushed against mine instead.

It had been very fleeting and light, however I'd felt the impact down to my toes.

"You little sneak!" Jackson had exclaimed, stepping back.

I'd laughed and said, "That'll teach you never to let your guard down with a Roberts woman."

"So you're a woman now, huh?" he'd asked, his right hand

unconsciously going to his mouth. I'd thought, then, that he hadn't been entirely unaffected by our kiss.

"I'm all the woman you'll ever need," I'd boldly replied.

And that was the first time we'd engaged in the sexy repartee we would fine-tune over the course of the next nine years.

I heard a noise downstairs and closed the book. I'd been writing so swiftly, my pen flying across the blank pages, that I hadn't noticed I'd recorded ten pages of memories in one sitting.

From that day onward, I vowed to write at least a page about me and Jackson each night before retiring. I was determined to get to the bottom of why I loved him: Was it an obsession with a childhood dream? Or did I truly love the man beneath the image I'd built up in my own mind?

Momma and Slim were in the kitchen getting something to drink when I got downstairs.

Momma looked up at me over her orange-juice glass. "I see the workmen have gone. Is everything finished?"

"Yeah, and the inspector came today, too. We're set," I replied going to her and kissing her cheek. "How did Slim's checkup go?"

"Ask him," Momma suggested, turning to smile in Slim's direction.

Slim had sat down at the kitchen table. He was drinking a glass of water.

"Well, Slim?" I prompted him. "How was your checkup?"

He set his glass on the table and met my eyes. "That quack says I should stop riding. He says it isn't good for my spine, or some such nonsense."

"When you get to be a certain age," Momma explained, coming around to join us at the table, "your bones get more brittle. Slim has been having some back pain, a fact he neglected to tell us about." She glared at Slim.

"Look what happened when I *did* tell someone," Slim interrupted, employing his usual one-sided reasoning. "I've been grounded."

"Did he say no riding at all?" I asked. "Or that you should cut back?"

"No getting on a horse," Slim said, sniffing. "A gawl durn

man who doesn't know one end of a horse from the other is telling me I can't ride anymore. Why that's like telling me I can't breathe anymore. Do you know how long I've been riding horses?"

In a fit, he continued before either Momma or I could reply to his query. "More than eighty years. I wasn't nothin' but a tadpole the first time my papa put me on a horse."

"Things change," Momma said sagely.

Slim pushed himself up from the table and went to put his glass in the sink. "I'm a man with no real vices," he said, his back to us. "I never had much use for liquor, didn't care for cigarettes, and was faithful to my wife. My main pleasure has been running this ranch. Tell me how I'm gonna do that if I can't ride?"

"You've been modifying the way you run this ranch for years now," Momma reminded him. "Because you didn't have the stamina for long rides, you've had someone drive you out and *then* you rode the fence on horseback. We'll come up with something."

"Maybe it's time I put myself out to pasture," Slim said, his voice low and tired. "It's unnatural for a man to outlive his son, his wife, and then become a burden to his daughter-in-law and grandchildren."

I couldn't take anymore of his self-pity. I went to him, caught him by the shoulders and forced him to face me. "Listen to me, old man, we love you. You're needed. And if you think, for one minute, that we're going to let you just sit around and will yourself into the grave, then you don't know how stubborn we can be.

"So what if you can't ride anymore? There're more sides to you than the part that sits on a horse!" I ended, hugging him fiercely.

"Although you can be a butthead sometimes," Momma joked.

"And you're the pain in my butt," Slim returned, to which we all laughed.

"Hey everybody!" Clancy called as she came through the back door.

She threw her book bag onto the table, and went straight for the refrigerator.

"Wash up!" Momma admonished.

I let go of Slim.

Clancy looked back at us as she washed her hands at the sink. "What's going on?"

"The doctor told Slim, today, that he can't ride anymore," Momma said.

"Can I have your saddle then?" Clancy asked as she reached for a paper towel.

Slim laughed. "Life goes on. Yeah, take the doggone saddle. I won't be needing it."

Clancy whooped and went to hug her grandfather's neck. Kissing his wizened cheek repeatedly, she exclaimed, "Thank you, Slim!"

"Well, at least one of us is happy," Slim said, still smiling.

Those were my sentiments, exactly, about two weeks later when I went into town to pick up some fresh cranberries. It was the day before Thanksgiving, and I'd forgotten the cranberries when I'd done the shopping at Big Fresh in Billings the previous day.

There was one small mom-and-pop market in Custer. I didn't hold out much hope of finding fresh cranberries. If all else failed, we would settle for the canned variety.

I parked Slim's red pickup in front of the store and climbed out, my booted foot hitting the pavement. It could be snowing out, and folks would still be standing outside the grocery store chatting. I spoke to the three men standing around exchanging gossip, and walked inside the store.

Mr. Cavendish, the owner, a tall, gaunt man with snow-white hair, brown eyes and sunken cheeks, greeted me cheerfully.

"Hi ya, Cheyenne. How's Riley? I don't see him much anymore."

People always asked after the oldsters in the family either out of respect, or morbid curiosity: there was a chance the elderly gent had died and they'd missed the funeral.

"Oh, Riley's just fine, Mr. Cavendish," I replied. Everyone in the family called Grandpa Slim because of his slight build. Acquaintances, or folks who knew him only by his reputation, referred to him as Riley Roberts, or just Riley.

"What can I help you find?" Mr. Cavendish asked, smiling.

His appearance belied his temperament. He reminded me of John Carradine, the tall, gaunt, somber-looking actor who portrayed undertakers in westerns. However, Mr. Cavendish was jolly and garrulous. When you patronized his store he'd sometimes follow you down the aisles, talking a mile a minute.

"Do you have any fresh cranberries?"

"As a matter of fact, I do!"

He came from behind the counter and walked over to me and crooked his finger at me, "This way, my dear."

I knew where the fresh fruits and vegetables were located in the store; but the place was empty except for us, and he seemed intent on giving me first-class service, so I let him.

"I just got them in yesterday, shipped all the way from Massachusetts, which is one of the four leading cranberry-growing states, the other three being: New Jersey, Wisconsin and Washington State."

I didn't know where he got all his trivia from, but he invariably passed out tidbits whenever I shopped there.

"The cranberry," he continued as we walked toward the back of the store, "grows in swampy or marshy areas. Do you know why it's called a cranberry?"

"I've often wondered about that," I lied, my voice sounding interested.

"It's because the stem of the cranberry curves like the neck of a crane. You get it? Crane . . . cranberry."

I laughed. "That's fascinating."

"It ain't algebra, but it's interesting," Mr. Cavendish agreed, smiling down at me. We'd arrived in the produce section, and he went over to the cranberries and picked up a handful, allowing them to sift through his bony fingers. "Help yourself, Cheyenne."

He turned away, then spun back around as though he'd forgotten something. "Oh, do you need oranges? A cranberry sauce without orange zest isn't cranberry sauce in my book."

"I'd better take a few, just in case," I told him. "I could get back home and Momma might remember she'd forgotten to tell me to get some."

Mr. Cavendish pointed at the Valencia oranges next to the pink grapefruit, then he left me to my picking and choosing.

I'd gotten about a pound and a half of cranberries, closed the plastic bag with a twist-tie, and was squeezing the oranges, when I heard the bell over the door jingle. More customers for Mr. Cavendish to regale with his prodigious memory for trivia.

I chose six oranges, bagged them and started walking back up front, when something on the baking ingredients aisle caught my eye. Baking powder. Momma was out of baking powder.

As I was reaching for the bright red can, someone rounded the corner of the row of shelves. I was looking down, so all I saw at first was a pair of feminine feet, small feet, in expensive suede boots.

The boots stopped in my aisle. I raised my eyes.

Marissa Claiborne smiled radiantly at me. "Cheyenne Roberts. It's been years since I've seen you. My, haven't you grown . . ." She craned her neck, "And grown. What are you, six feet?"

It took me a few seconds to recover from the shock of seeing her so suddenly. I was so taken aback, that I hadn't perceived the manner in which she was speaking to me. I'd heard her words, but not the underlying meaning behind them.

I smiled and said, "Hi, Marissa. I didn't know you were home."

"Then we're even, because I thought you were still living in Chicago," she said, her brown eyes narrowed. There was a smile on her lips, but it didn't reach her beautiful, almond-shaped eyes. "But, I was told that you've moved back to Montana indefinitely. What happened, did you lose your job?"

I really didn't believe we were close enough friends for me to discuss my personal life with her, but I indulged her curiosity.

"No, actually, I resigned so that I could come home and help my family with a new business venture."

"Oh? Then you'll be leaving again when your business gets on its feet?"

I wondered why she was so interested in when I'd be leaving town.

I must have taken too long to answer her last question because she flicked her auburn hair back with a quick toss of her head and smiled prettily, exposing perfect pearl-like teeth, and said, "I'm being nosy, I know. I'm just interested in learning what a young, attractive woman sees in a place like this."

"It's home," I said simply. "Everybody I love is here."

Frowning, she adjusted the gold bracelet on her slim wrist and peered up at me. "Is that really enough though? I mean, look at the men situation around here. Unless you go for white, Hispanic or Native American men, there isn't much of a selection."

"Is that why you left?" I asked, my smile just as false as hers was, no doubt.

"No, *I* left because it was impossible to pursue my career while living here."

"How is your career doing?" If she could ask if I'd been fired, I could inquire about her acting.

"I recently did a cold read for a movie," she said happily. "It may turn into something. I'm keeping my fingers crossed. Plus, I was understudy to the lead in a Broadway play last year. I never got to go on, but the experience was phenomenal. Commercials have been keeping food on the table. I've done regionals, mostly, but I also have a few nationals under my belt."

"You sound like you're doing all right," I complimented her.

I held up my bags of fruit and can of baking powder, indicating that I needed to go pay for them. She walked alongside of me.

"I'm doing well in New York," she said. I detected forced enthusiasm in her tone that time. "I do miss certain folks around here, though."

I placed my few purchases on the countertop, and Mr. Cavendish slowly weighed the fruit then rang everything up on his electronic cash register. When I was a girl, he'd had an old-fashioned one. Every time the cash drawer was opened, a bell rang.

"That'll be four sixty-nine, Cheyenne," he said.

Marissa touched my arm and said, "It was good seeing you, Cheyenne; give my best to your family."

"All right, Marissa," I said, my hand in my voluminous bag, trying to locate my wallet. "You do the same."

She turned down the canned goods aisle and I paid Mr. Cavendish and left the store with my purchases.

When I stepped outside and looked toward Slim's pickup, my attention was drawn to the truck parked next to it: Jackson's blue Explorer.

I could have been mistaken, but it was the only vehicle that was the same make, model and color of Jackson's Explorer. So I casually walked over to it and checked the license plate. It was his all right. I put on my sunglasses and looked around me. He hadn't come into the store, I was certain of that.

I climbed into Slim's truck and closed the door, then I waited. For what, I wasn't clear on; I just had a gut feeling that I should not go anywhere for the next few minutes.

I wasn't kept waiting long, because Marissa came out of the store, a large paper bag in her arms, waved at me, got into Jackson's Explorer, started it and backed out of the parking space.

I sat drumming my fingers on the steering wheel.

I knew then why she'd been so curious about when I would be leaving town: She'd seen my letter to Jackson. I was positive of it. Perhaps she'd only read my name on the envelope, but that had been enough to make her wonder at our relationship.

She was driving his car, so perhaps she was also back in his life. I had no way of knowing. I knew only this: She was thinking about it. Otherwise, why would she need to gather information on her competition?

Jackson had admitted that he still had feelings for Marissa. Maybe they had the convenient kind of relationship some ex-couples cultivated. Whenever one of them was in town . . . well, I didn't *want* to contemplate what they did when they got together.

After seeing Marissa behind the wheel of his truck, it was difficult to give Jackson the benefit of the doubt. But, I stubbornly hung on to my belief that he loved only me. I had faith.

TEN

"Has anybody seen Bear lately?" Momma asked the next morning over breakfast. It was around seven o'clock. None of us slept late.

Chad paused with a forkful of food halfway to his mouth. "You know Bear. He's probably visiting a lady friend on a neighboring ranch."

"Yeah, you and Lucas have certainly set a poor example for him," Clancy said, and laughed harder at her joke than anyone else.

Chad ignored her, eating his meal with obvious pleasure.

"I haven't seen him in at least four or five days," I said, picking up my coffee cup and taking a sip to clear my throat. I looked at Momma. "You don't think anything's happened to him, do you?"

We were used to Bear's frequent absences. The big, black, affectionate, husky usually found his way back home after a few days of joyous carousing, though.

"After breakfast, I'll ride along the perimeter of the woods and see if I can find him," Lucas offered.

"Thank you, sweetie," Momma said, smiling at her third son.

"It would be a waste of time," Slim told us. "He ain't nowhere except over at Jackson's with Miss Pris." Miss Pris was Jackson's golden retriever, so named because she was known for her manners.

Jackson had gotten her five years ago, when she was a pup. From day one, Miss Pris wouldn't eat dry dog food, she required canned, or, better yet, cooked beef. And she hated getting dirty. Every dog we'd ever owned loved to romp in the mud from time to time, but Miss Pris walked around puddles; she loved baths and sat patiently while her coat was being brushed. She was one fastidious pooch.

Which made me wonder what she saw in Bear, who was just the opposite. Bear loved mud puddles. He chased squirrels and raccoons through the woods, getting burrs and twigs, and whatever else he came in contact with, caught in his coat.

"I'll go over to Jackson's and see if he has an uninvited guest," Lucas said as he placed his utensils on his plate.

"That won't be necessary," I told him. "I'll be going over to Jackson's this afternoon anyway."

"You will?" Clancy said, intrigued.

She glanced in Momma's direction, probably hoping Momma would provide her with elucidation. Momma said nothing.

Slim said, "Why is *anyone* going over to Jackson's? Won't he be coming here for Thanksgiving dinner? He hasn't missed a year since his parents died. Is there something going on that I don't know about?"

We hadn't seen fit to tell him that Jackson and I had argued.

"How could there possibly be something going on that *you* don't know about?" I joked.

"Jackson does have a life apart from this family, you know," Momma said. "Maybe he'd like to spend Thanksgiving with a certain young woman this year, instead of coming here."

I knew what she was doing. I'd already said I was going to see Jackson later that afternoon. Momma was alluding that Jackson and I were spending the day alone at his place.

"Oh, all right," Slim said, satisfied.

Chad and Lucas exchanged looks.

"Wait a minute," Chad said, placing his fork on his empty plate, "something *is* going on here."

"Are you and Jackson . . ." Lucas looked at me, his brown eyes excited.

"Okay!" I cried as I rose and regarded Lucas and, then, Chad. "Jackson and I have . . . discovered each other. You'll have to be happy with that explanation for the time being."

Chad laughed. "You don't owe us any explanations, sis. It just amazes me that in a city as big as Chicago, you had to come back home to snag a man."

Lucas got up from his seat, his plate and utensils in his hand. He came around to my side of the table and, since I was also finished, took my place setting as well, but not before sweetly kissing my cheek. "Don't let him rib you, Chey. I'm happy for you and Jackson."

I smiled warmly at him. For two years before Clancy was born, Lucas had been the baby in the family, and I'd doted on him. He still had a special place in my heart.

"Well," Slim said, pushing his plate away and sucking his teeth, "I'm glad that's out in the open."

"Yeah, you must have been about to bust, trying to keep it a secret," Clancy put in with a grin, knowing, full well, that her grandfather had already spilled the beans to her.

"I love you all," Momma said, her eyes resting on each of our faces, one at a time. "But, just once, I'd like to have a quiet, uneventful meal at this table."

Following breakfast, Momma, Clancy and I got to work putting the finishing touches on the day's menu.

As always, Momma had roasted the turkey, baked the dressing and sweet potato pies the night before. She loathed being in the kitchen most of the day on Thanksgiving. With planning, she said, the time could be whittled down to a minimum.

So, when Cole, Enid and the boys arrived at around noon, the mustard greens, cooked with smoked turkey instead of pork, were simmering in a pot on the stove; the macaroni and cheese was bubbling in the oven, the corn bread alongside it; and the apple pies (little Cole's and Cody's favorite) were sitting on the block-top counter cooling.

Clancy had made a tossed salad with fresh iceberg lettuce, tomatoes, bell peppers, onions, carrots and purple cabbage.

I'd cooked the cranberries down to a sweet, chunky sauce with just a hint of orange zest.

Clancy took Cole and Cody out to the barn to see the new foal that had arrived the week before, while Cole and Enid stayed with Momma and me in the kitchen.

Enid was in her fifth month of pregnancy, and her golden-brown skin was slightly flushed. Momma, though, had taken one look at her and said, "It's a girl this time. You're positively glowing."

"Momma Roberts," Enid said, smiling, "you said I was glowing with Cody and little Cole, too."

"Yeah well, baby," Momma returned, pulling Enid into her arms for a warm hug, "you were."

Enid then began telling Momma all about her latest symptoms, as Momma nodded knowingly and gave advice where needed.

Cole pulled me aside, taking me by the arm and walking me over to the back door. "Jackson and I had a strange conversation last night," he said. He arched his bushy eyebrows questioningly at me and let go of my arm.

We stood facing each other: he, waiting on some explanation, and I, hoping he'd give me more to go on.

"I don't know what you mean by 'strange,' " I said, frowning. "Are you at liberty to tell me what he said to you?"

Cole blew air between full lips and met my eyes. "He didn't tell me it was between me and him, so I guess it's okay." He took at least ten seconds to compose what he wanted to say before continuing, however. "He told me that he was in love with you, Chey, but he didn't know what to do about it. He, then, confessed that he'd been in love with you since before his relationship with Marissa but, of course, he never would have done anything about it . . ."

"But, I forced the issue by telling him how I felt about him," I said.

Cole nodded in the affirmative. "You've got him confused. *I'm* confused. I knew you'd always had a crush on him . . ."

"You never ribbed me about it."

"I saw no reason to. It might've embarrassed both of you."

I smiled lovingly at him. "That was very sensitive of you."

"I loved you, sis, even though I didn't show it all the time. Back to the problem at hand." He was uncomfortable with displays of emotion. "Here is my take on the situation: Jackson loves you; you love Jackson. I believe you ought to pursue him, but in a subtle fashion. Be there. Don't alienate him with ultimatums, because that will only bring out your bullheadedness, *and* his. Make him believe that everything's as it used to be between you two. That should take the pressure off and allow things to develop naturally."

He'd recapped what I'd been planning on doing anyway. But I did not tell him that.

"Sounds like a plan," I said positively.

I tiptoed and kissed his cheek. "Thanks for being such a good friend to Jackson, Cole. And a great brother to me."

He hugged me tightly. "I hope everything turns out well for you two, Chey. I don't want to see either of you hurt."

I half expected Jackson to not be at home when I went calling later that afternoon. I hadn't phoned because I thought the element of surprise was in my favor. Then, again, *I* could be the one surprised if Marissa was there preparing an intimate dinner for two.

I pulled up in Slim's pickup and parked in front of the house, which was a lately built, two-story structure with wraparound porches. Pale blue in color, it was trimmed in white and had a captain's walk on the west side where Jackson's bedroom was.

The house was four years old. I'd often wondered if Jackson had built the house for him and Marissa to live in. They'd been a couple about a year before he began construction on it. By the time it was completed, Marissa had gone back to New York City in pursuit of her dreams.

I walked to the other side of the truck to get the picnic basket from the passenger seat. Momma had prepared Jackson a sampling of everything we'd cooked for the Thanksgiving meal, and she'd added a sweet potato pie because she knew Jackson loved her sweet potato pies.

With the basket in my hand, I approached the front porch. Beneath my coat, instead of my customary jeans, was a gray wool dress that clung to my curves. On my feet, I wore leather flats in the same shade as the dress. I'd worn my hair loose and combed away from my face.

My full lips were rose-colored. I pressed them together and moistened them before pressing the doorbell.

I breathed deeply and exhaled slowly. I was nervous.

I couldn't keep putting my foot in it where Jackson was concerned. He wanted a mature woman, and I'd been behaving like a lovesick teenager. I would curtail my impatient tendencies, somehow, if it was the only means by which I could win his trust.

Because that's what it boiled down to: trust. Jackson didn't trust what he was feeling. And he didn't believe I knew my own mind, that I sincerely loved him and was fully prepared to spend the rest of my life with him.

I stood there for more than five minutes, agonizing about what I should say to him, before I realized no one was going to come to the door.

I knocked and called, "Hello? Is anyone at home?!"

No response.

Upon pulling into the yard, I hadn't spotted Jackson's Explorer or his old blue Chevy pickup. He kept them in the barn behind the house, so I hadn't expected to see them parked out front.

I'd set the basket on the porch swing and I left it there as I stepped off the porch and began walking around the house toward the barn, which was also painted a pale blue and trimmed in white.

As I rounded the corner of the house, I was startled by a happy bark. I paused in my steps. Running in my direction, his tongue lolling out of his mouth, was Bear.

I braced myself for his usual assault. When he reared up, I grasped him by his forepaws and set him back on the ground, crouching low with him so as to discourage his putting his dirty paws on my coat or dress.

"Hello, pretty baby, we've missed you," I said, grinning and scratching him under his chin. Bear whined contentedly. "What's so important to you here that you can't come back home, huh, boy?"

I rose, and Bear ran toward the barn, paused, looked back at me, then ran on. Curious, I followed.

Jackson walked through the barn doors as I approached.

"Hey, I rang your bell but, of course, there was no answer. And then I ran in to Bear and he led me back here . . ."

I didn't want him thinking I was snooping, which I had been. I hadn't found him at home, so I was going to see whether or not his vehicles were in the barn.

A cold wind blew in, lifting my hair up off my neck. I pulled the heavy coat closer about me. Jackson still hadn't said a word.

His soft brown eyes were on my face. They moved lower to encompass all of me and I felt my body tremble.

I smiled, the muscles around my mouth quivering. "If this is a bad time . . ."

His features were frozen in a contemplative stare, while my resolve melted further and my thoughts ran from one possible reason for his continued silence, to the next.

"No, don't go, there's something inside that you should see," he said, finally. His voice was low, with little inflection.

We hadn't seen each other in five weeks, but could my appearance have shocked him so badly? I didn't believe that was a plausible explanation. Maybe he'd been thinking about me, and, *poof!*, I'd materialized before his eyes. That would be sufficient to send him into stunned silence. Anyway, I *wanted* that to be the explanation behind his reaction.

After all, he *had* just phoned Cole the night before and admitted that he loved me. He couldn't have changed his mind overnight, could he?

He turned and walked back inside the barn, I followed hesitantly. I thought, perhaps, one of his mares had foaled recently, as one of ours had done last week. He knew I was particularly fond of newborns.

Except for the light streaming in from the open doors, the barn was dim in most places, dark in others. We walked past empty stalls. Jackson had seven horses, all rather young. They were in the pasture grazing. The temperature was in the forties, however when there was no snow on the ground, he allowed them to graze, oftentimes wearing fitted horse blankets with the ranch's insignia, a large cursive *K,* emblazoned on the side.

"What is it?" I asked. "A new foal?"

"Something like that," he answered, and I thought his voice held a note of laughter. I calmed down a bit.

He paused at the last stall at the back of the barn and held open the door for me to precede him.

I stepped inside. Jackson reached around me and switched on a single light fixture attached to the wall.

Laying on a bed of hay was Miss Pris, and surrounding her were six puppies, four the golden color of their mother, two as pitch-black as their father.

Awed, I knelt. Miss Pris raised her head and allowed me to pat it, then she wagged her bushy tail and, tiredly, lay her head back down. The puppies hungrily pulled on her teats, their eyes barely opened.

I looked up at Jackson. "No wonder Bear has abandoned us. He has a family of his own now."

"Yeah, he's been pretty devoted to her, the old scamp. I figured he'd stop coming around after a while, but he appears to be here to stay."

I stood, my eyes on his face. "It's all right with you, then?"

"That Bear stays? Sure. I don't know what I'm going to do with six pups, though. I'll have to find them good homes once they're weaned. And Miss Pris will have to be spayed."

Bear came into the stall and lay down beside his family.

Jackson and I left them alone.

"When were they born?"

"Three days ago," Jackson replied. He paused, leaning against one of the stalls. Unzipping his brown leather jacket, and brushing a piece of hay off the thigh of his Wrangler's, he regarded me with a curious expression in his gaze.

I assumed he was about to ask me why I'd come to see him. What he said, though, was: "I must have read that note you sent a thousand times."

His comment floored me. I stared at him, my mouth agape.

Jackson grinned, reached over, placed his forefinger beneath my chin, and gently pushed upward. "It's good to know I'm able to turn the tables on you, and shock and confuse *you* for a change," he murmured with a soft laugh.

I stepped backward and spun on my heels, walking swiftly

toward the exit. I had to get out of there. I knew the signs, the symptoms of seduction when I saw them.

State your intentions, I told myself. *What did you come here to do? Don't be sidetracked by Jackson's charm. Stay focused.*

I heard his footfalls behind me, but I kept walking.

"Chey!"

I wondered what he was trying to do to me, telling me he'd read my note to him over and over, his voice filled with longing?

Didn't he know how weak I was for him? Wasn't he the one who'd wanted to take things slowly? How strong did he imagine my resolve to be, anyway?

"Cheyenne Josephine!"

I'd reached Slim's truck and had my hand on the driver's side door handle before I paused to look back at him.

Jackson's square-chinned face was tender as he stood two feet away, his gaze locked with mine.

"Now who's running away from what's happening between us?" he asked, his tone low and husky.

"I don't want my actions to be misinterpreted this time," I told him. I looked down.

He took a step toward me. "Explain yourself."

Our eyes met. "When you told me what my note, which could never be construed as a love letter, meant to you, I fell in love with you all over again. But, then the thought occurred to me: What would happen if I reacted the way I usually do? I wanted to take you into my arms and kiss you so hard . . . hard enough to make up for the five weeks we've been apart . . ."

Jackson covered the space between us in a step. I backed up, but I had nowhere to go. My backside was against the door of the truck, he'd placed an arm on either side of me, imprisoning me between them. "Then do it."

His clean-shaven face brushed against my cheek. I closed my eyes and breathed in the intoxicating male scent of him. My right hand caressed the back of his head, my fingers splayed between the soft waves. His hard-muscled body smelled of a masculine soap and his breath was warm and freshly sweet on my face. I had but to turn my head a fraction of an inch, and heaven would be mine.

"I missed you so much," he said in my ear, his voice a whisper. "When you love someone, you risk everything. You risk your safe, familiar world being turned upside down. You risk your heart being torn to shreds. I'm willing to risk that with you, Chey."

With a sigh, I turned into him. Our lips clenched, pulled back, clenched again. His tongue flicked out, mine did, too, and the kiss deepened. Warmth suffused my entire body as Jackson's big hands made sensuous circuits along it.

My hands were clasped behind his strong neck, and our bodies danced to the erotic music that our love for each other made in every cell, and the sinew of our physical selves.

My pulse had quickened, I could feel the thumping in my neck. I quivered when Jackson raised his head and licked me there, his tongue on the rhythmic beating. "Let me make love to you," he said, his voice raspy.

I threw my head back and said, "Yes, Jackson. I've been waiting for you to ask me all my life."

Jackson paused, his mouth on my cleavage. He lifted his head to stare at me. "What did you just say?"

"I said yes, Jackson . . ."

"No. After that."

"I've been waiting for you to ask me all my life."

"Then you *are* a virgin."

I smiled dreamily at him. "I'm willing to give up the title."

I saw, with utter disappointment, that the erotic fog was lifting from his eyes. He was breathing heavily as he tried to gain full control of his senses.

We'd come up against another Jackson Kincaid obstacle: Could a *real* man take a virgin to bed without being married to her?

He still had his arm around my waist and I seductively slid my body against his. "Jackson?"

He seemed to be deep in thought. "Mmm?"

"I want you."

"I want you, too," he replied, massaging my back. His brown eyes were intensely gazing into mine. "But not like this."

Then he bent his head and kissed my forehead. I groaned. "Oh, no, not the brotherly kiss. You aren't going to take me upstairs, are you?"

Jackson released me. I held on to his hands. He pried my hands from his. Stepping backward, he said, "You have to go, Cheyenne. I can't be alone with you right now."

"But why?" I asked plaintively.

My eyes, momentarily, lowered to the bulge in his pants, and I blushed.

Jackson laughed shortly. "That's why."

My cheeks grew hot. "Okay," I relented.

Jackson opened the door of the truck for me and handed me in. He closed the door and leaned in. "Come here."

We kissed slowly.

"Oh, I almost forgot, Momma sent you some dinner and your favorite pie. I left the basket on the front porch."

Jackson smiled at me, the crinkles around his eyes more noticeable. "I'll phone her and thank her."

"She'll be happy to hear from you."

"Give them all my best."

"I will."

I sat grasping the steering wheel with my left hand, my right, on my lap. Jackson placed a hand atop my left one. "How would you like to go out somewhere tomorrow night? Dinner, and a movie?"

"I'd like that," I said softly.

I turned the key in the ignition, then I casually said, "I saw Marissa in town yesterday."

"Yeah, she's here visiting her mother. Her mother's car is in the shop; she needed transportation, so I loaned her the Explorer."

A statement of facts, alone, nothing akin to surprise or irritation at the mention of Marissa's name. He was looking at me with such a tender expression in his beautiful eyes that my fears were instantly put to rest.

"That was sweet of you," I said.

"Just doing a favor for a neighbor," he said modestly.

He leaned in and kissed me again. "No need for concern, Chey. The moment I saw her again, I knew that my heart belonged to you."

"And the rest of you, too," I half-joked.

"And the rest of me, too," he promised with a sexy grin.

Satisfied, I left.

The next morning, Harry Johnson came over with a bushel of tomatoes he'd grown in his greenhouse. He knew Momma loved fresh tomatoes and, also, how difficult it was to find them in markets, at reasonable prices, that time of year.

I was upstairs writing in my journal when he arrived, so I wasn't there to see the reaction on Momma's face when he came bearing a gift he knew would please her.

Clancy had been present, however, and told me later that Momma shyly thanked Harry for the tomatoes and then invited him to stay for coffee, which Harry politely declined, saying he had to get back home because his brother, Ernest, was visiting from Bozeman and he didn't want to skip out on him for too long.

A couple of hours after Harry's departure, I went downstairs to help Momma get lunch on the table.

Chad and Lucas had driven down to the south field with Slim to check on the herd. The temperatures had been in the fifties in the daytime and in the thirties at night, so they wanted to make certain the younger cows, who hadn't put on enough fat to protect them from the cold, were doing all right with the colder climate.

Sometimes, orphaned calves had to be brought in to the barn because they didn't have mothers who shielded them from the elements, as other calves did.

We hated to lose any of the herd, but loss was a part of ranching. Every year we lost cows to exposure, especially in winter when the temperatures frequently dipped below freezing.

Clancy had switched on the radio as she, Momma and I prepared a meal of beef vegetable soup, grilled-cheese sandwiches and a garden salad.

She found an oldies station, unusual in Big Sky Country because country-western stations dominated the airwaves. Natalie Cole was singing, "Everlasting Love," and Clancy and I were dancing around the kitchen in our blue jeans, and T-shirts.

"What do you call that dance?" Clancy jokingly asked me after I'd executed a movement similar to the hula. "The Jackson-better-watch-out boogie?"

I swiveled my hips, grinned at her, and said, "Maybe."

Momma gave me a stern look, probably to remind me that my baby sister looked to me to set an example. Surely I wasn't leading her to believe that being intimate before marriage was perfectly fine?

I had never discussed my sexual life, or lack thereof, with Momma. But, I realized, that she took it for granted her daughters would remain untouched until their wedding night.

It was rather like, don't ask, don't tell. She gave all her children the basic birds-and-the-bees speech and then had faith that we would all use sound judgment when it came to the opposite sex.

"Strictly for the honeymoon," I corrected myself, smiling at my sister who arched her fine brows and laughed. She knew Momma as well as I did.

Lou Rawls sang, "You're gonna miss my lovin'," and Momma exclaimed, "That was one of your daddy's favorites."

She put down the lettuce she'd been rinsing at the sink and went and grabbed Clancy by the waist. "Dance with me, Clarisse Nancy."

"A two-step?" Clancy complained briefly. She saw the two-step as an "old folks" dance.

"I'll lead," Momma said.

"I'm taller," Clancy protested.

I stood aside, smiling at them. Clancy had a lanky figure, and Momma was short and slightly plump.

Momma was the better dancer, by far. She and Daddy had had plenty of practice over the years. At least once a month, they'd gone to a local tavern that had a live band. They had to dance to country-western (when in Rome . . .), but they learned to do-si-do with the best of them.

"Keep your back straight, Clancy," Momma instructed. "And

pick up the pace. You need to learn how to do more than the dances you mimic from *Soul Train* reruns."

"Why? I don't believe I've been asked to the cotillion this year," Clancy smart-mouthed.

"You should at least know how to do a two-step for when you dance with your groom for the first time at the reception," Momma said patiently.

"I'm never getting married," Clancy claimed, smiling. "I'm going to live here, with you, for the rest of my life."

"No you're not either," Momma told her emphatically. "You're *all* leaving this house, eventually, even if I have to physically put you out."

Clancy laughed. "You wouldn't know what to do with an empty house."

"I would find something to do with myself," Momma assured her lightly. "After you finish high school, you're going to college young lady, just as your brothers and sister have done before you. Chad is the only one who has expressed interest in ranching, so he can run the outfit. Me? I'm going to sit in my rocking chair on the front porch and watch the sunset."

"I'll believe it when I see it," I told her frankly. "You can't sit still for a minute. You'd go nuts without something to do with yourself."

"It might be fun to try it, though," Momma said.

I knew what she was saying. I was just having fun at her expense. What she meant was: she'd had the marriage, the children and the life as a ranch wife. She wanted time to rediscover herself without having to be responsible for someone else.

I tapped Clancy on the shoulder. "May I cut in?"

Clancy gladly relinquished her partner to me.

Momma and I did a near-perfect two-step together. I'd learned the dance when I was a teenager, even though, with the dearth of eligible males, I didn't get many chances to display my talent.

"Maybe you'll get married again someday," I said to Momma as I looked down into her upturned face.

"Why would I want to do that?"

"Because you miss real dance partners?"

"I've got my memories to keep me company," she said quietly, and from the tone of her voice, I perceived that she didn't want to talk about Daddy.

I wanted to know what she really thought of Harry Johnson and his bringing her courting gifts; but I'd wait until she was ready to tell me.

Clancy was at the stove, stirring the soup. "Mr. Johnson sure grows pretty tomatoes, doesn't he, Momma?"

Momma stopped dancing, we dropped our arms to our sides and she cut a glance in Clancy's direction. "Don't you go making more of that than it was."

Clancy put the top on the pot and set the ladle on the holder atop the stove. "I'm not, Momma. I was just wondering why he brought you his best tomatoes. He sells them to Mr. Cavendish in town, you know. Looks like he specially chose each one, not a bruise on them. As if they'd been plucked, with *love,* from the vine."

Momma turned and ran after Clancy, who hightailed it for the interior of the house, screaming, "I was just joking, Momma!"

"I'm gonna give you something to joke about," Momma threatened, but there was laughter in her tone, and she wasn't making much of an effort to catch my recalcitrant sister.

I went to the refrigerator to get the log of Cheddar cheese and slice it for the grilled-cheese sandwiches.

Marvin Gaye was singing "I Heard It Through the Grapevine."

A few hours later, I sat in the tub, bubbles up to my chin. I'd been there for twenty minutes, and I planned to soak another ten.

There was a knock at the door.

"I'm in the tub," I called.

"It's just me," Momma said, coming into the bedroom.

She walked through the bedroom to the bath and sat on the toilet seat, looking down at me. "Relishing the thought of Jackson coming over without the pretense of friendship?" she asked, her brown eyes alight with happiness.

"It's a major triumph, Momma," I said, having difficulty believing Jackson and I were unofficially a couple.

"He's a good man," she said philosophically. "I should tell you, though, that his parents were not overtly friendly people. They were probably very nice folks, I just didn't know them well.

I suppose they had to be all right, they raised a hardworking, loyal, individual between them. I do know, however, that they were very strict with Jackson. He was an only child and, I suppose, they wanted to be certain he'd be equipped to run the ranch he was due to inherit."

"There's one more thing, though," Momma continued, her expression serious. "When Jackson was a boy, I used to notice bruises on his face, arms and legs. I never asked him about them, but one day, when he was around ten, I think, he came over here and he was covered in fresh bruises. You know, on Jackson's skin, those types of coppery brown, bruises are highly visible. Anyway, when I saw him, I got so angry, that I got into my car and drove over to his parents' place. Your daddy wasn't at home, otherwise, he never would've let me go. Anyway, his mother, Ginny, came to the door when I got there; and by that time I was crying, I was so mad. I took one look at her, and said, 'Ginny Kincaid, I don't know what's going on around here, but that boy of yours has welts and bruises on him, no child should ever wear.' The poor mouse of a woman just stood there and took my tongue-lashing, she was so stunned. Then, when I was finished, she began to cry and I took her in my arms. She didn't say a word, but I knew instinctively that her man had reduced her to the sorry state she was in. I left her. Jackson didn't have anymore bruises after that incident. I don't know if she ever told her husband about my angry tirade, or not. But I think that after that, she found the strength to stand up to him. Or, perhaps Jackson was the one who stood up to his father. Either way, the beatings seemed to stop, for which I was very grateful."

Somewhat shocked, I sat back in the tub with my knees drawn up to my chin. I realized I didn't know Jackson as well as I thought I did. There were facets to him that I was yet to discover. It was an unsettling notion. However, what Momma had told me only made me love him more.

Momma got to her feet. "I just thought you should know," she said, her smile restored. "I don't know how much of an influence his father had on him. But, Jackson, like all men, has more than one side to him. You know the positive things, perhaps a few of the negative ones, like: *whatever* possessed him to get involved with that flighty Claiborne girl?"

I grinned at Momma. She had my back.

"Just be patient, sweetie, and learn the man behind the physical person you're so attracted to, that's all I'm suggesting," she ended. Then, "Want me to get your back while I'm here?"

I'd just been thinking that she, figuratively, had my back.

"No, thanks, I think I did a pretty good job on it already," I said, laughing softly. "Thanks for the talk, Momma."

In her absence, I got out of the tub and dried off with a thick bath towel and put on my robe.

Sitting in front of the vanity, I took the pins from my hair and shook it out. I looked into the eyes of the woman looking back at me. Did she know what she was doing? Was she prepared for a relationship with Jackson Kincaid, or was she only fooling herself?

ELEVEN

Jackson arrived promptly at seven. I was upstairs stepping into a pair of black leather pumps. I was wearing a black cotton-knit dress with a scoop neck, long sleeves, a zipper down the back, and a hem that fell two inches above my knees.

When I heard the doorbell, I rushed into the shoes and went to the walk-in closet to retrieve my overcoat.

A knock came shortly afterward. "Your date's downstairs," Clancy called. "How long are you going to keep him waiting?"

I flung the door open and breezed past her. She grinned impishly at my eagerness. Her dark brown eyes assessed my outfit. "Wow, may I borrow that dress if I should ever find a date?" she asked, close behind me. I paused at the top of the stairs and looked back at her. "You'd never get it past Momma," I told her, smiling down into her lovely doe-eyed face. My heart went out to her. When I was seventeen, I also thought that no male would ever give me a second glance. My confidence grew tremendously after I went away to college and discovered that some members of the opposite sex found my unique juxtaposition of facial features and the construction of my form desirable. "And I wouldn't worry about the lack of dates if I were you. Once you're at Howard University, you'll have so many men shooting at you, you'll have to pinch yourself to see if you're dreaming."

"That sounds like a dream I wouldn't want to wake up from," she said happily. She nudged my shoulder. "Jackson's waiting. But don't slide down the railing, it's undignified."

I expected Jackson to be waiting at the foot of the stairs, but he was in the company room with Momma and Slim. Momma had served him a cup of coffee and they were seated near the fireplace; Slim in his favorite wing chair, Momma on the sofa and Jackson on the matching wing chair across from Slim.

They looked up when I entered the room. Jackson rose, walked over to me and clasped both my hands in his. Warm brown eyes targeted my face and stayed there. "You look beautiful," he said, his lopsided smile making my heart do flip-flops.

He was also beautiful in a crisp white long-sleeved cotton shirt and a black bolo tie with a silver clip at his neck. The immaculate shirt was tucked into black slacks. He wore his favorite pair of black leather, highly polished dress boots.

He was freshly shaved, and the black, shiny waves of his natural hair looked as if they were still damp from his shower. I reached up and caressed his cheek. "Thank you. And you look as yummy as ever." This was said in a very low voice so that Momma and Slim wouldn't overhear.

We walked back over to where Momma and Slim were sitting to say good night to them. Slim smiled enigmatically at me. I knew from experience that he was dying to whisper something in my ear, so I went to him and leaned down. He kissed my cheek. "If you play your cards right," he said. "There could be a great-grandchild in it for me."

I laughed softly and said, "Isn't it past your bedtime?"

I straightened up and Slim said loudly, "Have her back by next week, boy. I want her to drive me into Billings so I can take a look at the new tractor models."

Laughing, Jackson said, "She'll be back long before then."

Momma rose and tiptoed to kiss my cheek and said in a low voice, "Bundle up, baby. I don't want you to catch a chest cold."

I self-consciously tugged at my bodice. "Is it too low cut?"

"Nah," she denied, her hand on my arm. "Just trying to get you to relax."

I sighed. "I *am* nervous."

"It's just Jackson," she said lightly. "You've known him all your life."

While Momma tried to put me at ease, Jackson and Slim were debating the merits of a John Deere tractor as opposed to a McCormick.

"Go and have a good time," Momma said.

She saw us to the door.

Jackson bent to kiss her satiny cheek. "Thanks for the coffee, Miss Peaches; and don't worry. I'll bring Chey back safely."

Momma smiled and said, "I know you will. Good night."

She abruptly closed the door in our faces.

I laughed. "I think that's her way of telling us to go already." Facing him, I said, "Kiss me."

"Here?"

"She's looking out the peephole, I know it. Kiss me."

I put my arms around his neck and brought him lower. Our mouths met in a brief, dry kiss. The porch light flicked off, then back on again.

"I told you she was watching," I said, laughing. I took his hand and we walked down the steps to his waiting Chevy truck.

He opened the passenger side door for me and I slid onto the vinyl seat. The inside of the truck was still warm from his drive over and after he'd securely closed the door, I settled back on the seat and fastened the seat belt.

Jackson got behind the wheel, shut his door and turned to me. "We never discussed where we were going tonight. Do you have any preferences? Seafood? Italian? Chinese?"

"Definitely not beef," I told him.

The top of his head was about two inches from the ceiling of the truck and I could barely make out his face in the dim light. His voice, though, in the silence and stillness of the night, was deliciously sensual.

He started the Chevy. "All right, then. I know this great seafood place near Rimrock Mall. We'll eat there and then catch a flick at the cinema at the mall."

"Sounds good to me," I agreed.

"Sorry about the old wheels," he said.

"No need to apologize," I told him sincerely. "I like older trucks. You may have noticed how often I drive Slim's old Ford."

He didn't have to tell me that Marissa was still in possession of his Explorer. It didn't matter to me. She had the Explorer. *I* had him. I felt I was the fortunate one.

"I bet I know what you like about the Ford," Jackson said

speculatively. "It's the gears, right? You like the power you feel when you shift the gears."

"You *do* know me."

"I'm learning you. Tell me more."

The Chevy's suspension was no match for the unpaved two-mile dirt road that led to the house. We felt each bump and pothole.

"What do you want to know?"

"What's the title of the best book you ever read?"

That was difficult to decide upon. I'd read so many wonderful books in my lifetime. "That's hard to say," I finally replied. "I believe *Song of Solomon* by Toni Morrison was exquisite. But, for the sheer beauty of words, I'd say *The Wedding* by Dorothy West. How about you?"

"I liked *Native Son,*" Jackson said. "And I read all of Walter Mosley's books. But as for impact, *A Lesson Before Dying* by Ernest Gaines really affected me."

"Oh, I loved that book!"

I'd noticed that he'd only mentioned male writers.

"Do you ever read female writers?"

"Sure. I've read a couple of Toni Morrison's novels. She's deep. I have to read her books twice before I get what she's trying to say. Maybe I'm dense . . ."

"You aren't dense," I told him reassuringly. "I read *Song of Solomon* when I was in high school and didn't understand it. Then, just last year, I read it again, and it was lyrically beautiful to me. Each reader perceives words differently, and when you read a book, you sift the words through your own life experiences. Therefore, my perception matured, and *Song of Solomon* meant more to me at twenty-six than it did at seventeen."

"All right. What's your favorite movie?"

"I look at movies," I told him, "as plain escapist fun. Give me something adventurous like the *Indiana Jones* films. And I'm a *Star Wars* fan. I like spies and pirates and aliens."

"In other words, you're a kid at heart when you watch a film."

Looking at his profile, I nodded. "Yeah, I just want to be entertained."

"I go for those kinds of movies. But I also like more serious films. For instance, Spike Lee's *Malcolm X*. I believe that's his best work to date."

I shifted my body on the seat so that I was turned toward him.

"Okay, I'll give you that. But I thought that *Get on the Bus* was also powerful because it gave me insights into the workings of the black man's mind," I said, getting into our give and take.

"What insights?" Jackson asked, sounding a bit skeptical.

"All right." I paused, choosing my words carefully. "I know sisters who believe there are no good black men out there. The usual cry is that black men are not ambitious enough. They don't pull together with their women in order to improve their lot in life. Statistically, black women outpace black men. More black women than black men are going to college, getting advanced degrees and becoming successes. So, what's the reason behind the statistics?"

"Racism, a feeling of hopelessness in a society run by white males?" Jackson commented dryly. "It's easy to get sucked in to the belief that no matter how hard you try, you'll never succeed because 'the man' will hold you down. You know *our* environment. There are so few blacks here, that we know that the ones who *are* still here fought to stay, and absolutely no one is going to keep them from making a living in this, oftentimes, brutal land we live on."

"So, are you saying that all black men ought to take the attitude of not allowing anyone to stand in their way? No matter where they live, be it city, suburb or small town?"

"Exactly," Jackson said enthusiastically. "We give ourselves all kinds of reasons for failure. It's time we gave ourselves reasons to succeed. Such as a stronger community. Better relationships with our women, who have cause to believe we're shiftless if we aren't giving it our best shot. You want to know why black women are doing it for themselves? Because experience taught them that they couldn't depend on the men in their lives, that's why."

His voice, in the confines of the cab of the truck, was electrifying to me. My body tingled all over, and I wanted him to stop the truck so that I could throw my arms around him and kiss him long and hard.

Instead of attacking him, I said, "Back to the insight I gained from *Get on the Bus:* I learned that black men truly want to be everything their women want them to be, and more. I have to admit that until I moved to Chicago, I wasn't aware of there being such a gulf between the sexes. All the black men I knew when I was growing up, my father, grandfather, you, Cole, you all were single-mindedly devoted to your families. And your devotion meant that you did everything within your power to make sure your family was taken care of."

Jackson was silent for a few minutes, then he said, "You had a great dad, Chey. Some of us weren't as fortunate."

I fought against asking him what he had meant by that. I firmly believed it was best if he volunteered the information and that I not attempt to wring it from him.

The silence grew thick between us, and I got the uncomfortable feeling that he was about to disclose something vital from his past to me, had thought better of it, and then didn't know how to proceed with our conversation.

We had turned onto Highway 94 and were perhaps thirty-five miles from Billings. I would have to say something and possibly interrupt his flashback to the horror of being an abused child.

I cleared my throat.

Jackson briefly looked at me and smiled. "I'm sorry. I haven't forgotten that you're here. My mind was just elsewhere for a moment."

"That's all right," I assured him.

He reached over and clasped my left hand in his right one and gently squeezed it, his eyes on the road. "My father beat me when I was kid, Chey. Not the sort of punishment your parents dispense when you've misbehaved. No, he beat me with his fists until I passed out, or until he grew tired, whichever came first. And you want to know why he did it?"

Tears rolled down my cheeks, my throat was full, and I didn't believe I could disguise my state if I spoke, so I remained silent.

"It was because I defended my mother from him whenever he jumped on *her.* He called her a mealymouthed witch who wasn't worth the cost of the food he provided for her. You see, he wanted a house full of children, more hands to help him with the ranch;

but after I was born, the doctor told Ma that she could never have anymore children."

A sob escaped from my throat, and then the deluge came.

Jackson looked behind him to make sure there was no car so close to his that the driver wouldn't have sufficient time to brake as he pulled onto the soft shoulder of the road.

He then pulled over, braked and put the truck in park. Unfastening his seat belt, he undid mine as well and, with a groan, pulled me into his strong arms.

"I'm sorry. I don't know why I told you. I shouldn't have said anything," he said, his voice low in my ear. "Don't cry. It's all right. It was a long time ago. I just thought you should know, Chey. I love you, and I want you to know everything about me, so that you can judge whether or not you want to spend the rest of your life with me. If I have funny quirks, you should know about them."

He laughed shortly. "If I get nuts when the food on my plate touches, you should know about it."

"You don 't."

"No, I don't."

I twisted on the seat and reached up to take his face between my two hands. "I love you, Jackson. And I'm not crying for the man you are now; I'm crying for the little boy you were. That boy who couldn't defend himself against his father. I know you're all right now. I just wish someone had been there for you."

Jackson took one of my hands in his, brought it to his mouth and kissed the palm. "Someone *was* there for me, Chey. Your whole family. Being around you made me realize that normal families existed. Families in which the father loved and protected. Families in which the mothers were strict yet loving, like Miss Peaches. I cherished the times I spent with your family."

Fresh tears made their way down my already sodden face. "I'm glad."

"I patterned my behavior after your father's and grandfather's. I knew I wasn't going to grow up to be like Joseph."

Joseph was his father's Christian name.

"You do have a lot of ways like Daddy's" I agreed with him "But . . ."

"But?" He kissed the corner of my mouth.

"You don't dance."

He kissed me fully on the lips and my arms went around his powerful neck, drawing him closer.

He ended it. Otherwise, I would have been perfectly happy to spend the rest of the evening necking in his Chevy.

Raising his head, he kissed the tip of my nose. "You taste salty from all those tears. Come on, girl, let's get going, or it'll be 2:00 A.M. before I get you back home."

"Slim gave you until next week," I joked as I sat up straighter on the seat and refastened the seat belt.

Jackson buckled his seat belt and turned the key in the ignition. Pulling back onto the blacktop, he said, "We should set some ground rules."

I knew what was coming next: He wanted to know how we were going to avoid becoming intimate. Since he was armed with the knowledge of my virginity, it was his sacred duty to guard it. Every other man I'd ever dated made it their objective to get me into bed. I hadn't given in to them because I was adamant about being in love and in a committed relationship before consenting to sexual relations. I hadn't been in love with any of them, so I hadn't relented. The *one* man I loved, and the only man I'd dreamed of (both literally and figuratively) making love to, was going to make me wait until our wedding night.

"You're going to have one frustrated woman on your hands if you're about to say what I *think* you're about to say," I told him honestly, looking at him out of the corner of my eye.

Jackson chuckled. "No sex before marriage, Cheyenne."

"What?!"

"We both know it would be inadvisable. What if something went wrong? You may regret having given yourself to me. I'd feel guilty . . ."

"Speak for yourself," I cut him off. "I wouldn't regret a *second* I spent in bed with you, Jackson. I've been lusting after you for years. Are you trying to tell me I'm going to have to wait until you put a ring on my finger before my fantasies can be realized?"

"That's what I'm saying," he stated calmly.

I tried reasoning with him. "All right. No intercourse. What about heavy petting? Can I undress you and rub my hands all over your body?"

"I wouldn't do that if I were you. I'm getting hot just thinking about it."

"Well then nudity is out of the question," I said regrettably.

Sighing, Jackson said. "This is how I see it: kissing while fully clothed. Hands may travel wherever they wish, except too far north, and *front*. We cannot be alone together except when traveling to or from a public place . . ."

"You sound like my mother," I protested.

Jackson laughed. "I'm just trying to refrain from ravishing you so thoroughly that neither of us would walk right for a week, Chey. I could use some help here."

"After that description, you won't get any help from me."

The restaurant turned out to be elegantly understated, not a mounted fish in sight. Jackson and I were seated at a secluded table toward the rear of the dining room. I chose the broiled shrimp and he had the fried catfish.

After we were served our meals, I smiled at him and said, "Don't you get tired of catfish?"

Like Momma, Jackson was an avid fisherman. When he went fishing on the Yellowstone River, he caught catfish on a regular basis. Our freezer was well-stocked with his, and Momma's, catfish, trout and walleye.

"I know what I like," he said, sending me naughty signals with his eyes. "And what I like, I like for a long time."

"Well, all right!" I responded enthusiastically. I speared a shrimp with my fork, looked into his eyes, sensuously brought the shrimp to my mouth, licked it, then bit it in half and slowly chewed, my eyes never leaving his.

"An addendum to our rules," he said, his eyes on my mouth. "What you just did . . . From now on, that's prohibited."

I ate the other half of the shrimp and smiled at him. "Let's face it, Jackson. Just *being* in your presence turns me on. I've been known to require a cold shower after a conversation with you. You can't legislate emotions."

"Tell me about the lodge," Jackson suggested. A thin layer of sweat lay on his forehead, and it wasn't at all warm in the restaurant. "What do you have left to do before your grand opening?"

I dabbed at his forehead with my napkin. "We've already got the license. Momma and I are going to take a class in hotel management in December. It lasts until mid-January. Following the course, I'll get started on the advertising. Plus, we'll be visiting some of the area's most successful lodges to see how they manage their businesses."

"Sounds as if you have things well thought out," Jackson said.

I was observing how his warm brown skin, against the stark white of his shirt, was the color of burnished copper.

"I'm committed to making a success of the lodge. And I intend to set up the business so that my family can operate it in my absence. I'm not always going to be there, so they need to be capable of running it on their own."

I took a sip from my glass of white wine, and reached up to push a strand of hair behind my right ear.

Jackson leaned forward, his lips curved in a small smile. "When you did that, it reminded me of the time when you were eighteen and you tricked me into kissing you under the mistletoe."

"You remember that?"

"Of course."

"I lay in wait for you all morning. You were late."

"I had trouble with my truck. I wasn't as prosperous back then. After my parents died, I almost lost the ranch to the bank. . . ."

"We didn't know that!"

"Another thing I inherited from my parents: their idea that you don't broadcast your troubles to the world. I got through it. It took me three years to turn a profit, though. Anyway, the truck threw a gasket that day. I replaced it and arrived at your place two hours after I was supposed to have been there."

"You must have thought I was some nutty teenager, throwing myself at you the way I did," I told him, laughing softly.

"Actually," he replied, his eyes narrowing a bit, "I was flattered. You always had a knack for making me feel better, Chey. Even when you were a little girl, your open admiration made me feel loved. Not much emotion was displayed in my house. Ma was depressed half the time. Who wouldn't be, married to a man like Joseph? Joseph, I think, resented me. I could never do anything to please that man."

"I've always been curious about something, Jackson," I said, placing my fork on my plate and folding my hands on my lap. "Did they ever find out how your father lost control of the car the night your parents were killed?"

Jackson scowled and put the beer mug he'd been drinking from onto the tabletop. "No, they never did," he said, his eyes on his hands. His voice was hard, discouraging further questions.

I picked up my fork and tore into my food.

Jackson sat quietly, not eating or drinking.

I tried to will him to meet my gaze, but he continued studying his hands as if he was afraid to meet my eyes. I knew I'd made a faux pas, however I didn't know why. Why did the mention of the accident upset him?

I couldn't take anymore of the silence. "Forgive me for reminding you of that awful night. I wasn't thinking."

Jackson sighed and looked straight into my eyes. "One revelation at a time, Chey. I'll tell you about the night my parents died, someday, but not tonight."

I reached across the table and cut off a piece of his catfish with my fork and ate it. "That's scrumptious."

I wanted him to understand that I was not hurt because he wasn't prepared to discuss a night that must have had an earth-shattering effect on him.

Shaking his head, he smiled at me and said, "Help yourself."

So I did. I took a fillet from his plate and gave him part of my shrimp in exchange.

We drove around the Rimrock Mall parking lot for several minutes before we located a parking space. The mall was invariably busy on the weekend. Billings was the largest city in Montana, and numerous folks from the neighboring towns of Laurel, Hardin, Ballantine, Custer, Pompeys Pillar, Huntley, Shepherd, Worden and others, came to Billings in order to shop, go out to dinner and enjoy the various forms of recreation their smaller towns didn't provide.

The mall had all the major department stores under its roof; restaurants, movie theaters, everything a shopper desired. We Montanans were simple people, but we didn't like to think we were missing out on the latest fashions, or being deprived of culture just because we lived in a state with wide, open spaces.

Jackson and I both enjoyed sitting in the rear of the theater so that we could see the entire screen with no difficulty. We were fortunate to have arrived at the theater for the final showing of the latest Will Smith vehicle, a western.

After sitting on the plush seat, I settled back and Jackson placed his arm on the back of my seat.

The movie hadn't started so Jackson leaned over and whispered, "Would you like something from the concession?"

"No, thanks, I'm fine."

"What? No popcorn, candy or a drink? What's a movie without junk food?"

Smiling into his handsome face, I said, "Oh, all right. I'll have a small popcorn, no butter, and a Diet Coke."

He unfolded his long legs and rose. "Be right back."

In his absence, I looked around the still-lit theater, trying to see if I recognized anyone in the room.

We were surrounded by teenagers out on dates. Older couples made up maybe ten percent of the audience.

The voices in the theater sounded like bees buzzing.

I'd been sitting there perhaps five minutes, ruminating on how the evening had gone so far, when, from behind me, a feminine voice said, "Cheyenne, is that you?"

I turned my head and looked into the face of Marissa Claiborne. She was walking down the aisle with a good-looking African-American man of perhaps thirty.

Her coat hung open, revealing a skintight miniskirt, a matching vest over a blouse and calf-length leather boots. Her short auburn hair was combed away from her perfectly made-up face.

She came toward me, pulling the man with her. "Hello," she said. Turning to glance up at her date, she continued. "I told you there were more black folks here," she joked. Her eyes were on me again, "Cheyenne, I'd like you to meet Calvin Hathaway, a close friend of mine from New York. Calvin, Cheyenne Roberts."

Smiling warmly, Calvin came forward and reached for my hand, which I graciously offered. "Good to meet you, Cheyenne."

"Same here," I told him, returning his smile. "Is this your first time in Montana?"

"This is my first time this far north, period," Calvin said, his green-brown eyes full of goodwill. His skin was medium-brown, and he wore his brown hair in short dreadlocks. Five-ten, and stockily built, he had an energetic aura about him that seemed to encompass those around him.

They sat down in the two empty seats on my left.

"Cheyenne is an accountant who just moved back home from Chicago," Marissa told Calvin. She regarded me. "Who're you here with? You didn't come *alone,* did you?" The note of sympathy in her voice irritated me a little. Did she believe I couldn't get a date?

I didn't have to answer her question, because Jackson returned at that moment and sat down on my right. He hadn't even noticed the couple on my left.

Handing me the popcorn and plastic cup of Diet Coke, he looked directly into my face and was about to lower his head to plant a quick kiss on my mouth, when he frowned and pulled back.

"Marissa!"

Marissa laughed at the shocked expression on her ex's face.

Jackson's eyes met mine and I raised my eyebrows in resignation, denoting my utter disbelief at the turn of events.

Then I heard him laugh deep in his throat, and I relaxed.

He rose and shook hands with Calvin. "Hello, you must be Calvin Hathaway."

Calvin pumped his hand. "And you must be Jackson Kincaid. Good to meet you."

Marissa looked over at me, an entirely friendly expression in her almond-shaped eyes. I smiled. I believe we had an under-standing. She was moving on with her life. She further demon-strated this by taking Calvin by the hand when he returned to his seat and suggesting they find another spot from which to watch the movie. They found seats in the middle section of the theater.

"Then you've heard of Calvin before," I said to Jackson after Marissa and Calvin had departed.

Jackson placed his arm about my shoulders. "He's an actor. They met about a year ago. She says she's in love with him."

"Really? It would've been nice if you'd told me about him when she first put in an appearance. I was under the impression she might still have feelings for you."

He looked down into my eyes. "Oh? Whatever gave you that impression?"

I briefly told him about Marissa's behavior in Mr. Cavendish's store. "Plus, she was driving your truck."

"But I told you that the moment I saw her again, I knew I was in love with you," Jackson reminded me.

"Yes, but if you'd told me *she* was in love with someone else, then I wouldn't have thought of her as the competition," I logi-cally pointed out. "There's only one reason you wouldn't tell me about Calvin," I deduced.

Smiling, Jackson said, "And what is that?"

"You wanted to see if I'd be jealous. Which I was . . ."

"Okay. Maybe I needed an ego boost."

"If you'd relax your rules and let me give you a massage, you wouldn't be in need of an ego boost."

He bent his head and covered my mouth with his own. Ending the all-too-brief kiss, he said, "Watch your mouth, little girl."

"Well, you left yourself wide open," I countered.

The lights dimmed, then went out. The audience applauded the beginning of the film, and Jackson and I sat back in our seats, his right arm on the back of my seat and my left hand on his muscular thigh. He reached over and removed it, placing it on my lap. I laughed softly and lay my head on his shoulder.

Will Smith was his inimitable self. The audience participated in the film: laughing, talking back to the characters on the screen.

I got so interested in the film, that I sat up straighter in my seat, my body no longer touching Jackson's. He must have missed my warmth, because he pulled his eyes from the screen, looked at me and said, "Your muscles tired?" He then reached over and began massaging my shoulder, working his way up to my neck.

I believe he intended to soothe my sore muscles, however his touch had the opposite effect: It aroused me.

I grasped his hand. "I'm okay."

I was trying to abide by his rules.

He leaned toward me, his mouth near my ear. "What's the matter?"

"Your hands were exciting me," I told him honestly.

He kissed the side of my neck.

"Is this allowed?" I asked, turning my head so that he'd have better access to my neck.

"We're fully clothed."

Several erotic images played out in my mind. In all of them, I was fully clothed, however Jackson didn't have a stitch on.

I laughed softly.

"What?" Jackson asked curiously.

"I can imagine myself in clinches with you while I'm wearing clothes. But, I can't help it, I always imagine you naked."

"Me, too," Jackson admitted.

"Me or you?"

"You."

We returned our attention to the screen. I kept stealing glances at him, enjoying observing him without his knowledge. I considered that night our first date, even though we'd gone out to dinner together in Chicago.

In Chicago, his intentions had been vague. However, that night out together in Montana, I'd become privy to some of his darkest thoughts. I felt closer to him than I ever had before.

When the movie ended, and the lights came up, Jackson and I stood and stretched our legs. I looked over at the section I'd seen Marissa and Calvin find seats in at the start of the film. They were also rising and getting into their coats.

Marissa raised her eyes to mine and waved. "Marissa's saying good night," I told Jackson as I waved back.

Jackson was in the process of pulling on his coat. Finished, he looked up and waved at Marissa and Calvin, who nodded and turned to leave. Then he helped me with my coat, and we left the theater by a side exit.

He held my hand securely in his as we leisurely strolled across the parking lot in search of the truck. I glanced up. The night sky was sprinkled with brilliant stars. Even the glare of the parking lot's lights couldn't distract from the beauty of God's display.

"You know," Jackson commented. "For a woman who spent the last ten years of her life in the city, you seem to get a kick out of the simple pleasures."

An icy breeze whipped about us, and Jackson pulled me closer to him, shielding my body with his own.

We picked up our pace, almost running toward the truck. When we arrived at the truck, Jackson unlocked the passenger-side door and handed me in, whereupon I leaned over and unlocked his door.

He climbed in and firmly shut the door. The keys jangled as he turned them in the ignition. The trusty old Chevy immediately rumbled to life and Jackson let her warm up a minute before switching on the heater.

"It must be thirty degrees out there," he said, rubbing his hands together. He looked at me out of the corner of his eye. "What're you doing way over there? Get over here, girl."

I didn't have to be asked twice. I scooted across the vinyl seat until my hip bumped his. "Is that better?"

Jackson wrapped his strong arms around me. "Much."

My nose was buried in his chest. I turned my head so that I could look up into his eyes. "I had a great time tonight."

"The night isn't over yet. Wait until I get you safely home before you get generous with the compliments."

"Wanna steam up the windows?" I asked mischievously. "We're fully clothed."

TWELVE

Harry Johnson had been serious when he began his campaign of wooing Momma by bringing her courting gifts. Knowing the way to her heart wasn't through expensive jewelry or flattery, he chose a more practical route: fresh produce.

The first week of December, Momma and I spent the better part of a day canning tomatoes. The following week, it was collard greens, which grow well in cold weather. We blanched them, put them in plastic bags, and stored them in the freezer.

Before the pungent odor of all those collards could dissipate, Harry drove up to our back door with two bushels of butter beans.

Momma and I were in the company room, lounging on the sofa, our feet up, studying for a test in hotel management that would determine whether or not we received certificates proving we'd passed the course. We had two weeks to prepare for the test.

I heard Harry's truck and looked up from my book. When you live out in the country, your ears become attuned to the motor sounds of vehicles you're familiar with. Harry had been coming by so often, I knew the sound of his Ford Ranger XLT.

I peered at Momma. "It's for you."

Momma sprang to her feet. She complained vociferously about Harry's edible gifts, calling him a lonely widower with too much time on his hands. But, I'd observed how she'd blossomed since Harry started laying vegetables at her feet. Whether she cared to admit to it, or not, she was becoming fond of Harry.

"I wonder what it could be this time," she said, pretending consternation. I'd noticed a mirthful glint in her golden-brown depths, though. She wasn't fooling me.

I remained on the sofa as I watched her walk swiftly from the room. "You're going to have to tell him to quit," I called after her. "Otherwise, we're going to run out of space in the freezer!"

I heard her laughter, like tinkling crystal bells, coming from the hallway.

I waited a good ten minutes, to allow them a private greeting and some time to talk without others about; then I got up and went to the kitchen to help transport whatever Harry had brought, from his truck's bed to the kitchen. Chad and Lucas were out in the barn cleaning the stalls. Earlier that morning, Clancy and I had groomed all six horses and had put blankets on them and led them out to the paddock. After Chad and Lucas cleaned the stalls, they would lead the horses back into the barn. Clancy had gone to visit her friend Laura at a neighboring ranch. Therefore I was the only one available to help get Harry's latest offering into the house.

I cleared my throat before entering the kitchen. Not that I believed they'd be in a passionate clinch when I walked in. But, just in case.

Harry had recently had his salt-and-pepper hair cut, and the new style made him look ten years younger. His blue eyes twinkled in his strong (according to Momma) . . . lightly done toast-colored face.

"Cheyenne," Momma said excitedly, "Harry wants to ask you something."

Eyebrows arched with curiosity, I regarded Harry with a half-smile. "What is it, Mr. Johnson?"

Harry nervously rolled his felt hat in his hands. I wished he'd stop. It was too much like watching a pimply-faced teen-aged boy around a pretty girl. Very uncomfortable for all concerned.

"Peaches was telling me how you were thinking of starting your own business one day soon, and I was thinking: maybe you could start with me. My books need a good going over. And maybe you could also do my taxes this year. If I had a professional doing them, I might not be tempted to wait until the last minute."

His suggestion caught me by surprise. The nearly three months I'd been home, not once had I thought about working as an accountant. I was enjoying preparing to open the lodge. I hadn't given much thought as to what I would do when the lodge was under way and Momma had become adept at managing it by herself.

I had to face reality. From the beginning, I'd said that if things didn't work out between Jackson and myself, I was not going to stick around to watch him live out his life with another woman who would, undoubtedly, bear him beautiful children. I would not be that bitter woman with a life full of regrets and missed opportunities. I was a romantic at heart. But I was also a hard-headed woman of the nineties who always had to have a backup plan.

"All right," I told Harry after thinking about it. "When would you like me to begin?"

Harry had smiled with pleasure. "How about tomorrow morning?"

Tomorrow would be a Friday. "That's good. Ten o'clock?"

"That's fine with me," Harry agreed, his eyes on Momma's glowing face.

I slapped my hands on my jeans-clad thighs. "Umm . . . Momma. Do you need my help with anything?" I felt like a third wheel.

"No, sweetie. Harry and I can manage. You run along," Momma replied as she smoothed her hair. She'd put her long, black hair with silver streaks in a chignon. Not a tendril was out of place, but, apparently, Harry made her self-conscious.

"All right," I said, backing out of the room. I suddenly had an urge to defend Daddy's memory. But that foolish impulse evaporated as quickly as it had materialized. Momma had been widowed for more than seven years. And she was well past the age of consent.

It's true that you never know how you'll react to a situation until you're faced with it. I had misgivings about Momma getting seriously involved with Harry. Did that mean I was a bigot? Or was I simply concerned for her personal safety? There were still people out there who thought nothing of burning a black person's house down in order to get their point across. It was a frightening world we lived in.

I returned to the company room and picked up my hotel-management textbook. Kicking off my flats, I sat down on the brown leather sofa and put my legs under me, getting comfortable.

I was facing the three picture windows that made up the east wall. Outside, the sky was overcast. The weatherman on the local news that morning had promised no snow for at least another week. Slim, however, swore by the white color of the ptarmigan's feathers. They predicted an early snowfall.

I didn't mind winter in Montana. Since our chores around the ranch were limited to making certain the cattle were salted, fed their grain, given fresh water and the horses were also taken care of, our time out in the elements was cut down to a minimum.

Everyone respected Father Winter. In heavy snow, a rope was strung from the house to the barn, to prevent getting lost in all that whiteness. We usually sent the bulk of the herd to market before deep winter, which was January-February. Sometimes, though, a blizzard sneaked up on us and the herd was left to fend for itself. That's why, in winter, we moved the herd to the south field.

The south field was closer to the homestead, from which we could keep a closer eye on the herd. Plus, there were numerous trees that the cattle could huddle underneath for added warmth and protection from snow and rain.

When I was growing up on the ranch, wintertime meant the opportunity to read more. So over the course of the year, I would buy up books at a discount from bookstores in Billings. When we were snowed in my nose would invariably be in a book, while my brothers and sister ran wild in the house, trying to find something to entertain themselves with. I'd be so engrossed in my books that the racket they made would recede into the background, and nothing, and no one could interrupt me unless they repeatedly banged on my bedroom door.

I closed my textbook, grabbed the sofa pillow and placed it behind my head, laying back. I couldn't concentrate. Jackson was on my mind. Two days earlier, he'd embarked on a cattle drive that would take him on a route cattlemen had been using for decades. It began in southern Montana and ended in northern Wyoming. Jackson's destination was the stockyards in Sheridan, Wyoming. It was on a similar cattle drive that we lost Daddy.

Now, every time someone mentioned that route, I inwardly cringed. It would take Jackson and his men seven to ten days to get the cattle across Montana to Wyoming. They would have to allow for weather, downtime for the men and the cattle who could only walk so far each day. Plus, you didn't want the herd to shed too many pounds before reaching market. Therefore, they couldn't be pushed too hard and they must be allowed to graze and replenish their energy reserves.

Using his mobile phone, Jackson called me each night. I hadn't tried to talk him out of going. I knew the vicissitudes of ranch life. It was Slim's opinion that one should live life by the seat of one's pants. I amended that philosophy somewhat. I believed that one should accept change in one's life as the natural course of living.

Jackson had become a part of my life. Therefore I had to accept his way of life, a life that entailed going on cattle drives at least once, sometimes twice, a year.

The phone rang and I sat up. It was located on the end table on my right. I sounded a bit hoarse when I answered. "Hello?"

"Is this the Robertses' residence?"

"Yes it is. With whom would you like to speak?"

"Cheyenne Roberts."

"I'm Chey . . ."

"Cheyenne, have you been away from the office so long, you don't recognize my voice?" the woman asked incredulously.

The synapses in my brain connected then. It was Janet, the receptionist, calling from Streiber and Farrar. She was right. I had happily put Streiber and Farrar far behind me.

"Janet?"

"Yes! How are you doing?"

"I'm doing just fine," I said, wondering why she was calling. "And how are you?"

"I'm hanging in there. Listen, Cheyenne, Mr. Streiber would like to speak with you. Here he is . . ."

My mind began racing at the mention of Garrett's name. I sat with the receiver to my ear, a frown creasing my brow. What could Garrett Streiber possibly have to say to me?

"Cheyenne!" came Garrett's enthusiastic baritone. "How are

things going for you up there? Have you had any luck getting your business started?"

"Hello, Garrett," I said quietly. "Yes, I'm doing just fine, thank you. How are things with you and Stu?"

I wasn't actually concerned about Stu's well-being, but it was only polite to ask.

Garrett paused before replying. Then he said, he voice grave, "Stu had a massive heart attack three days ago, Cheyenne. He'll recover; but, in his absence, there have been some interesting developments here at Streiber and Farrar. I suppose it's my fault for being so inobservant . . ."

His voice broke and he went silent. He sounded extremely upset. He had piqued my curiosity, and I was afraid he wouldn't continue.

"Garrett?" I said softly.

"I need you, Cheyenne. Stu has done some creative cooking of the books. He's transferred funds to various accounts all over the world. I haven't been able to retrieve those funds. I don't know what to do. I know how good you are with international funds. I wondered if you'd come and see what you can do about it? Please. You know I wouldn't ask if I wasn't desperate. It isn't just me he's royally screwed, Cheyenne. He's completely emptied the employees' savings plan. I swear, I don't know how he did it. I just know I've got to do something about it."

"Everything you've described is illegal, Garrett. Have you gone to the authorities?"

"No. I want to try to retrieve the funds first. Do you know what Stu would get if convicted, Cheyenne? Two years in a country-club prison. It'd be like he was on *vacation*. No. If I cannot get the funds back, I'm going to go to the hospital and blow his brains out."

"I'll get the first plane out of here, Garrett," I hastily promised. "I'll call you back with the details."

Garrett sighed with relief. "Thanks, Cheyenne."

"Don't thank me yet," I told him. "I might not be able to reverse the damage that rat has done."

We rang off. I sat there feeling guilty for not having told Garrett what I suspected Stu of months ago. If I had told him, he would have been forewarned. Although, knowing Garrett's good nature, he might not have believed his partner was capable of the sort of perfidy I would have been accusing him of.

At any rate, I felt as if I'd taken the money and run, leaving Garrett and the employees of the firm to suffer the consequences of Stu's greed.

With a sense of urgency, I rose and gathered my books and papers from the sofa. Momma and I had planned to go to Billings that afternoon to attend our hotel-management class. I glanced at my watch. It was nearly two o'clock.

I ran upstairs to put my study materials in my bedroom and to get my American Express card from my wallet.

Sitting on the bed, I reached for the phone book on the nightstand. I located the phone number of the travel agent I used when in a pinch. I could have found a flight out of Billings and booked a room in a Chicago hotel myself, but it would've taken me longer.

You paid for convenience.

By the time I got off the phone ten minutes later, the agent had booked me on a 5:15 flight out of Billings, making the ticket open-ended. Plus, she'd made a reservation for me at a hotel along The Miracle Mile, a posh section of Chicago within walking distance of Streiber and Farrar.

Going back downstairs, I encountered Momma in the hallway between the kitchen and the company room.

Harry had recently departed, and she was still on her Harry high. I hated to tell her I had to leave.

Her golden-brown skin looked flushed and her eyes were strangely serene. I wondered if I looked like that after spending time with Jackson.

"Sorry about the interruption," she apologized. "Shall we get back to the books?"

I took her by the shoulders. "Momma, I need to go out of town for a few days. Garrett Streiber phoned while you were talking to Mr. Johnson. He's got troubles and he asked me to come and see if I can help him out of them."

Her brow furrowed in a frown. "Your ex-boss? It's nothing dangerous, is it?"

Momma's initial concern was always for the personal safety of her children.

"I don't believe so. Stu Farrar apparently embezzled money from the firm. Garrett wants to try and get it back . . ."

"But is that possible?"

"All we can do is try," I said, not sounding too confident.

Momma's tendency to be our No. 1 cheerleader awakened at the note of skepticism in my voice.

"You'll go and do your best," she said. "When do you have to leave?"

"My flight's at 5:15."

"Then we'd better get you packed. I'll go to the class by myself tonight. I'll leave a note for Clancy. While you go and throw some things into a bag, I'll run upstairs and explain what's going on to Slim. The boys can get the news from Clancy."

Momma was a rock during an emergency.

A little more than three hours after I'd received the phone call from Garrett, I was sitting in coach going over our conversation in my head.

When I'd phoned him with the time of my arrival in Chicago, he'd said he would pick me up at the airport. It was then that I'd told him that if he hadn't discussed what was going on with any of the other accountants or the office staff, it was best if he refrained from doing so. The less people who knew about it, the better.

He'd said he hadn't told anyone, save his wife, Denise.

I left further questions for when we met face-to-face.

We were over South Dakota when a pertinent fact occurred to me: In order for Stu to access the firm's various accounts and make wire transfers, both his and Garrett's terminals had to be utilized. It worked like this: Stu would have to type in his secret code from his terminal, which the financial institution would receive and then wait for Garrett to enter his secret code from his personal terminal. After those steps, the wire transfers would be put through.

Stu and Garrett had set it up this way from the beginning. I knew about it because one night when we were at a cocktail party, given for the clients of the firm, Stu had gotten tipsy and blabbed about it in an effort to impress a client with the firm's practice of maintaining tight security.

Therefore, Stu had an accomplice. He couldn't be at two terminals at once. The rule was, the second code had to be punched in within ten seconds of the first one. Stu's stubby legs couldn't possibly get him down the hall to Garrett's office within that space of time.

That left Stu's weaselly nephew, Monte Pepper. Monte, whom I'd kneed in the privates the last time I'd seen him. I wondered where Monte was while his uncle was laid up in the hospital with a coronary?

At Chicago's O'Hare International Airport, I spotted Garrett before he saw me. He was standing in the waiting area of the carrier I'd used. In a dark suit with a white shirt and a Hermes tie at his neck, he looked impeccable, as usual.

His brown eyes lacked their normal fire, however. And he had dark circles under them, too.

He made an effort to muster up some pep when he saw me walking toward him. "Cheyenne!" he called, grinning. "Montana must agree with you. You've never looked better."

"It must be my mother's cooking," I half-joked. The truth was, I'd gained nearly ten pounds since I'd been home. I wasn't jogging on a regular basis any longer. I hadn't run since Jackson and I stopped meeting secretly in the mornings between our place and his.

Momma said I was getting fat and happy. The extra pounds weren't unsightly on my five-ten inch frame, but if I got any happier, my behind would get so big, it would appear as if someone was following me when no one was really there.

Garrett gave me a bear hug. "Thanks for coming," he said. He glanced down at the single bag I was carrying. "You sure do pack lightly."

"Force of habit," I commented.

He reached for the folded-over suit bag. I gave it to him.

"This way," he said, turning toward the exit.

We walked side by side through the electric doors and turned to the right in the direction of the lot designated for temporary parking. A blast of arctic air hit me in the face the moment we stepped outside. "Yeah, I missed you, too," I said to the wind.

"What did you say?" Garrett asked.

"Nothing."

What I had to tell Garrett was best said in the comfort of his Lexus. So I waited until we were in the car and pulling out of the parking lot before broaching the subject of my replacement, Monte Pepper.

Garrett smoothly maneuvered the luxury car through the congested airport traffic. I sat next to him, gathering my thoughts. After a few moments of silence, I said, "Garrett, I'm afraid I need to ask for your forgiveness before we proceed."

Puzzled, Garrett frowned at me before returning his attention to his driving. "I don't understand, Cheyenne."

"You see, I suspected Stu might be up to something when he hired his nephew to replace me . . ."

"His nephew? You mean Monte?"

So he hadn't been aware that Monte Pepper was Stu's nephew. I had wondered about that when I'd found out about Stu's actions months before.

"Yes, Monte. We were in his office one day when he slipped and referred to Stu as his uncle," I informed him, my gaze on his profile. "I didn't know what to make of it. He said Stu wished to keep it a secret. He didn't explain why. The first thing that popped into my head was that if Monte eventually became a partner in the firm, Stu would then control two-thirds of the business. I wish I'd gone to you back then, but I only had my suspicions and, to be honest, they were fueled by my dislike of Stu; so I don't think my opinion was exactly unbiased."

Garrett laughed shortly, shaking his head. "I probably wouldn't have believed a word of it." He briefly glanced at me. "Do you know how long I've known Stuart Farrar? Most of my adult life. We met in college—Loyola. That's probably another reason I didn't look into Monte's background when Stu recommended him. He's also a Loyola graduate.

"This gets even stranger, Cheyenne. I should have known something was going on. It was Monte Pepper who brought the discrepancies to my attention."

"How?" I asked, my voice rising an octave in disbelief.

"He was with Stu when he had the heart attack. They'd been working together in Stu's office. Before the paramedics arrived, Monte pulled me aside and asked if it wouldn't be best if the sensitive material on Stu's computer monitor was deleted before some unauthorized person got a look at it. I asked him why he hadn't already cleared the screen himself, and he said Stu had told him, and others in the office, never to touch his computer. But since I was Stu's partner, it should be all right for me to do it. So, there I was, reading the material on the screen, while Stu lay flat on his back a few feet away. I don't know what upset me more, seeing my best friend turning blue, possibly dying, or reading what was on his computer screen. He'd been checking on his accounts at a Cayman Island bank. The sum of all three accounts amounted to more than two million dollars, Cheyenne. I was horrified. I left Stu with Monte and went to my office and methodically checked all of our accounts. Except for the office maintenance fund, which was minimal anyway, he'd wiped us out." His voice sounded tired and hopeless.

"So you had no reason to suspect Monte, too?" I asked.

"No, of course I didn't. I thought he was still wet behind the ears. You know, getting brownie points by ingratiating himself with the boss."

"You do realize that Monte probably helped Stu get his hands on the accounts?" I asked.

"How else could Stu have done it? He had to have someone on my terminal putting in my access code. My question is: How did they get my code? I hadn't written them down anywhere. I hadn't told anyone the code I use, not even Denise."

"Who knows you better than your best friend?" I asked. "Stu's known you longer than your wife has. Plus, you're a sentimental man, Garrett. You're in love with your wife and you adore your children. Nine times out of ten, your code is the abbreviated name of someone close to you. Or it could be the date of your anniversary: your children's birth dates, your favorite romantic vacation destination. Stu would know all of that."

"You're absolutely right. It was September 27, the birth date of Brice, my youngest son. Stu's his godfather."

"What we need to do," I proposed, feeling excited about the prospect, "is figure out what Stu's code is. So rack your brain, Garrett."

Garrett humphed. "The thing is, Stu was never as forthcoming about *his* personal life as I've always been about mine. I should have known there was something innately wrong with him all these years; but I chalked it up to his having a bad childhood. He once told me that his mother skipped out on the family when he was a kid. I figured a person who'd been abandoned at such an early age would have difficulty putting their trust in anyone."

"Well don't beat yourself up about it," I said, hoping to remind him we had more pressing matters to attend to. I looked down at the Lexus' clock. It was 9:10 P.M. "We should go to the office now," I suggested.

"I was hoping you'd say that," Garrett told me frankly.

The security guard in the lobby of the building knew both of us by sight. His name was Alvin Williams and he was a portly black man in his middle forties. He didn't express surprise at seeing us at that hour of the night when he let us in the building.

Grinning at me, he said: "Miss Roberts. I hope this means you're back to stay."

"How are you, Mr. Williams?" I asked nicely.

Garrett took Alvin by the arm. "Alvin, I need to ask a favor of you; and I know I can count on you. You are not to mention you've seen Miss Roberts here tonight, do you understand?"

"Yes sir!" Alvin said immediately.

Garrett was always generous with the people whose services he availed himself of. I was sure there would be a nice fat bonus in Alvin's pay packet that week.

Garrett and I walked to the bank of elevators in the lobby, and Garrett pressed the button for the fifth floor.

Garrett turned to me. "I didn't even think to ask if you've eaten, or if you're fatigued." He smiled. "I haven't thought much about eating or sleeping, myself, the past three days."

"We can order sandwiches and coffee from that all-night diner near the park," I said. "They deliver until eleven."

"Was I such a slave driver that you know how late the local takeout places stay open?" Garrett joked.

"A girl had to eat," I returned.

Five minutes later, I was sitting at the terminal in Stu's office typing in access codes. I tried every word that I associated with Stu: his wife Dolores' name; his sons Dominic and Anthony; his daughter, Catarina.

"Talk to me," I urged Garrett, who was pacing the room.

"His mother's name was Gina," he offered.

"With a *G*, or a *J?*" I asked.

"G, I think."

I typed it in. *Access denied* the screen read.

"What year, month and date did you start the firm?"

"January 2, 1984."

I typed in the information. Nothing.

"Do you remember the day of the week?"

"I believe it was a Monday," Garrett said. He'd gone around to sit behind the desk and was going through the drawers, probably hoping to find something that would trigger some memory deep inside him concerning his erstwhile friend.

I threw a battery of questions at him.

"What are Stu's hobbies?"

"I don't think he has any. He sails a little."

"Does he own a boat?"

"Nah . . ."

"Is his father still living?"

"No, he died years ago."

"Do you know what his name was?"

"Benito," Garrett said absentmindedly. He was reading Stu's appointment book."

"Had Stu ever been married before he met Dolores?"

"Not that I know of."

"Did he pledge a fraternity while he was in college?"

"Neither of us did."

"Was there a special girl in Stu's life when you were in college? Maybe a steady girlfriend?"

"There was a girl called Valerie that he particularly liked, but she wouldn't give him the time of day."

"That isn't it," I told him after I'd tried the name.

Garrett raised his brown eyes to mine and smiled. "Look at this," he said, his mood more optimistic than it'd been all night.

I rose to go stand next to him. Looking over his shoulder, I watched as he pointed to several entries in Stu's appointment book.

For months, Stu had scribbled the notation, VS, next to the Wednesday space in his book. The appointment had invariably been at three in the afternoon.

"A little love in the afternoon?" Garrett submitted for my consideration.

"Could be," I said.

Then I remembered all the times Dotty had insisted that quite a few people in the office engaged in illicit affairs. She'd named names. I'd been oblivious to all the hanky-panky going on around me. I kept my nose to the grindstone.

"Go to your office and check the employee roster and see if there's anyone with the initials VS on the payroll," I suggested.

I knew a few of the secretaries. However, there was a support staff of more than twenty full- and part-time employees, and I couldn't recall all of their names.

In Garrett's absence, I picked up the receiver and dialed the ranch in Custer.

It was an hour earlier there so it would only be a little after nine P.M.

Clancy answered on the third ring. "Robertses' residence, Clancy speaking."

"Hey, girl."

"Chey, Jackson just called. Momma gave him the number at the hotel and your cell phone number because she was afraid you might not be at the hotel."

"How long ago was that?"

"Five minutes?"

"I've got to go. Tell Momma everything's fine here. I'll phone again in the morning. 'Bye, Clance."

" 'Bye."

I replaced the receiver and glanced at my shoulder bag, which I'd hung on the brass hat tree next to the door when we'd entered the office. *Ring,* I willed the cellular phone inside it to do. *Ring!*

My mental powers weren't up to par that night, because it didn't ring. Garrett returned ten minutes later, his chin dragging on the floor.

"No luck, huh?"

"Not a VS in the whole bunch."

We ordered sandwiches and coffee and kept at it until two in the morning, at which time Garrett insisted on driving me to the hotel so that I could get some rest.

By three, I'd showered and stretched out between the cool, lavender-scented sheets of the Hyatt Regency.

I'd put my cell phone on the nightstand next to the bed within easy reach, and my mind was firmly on Jackson and what he might be doing at that time. Asleep under the stars? Laying awake wondering why I wasn't at home awaiting his return?

I didn't phone him because of the obvious reason: sudden noises startled cattle. They wouldn't react favorably to a 3:00 A.M. phone call.

I drifted off with Jackson's handsome face in my mind's eye, and I dreamed I was laying with him in his bedroll. The black blanket of sky above us was solely illuminated by the full moon and there wasn't another soul around.

We did not speak. The only form of communication was the eloquent language of our bodies touching. The insouciant joy of flesh molding to flesh. And at the penultimate moment, just as my dreamself was about to ascend to orgasmic heights, I awakened to the insistent ringing of the cell phone.

"Hullo," I mumbled. I was still shaking off the effects of that splendid dream.

"I know it's late, but this is the first opportunity I had to phone. One of the hands, a rookie, didn't heed our warnings about proper clothing and got himself a case of pneumonia. I'm at the sheriff's office in Saint Xavier. They're getting ready to transport him to the hospital in Billings."

"Jackson. Thank God," I breathed with relief. "Is he bad off?"

"The doc here says he'll make it, but he'll have to be hospitalized for a few days."

"Well that's good . . ."

"What is this I hear about your having to fly to Chicago to help your former boss salvage his business?"

I gave him the story in abbreviated form. "I don't know if I'm going to be of any help. We haven't even been able to come up with his code."

"I'm sure you'll stick with it until you solve it. You were always good with puzzles," he said huskily.

His voice sounded as though he was standing in a cavernous building. I hoped the battery in his cell phone wasn't going dead.

"I love you, Jackson," I told him before our connection started breaking up.

"I dream of your sweet face," I heard him say before the static got so bad that his words became unintelligible.

"Jackson!"

Nothing on the line except white noise.

I turned off my phone and climbed back under the covers. Laying my head on the pillow, I closed my eyes and tried to conjure up the images of the dream Jackson had awakened me out of.

A good night's rest did me a world of good. The next day, I awakened with renewed vigor. I felt confident that Garrett and I would break Stu's code that night.

In the meanwhile, I had the whole of Friday to get through. I phoned Dotty's apartment at eleven.

Her son, Bailey, barely two, answered the phone.

"Hi, Bailey, it's Auntie Cheyenne," I said cheerfully.

"Chey, Chey, Chey," he chanted happily.

"Let me speak to your mommy, sweetie," I interrupted. Bailey liked the sound of his own singsong voice.

"Cheyenne, is that you?" Dotty asked, laughing. To Bailey, she said, "Go ask your daddy to clean your nose, boy, you look like you're trying to slurp spaghetti through your nostrils."

"That image is a little too vivid for my taste," I joked.

"My Caller ID says you're phoning from the Hyatt Regency here in town. What are you doing back? And why didn't you tell me you were coming?"

"Because I'm on a secret mission and information is on a

need-to-know basis; and you didn't need to know," I said, laughing. "I missed you, Dotty."

"Of course you missed me. I'm the original. When God made me, he wanted to keep me for himself. But we were incompatible, the spirit/flesh thing, you know, so he, regrettably, had to send me down here."

"I don't know, Dotty, but your joking about God wanting to keep you for his woman might be hitting close to blasphemy. You'd better go to church Sunday and beg his forgiveness."

"Girl, I go to church every Sunday. And God is an expert on jokes. Look at the duck-billed platypus."

We chatted over the phone for more than twenty minutes, after which I invited her and Pete to meet me downtown for lunch, my treat. They accepted, and I got up to get dressed.

THIRTEEN

The firm Dotty worked for allowed their employees to share jobs. Dotty's partner worked mornings. Dotty worked afternoons. They shared a salary but had full benefits. As for Pete, he was a freelance writer who picked and chose his own assignments.

I was delighted they were both free to spend some time with me that afternoon. I'd been waiting ten minutes when they arrived.

A striking couple, Dotty was wearing a stylish dark gray pantsuit that tied at her small waist, and Pete wore a white New Boxer shirt with a mandarin collar and a pair of slate-gray trousers. Dotty, with her hourglass figure, dark-chocolate skin and expressive eyes was the perfect complement to Pete's tall, muscular, honey-colored pulchritude.

I rose and hugged Dotty. Pete bent over and kissed my proffered cheek.

Seated, we smiled at one another. "You two look footloose and fancy free," I complimented them.

"We have a whole four hours to do as we please," Dotty said, dimples showing in both cheeks. "My mom and dad kidnapped the tykes and are taking them to a movie, then to a pizza place. Of course I warned Mom that four hours with them would age her ten years, but she was willing to risk it."

"Grandmothers are the bravest of the brave," I said.

"So," Dotty said, obviously bored with chitchat. "Why are you in town?"

Our waiter, a young African-American man who looked as if

he pumped iron, appeared at our table and handed the menus around. He then stood poised with the order pad and pen in his hands.

Pete met the young man's eyes. "Would you give us about five minutes?" he asked.

The waiter smiled in Pete's direction and sauntered away.

"Stu Farrar, has embezzled more than two million dollars from the firm," I told them.

I saw no reason not to tell Dotty and Pete. Dotty had been working as an accountant with another firm for three months by then. Dale Parsigian had become one of her clients, as had three other of my former clients who were professional athletes.

"I never liked him," Dotty said, as if her opinion of Stu had been confirmed. "He was always ordering me around."

"He was your boss," Pete pointed out.

I knew what Dotty meant. The preferred employer issued orders in such a way that she made them sound like requests. Stu enjoyed throwing his weight around. He trampled on other people's feelings, oftentimes belittling them.

"She's right," I told Pete. "Nobody that I know liked working for him."

"See!" Dotty said, cocking her head toward her husband, undoubtedly feeling vindicated.

She turned to look at me. "Where do *you* come in?"

I told her and Pete what Garrett and I had been up to the previous night, and how we'd discovered nothing about Stu except that he kept an appointment every Wednesday afternoon with someone, or something, whose initials were VS.

The waiter returned, we placed our orders and after he'd left, we resumed our conversation.

"There could be something to that," Dotty said. "Stu was usually gone home for the day by 2:45 in the afternoon every Wednesday. He worked until around six every other day. But, Wednesday? He was out of there, his gym bag in his fat little hand. A smile on his greasy lips."

"You really *didn't* like him, did you?" Pete commented dryly, smiling at his wife.

Dotty ignored him. "He definitely wasn't going to a gym," she concluded.

"Sounds like he was having an affair," Pete said.

Dotty and I gave each other knowing looks and said, "Yuck!" in unison.

"What woman in her right mind would lay down with him?" I wondered aloud.

"His wife did it for years," Pete put in.

"She isn't *in* her right mind," Dotty informed him without cracking a smile. "She used to come to the office ranting and raving about that dog of theirs. The meanest Chihuahua from south of the border. He'd be in her arms, baring his sharp little teeth at me, looking smug. I wanted to throw her *and* her dog out on their butts. But I'd smile and buzz Stu's office and tell him they were there. He always made them wait until he was good and ready to see them."

"Then his nutty wife drove him into the arms of another woman," Pete said.

Dotty cast him a sour glance. "Why is the wife always blamed?"

"You just said . . ."

"Stu was twice as nutty as she was. She was just a lonely, middle-aged woman trying to find happiness. All of her kids were out of the house. She showered her love on the mutt, because Stu was obviously ignoring her. She might need therapy, but Stu needs a personality transplant," Dotty said hotly.

"Children," I said, breaking it up. "The differences between men and women will remain a mystery long after we're all dead. Shall we get back to the problem at hand? Who, or what is VS?"

"Some hoochy momma," Dotty guessed.

"Maybe, and maybe not," Pete said cautiously. "When a man has a flamboyant woman at home, as you describe Mrs. Farrar, he might go for something more refined when he steps out."

Dotty stared at her husband, the expression in her beautiful dark, almond-shaped eyes changing from irritation to admiration.

When she grinned, I knew that something pertinent had dawned on her.

"Oh my," she said. "That's it."

"What?" I asked, wishing she'd speak up.

"About a week before I left the firm, a woman came in. She was a tall, elegant brunette in her late forties, or it appeared so. She might have been older. She reeked of money and class. Not the kind you buy, the kind you're born with. She was 'old money,' I know it. Anyway, she stood there in a Christian Dior suit, diamonds on her fingers and in her earlobes. Expensive perfume wafting off her. Then she opened her mouth and asked for Stu. I almost went *splat!* What would Stuart Farrar be doing with a dame like that? I buzzed Stu's office though, and he said to send her right in. I looked up at her and said, 'You can go straight back, Ms. . . .' And she immediately replied, 'Snyder. Thank you, dear.' "

"That's the *S,* " I cried. "You didn't get her first name, huh?"

Dotty nodded regrettably. "No. Sorry."

After we'd eaten, Dotty and I excused ourselves to go freshen up. Once we were in the ladies' room, she grasped me by the arm, turning me around to face her. "I've been dying to ask," she said. "Have you and Jackson done the horizontal mambo yet?"

Laughing, I told her, "We've decided to wait until after the wedding."

"How do you manage?" she asked seriously.

"Wet dreams and cold showers."

"The old standbys," she said knowingly.

Following lunch and that enlightening conversation with Dotty and Pete, I hailed a cab and went back to my hotel.

I was tempted to phone Garrett at the office and tell him what I'd learned from Dotty. However I couldn't chance it. What if Monte was strolling past the reception desk when Janet answered the phone and inadvertently heard her say my name?

After he was done cringing at the mention of my name, his active brain cells would kick in and then he'd start putting two and two together. I had yet to figure out why he'd brought

Garrett's attention to Stu's computer screen the day of Stu's heart attack.

Had he and Stu been arguing just before Stu collapsed?

It was a possibility that Stu had used Monte, and having completed the theft, Monte was no longer of any use to him.

Stu was a braggart. He could have pulled up the information on the screen to demonstrate to Monte how rich, and therefore, powerful he was now. His body, however, had conspired against him.

In the middle of his gloating, he'd clutched his chest and fallen to the floor, while his young, robust nephew looked down upon his stricken face, claiming revenge without having to lift a finger against his uncle.

Monte could have then suggested to Garrett that he clear the screen because he knew Garrett would read what was on the screen before deleting the information. Therefore Monte would have accomplished two things: He would have implicated his uncle in the theft of the firm's funds; and he, himself, would've appeared to have been seeking to ingratiate himself with Garrett. Which, as it turned out, was Garrett's interpretation of the young accountant's behavior.

There could be other reasons Monte reacted the way he did. Among them: Foreseeing that Garrett would notice the information on the screen without *his* hints or assistance, he needed Garrett to believe in his innocence. So he'd been the one to point Garrett to the info. Then, too, and this one got my vote: Monte might have tried and failed to get his hands on the money. Seeing no way to do so, he'd reluctantly given away his uncle's plot to sink the firm.

That also meant he could still be trying to break Stu's code at the same time Garrett and I were. I made a mental note to mention the possibility to Garrett when I met him at the office later that evening.

In the interim, I wondered about the woman Dotty said had visited Stu at the office. The night before, Garrett informed me that when he and Stu were at Loyola, Stu had been quite taken with a woman named Valerie.

At that point in the evening, Garrett hadn't run across the

entries in Stu's appointment book; therefore we hadn't associated the Valerie Stu had been infatuated with in college with the VS in his 1999 appointment book. Could they be connected?

Garrett had been meeting with his lawyers all day to find out what sort of legal recourse, if any, he would have if we weren't able to retrieve the stolen funds.

Consequently, when he wasn't on time, and I had spent more than half an hour alone in Stu's office testing my theory about the Snyder woman, and coming up with zilch, I decided to try his cell phone number.

He answered immediately.

"Garrett," I said, "Cheyenne here. What's the holdup?"

"Stu died tonight, Cheyenne," he whispered into the mouthpiece.

I heard voices in the background. He wasn't alone.

"I'm going to step outside for a minute," I overheard him tell someone. Then he continued in a clearer voice. "Cheyenne, listen, I want you to leave the office at once. The nurse who was on duty when Stu died said that he was visited by a young white male with dark hair and olive coloring minutes before they found Stu with a pillow over his face. I believe Monte asphyxiated Stu; and if he was desperate enough to do that, there's no telling what else he's capable of."

"He knows the code," I said, my voice breaking.

"I think it's safe to assume he does," Garrett readily agreed. "It's over, Cheyenne. Get out of there. I've already called the police and they're supposed to be watching the building in case Monte shows up there. But, I don't trust that; get out now."

I was walking toward the exit as he was speaking. I grabbed my bag from the hat tree by the door and opened the door. That was when I heard the unmistakable sound of the elevator doors sliding open, and I froze in my tracks. Ducking back inside Stu's office, I quietly closed and locked the door.

"Someone's getting off the elevator," I whispered into the receiver. A chill came over my body.

"Hide, Cheyenne. Don't let him see you. I'm on the way,"

Garrett cried. I heard his heavy footfalls as he ran for the nearest exit.

I switched off the overhead light and hurried to Stu's desk to turn off the gooseneck lamp sitting upon it. I then crouched behind the desk and tried to will my rapidly beating heart to slow down.

"Cheyenne, I'm still here," I heard Garrett's concerned voice say. I'd taken my cell phone from my ear, holding it in my trembling left hand. I brought it back to my ear.

"I turned off the lights and hid behind Stu's desk," I told him.

"All right, I'll tell the cops that's where you are. Keep talking to me. Do you hear anything else?"

"No, not yet."

"I'm sorry I got you involved in this, Cheyenne. I should have left you at peace in Montana," Garrett said breathlessly.

"Shut up, Garrett. They always say that kind of sentimental crap to the character who gets killed in the horror film. Just get your apologetic butt over here and rescue me."

It occurred to me, as I huddled next to Stu's desk, that if the intruder was Monte, he would've come directly to Stu's office. What was keeping him? He had the code. All he had to do now was use it to transfer the money from Stu's accounts in the Cayman Islands to his own account. He had his choice of any number of world capitals. If he'd done any planning ahead at all, he'd already opened an account in a foreign bank somewhere. The transference of the funds would take less than five minutes on Stu's terminal, less on more up-to-date models.

I got the answer to my query when I heard the sound of breaking glass several doors down.

For an instant, my fears lessened somewhat. Maybe it was just vandals who'd sneaked past the security guard in order to have some destructive fun. After a few minutes of unbridled violence, perpetrated against the office equipment, they'd leave before the police arrived to haul them off to jail.

Or so I hoped.

The cacophony ended after three minutes, not time enough to trash the entire floor. They couldn't have ransacked more than one office in that length of time.

The ensuing silence was more frightening than the sound of breaking glass had been. I held my breath, then remembered to breathe, and heard myself sigh. Someone rattled the doorknob. I sucked in air. Whomever was on the other side of the door then tried to kick it in with no result. He hurled guttural expletives at the door.

I didn't recognize the voice as Monte's, but then I'd never witnessed him having an angry altercation with a door.

I put the phone back to my ear to determine if I could still hear Garrett coming to the rescue. He must have accidentally hit the disconnect button because all I got was a dial tone.

I pressed the end call button on my phone and reached up to grab Stu's desk phone, pulling it onto the floor. I dialed 911.

The dispatcher picked up on the second ring. "State your emergency, please."

"I'm trapped in an office building by a homicidal maniac. He's pounding on the door. I don't believe it's going to hold up much longer."

"My name is Lynn. I have someone on the way to you now, miss. Stay on the line."

"I'm not going anywhere, Lynn."

"Do you have anything with you that you can protect yourself with?"

"I don't have a weapon, if that's what you mean."

"Do you have your purse handy?"

"I'm holding it right now."

"You got any hair spray or breath spray? Any kind of chemical you can shoot into his eyes?"

I had a small bottle of spray cologne in my purse. I pulled it out and held it at the ready. "I'm packing cologne," I told the dispatcher.

"Good. If he gets in, the moment he lunges toward you, let him have it, then kick him and run. Got that?"

"Is that standard police advice for a woman who's about to be assaulted?" I asked, using humor to calm my frayed nerves.

Lynn laughed. "No. Just trying to keep you lucid and alert."

I nearly gave myself away by screaming in panic when a swivel chair came flying through the sheet of glass in the upper part of the door. Tiny shards of glass momentarily made a sparkling trail in the electrified air. Thinking some might get in my eyes, I shut them tightly and huddled closer to the desk.

The chair skidded across the floor and came to a stop against the front of the desk.

"That doesn't sound good," I heard Lynn say. "Get your spray ready."

Hearing the doorknob jiggle and then the sound of the door creaking open, I knew he was inside the room.

Still crouched behind the desk, I had the phone in one hand and the bottle of cologne in the other, my finger poised on the nozzle.

He was breathing hard from the exertion. I strained to hear his every movement. I wanted to be ready to jump up and spray him in the eyes if I heard him approaching my side of the desk.

"Locked doors." I recognized Monte's voice that time. "Why lock each office, when you have security downstairs?"

It was the insane blathering of someone uncomfortable with his inner thoughts. Was he going over the edge, or had he already gone? If Garrett was right, and he'd smothered Stu with a pillow, then he had nothing left to lose.

"You had to have it all, didn't you? You got my hands dirty, and then rubbed my nose in it, too. Selfish Uncle Stu, you were a snake. Slime. Pond scum. What I should have done was tell Aunt Dolores about your classy number on the side. Then *she* would have had the pleasure of snuffing your miserable life out. That's what I should have done."

Then, to my amazement, he began to weep, making convulsive choking sounds. I wondered if he was experiencing guilt after killing his uncle, or if the crying was a form of stress release. After he'd let off some steam, he would think more clearly, then get on with his plans.

He stomped around the room, the soles of his shoes making crunching noises due to the broken glass littering the floor.

"My life is ruined because of you. I've got to leave the country and, possibly, never see my family again because of you. I should never have let you lure me here with your empty promises:

'Come work for me, Monte, and you'll be a rich man inside of five years.' I trusted you. I believed in you!"

He swept everything off the desktop in a fit of rage, and as he was bending down, he saw me. His brown eyes widened and his mouth hung open in surprise and shock. I'm sure he never expected to see me again, let alone at that moment.

I took advantage of his surprise and my right hand came up and I pressed the nozzle down. A stream of cologne shot out of the nozzle, into his eyes and he screamed.

I leaped to my feet and across the desk, shoving him out of the way as I did so.

He growled like an angry bear encountering an interloper in his den and lunged after me, catching me around the waist and we both fell to the floor. I felt a piece of glass penetrate the upper part of my left thigh and I cried out in pain.

Monte's hands were climbing up my body trying to gain purchase.

I was wriggling so ferociously, it must have been like trying to hold on to an eel.

He was grunting and wheezing with the effort, his eyes partially closed, and I was clawing my way toward the door.

"You got away from me before," he said menacingly. "You won't get away this time."

Using his powerful thigh muscles, he caught me and held me. I lay on my stomach, snuffling. Nicks and cuts covered my face and body and whenever he applied pressure with his thighs, I gasped for breath. "Sweet Cheyenne. Don't struggle," he said softly. "I won't hurt you if you don't make me. This is poetic justice, don't you think?" Leaning closer, he asked, "What are you doing here? Garrett beg you to come help him save his precious firm? Is that it?" He laughed. "Did he think you could figure out Uncle Stu's code?"

"I did figure it out," I said. I was buying time. Garrett had to be there shortly. My frightened mind would accept no other scenario. I *would* survive this horrific night.

"Impossible. You don't know Uncle Stu well enough. Nobody here knew him. You would have had to live in his world to know him, and I did. His own wife didn't know he went to Victoria's

Secret every Wednesday afternoon and bought his lover something alluring to stoke the old sexual fires. Nobody knew that except he, his lover . . ."

"The mysterious Ms. Snyder?" I asked.

He squeezed me tighter. "How did you know that?"

"You're hurting me. . . ."

He wanted to hear my explanation badly enough to let up on the pressure. I took great gulps of air before continuing.

"She came to the office once when I was working here. She isn't easy to forget. After Garrett called me, I remembered her. It took me a while to track her down, but I found her. When I located her, she was in the mood to talk. She was very upset over Stu's condition. They're supposed to go away together."

"That'll never happen now," Monte said smugly.

"What do you mean?" I asked, feigning ignorance.

"Uncle Stu drew his last breath about two hours ago," he stated matter of factly.

"What happened?"

"He stopped breathing. What's the difference? He's dead," Monte replied. "Shall we get on with this? I've never been much of a talker before or afterward. So don't expect me to cuddle later."

With that, he ripped my blouse up the back, exposing the camisole underneath. I screamed, and he shoved my face hard into the floor.

"I don't want to have to tell you again, Cheyenne. Be quiet, or I'll beat you into submission."

"And I don't want to have to tell you twice, mister. Get up off the woman *now,*" a male voice said authoritatively from the doorway.

I couldn't turn my head, so I didn't know whether the man was one of the security guards, or a Chicago policeman. The voice certainly wasn't Garrett's.

Monte slowly rose and stepped across my body. I went to get up and winced in pain. My face, hands, the fronts of my legs and thighs all had pieces of glass embedded in them.

Two uniformed officers quickly came forward and each of

them took an arm, pulling me to my feet, and out of the room into the hallway.

After the semidarkened office, the lights in the hallway were glaring; or maybe I was suffering from shock and the intensity of the lights had become heightened to me. I wasn't certain.

Garrett appeared in front of me and put his arms around my battered body, taking me off the hands of the policemen.

I collapsed into his arms.

He walked-carried me to the office next door where he sat me down on a couch. His shirtfront was covered with my blood. "The paramedics are on the way," he said soothingly.

"I've got the code," I told him.

"That isn't important right now," he said earnestly. He gingerly held my abraded hands, looking down at the pinpoints of blood in the palms. He sighed, his brown eyes were regretful. "I'm so sorry, Cheyenne. I'd understand if you aren't able to forgive me for bringing you into this crazy mess. I should have handled it on my own. I should have just let the business go down the drain."

It was funny, but as he was speaking, I was thinking of one of the Josie stories Slim loved to tell us. It went like this: Once when Jacob was off checking his traps, a couple of men happened by and seeing Josie alone with a toddler and an infant, assumed she was helpless. One of them held her down, while the other pulled her skirt up. When he did that, the assailant spied the knife Josie kept strapped to her inner thigh. Taking advantage of his surprise, she grabbed the knife and cut him good on the belly. Panicked, believing he was bleeding to death, the first man stumbled toward the door. Seeing what was unfolding before him, the man who'd been holding her down, released her and ran to get the rifle he'd confidently left propped against the doorjamb earlier.

Josie threw the knife and pierced him in the back. He expired on her cabin floor.

The other man's body was found in the woods the next day.

I don't know if half of Slim's stories about Josie were true, or not. At that instance, however, thinking of my brave ancestor kept me from falling to pieces.

I actually smiled at Garrett. "Do you suppose someone could get me a sandwich? I haven't had a bite to eat in hours."

"I'll cook you a gourmet meal," Garrett promised. "Just let the paramedics check you out first."

Assisted by Garrett, I walked out of the building. We were greeted by the flash of newspaper photographers' cameras and the glare of lights attached to television cameras, as well.

I kept my head lowered and my eyes on the steps we were descending.

"Who called *them?*" Garrett grumbled about the reporters and their support crews.

"They have their ways," I said just as a male TV reporter shoved a microphone in my face and demanded, "Talk to us! You're the victim in this drama. Can you tell us what happened? Is it true that the assailant, Monte Pepper, killed his uncle only minutes before he tried to harm *you?*"

The lights were so bright, I couldn't make out the reporter's face. I saw only a flash of teeth, a dark suit and a white shirt underneath.

"No comment," I said, and turned away. My bulldog of an ex-boss placed his body between mine and the reporter's.

"You heard her," he said forcefully. "Get your story else-where."

That wasn't the end of it, however. There were three other reporters who had to give it a shot. Garrett and I wound up racing down the remaining steps to his waiting Lexus, and speeding away.

I looked back at the news vans lined along South Wacker Drive and recognized a logo on one of them. The van was owned by a national network that my family watched on a regular basis.

I hadn't been concerned about them seeing news footage about the story on any of the local affiliates. However, there was a real possibility Momma or Clancy was watching WGN that night.

I told Garrett about my fears.

"You'd better phone them and tell them what happened, before they hear it from another source," Garrett said.

He pulled away from the curb and into traffic, heading downtown to my hotel. As it turned out, I had only one cut that needed stitches: the gash on my left thigh. The rest of the wounds were superficial and required the removal of glass fragments, followed by cleansing and disinfecting.

I was told to go soak in a tub and get some rest. If I had any pain, I was to take aspirin or Tylenol. Their suggestions were satisfactory with me. I didn't want to go to a hospital and, besides, I felt much better once I saw Monte being led away in handcuffs.

The detective in charge had taken my statement on the spot and informed me that I could be called to testify when Monte's trial was scheduled. I gave him my number and address in Montana and told him he could reach me there. I was leaving town as soon as possible.

In my hotel room, Garrett made me sit down on the couch and he put pillows behind me. "You relax," he said, as he walked over to the phone on the desk and picked up the receiver. "What would you like from room service?"

"A turkey sandwich and a bowl of vegetable soup, please."

He briefly spoke into the receiver and then hung up. "I ordered you a glass of white wine, too. It'll help you relax."

He brought the phone to me. "Here, call your folks."

I accepted the phone, but didn't dial right away. Looking up at him, I said, "Go home, Garrett. Your wife must be worried sick about you."

"I'm not going anywhere until I know you're all right," he adamantly refused.

I laughed. "Well what are you going to do for me, personally put me in the tub? I'll be fine, Garrett. Monte's behind bars. You have the code. Go home to your family."

I had persuaded him to go try the code: VICSEC, an abbreviated version of Victoria's Secret, while the paramedics were patching me up. He had returned a few minutes later with a triumphant expression in his formerly woebegone eyes. It had worked. He had his company back.

"I'll leave if you promise to call me if you need anything during the night. Anything! Do you promise?"

"I do," I assured him, rolling my eyes.

"Okay then," he agreed. He came to me and gently kissed my forehead. "Good night, Cheyenne. I'll see you in the morning."

Alone, I got up to go into the bathroom to assess the damage to my person. I had sore spots on my face where pieces of glass had been embedded, in the palms of my hands, in my back where Monte had sat in his attempt to hold me down. Compared to that pain, the discomfort from the gash in my thigh was barely noticeable.

I switched on the light over the sink and grimaced at my reflection. There were scratches on my forehead, both cheeks, and my chin. Some were from a quarter inch to half an inch in length; one on my right cheek was an inch long or better, and was an angry red color. Monte must have scratched me. I was sure I'd gotten him good a few times.

My curly black hair had bits of debris in it. I reached up and plucked them out. Tiny pieces of paper, lint, wood shavings. We must have knocked over the wastebasket when we were rolling around on the floor. I couldn't recall that happening, either.

I touched my face. I was pretty certain the scratches would heal without leaving permanent scars. I'd gotten worse scratches than those in school yard fracases.

Satisfied that my face had survived the ordeal, I began to peel off my clothes, what was left of them. Since Monte had ripped my blouse, I'd surrendered it to the police as physical evidence.

So I pulled off my jacket and camisole, then undid my button-fly jeans. The kind paramedic who'd bandaged the wound on my thigh had cut the left leg of the jeans nearly all the way up to my crotch. They were a total loss.

I pulled them off and dropped them into the wastebasket next to the toilet. Then I sat on the edge of the tub and removed my leather boots. They were scuffed and the soles had pieces of glass stuck in them, but leather could take a beating. It gave it character.

In my underwear, I walked back to the outer room and sat down on the couch. I felt I could talk to my mother now without sounding too emotional.

I dialed the number, pulled my feet up and stretched out on the sofa.

Momma answered on the third ring.

"Cheyenne, that had better be you."

"Are you psychic?"

"Caller ID, dear. Where have you been all day, and night? It's ten o'clock here, so it's eleven there. I've been worried."

"Momma, remember when I was preparing to leave for Chicago and you asked if it could be dangerous?"

Half an hour later, after I'd been through the whole story with her and assured her that I was all right more than once, she said, "Well that's it for you, young lady. When you get back to Montana, you're grounded."

Thinking she was joking, I laughed. "Momma, I'm twenty-seven."

"I don't care how old you are. I'm still your mother. And I'm angry with you, Cheyenne Josephine. You jumped into a situation without thinking it through. You didn't show sound judgment."

"But I had no way of knowing this could be dangerous," I said in my defense.

"A man embezzles two million dollars and you don't believe some type of evil is at work there? Now Stuart Farrar is dead, you're beaten and battered. But Garrett Streiber has his business back. All's well that ends well? I think not. It's going to take me a while to get over this, so I'm going to say good night now. Go to bed. And you be on a plane for home tomorrow, you hear me?"

Sighing, I said, "All right, Momma. Good night."

It was then that the impact of the consequences of my actions hit me like a ton of bricks. Momma had been right. I hadn't thought before jumping in with both feet. I'd heard the note of desperation in Garrett's voice and had gotten the next plane to Chicago.

Why? Because I felt guilty for not having warned Garrett about my suspicions concerning Stu.

There was a knock at the door. I walked over to it. "Who's there?"

"Room service, madame."

"One moment."

I went to get my robe from the bedroom and put it on. Going

back to the outer room, I looked through the peephole before opening the door.

The young woman carried the tray inside. "Where would you like it, miss?"

"I'll take it, thanks."

I took the tray and when I had it balanced on my left arm, I handed her a generous tip.

I closed and locked the door behind her then went to set the tray on the coffee table in front of the couch.

Picking up the remote from the table, I switched on the television set.

I turned to WGN to see if they'd gotten the Streiber and Farrar story on the late edition of their newscast.

To my relief, the only film clip they showed was of Monte being put into a police car, the policeman assisting him holding his head down so that he wouldn't bump it. Monte had been smiling for the cameras. In court, the prosecuting attorney would probably make a point of running that tape to demonstrate Monte's lack of remorse for his crimes.

I consumed the soup and sandwich and drank the wine, after which I soaked in the tub until I got drowsy.

As I was drying off, my cellular phone rang. I dropped the towel I'd been using and ran, naked, into the next room where I'd left my purse. Opening my bag I grabbed the phone, flipped it open and cried, "Jackson?"

"I love you, Cheyenne. I'm telling you right now, because I got cut off before I could tell you last time."

"You don't know how much that means to me. . . ."

"What's wrong, Chey?"

"Jackson, I've done something really stupid. . . ."

FOURTEEN

"You gave me the impression you were there to do a little computer work," Jackson said after I'd told him what had happened. I slipped into my robe, the phone held at my ear by a bit of shoulder action, as he said this. Finished, I paced back and forth in the sitting room.

"Believe me, Jackson. If I'd known Monte was going to go ballistic, I never would have gotten on that plane."

Jackson sighed. "Are you really all right?"

"I'm fine," I said, my voice husky.

"I'm not going to berate you over the phone, Chey. But, when I see you, I don't know how I'll react. If I'm as mad as I am right now, I'm liable to put you over my knee and spank your bottom."

"That might be . . . interesting."

He laughed in spite of his irritation. "I don't know what I'm going to do with you." The sensual tone in his voice, however, indicated he had a few ideas. "I adore you. And, then again, sometimes I'd like to throttle you."

"It's still safe to love me. It isn't as if I'm going to be sleuthing every day of our lives together," I said jokingly.

"You're *never* going to do it again," Jackson emphatically stated. "I'd like to hear you say that, Chey."

"You don't have to worry, Jackson. I'll behave myself. All I want now is to go home and be surrounded by the people I love."

"You voiced similar sentiments three months ago when you told me you wanted to get married and have babies. Then you went running back to Chicago when your ex-boss phoned. Are you sure you aren't going to take off again when boredom strikes?"

"Are you saying I was bored with home, and that's why I didn't hesitate when Garrett phoned?"

"You *have* been out there for ten years, Chey. That way of life gets in the blood."

Blowing air between my lips, I said, *"You* are the only thing in my blood, Jackson. If you're so afraid I might leave you, then marry me and get me pregnant. Put up or shut up."

Laughing, Jackson replied, "We aren't getting married until I'm convinced that you'll be content living on the ranch."

"So this little stunt has set me back a notch or two, huh?" I asked.

"I'm not keeping score, Chey. But, your actions have made me wonder if you're going to be happy with my boring way of life."

"You don't know me as well as you think you do if you believe that of me, Jackson."

"That's just it, Chey. We don't know each other well. We're familiar with the outer persons, but neither of us really knows what motivates the other."

"All you have to do to know me is to pay attention to how I've lived the last twenty-seven years. Sure, I've been a city girl, but my heart was always back home. When my family needed me, I was there for them. Haven't I spent the last three months trying to make certain that their business gets launched properly? You do know me, Jackson. You're simply not ready to let down your guard yet. Somewhere in the back of your mind, you believe I'll use you and toss you aside if something better comes along. But that isn't me. I'm loyal to the people I love. . . ."

"This isn't my insecurity speaking now, Chey: I could wring your neck for putting your life in jeopardy. When you blithely do something like that, you're disregarding all the people who care about you. It isn't just your life anymore, it's mine, too."

"I know, Jackson," I said, my voice breaking.

"Do you truly know?" he asked softly. "I've invested my heart, my soul in you, girl. They're in your hands, and if something should happen to you, I don't think I'd ever be able to put myself back together again."

My body had gone weak, and I sat down on the couch, reclining on the pillows Garrett had propped behind me earlier.

Tears trickled down my face into my mouth.

"Jackson, do you know what you do to me when you talk like that?"

"If it's anything like the way I feel at the sound of your voice, I'd say it's a pleasurable sensation," he said, his tone devoid of anger now. "I've got to go, baby. I'll be home in three days' time."

"I'll be waiting," I assured him.

"Take care of my body."

"Take care of mine," I returned. "I love you."

"I love you."

And with that, our connection was severed. I sat there a long while, smiling through my tears.

Saturday morning, I awakened, went to get out of bed and thought better of it. I was sore all over. Every place where Monte had mauled me ached.

I swung my legs down anyway, though, and rose. A hot shower and a couple of aspirin would work miracles. I baby-walked to the bathroom where I turned on the water full blast.

Stripping out of my gown, I let it fall to the floor, then I stepped under the spray of water, closed my eyes and let it rain down over my head. Reaching for the loofah and liquid soap, I lathered, vigorously massaging my sore muscles as I did so.

It felt so good, after a while, that I stood there for nearly half an hour until the water started getting tepid, at which time I got out and toweled off.

Feeling almost whole again, I decided to forego the aspirin until after breakfast. I got on the phone and ordered a large breakfast, then went into the walk-in closet to get something to put on. I didn't have a great selection to choose from. I'd brought two pairs of jeans. One pair was totaled. That left the powder-blue pair with the button-fly. A navy cardigan with a short-sleeved shell went nicely with the jeans, and my leather boots, once I'd dug the glass out of the soles, completed the outfit.

Someone knocked on the door a few minutes after I'd finished dressing. Thinking it was room service, I hurried to the door, my stomach growling. Looking through the peephole, I grimaced. It was Garrett. I hoped he wasn't there to check up on me as he'd promised to do last night. Gratitude was one thing, but as far as I was concerned, we were even. My guilt was eradicated, and he had his business back.

I opened the door and was surprised to see he wasn't alone. His wife, Denise, a plump, petite blonde in her late forties, was with him.

"I hope we aren't too early," he said. "Denise and I were concerned that you might not have been able to sleep, what with the beating you took last night."

They came into the room. They were both dressed casually. Garrett in a bulky sweater and jeans beneath his overcoat and Denise in a wool blazer in mocha over a mock turtleneck sweater in the same shade with a pair of off-white trousers.

I knew Denise from various office parties and, three or four times a year, I'd been invited to their home for dinner. She'd always been a kind, solicitous hostess.

She came forward and gave me a warm hug, which wasn't too firm, thank God. "She's up and about, Garrett. So we can't be disturbing her too much." Smiling up at me, she said, "I had to come to personally tell you how much we appreciate your help, Cheyenne. And also to say how sorry I am about what happened to you last night. I don't think any of us would have suspected Stu of embezzlement, or Monte Pepper capable of murder. My head is *still* spinning."

"Yours isn't the only one," I told her, returning her smile. "Please. Have a seat."

We walked over to the seating group, where Garrett sat on the chair facing the sofa and Denise and I sat on the sofa.

"Denise and I have talked about it and we have a proposition for you, Cheyenne. Now, you don't need to answer at once. Take your time. But, we were wondering if you'd consider becoming my partner in the firm. We'd split the profits down the middle. I'm not a greedy man, I just want to make certain the business is run in the right way, and I'd like to relax and not have to be watching my back every minute. I know I can trust you. So the arrangement would be ideal for me."

I was sore, hungry and ready to be on a plane back to Montana, so I wasn't in the best of moods. Plus, there was something Daddy had once told me about working for someone. He'd said that when you worked for someone other than yourself, that person sometimes came to believe he owned you. That your time, your life, your very being belonged to them.

The Streibers were beaming at me; their cheeks rosy from the frosty weather outside; their brown eyes shining in expectation of a positive reply. I almost hated to turn them down.

"But it wouldn't be ideal for me, Garrett," I said, trying to keep the friendliness evident in my tone. I wanted to part with Garrett on good terms. I'd always liked him. He'd been more than fair with me on my severance agreement. I felt no animosity toward him. It just rankled that he wasn't sensitive enough to my needs to inquire about my plans before putting his offer on the table.

And, hedging my bets wasn't important to me any longer. I was positive Jackson loved me; therefore, I didn't need a backup plan in case he refused to marry me. I *was* going to become Mrs. Jackson Kincaid one day, sooner or later.

While Garrett looked surprised, and Denise painted a smile on her attractive face, I explained: "You see, when I left the firm I had no plans of ever returning. Montana's where I want to be for the rest of my life. And even though your offer is very generous, I couldn't accept." I'd been looking at Garrett. I turned my gaze on Denise now. "There's a man."

Denise jerked as if startled by that revelation. Her smile broadened. "You don't have to say more. I understand." Looking into her husband's eyes, she said, "Try to remember how it was when you and I fell in love, Garrett. You would've moved heaven and earth to be with me."

She returned her eyes to mine. "I'm happy for you, Cheyenne. Being in love . . ." she said wistfully, "is worth any sacrifice."

"Yes!" Garrett agreed enthusiastically. He appeared to have just awakened from a mental stupor. I suppose it had finally dawned on him that I was serious about turning down his offer.

However, since he was also a practical businessman, he added, "If things don't work out, though, you will always have a place with us."

I smiled at him. "All right, Garrett. Thank you."

They hastily rose to their feet then and Garrett placed his hand on the small of his wife's back, directing her to the door. "We're going to say so long, Cheyenne. I've already spoken with the person at the front desk and I've taken care of your bill. And, this is to say thanks." He withdrew an envelope from his coat pocket and gave it to me. I accepted it and opened it, peering inside. There was a check for ten thousand dollars inside.

I reached for his hand, placed the envelope in it and said, "This one was on me, Garrett. My guilt's assuaged. That's why I came. You've already been more than generous with me. Let's part as friends, shall we? Not as employee, employer."

"But . . ." Garrett began. He was so used to compensating those who did him a service.

"You can't always have your way, dear," Denise said, grasping her husband's hand. She paused to kiss me on the cheek. "It's been a pleasure, Cheyenne. You take care. And don't forget to send us an invitation to the wedding."

"I'll be sure to do that," I promised with a smile.

When I opened the door to see them out, I spotted the woman from room service approaching with my breakfast tray.

I waved good-bye to the Streibers and walked back inside to get a few bills from my purse to tip the food-service employee with. By the time I returned to the door, she'd arrived and I took the tray from her and handed her the gratuity.

After closing and locking the door, I crossed the room to the sitting area where I set the tray on the coffee table and lifted the silver food covers to reveal soft scrambled eggs, hash browns, toast, jam, orange juice and coffee.

I sat down and devoured it all.

I was able to get a 3:20 flight out of Chicago. Chad and Clancy met me at the airport in Billings.

Clancy merrily informed me that Momma was still angry

with me and that I should tread lightly for the next few days. We were rarely witnesses to Momma's fury and, frankly, didn't want to be.

Chad ran his eyes over me. "I'd hate to see the other guy if *you* look this bad."

"He's going where he can't harm anyone else," I said, handing him my bag. "Here, make yourself useful."

"That'd be a first," Clancy quipped. She put her arm about my waist. "I saw that guy on the news. The way he was grinning at the cameras, he looked out of his mind. His face was all scratched up and bleeding. So you must have given him a hard time."

She was smiling, but her dark-brown eyes held a serious expression in their depths. It brought home to me what Jackson had told me the night before: My actions affected everyone who cared about me. I'd learned my lesson. I wouldn't go off half-cocked again.

As we walked toward the exit, I put my arm about her waist and drew her close to my side. "You know I made a big mistake, right?"

Her eyes met mine. "Momma made that perfectly clear."

Chad had moved ahead of us, his long legs putting some distance between us. When he was several feet in advance of us, he turned and said, "Would you get the lead out? I've got a date tonight. I need time to get pretty."

"There ain't enough time in the world," Clancy said.

Momma's reception was as warm as ever. She took me in her arms and squeezed me tightly. Then she set me away from her, her golden-brown eyes encompassing my face and body. Shaking her head, she murmured. "And all these years, I thought you were the sensible one."

The disappointment in her voice hurt me. I figured I had it coming though. I would endure her chastisement.

Smiling down into her much-loved face, I said, "I've repented. Both you and Jackson have pointed out to me the selfishness of my behavior. I'm done defending myself." I raised both hands as in surrender. "I'm ready to take my punishment."

Momma laughed shortly and reached up to touch my cheek. "You look as if you've already been punished enough. But, I would like to make a suggestion."

"Anything."

"The next time someone calls and asks for your help with something, tell them you'll call them back the following day. You'd at least get to sleep on it before making a decision."

"All right, I'll do that."

We were in the foyer. Momma crooked a finger at me. "Come on back to the kitchen, I was peeling eggplant. You can wash up and help."

The next three days I spent putting finishing touches on the cabins. Chad, Lucas and Clancy were on Christmas vacation. They had most of December away from their studies.

When Chad and Lucas weren't doing chores around the ranch, they were with their girlfriends, whom we'd heard a lot about, but hadn't had the pleasure of meeting. Momma told them that if they dated a girl for more than two months, they were obligated to bring her home so that she could meet her. I don't believe my brothers had ever dated any one girl for more than a month. They had roving eyes.

At nineteen and twenty-one, I suppose I shouldn't expect more from them. Cole had been the same way until he met Enid, and after he saw her, he had eyes for no one else. I suspect Chad and Lucas would also be struck by love just as suddenly.

Clancy spent her free time dreaming of her imminent departure from Montana. Both she and her friend Laura Peterson were planning to attend college in Washington, DC: Clancy at Howard University and Laura, whose father had graduated from Georgetown, at his alma mater.

Slim was still riding the fence; only now, he was doing it from his seat in his truck. Every now and then, he'd go out and watch the horses running in the paddock with a sad longing in his eyes.

Momma often helped me in the cabins.

Three days after my return, she and I were in Cabin B sprucing up the bathroom. We'd chosen different color schemes for all four cabins. Cabin B was the blue cabin. So the tile on the wall of the shower was white, the tile on the floor, blue. The curtains hanging at the single window were blue. And the shower curtain was white, trimmed in blue.

There was a rattan étagère above the commode, which had shelves that would hold towels, linen and toiletries.

Momma was standing in the tub hanging the shower curtain while I was putting the étagère together. I'd already assembled a similar étagère for Cabin A, so my work was going relatively smoothly with the second one.

"Momma," I said, looking over at her, "are you growing fond of Harry Johnson?"

"I've been fond of Harry for years now, Chey. He was Cole's good friend. And over the years, he's become mine. Yes, I like Harry."

She was wearing her black hair with silver streaks, in a bun that day, and she had put an apron on over her tan sweater and brown slacks. I'd always thought of my mother as beautiful. Lately, she'd been radiant. I stood up to straighten one of the two poles on the étagère, stretching my lithe body until my sweater rode up, revealing my midriff. "I don't mean fond, Momma. I mean *fond*. As in, you'd actually consider dating him. Does Harry make you feel that way?"

She'd finished putting the last hook through the rings in the curtain. Smiling at me, her eyes alight with humor, she said, "Harry reminds me that I'm a woman, Cheyenne. There, I've said it. Since your father died, I've had many roles. I've been the mother, the dutiful daughter-in-law, the grieving widow. Cole and I loved each other so much . . . I still wake up in the middle of the night expecting him to be there. I feel his presence all through the day. You get into a certain routine when you've lived with a man a number of years; and when you continue to go about your day, after he's been taken from you, there's a gaping hole where he used to be."

"Love always comes with a price," she continued. "I like

Harry Johnson, but I'm not willing to risk my heart any longer, Chey. I've given all I have to give."

Listening to her, I had an epiphany. It all became clear to me. To have my father die in my arms, and then to witness my mother's suffering, all worked to build a shield around my heart. Neither Ahmad nor Tad ever had a chance at breaking through that barrier.

I'd seen the outcome of devotion: pain. I wanted no part of it. But, Jackson, the man whom I'd assumed I had a childish crush on, proved to be a bulwark, my protection. Consequently, because of who he was, the barrier came down. It astounded me that I could love him so completely, in spite of my fear of one day losing him.

"I can't possibly know how it feels to love someone for as long as you loved Daddy," I told her honestly. "And I would not dare presume to know what it feels like to open yourself up to more pain. But it makes me sad to hear you say you don't ever expect to love again. I don't believe Daddy would want you to be alone the rest of your life. You're a vital, beautiful, interesting, intelligent woman. And you deserve all the happiness in the world."

"It's good to know my daughter thinks that of me," Momma replied, her eyes misty. "And I *am* happy. I really have no complaints. But, as for Harry and me, it's just platonic. He knows my views on romance. He wants more, but I'm just not ready. I don't believe I ever will be. Your father was a hard act to follow."

She sighed. "How far we'll go with this relationship is yet to be seen. But, I'd really like to hit the dance floor with a willing partner one last time," she ended with a wistful smile.

She wasn't aware of it, but when she smiled, she looked luminous. And I figured if Harry's attention had done that for her, he'd been a positive influence on her.

"Does Harry dance?"

"Does he ever! I never told you Harry spent some time in Argentina when he was a young man. He swears he learned to tango from a lady of the evening who worked out of a dive in Buenos Aires."

"You'd better watch out. If Harry teaches you how to tango, you might just change your mind about him," I joked.

Momma laughed. "It's going to take more than a dance to change *my* mind."

She stepped out of the tub and walked past me, into the hallway of the cabin. Turning to look at me, she said, "Now that you've interrogated me about Harry, I have a few questions about Jackson."

I was in the process of straightening the poles on the étagère. This done, I met Momma's eyes. "Ask away."

"Just an observation, really. I know what passion is, Chey. I want to make sure you're taking care of yourself . . ."

I blinked. "You mean as in sex?"

Momma smiled slowly. "I've noticed the way Jackson looks at you. If he could, he'd devour you. And you? You are probably as hotblooded as I was at your age. That makes for a dangerous combination. Yes, I'm talking about sex."

I laughed. "You don't have to worry, because after I told Jackson I was a virgin, he insisted that we wait until we're married to get naked."

Momma was staring at me with an expression akin to awe in her eyes. She quickly drew me into her arms and hugged me to her ample bosom. "You *were* listening to me when I was talking to you."

Shortly after that, she went up to the main house to prepare lunch while I stayed behind to sweep and scrub the bathroom floor.

Alone, I thought about my comment to her concerning Jackson's and my pledge to wait until marriage to hit the sheets. I had to admit, I would have brazenly broken that pledge at the drop of a hat if he gave me one indication of acquiescence. Call me weak. Call me hot-to-trot. Call me a sin waiting to happen. But call me honest. I wanted him so badly, I could taste it.

My dreams about him had become ultra vivid. I'd begun to look forward to going to bed at night. Last night, following a chat with him during which he'd said he'd be home today, I'd gone to sleep and dreamed I was waiting in his house when he returned from Wyoming.

His housekeeper, Mrs. Anderson, had gone home for the day, and when I heard him coming into the house, I walked from the kitchen to the living room, wearing the negligee I'd described to him in the cab when we were leaving the Cattlemen's Association conference that day in Chicago. A diaphanous number that left little to the imagination.

I was scrubbing the floor with a mop as I recalled how sexy Jackson had been in my dream: He had a day's growth of beard, which gave his square-chinned face a roguish, bad-boy countenance.

In his boots, he was six feet, six inches tall. When he opened the door, he stood watching me. He then dropped his saddlebags on the foyer floor and crossed the room, his thigh muscles flexing beneath his Wrangler's. His denim shirt was open at the neck revealing a well-shaped clavicle. I longed to go to him and unbutton his shirt the rest of the way.

But I remained on my side of the room, willing him to come to me. When he did reach me, we embraced; my arms went around his neck and he lifted me off the floor. To my chagrin, I awakened at that juncture in the dream.

It had nonetheless been a pleasurable imaginary interlude and I awakened quite happy to have experienced it.

"They got you out here by yourself doing the Cinderella bit?"

I calmly, more calmly than I felt, propped the mop against the doorjamb and turned.

"A girl has to do what she has to until her prince comes along and takes her away from all this drudgery," I replied, my heart doing double-time.

The breadth of his shoulders blocked out the light coming in from the window behind him. His tan coat hung open, revealing a checked blue-and-tan shirt and Wrangler's. He held his tan Stetson in his hand, and he stood with his legs slightly apart, the tan boots he was wearing making him appear even taller than he was.

"You're early," I said as I slowly closed the space between us.

He smiled, revealing perfect teeth in his copper-colored face.

"Actually, I'm late. I *wanted* to be here sooner."

When I was within two feet of him, I stopped and peered up

at him. He was clean-shaven, and his curly hair was still damp from a shower. He had a habit of doing that, leaving the house with wet hair. I had to remind him that he could catch cold that way.

Jackson was watching me as intently. He moved closer and reached out, gently touching my cheek with his right hand. "They'll heal," he murmured softly, referring to the scratches on my face.

Something inside of me melted when he said that and I pressed my body into his. He wrapped his arms around me, the warmth and strength of his body caressing, enveloping me.

His chin was on the top of my head as my nose pressed against his chest, breathing in the intoxicating male scent of him.

Looking upward, he cried, "What's happening to me? I couldn't bear to be away from you another day."

"This isn't exactly how I planned our reunion," I told him, my eyes raking over his beloved face. "I wanted to be all dolled up for you."

He kissed my forehead. "You're beautiful, Chey . . ."

"I'm perspiring, my hair has spiderwebs in it and these jeans have seen better days."

"Your skin is glowing, your hair's sexy like that, and, baby, you make those jeans look good. Now be quiet and give your man a proper welcome."

Just as he bent his head to kiss me, I heard footsteps in the next room. Jackson did too, because he let go of me and took a step backward. Smiling ruefully, he said, "I'm going to have to wait a while for that kiss."

Clancy stuck her head through the entrance to the hallway. "Hey you guys, Momma asked me to tell you that lunch will be ready in ten minutes." She spun on her heels after delivering the message. "I'm leaving now. I promise not to double back and try to catch you kissing!"

Laughing, I said, "Tell Momma we'll be right in."

After Clancy had gone, Jackson turned to me, "I don't know about you, but I don't want to wait any longer to kiss you. I spent seven days and six nights under the Montana sky, remembering how you feel, how you taste; and, I want more than my memories to . . ."

I reached up, grabbed him by his coat's lapels and pulled him down to me. With my mouth about an inch from his, I admonished, "Shut up already!"

Jackson firmly pulled me against him and bent his head. His mouth tentatively brushed against mine. "I like it when you play rough," he whispered. Then our lips met and our mouths hungrily teased and tasted. With my eyes closed, I gave myself to him, allowing my emotions to dip, then soar with each tantalizing movement of his tongue inside my mouth.

If this was a preview of what sex was going to be like with him, then I was ready for the main event to begin.

His right hand cupped my breast, and, remembering his rules, I thought, *violation*. But, then *my* hands had moved downward to rest on his fabulously toned buns, so who was I to call foul?

In his slow circuit of my body, his hand paused on my left thigh and I knew he'd found the bandaged wound there. I reached down and took his hand, moving it upward to my breast again.

He moaned deep in his throat and pulled away. "What is that?"

"Just a cut I got when I was fighting off Monte Pepper," I said lightly. Kissing his chin, I murmured, "It's nothing, really."

I sensed the spell had been broken, however. In his warm, brown, thickly fringed eyes, I saw a flicker of sadness.

"It *is* something, Chey. It'll be a constant reminder of my inability to protect you."

Gaping at him, I said, "Come on, Jackson. I made a stupid error. It had nothing to do with you. It was my decision to go to Chicago. It was my decision to be there that night. You can't always protect the people you love. They have to be capable of looking out for themselves. I'm here. I'm safe and sound."

"But he could have . . ."

"He didn't though," I firmly reiterated.

He had his arms around my waist, the lower halves of our bodies were pressed together. I smiled up at him. "Your voice over the phone that night is what kept me from breaking down. I'd never been in a situation like that before. I mean while it was happening, the adrenaline rush must have served to buoy my strength. I would have fought him off all night, and I was confident I would've. But, when it was all over and I thought about what could have happened, and how it would have affected you and my family, I wanted to dissolve into nothingness. I'm sorry. I didn't think, Jackson. Can you forgive me?" I was fighting back tears when I finished. His eyes bored into mine.

"You've got to curtail those Josie tendencies of yours," he said, smiling. Over the years, he'd also heard the Josie stories from various members of the Roberts clan.

Taking him by the hand, I led him to the front door where I regarded him with keen eyes. "Jackson, there's something you should know about the Roberts women: We are loyal to our men, but you never can tell what we'll do next."

"Oh?" he said, tickling me beneath my rib cage.

I giggled, wriggled out of his hold and ran down the front steps. "Don't ever tickle me, Jackson. I hate that!"

He was right on my heels and caught me before my feet hit the lawn good. His smile was slow and wicked when he looked down into my upturned face. "Your days are numbered, Cheyenne Josephine."

I grinned at him. "Meaning?"

"Meaning I'm going to marry you and tie you down so you'll never go roaming again. I'm going to have you barefoot and pregnant year-round."

"Promises, promises," I cooed as I walked into his arms and kissed him long and hard once more before going on to the house.

The next day, I kept my word to Harry Johnson and went over to his place to go over his books.

I arrived at around ten, walked up onto the porch and knocked on the door. I admired the intricate stained-glass design in the top half of the door. Harry's house had many decorative touches. It was one of the oldest homes in the county. Victorian, it'd been built by Harry's father in 1920. The house sat on a hill among gnarled Ponderosa pines that were even older than the house itself.

Just as I was about to knock again, the door was flung open

and Harry's eldest daughter, Iris, pushed the screen door open, barely missing hitting me with it.

Harry followed close behind, a thunderous expression on his face.

Iris cut a glance at me, her blue eyes condescending. "What are *you* doing here?"

Iris was three years ahead of me in school, which placed her age at around thirty, I suppose. She wore her dirty-blond hair in a tousled chin-length cut. Mascara thickly covered her dark lashes and her mouth was a thin, red slash.

Her eyes were red-rimmed, either from crying or too little sleep; and her long, straight nose was also red. She held a crumpled tissue in her right hand.

I moved out of her way.

Harry smiled faintly in my general direction as he came out of the house. "Sorry about this," he said sheepishly.

"Don't apologize for me," Iris said, after hearing her father's words. She turned her angry gaze on Harry. "If you want to act like a fool over that woman, that's you. But they need to know that your family ain't pleased about it."

She stomped down the steps, heading for the dark sedan parked beside Harry's pickup in the yard.

The poisonous, spiteful tone of her voice raised my ire. I unconsciously took a step toward her. Harry placed a hand on my arm.

"She's not in her right mind, Cheyenne. She's been out all night with people she shouldn't be associating with. Her life's a mess and she's trying to make everyone around her miserable, too."

I hadn't smelled alcohol on her breath, even though the rest of her had been rank and stale smelling. I wondered if she could be on drugs.

Iris started the sedan and hit the accelerator; the tires of the car spit dirt and grass in her wake.

Sighing tiredly, Harry looked after her. "She hasn't been the same since the divorce. And now she's found out that Paul is getting remarried and his girlfriend's expecting. She's never had children, you know."

He turned back and held the door open for me. "Come on in, Cheyenne. That is, if you'll willing to help me after that little scene."

I looked into his eyes. "She might not be herself at this moment, Mr. Johnson . . ."

"Just call me Harry."

Looking into his eyes, it occurred to me that he and Momma had more in common than I'd initially thought. He'd lived through times when it was against the law for races to mix, just as Momma had. But it hadn't influenced him. He didn't care about a person's skin color. And he was just as stubborn as Momma was about sticking to his convictions. They were a pair.

Standing on Harry Johnson's front porch, staring into his faintly smiling face, I had a frightening revelation.

"You're in love with my mother, aren't you?"

"For quite some time now."

FIFTEEN

Apparently, while I was busy going over his books, Harry phoned Momma and told her what had transpired that morning. By the time I got back home, she was waiting for me.

The moment I walked through the back door, she placed the knife she'd been using to chop onions with on the cutting board, and wiped her hands on her apron.

I hung my coat on the hat tree next to the door and walked into the room, prepared to launch into my tale.

"Cheyenne, Harry phoned and told me what Iris said to you." She came to me and grasped me by the shoulders. "I don't want you getting into a fistfight with Harry's daughter. It won't solve anything."

"Iris Johnson is a hateful bigot. Somebody needs to set her straight."

"So, do you think a good whipping is going to change her attitude? Harry lived with his family's griping for years when he and Cole were friends. I believe he can handle his daughter," Momma said reasonably. "Her mother had some of the same views . . ."

"I always assumed Annie Johnson thought like her husband did," I naively said, my eyes on her face. "She was always nice to me. She would comment on how pretty my hair was, or my eyes. She made me feel as though she thought I was the cutest little girl in the world."

"A penny for a pickaninny," Momma said cynically.

She let go of me and went back to her task. "We were at a community picnic once and she sidled up to me: 'What does my

Harry see in that man of yours?' she asked. 'Decent folks won't
have anything to do with him because he insists on being friends
with *him.*' Then she cried, "Harry is a fool, we're never going to
get anywhere until he learns not to associate with you people.' I
told her as far as I was concerned, she could kiss my butt, my
husband's butt, all our children's, *and* our future grandchildren!"

"That's a lot of butt-kissing, Momma," I said, chuckling.

"After that, she and I didn't speak. I told Cole what she'd said,
and he just laughed. He already knew how she felt."

I stood next to her as I washed my hands at the sink. "I get it.
You're saying Iris takes after her mother."

"Just as their other two children, Deana and Harry, Jr., took
after their father in that respect. You can't control which way a
child will go. All you can do is try to set a good example. Then
too, Cheyenne: You need to develop a thicker skin. When someone says something that you interpret as prejudiced, you can't
let it get your goat every time. You're young. But the longer you
live in this world, you come to realize that most of the people
expressing those views are idiots anyway, and it isn't worth your
time and effort to refute what they say."

"All right," I agreed. She made sense. Iris Johnson wasn't my
problem. She was Harry's; and Harry seemed capable of dealing
with her without *my* aid.

Going to the refrigerator to get a carton of orange juice, I
asked, "Have you seen Slim since breakfast?"

"No. I believe he's upstairs in his apartment."

I poured a glass of juice and returned the carton to the refrigerator. "He's been pretty quiet lately."

Momma laughed shortly. "He's still a little sore over the doctor's orders."

I took a swig of the juice. It was tart, but sweet and icy-cold.
"I think I'll go up and see what he's up to."

"While you're up there, ask him if he remembered to take his
calcium this morning. He's always forgetting that."

I finished my drink and went to the faucet to rinse the glass
and place it in the sink.

Running up the back stairs, I wondered if Momma was aware
Harry was in love with her. They seemed to discuss everything;

surely he hadn't been remiss in sharing that bit of information with her.

Knowing Momma, she already knew without his having to tell her in words. She probably read it in his actions; in the way he looked at her. She undoubtedly recognized his devotion masquerading behind the prize tomatoes he delivered to her back door. She was perceptive that way.

I knocked on Slim's door. "Slim! I was wondering if you wanted to drive to Billings to check out the new year 2000 tractors at Beau Bradley's." Even if he didn't particularly feel up to company, the mention of his favorite pastime was sure to draw a reaction.

Nothing. Thinking he might be ill, he *was* eighty-five, after all, I turned the doorknob and strode into the apartment. Slim's sanctuary had a living room, a kitchenette (which held a stove, sink and a refrigerator), a bathroom and a bedroom. With a sweep of your eyes, you could cover the entire area. I went to his bedroom. His bed was neatly made. On his nightstand was a framed photograph of Grandma Penelope. She was wearing her wedding gown in the photo. Standing alone in the entrance of a whitewashed church. She'd been no more than nineteen. A petite brown-skinned child with an angelic face.

I picked up the photograph and peered down at it, trying to see my own features in her face. There was something about the shape of her eyes that was so like Daddy's. And all of us children had eyes shaped like Daddy's: large, thickly fringed, slightly downward sloping. A gift from Grandma Penelope.

I returned the photograph to its place on the nightstand and swiftly left the room. I had an idea where I could find Slim. I knew that if I'd been denied my favorite habit, it would be difficult to give it up cold turkey. I'd slip a few times. I might have to sneak around in order to indulge, but I would definitely engage in the forbidden act a few more times before I arrived at the point where I became sufficiently strong enough to resist it for the rest of my life.

When I'd come back home, after my work at Harry's, no one was on the ranch except Momma and Slim. I was willing to bet that Slim waited until Clancy had driven away in Momma's Taurus, and the boys had pulled out of the yard in the King Cab. Then he'd gone downstairs to see what Momma was up to. When he saw her engrossed in her work in the kitchen, he'd sneaked down the back stairs and out to the barn. Big Red, a sorrel, Slim's favorite quarter horse was gentle with his master, therefore I wasn't unduly concerned. I simply wanted to know if my hunch had been correct.

Therefore I ran down the back stairs. Momma was on the phone. She looked up when she heard me. Putting her hand over the receiver, she said, "Hattie Stephens. Is Slim all right?"

"He isn't up there," I told her, smiling. "I'm going out to the stable to see if he's there."

She nodded and returned to her conversation with Hattie Stephens who was a friend of hers from Mt. Carmel Baptist Church.

I grabbed my coat and shrugged into it. The temperature had peaked at thirty-five degrees on that fine December day. The sky above was a clear blue, but, in the distance, cumulus clouds were rolling in. Snow would probably be falling by dusk.

It was still early though, so Slim had plenty of time to get home before inclement weather impeded his progress.

Big Red had the third stall in. I went straight to it. Just as I'd thought, he wasn't there. I hurried around the corner to the tack room. Slim's soft leather saddle, the one he'd generously given to Clancy, was missing, too.

I walked back toward the exit, trying to figure out what to do next. I could wait there until he returned, but the trouble with that plan was I didn't know how long he'd been gone. If he truly was in trouble somewhere on the property, then time could be of the essence.

Sighing, I turned back toward the stalls. I went to Pie's stall and unlatched the gate. He eyed me and whinnied softly in recognition.

"Looks like you and I are going in search of the master," I said.

I made short work of outfitting Pie, then led him out of the stables. I walked him up to the back of the house where I tethered his reins to the post on the back porch.

Momma met me at the door with a concerned expression on her face.

"What's going on? Why do you have Pie saddled?"

"Slim's gone, Momma. He and Big Red are gallivanting all over the property . . ."

"What?! Why that sneaky old coot!"

I walked past her to the pantry where we kept the bottled water and an extra first-aid kit. I grabbed a bottle of water and the first-aid kit and stashed them in the saddlebag I'd thrown over my shoulder while in the stables.

Glancing up at the wall clock, I said, "It's 2:12. If I'm not back in two hours, send reinforcements. I'll cover the southern section first, then, west. He likes the meadows out that way."

"Okay," Momma said. "I'll get on the phone and see if I can get Clancy back here, at least. I don't know how to contact Chad and Lucas. Those boys are going to have to get beepers or something . . ."

She was rattling in her anxiety. She and Slim were often at odds, but she loved the mischievous rascal like a father.

With my hand on the doorknob I paused to reassure her. "Slim's probably just fine, Momma. He knows this place better than anyone. But, like I've said, if I'm not back in a couple of hours, call Jackson. If you can't get Jackson, then you'll have to call the sheriff."

"I know the drill, sweetie," Momma said. "Go find him. And you be careful."

"My cellular phone," I said, almost forgetting it. "I'll phone if I have any problems."

Momma brightened. "Well now you're thinking, baby."

I ran upstairs to get the cellular. By the time I got back down, Momma was on the phone to the Petersons, trying to locate Clancy.

I nodded in her direction, she nodded back and I hurried outside. Pie stood patiently, contentedly waving his tail back and forth.

Pie was eighteen hands high, which made him large for a quarter horse. He stood still while I placed the saddlebags on his back and then mounted him.

I jerked on the reins, indicating that we were heading south and he promptly complied, cantering across the yard down the slope and past the cabins.

I was wearing sunglasses so that I wouldn't squint against the glare of the afternoon sun. My hair was pulled away from my face and tied with a kerchief. I'd left my jacket open, but I was wearing a T-shirt under a denim shirt and a leather vest over the shirt, so I was well-insulated from the cold.

The Levi's, tucked into a pair of well-worn leather boots, were the heavy-duty kind worn in winter. I hoped Slim had remembered to dress warmly.

Half an hour into my ride, I'd come to the pasture where the cattle were grazing. I pulled up on the reins and Pie slowed to a saunter. Surveying the area, my eyes searched for a sign of anything out of the ordinary. Many of the cows were gathered around the pond central to the southern section of the ranch. The sound of their bleating was that of animals undisturbed by outside stimuli.

I knew, too well, the sound they made when under duress. All was normal here. I pulled left on the reins and Pie galloped in that direction.

Slim sometimes liked to sit by the stream that ran through the western section of the property. He would go down there and skim stones along the surface of the water. Occasionally, he'd pack a lunch and spend hours in that spot.

I'd never asked him why. Maybe that had been a favorite retreat of his and Grandma Penelope's when they were living alone here. It was a lovely oasis boasting some of nature's most exquisite palette of colors. In spring, lavender crocus and yellow bells abound there. In winter, the stream froze over and snow blanketed the ground, but the meadow was still beautiful in repose.

I couldn't begin to imagine how much more pristine this land had been when Slim was a boy. He'd lived here all his life. He played hide-and-seek in these woods. He and his dogs chased rabbits through the brush and returned home sweaty, filthy and extremely happy. This land was such an intrinsic part of who Slim had become, he undoubtedly thought of it as a living, breathing entity; an extension of himself.

I was coming through a thick copse of pine trees when I spotted Big Red tethered to a tree, nibbling at the grass around him. I slowed Pie with a pat to his muscular neck and sat tall in the saddle looking in all directions. Then, I saw Slim stretched out on a blanket, near the bank of the stream. His boots were still on; he'd folded his hands across his stomach and his hat sat over his face.

I couldn't discern whether he was breathing or not from my vantage point. So I dismounted, tied Pie's reins to a low branch of one of the older pine trees, grabbed the cellular phone and began walking toward Slim. I paused to pat Big Red's flank with my gloved hand when I passed him. "Hey, boy."

I refused to allow the thought of Slim's having expired to linger in my imagination. He was all right. He was just taking a snooze in the afternoon, in the middle of the wilderness, when it was thirty-five degrees out. Not logical behavior for a man who knew what exposure could do to the human body, especially one as old as his was; but I continued to hold on to that image nonetheless. He was all right.

I approached him as quietly as I could, given the amount of fallen pine needles and twigs on the ground. Standing directly over him, I bent and lifted his hat. His eyes slowly opened.

"What are you doing here?" he asked, irritated.

"Tracking an ornery cuss who cares nothing about his family's level of panic at finding him missing," I said, frowning.

He placed the hat back over his face. "Can't a man die in peace?"

I didn't respond to that. I calmly flipped the cellular phone open and dialed the number at the main house.

Momma answered immediately. "You find him?"

"He's all right. He's down by the stream in the west section. He thought it was a good day to die."

"That again?" Momma said, sighing. "Then come on back home and let him die. I'm tired of his shenanigans."

"Hold on a minute," I said into the receiver. Looking down at Slim's prostrate form, I said, "Momma says to just leave you. And since you are adamant about wanting to die, I suppose I'll have to respect your wishes." I spoke back to Momma. "I'm coming in."

"I'll phone the funeral home in Billings and start making arrangements. Ask Slim if a pine box is sufficient, or if he'd rather be cremated. That *is* much cheaper," Momma said.

Suppressing laughter, I relayed her message.

Slim sat up, his hat falling to the ground. His dark eyes flashed with anger. "Give me that contraption," he cried, reaching for the phone.

I handed it to him and took a step back to watch the fireworks.

"You mercenary harpy," he accused Momma. "You know my insurance will cover a funeral with all the trimmings. What are you going to do with the extra money, go to Las Vegas and gamble it away?"

I had no way of knowing what Momma's reply to that had been, but whatever she said got Slim on his feet. He pushed himself slowly to a stand and stomped the hard earth several times with his booted feet. "You know my will doesn't stipulate how I want to be buried. I thought I could trust you to put me away with some dignity and respect. I ain't going in no pine box. And if you try to torch my body, I'm going to come back and get you. . . ."

I bent and picked up the blanket, folding it. Then I turned and walked to where Big Red was tethered.

I placed the blanket into the saddlebags Slim had thrown over Big Red's back. After that, I untied his reins and led him to where Slim stood yelling into the cellular phone.

I waited several minutes, observing how the surface of the water rippled when the wind blew across it. Once, Big Red tried to nibble my shoulder. I boxed his nose and he chuffed. "Then be nice," I admonished him.

Slim finally pulled the phone from his ear, and his face was a mass of frowns. He raised the hand he was holding the phone in, preparing to fling it into the stream.

"Whoa," I cried, going to snatch it out of his grasp. "That's an expensive piece of equipment."

"I'm ready," Slim announced. "I need to go see my lawyer. I'm writing that woman out of my will."

When we were both on horseback and heading in the direction of the main house, I looked over at him and said, "She got your juices going, huh?"

"That woman can make me so mad; if I still had the strength in my hands, I would put them around her neck and squeeze."

"But you no longer believe it's a good day to die, do you?"

"I ain't got time to die. I've got business to see to. When I'm through with her, she won't have a pot to pee in. . . ."

He stopped abruptly and his eyes met mine. I smiled. He grimaced. "She got me again. That sneaky little . . ."

"It takes one to know one," I reminded him sweetly, to which he smiled for the first time during that whole ordeal.

He clucked his tongue at Big Red. "Hah!"

They took off at a gallop across the meadow, with me and Pie following close behind.

Slim's time dying in the meadow must have made him ravenous because he downed two helpings of Momma's beef stew when he got back to the house. And there was no more talk about writing Momma out of his will. They embraced. Momma called him a pain. And he called her the wicked witch of the west. Things were back to normal.

After our meal, I went upstairs to my bedroom to commune with my journal awhile. The last few days had given me lots of material to write about.

Soon, Christmas Eve was upon us and we planned on celebrating it in the same manner we did every year: The family would gather in the company room, where each of us would open one gift.

Cole, Enid and the boys had arrived the night before, and early that morning, I'd driven to Lame Deer to pick up Grandma Isabella, Momma's seventy-five-year-old mother.

Momma had tried to persuade Grandma to come for a visit around Thanksgiving and stay until after Christmas, but Grandma Isabella was as stubborn and independent-minded as her daughter; besides, before Thanksgiving somebody had told her there was good fishing at the Tongue River Reservoir, so she and some of her cronies drove there and spent several days fishing for bass, crappie, walleye and northern pike.

She was a small woman. Trim, with golden-brown skin, white hair that was wavy and fell to her waist. She invariably wore it in a bun at the back of her head. Isabella Rainwater was half black and half Cheyenne. Her father had been black, her mother, Cheyenne. She'd married Benjamin Rainwater, a black man. Where he got his last name from, no one ever found out. Ben had been an orphan and could have easily named himself. In the photographs Grandma Isabella and Momma had of him, he appeared to have been very dark-skinned. Hence, we'd assumed his ancestry was African-American.

He died before I was born, so I'd never met him.

My Uncle Sammy, Momma's only brother, had been there when I'd arrived at Grandma Isabella's bungalow that morning.

Uncle Sammy lived on the res, as the locals called the reservation, and was married to a Cheyenne woman, Aunt Ruby. They had four grown children whom we used to love playing with in the summertime when we'd go stay with Grandma Isabella for a few weeks.

Of Uncle Sammy's two sons and two daughters, none lived on the reservation. Like many of the younger ones, they had sought their fortunes in the outside world.

The first thing you saw when you walked through Grandma Isabella's door was a long row of photographs lining her foyer wall. Several were of her and Grandpa Ben together. Others were of Uncle Sammy and Momma as children. Then, there were the grandchildren and the great-grandchildren.

But the three most prominent portraits on her wall were of John F. Kennedy, Martin Luther King, Jr., and Bobby Kennedy. Grandma believed that there hadn't been a decent president in office since Jack Kennedy was assassinated. Bobby, she thought, would have been a worthy replacement for his brother, if he'd lived. And as for Martin Luther King? He was a saint, plain and simple.

Uncle Sammy was there doing some plumbing repairs in Grandma's kitchen when I rang the bell.

Grandma answered the door. She was in one of her ever-present housecoats. This one had a dark-blue background with huge yellow tulips all over it. I smiled as I stepped inside and went into her outstretched arms.

We hugged tightly then regarded each other.

"Where's the ring?" she asked, peering at my hands.

"What ring?" I inquired, laughing. She and Momma were on the phone gossiping practically every day. So what she wanted to know was how my relationship with Jackson was going.

She scowled, and put her hands on her hips. "Don't be coy with me." She turned away, heading toward the back of the house, expecting me to follow her, which I did. "You've known each other all your lives, what do you need with a long engagement? I say go ahead and get married, what are you waiting for?"

She was a woman after my own heart.

Stopping at her bedroom door, she opened it and went inside. Going to the closet, she tiptoed and tried to grasp the handle of a suitcase on the top shelf. Unable to reach it, she looked up at me, then stepped to the side. I easily reached up and retrieved the suitcase for her, handing it to her.

We went back into the bedroom where she went to the bureau and began tossing clothes into the open suitcase on the bed.

"Young people these days," she expounded, "don't know how to court one another properly. The mystery is gone. What is there left to the imagination when some of them go to bed together on the first date?"

My features must have expressed surprise, because she laughed and said, "Don't give me that look; I might be old, but I pay attention. Jackson is a good man. I'm sure he respects you. But, did you know your cousin, Joann, is living with a man in Cody? Sammy thinks I don't know it, but Ruby told me. She's real upset over it. I told her until Joann realizes her own self-worth, she'll allow men to take advantage of her."

That was my Grandma. The fact that couples lived together without marriage was a common occurrence in today's society, had not escaped her notice. With Isabella Rainwater, there were no two ways about it. When something was wrong, it was wrong.

At that point in our conversation, I heard someone banging on a pipe elsewhere in the house. "You aren't alone?"

"No, your Uncle Sammy's in the kitchen fixing the leaky faucet."

I rolled my eyes. "What if he had come in here when you were talking about Joann?"

"You know I never hold my tongue with you children." She referred to all of us, her son and daughter, her grandchildren, the myriad great-grandchildren, as children.

"I'm going to say hello," I told her as I turned to leave the room.

She went on with her packing. I walked down the hall, through the small living room and into the kitchen. Uncle Sammy was lying on his back, his head stuck underneath the sink.

"Uncle Sammy."

"Hey, Chey, I heard you when you came in, but I was busy changing a washer. I'm almost finished. How you doin', baby girl?" He spoke without moving.

I went to squat next to him. "I'm fine."

"And Diana and the rest of the family?"

"They're all doing great. How's Aunt Ruby? You heard anything from Joann, Clint, Jodie or Wyatt lately?"

"Well," he began, sounding tired, "your Aunt Ruby's doing just fine. She found a lump in her right breast, but it turned out to be benign, so that was a relief. We went out to celebrate when we got the news. Your cousin Wyatt just got a promotion to manager at the Wal-Mart in Roundup . . ."

"Oh, that's great about Aunt Ruby. I'll go over and say hi before we head back to Custer. And Wyatt's really doing good, huh? Momma told me he and Mako were expecting a baby."

"That's right," Uncle Sammy said, his voice more sprightly. "She's due in March."

"March? That's when Enid is due!"

Uncle Sammy chuckled. "Wouldn't it be funny if they were born on the same day?"

"That would be something," I agreed.

"I'm sort of worried about Joann," Uncle Sammy continued. "The last I heard, she'd moved in with some cowboy who drinks too much and likes to shove women around. I don't want to have to go down there and put a bullet in his backside."

Sighing, I said, "Joann. She's a smart girl. Why does she get involved with bad boys?"

"I don't know," Uncle Sammy replied with a hopeless note in his voice. "We raised all of them to be proud of who they are. Maybe it didn't sink in with her. She seems to believe that's all she deserves; so she doesn't try to do any better."

I believe he knew his youngest daughter quite well. What other reason would a woman with a degree in computer science, who had absolutely no trouble finding and keeping good jobs, who was physically strikingly beautiful, want a man who mistreated her?

"I wish I could help," I said regrettably.

"Her mother and I have talked to her until we were both blue in the face. It hasn't done any good. But, we keep trying."

"Yeah, you keep trying," I encouraged him. "What about Jodie and Clint? They doing okay?"

"Oh sure. Clint's construction company is doing great. Although he says he can't get used to the heat in California. And Jodie's making good grades at Howard University. She phones home for money every couple of months. She hasn't learned to budget her funds yet, but I'm sure she'll get the hang of it."

"Clancy's going there next year. What will Jodie be, a sophomore? Clancy can't wait to get out of Montana."

"Jodie was the same way. Now she gets homesick," Uncle Sammy said, laughing.

He scooted from under the sink and grinned at me. I rose to my feet and offered him a hand, pulling him to his feet.

We were about the same height. He had golden-brown skin similar to Momma's, except his was of a bit deeper hue because he loved being outdoors. He had a silver streak down the middle of his black hair. Long and wavy, he kept it tied back with a leather strap.

I always thought my uncle was the coolest because of his attitude toward life: He invariably sought the sunny side of the street. And that ponytail didn't hurt.

We hugged and his golden-speckled brown eyes met mine. "I've been hearing good news about *you* lately. What's up with you and Jackson?"

I shrugged and gave him an enigmatic smile.

"Don't want to jinx it, huh?" he said of my reluctance to define my relationship with Jackson.

"No, that isn't it. It's just that I don't know what you'd call it. We're dating. Calling him my boyfriend sounds a little like we're in high school."

"Why do you have to call it anything? All that matters is that you're happy. You *are* happy, aren't you?"

I grinned like a Cheshire cat. "I am."

Shortly after that, Grandma Isabella came into the kitchen and announced that she was packed and then issued an order for me to get the large cooler from the pantry, then go downstairs to the cellar, get two bags of fish from the freezer, put them in the cooler then put the cooler in the bed of the King Cab.

She was just like Momma when it came to giving orders. Both women would have excelled as Marine Corp staff sergeants.

As we were waving good-bye to Uncle Sammy from the King Cab, I told her: "I promised Uncle Sammy I'd go by and say hello to Aunt Ruby before leaving the res, so hang tight."

"Honey, I'm seventy-five years old, there's nothing tight on me anymore. But I can manage the hanging part."

Everyone spilled out of the house to welcome Grandma Isabella when we got home. Cole and Enid led the procession, Enid looking radiant in her sixth month of pregnancy. Her perfectly round belly made her appear as though she was concealing a basketball under her blouse and she kept a hand atop it as if protecting the unborn child inside from unforeseen dangers.

She and Cole were at their most contented when they were readying the nest for another member of the family.

Momma outpaced the slow-moving Enid and reached the truck first and went around to Grandma's side to greet her mother.

Grandma climbed out of the cab into her daughter's waiting arms and they hugged, after which they kissed each other's cheeks.

I got out and told Chad to get Grandma's suitcase and Lucas

to get the cooler out of the bed of the truck. It seemed I was also adept at giving orders.

Everyone took their turn hugging Grandma Isabella, who was clearly enjoying the attention. She was beaming.

I noticed Slim sitting in his favorite rocker on the front porch. I walked onto the porch and smiled down at him. It was three o'clock in the afternoon, and he smelled as if he'd just showered. He also reeked of Old Spice. Slim only bothered to shave once a week, and that was on Sunday morning. *If* he felt like it. It was Friday, December 24. He was two days early.

I didn't have to ask why he'd gussied up a bit. He and Grandma engaged in a mild flirtation every time she visited. They'd both been widowed for many years. Neither had ever gotten remarried. But that didn't mean they didn't enjoy the company of members of the opposite sex.

Grandma Isabella stepped onto the porch and stopped beside Slim's chair. "I see you're still breathing," she said, her eyes sparkling.

"I see you're still walking without a cane," Slim returned, a smile on his thin lips. "Hip replacement?"

"No. I've still got it, that's all," Grandma replied saucily.

"You've still got it because no one else wants it," Slim quickly parried. He sat up straighter on his chair.

Grandma Isabella threw her head back and laughed delightedly. She bent and kissed his cheek. "Yes, I missed you, too."

They held hands. The rest of us moved around Grandma Isabella, going on into the house. They looked as though they wanted a moment alone.

"Good trip, baby?" Momma asked me once we were inside.

I told her all about the visit with Uncle Sammy, Aunt Ruby and filled her in on what my cousins were up to as we walked through the house to the kitchen.

In my absence, she, Clancy, Enid and Cole had been preparing Christmas dinner. Cole didn't do much cooking, but he was a whiz at baking. His pies rivaled Momma's. A fact Enid bemoaned. She accused him of putting those extra pounds on her hips. And, whenever she was pregnant, he spoiled her continually by baking her favorite pie, coconut custard, at least once a week.

About an hour after I got home, the phone rang and Momma answered it. We were all sitting around the kitchen, chopping, mixing, shredding some foodstuff or another.

Enid was telling me about little Cole's Christmas play at his day-care facility. He'd been a sheep in the manger scene and she said that when it came time for him to baa, he mooed instead. The audience laughed uproariously and little Cole didn't know why they had done that until his mother explained it to him at home later.

"Cheyenne!" Momma called.

I looked up at her.

"It's the hospital in Billings. They say Jackson was brought in a few minutes ago. They won't say how badly he's hurt . . ."

I was up off my chair the moment I heard Jackson's name.

I went to Momma and took the receiver out of her hand.

"Hello? This is Cheyenne Roberts. What happened? May I speak with him?"

"I'm sorry," the woman on the other end said. "He's in surgery at the moment. I phoned you because you're on his admission form as next of kin. You *are* related to him, right? Sometimes the patients aren't too lucid when they give us information."

"Yes," I lied. "Can you tell me anything about what happened? Was he in an accident? What?"

The woman paused for a moment. "It says here that it was a car accident. He was brought in by paramedics. His leg is broken, and there could be internal injuries as well. I'm sorry, but that's all I can tell you right now."

"Thank you for calling," I told her and hung up.

Everyone's eyes were on me, awaiting some news about Jackson.

"It was a car accident. He has a broken leg, possible internal injuries and he's presently in surgery," I said my voice breaking toward the end.

I walked purposefully toward the hat tree next to the back door. When I'd come in earlier, I'd hung my coat and my shoulder bag there. Now they were conveniently within easy reach.

I grabbed them and turned to look into the faces of my family.

"I've got to go. I'll phone when I get to the hospital . . ."

"You're not driving," Momma said vehemently.

Cole was already getting into his coat. "Of course she isn't. I'm driving."

I rummaged in my bag for the keys to the King Cab and placed them in his outstretched hand.

Our eyes met momentarily, and I'd never been more grateful to have him for a big brother.

Momma rushed to me and kissed my cheek. "Be strong, sweetheart. Don't let Jackson see how scared you are. He's going to need your strength now."

I nodded, too full to speak.

Cole and I left by the back door.

A car accident, I thought, as Cole pulled out of the yard. What is this, fate trying to reassert itself? Thirteen years ago Jackson's parents had been killed in a car crash. He hadn't been in the car with them, so now he was to suffer the consequences he should have undergone thirteen years ago? It was amazing where your mind took you when you were in a panic.

Cole reached over and grasped my hand in his, squeezing it reassuringly. "He'll be okay, Cheyenne. Jackson's tough. He always has been."

I looked at his chiseled profile through tear-glazed eyes. "He has to be, Cole."

Then I remembered: Cole was Jackson's best friend. He loved him, too. They had been through everything together. Cole had gone with Jackson to identify his parents' bodies when they'd died in that car crash. Jackson had been Cole's best man in his wedding. Cole had helped Jackson build his house. And Jackson had, in turn, helped Cole build his and Enid's home a few years later.

I squeezed his hand. "You're right, Cole. Jackson will be just fine. You're going to be best man at our wedding."

"That would make me very happy," my wonderful brother said.

SIXTEEN

Cole and I were directed to the waiting room on the third floor. The physician who was operating on Jackson, Dr. Ashland, would come out and give us an update on his condition shortly after the operation was concluded.

Cole sat reading a *Sports Illustrated,* while I fidgeted. My mind was racing. I wondered what Jackson had been doing in Billings on Christmas Eve. Some late shopping?

The night before, I'd gone for a drive with him and I'd reminded him of our annual Christmas Eve dinner and gift exchange. He'd always been included in the past. The only times, I could recall, he hadn't shown up was when he was dating Marissa, and he had been obligated to spend holidays with her and her family.

He'd promised to be there promptly at seven o'clock. Since he'd sold part of his stock two weeks previously, his duties on the ranch had been reduced considerably. His foreman, Al Armstrong, the only employee he had who lived on the ranch year-round, had already left for his vacation, and wouldn't be back until March.

The other men who worked for him lived with their families.

Therefore, except for Mrs. Anderson who came in every weekday to cook and clean for him, he was basically alone out there.

Alone. Jackson had no relatives nearby. His mother, Ginny, had been from Helena. He'd told me she had a sister there. He'd called her Aunt Bette. He never talked about his father's relatives, if he'd had any.

But, of his parents, it was obvious to me that his mother was the only one he'd wholly loved. He had never expressed any warm feelings for his father, Joseph.

"Cheyenne . . ."

I looked up at Cole. He was sitting beside me in the waiting area. The room was nearly filled with other people who were also anxiously awaiting news of their loved ones.

"Would you stop tapping your heels on the floor? Listen, why don't you go downstairs to the cafeteria and get us some coffee? You could work off some of that nervous energy," he suggested, smiling at me. "I'll come get you if Dr. Ashland shows up . . ."

"I'm not going anywhere until I hear something," I said, crossing my legs. I hadn't been aware I'd been tapping my heels on the floor. It was a nervous habit.

"All right, then," Cole said patiently. "I'll go get us some coffee. What do you want in yours?"

"I don't want any coffee, Cole."

"A cold drink?"

"Nothing, thanks."

Cole rose and glared down at me. "You haven't had anything to eat since this morning." He glanced at his watch. "It's after six. Now unless you want me to drag you downstairs to the cafeteria to get a meal, you're going to drink a cup of coffee, or something!"

I laughed suddenly and got to my feet. "You sounded just like Daddy when you said that," I told him.

Cole hugged me to him. I think we both realized we'd been allowing our fears to get the best of us.

"I'm sorry," I murmured, my nose pressed to his chest. "I know you're just trying to look out for me."

He smiled. "I'm worried, too, Chey. I was sitting there remembering the night Jackson and I went to the morgue to identify his parents' bodies. God, it was awful . . ." He stopped, probably because he didn't think it was wise to be discussing such a macabre subject when we didn't know whether Jackson would survive or not. Our eyes met. "So many weird things go through your mind when you're in a situation like this."

"I know. I'd also been thinking about the Kincaids."

"You were?"

"Yeah, except I was asking myself if fate was trying to reassert itself thirteen years later by claiming Jackson."

"Banish that thought, Chey. Jackson is going to make it."

"Anyone here for Jackson Kincaid?" a male voice asked from the doorway.

Cole released me and we turned in the direction of the questioner. "Right here," Cole said.

Dr. Ashland appeared to be in his late forties. He had dark hair and eyes, was around five-eleven and wore horn-rimmed glasses. His face was set with an unreadable expression.

As he crossed the room, I whispered to Cole, "Look at his face. Not even a semblance of a smile."

"The man's probably tired, Chey," Cole said from experience. He was a veterinary surgeon, so he knew the energy-sapping intensity of the occupation firsthand.

The two men shook hands and then Dr. Ashland reached for mine. His hand felt cool and firm in my own. A thought flashed in my mind as we shook: His hands had just touched Jackson. Was it possible to discern how Jackson was through this man's touch?

I looked into his eyes, and he smiled. My heart started to beat again and my stomach muscles relaxed.

"He's going to be just fine. Concerning the leg: It was a clean break. It should heal in about six to eight weeks if he takes care of it. The lungs were another matter. One of his ribs punctured his left lung. We were able to get to it, though, before there was too much damage done. He'll be perfectly fine; a bit of pain when he breathes for a while, but once everything heals, he will be as good as new."

Once the doctor got started, he was rather garrulous, I was happy to note.

"Imagine if he hadn't been wearing his seat belt . . ." the good doctor continued. He laughed shortly. "He was lucky. The elderly man who broadsided him had a heart attack at the wheel. He's undergoing a bypass as we speak. His wife got only a few scratches. Miraculous!"

"When can we see him?" I asked when I could get a word in edgewise.

"Give them a few minutes to get him situated in intensive care, then you go up and tell the nurses who you are, all right?"

He finally gave me back my hand. "By the way, you wouldn't be Chey, would you?"

I thought he'd asked if I was shy. "I beg your pardon?"

Dr. Ashland smiled sheepishly. "I'm sorry, I thought it was someone's name he was murmuring when the anesthesiologist was putting him under."

"Yes," I said, grinning. "That's me, Cheyenne."

Dr. Ashland squeezed my shoulder. "Well, you take good care of Jackson, Cheyenne."

"Thank you, doctor," Cole said.

Dr. Ashland smiled his appreciation and with one more glance in my direction, left us.

Cole and I hugged fiercely.

"You see?" he said. "You were worrying needlessly."

Grasping his hand, I said, "Let's go on up. I can't wait to see him."

Laughing, Cole refused to move. "No, Chey. We're going to phone the house first. Then we're going downstairs to get something to eat. After that, we can go up. They need time to get Jackson in a room, get his IV set up and various other things. So be reasonable."

"Thank God," Momma said over the phone a few minutes later, her voice rife with relief. "I can rest easy tonight. When you see him you tell him for me, that he is dearly loved."

"I'll be sure to do that," I promised.

"And, Chey?"

"Hmmm?"

"I was worried about you, too, baby. Now that Jackson seems to be out of the woods, are you feeling better?"

"I'm all right, Momma."

"I'm going to take your word for it, sweetie. May I speak with Cole?"

We were standing near the bank of phones adjacent to the emergency room entrance. I arched my brows at Cole, who'd been observing me throughout my conversation with Momma. Handing the phone to him, I said, "Momma wants to talk to you."

He took it and turned his back to me. I leaned against the wall and waited. I could imagine what Momma had to ask him: Is she really all right, Cole? Keep an eye on her. This was a big shock for her and I don't want her getting ill behind it.

"Hmmm huh," was all I heard my brother say.

He hung up the phone and turned to smile at me. "You know Momma. She wanted verification that you are, indeed, just fine."

My stomach was growling. "Let's go eat," I said.

No use discussing Momma's protective proclivities. She wasn't going to change anytime soon. And it was rather comforting to know she loved us so much.

"You're putting away the food pretty well for someone who didn't want anything a few minutes ago," Cole said a quarter of an hour later.

The hospital cafeteria was an assembly-line operation. They were serving dinner, and the choices were standard American fare. I got the baked chicken, mashed potatoes, broccoli and a green salad. Cole had the meatloaf, mashed potatoes, green beans and rolls.

I looked down at his plate. "How's the meatloaf?"

"It's good, you want to try it?"

I reached over and cut off a piece with my fork and ate it.

"Mmm, sort of spicy. It is good."

Cole smiled, his eyes on my face.

"You're rather mercurial. Your mood changes as swiftly as the weather outside." His expression became more serious. He sighed. "You realize it's going to take weeks and weeks before Jackson's back to normal. He's going to be irritable, impatient, mean. A major injury isn't easy for a person like him to take. He's never been sick a day in his life."

I smiled serenely. "I know all of that," I assured him. "He'll be a bear. Knowing him, he'll use this as an excuse to push me away. What if he never regains full use of his leg? Every negative aspect of his situation will surface. But he won't chase me away."

"Okay . . ." Cole said skeptically.

* * *

The nurse at the nurses' station in the intensive care unit warned us that Jackson was still unconscious. But she said it was all right if we wanted to see him anyway.

Cole and I walked down to Room 303 and he pushed the door open, allowing me to precede him.

The quietness of the room was what struck me first. The sounds seemed muffled, subdued. Jackson lay on his back in the hospital bed, his right leg raised. On closer inspection, I saw that the leg was encased in a thick, white cast halfway up his thigh.

They had him hooked up to several monitors; one that kept track of his breathing, another, his heart. An IV drip was in his right arm. I stood next to him, peering down into his ashen face. His breathing was steady, rhythmic. I was grateful he didn't sound congested. I'd never seen him sleeping before. He looked so peaceful, almost like a small child. I placed my hand on his forehead. His skin was warm and soft to the touch. I bent and kissed his face. "I love you," I whispered, my breath on his cheek.

Cole appeared at my side, a frown on his face. "I suppose he looks better than I'd imagined he would."

I was content to stand there marveling at God's perfect handiwork. "He's beautiful."

Laughing quietly and shaking his head, Cole said, "Girl, you've got it bad."

He moved down to the foot of the bed and picked up the chart that hung on a clip there and started reading it.

"His vital signs are good. Looks like the big beau hunk will survive."

I'd gone over to the window to see what kind of view Jackson would be greeted with in the morning. Lights illuminated a man-made pond over which a footbridge had been erected. A few people were walking across the bridge to the eastern wing of the hospital. We were in the west wing.

"Don't talk about him like that," I cautioned Cole. "They say people who are unconscious can hear what's being said around them."

"I don't know about unconscious people, but I can hear you just fine," Jackson said, his voice low and noticeably weak.

I was instantly at his side.

He looked at me and smiled slowly. "I was hoping yours would be the first face I'd see when I woke up."

"Hey, bud," Cole said, coming around to stand next to me. "Did your life flash before your eyes?"

"Yeah," Jackson said, "and your ugly mug was in most of it."

Grinning, Cole replied, "I wouldn't talk about looks if I were you." He placed his hand on the small of my back. "Listen you two, I'm going to get lost for a few minutes in case you want to get mushy. Brothers can't stomach that kind of behavior."

"You do that," Jackson said.

In Cole's absence, I placed my arms around Jackson as best I could. "I was so afraid of losing you. . . ."

"Cheyenne, it hurts to breathe and I'm groggy, so I don't know how long I'm going to be conscious. Just know this: I'll be the man you fell in love with again one day soon. You can count on it."

I didn't want him to see me crying, so I fought back the tears that were threatening to fall. "You're already the man I fell in love with, Jackson."

His eyes closed and I was loath to awaken him in order to press a point. However, his words had made my pulse quicken with apprehension. What sort of fatalistic reasoning was he allowing to take hold of him?

I left the room and went in search of Cole.

The next day, Jackson was more himself. Dr. Gray, his personal physician, had put him on solid food, so his energy level was steadily rising. My entire family, excluding the grandparents who didn't feel up to climbing the stairs at the hospital, went to see him.

On the third day of his recuperation, a physical therapist, Dave Carey, got him up on his feet in order to begin to teach him how to use crutches properly.

I was there when Dave came into the room. He was tall, in his early twenties with curly brown hair and dark brown eyes. He had an optimistic way about him, which I appreciated.

"Hi, I'm Dave," he said, going to shake Jackson's hand.

From his bed, Jackson regarded Dave with a cool smile. He'd been poked and prodded so much, that he was understandably wary of new hospital personnel when they came into his room.

"I'm the physical therapist," Dave said. "I hear you're eager to get out of here. Well, this is the first step, so to speak. I'm here to get you up on your feet and to teach you how to use your crutches."

They allowed their hands to drop and Jackson gestured at me. "This is Cheyenne Roberts, my . . ."

"Good friend," I answered for him stepping forward and offering Dave my hand.

"Good to meet you, Miss Roberts."

I looked at Jackson. "I'll go downstairs . . ." I was giving him an out if he'd rather I not be present during his first session with his therapist.

"All right," he agreed.

I understood. It must have been difficult for him to depend on anyone else. He'd been the strong one all his life. And it embarrassed him for me to see him in his present weakened state. What if he failed when he went to stand on his own?

So I gave him a quick peck on the cheek and made myself scarce.

I returned an hour later and he was back in bed with his leg in traction. Smiling as I came through the door, I cheerfully inquired as to how his first session had gone.

"Cheyenne, don't you have anywhere else to be? You've been here continually for three days straight," he snapped. "Go home, please. Go get your cabins ready for the spring season."

He didn't even look at me; his eyes were trained on the conifer outside his window.

I went and stood directly in his line of sight. He cut his eyes at me. "Can't you see I don't want you here?"

I walked slowly toward him, my boots making clicking sounds on the tile. I'm sure, if he could have, he would have turned and gone in the opposite direction, away from me. But he couldn't do anything except sit there and wait to see what my next move would be.

"It didn't go well, huh?"

"I'm not going to talk about it." The expression in his eyes had gone from indignant to cautious. Sometimes it paid to be an unpredictable woman.

I stopped about two feet from his bed. "You don't have to say a word. But, you'd better listen up."

I quickly went to him, firmly took his face between my hands and kissed him hard on the mouth. He struggled at first, but I could feel his resolve melting and, sure enough, he kissed me back, hungrily, as if my mouth, my tongue, my breath were the only things keeping him alive.

I pulled my mouth from his and looked into his eyes, which were regarding me with such adoration that my stomach muscles constricted painfully at the sight of them. "Jackson, I know you're afraid. I'm afraid *for* you. You can yell at me. You can threaten me. You can be as mean as a bull with a thorn in its hoof. I'll be here for the duration. But, if you've stopped loving me, just tell me." I brushed my cheek against his. "Have you stopped loving me?"

"God, no. I'll never stop loving you," he breathed.

I kissed his lips gently and smiled at him. "I didn't hurt you, did I?"

He smiled, the crinkles at the corners of his eyes becoming more pronounced. "Only my pride. *Why* do you love me, Chey?"

With my gaze on his face, I straightened up and took a step away from the bed. "Why do I love you? Because you're the kindest man I know. You're also loyal to your friends. And when a neighbor's in need, you're always the first to offer aid. Those are the surface reasons I love you. On a deeper level, I love you because you make me *feel* good. Just being near you causes endorphins to flow throughout my body like a potent drug."

He laughed, then winced and gingerly touched his bandaged torso.

I went to him and placed my hand on his forehead, a bead of sweat had broken out there. "What's wrong?"

"Just a pain," he said, smiling again. "Don't stop. I'm enjoying this."

I grasped his hand and brought it to my mouth, kissing his knuckles. My cheek rested in his palm as I went on: "I love you because when I was five, you rescued me from a bunch of hateful girls who made fun of me when I unwittingly flashed them."

He laughed again. "I'm glad you were able to break that habit."

Getting into it, I moved away from the bed and threw my arms open wide. "I love you," I said with gusto and conviction, "because you have the best buns I've ever seen on a male specimen! I love you because when you kiss me, my toes curl and my spirit rises up out of my body and does the boogaloo!"

"Now that's love," Dr. Ashland said as he strode into the room.

Startled, I turned and stumbled against Jackson's bed. Jackson grasped my arm, steadying me. I peered into his face. He seemed infused with new vitality and strength. I knew then that together, we were a force to be reckoned with. We would make it.

The weather service issued its first snowstorm warning of the season the day Jackson came home from the hospital. I drove carefully as the gray, snow-laden sky shed its white mantle upon the earth.

We arrived at his doorstep safe and sound, and I got out of the King Cab and ran around to get his door.

Having heard the truck, Mrs. Anderson, a stout black woman in her early sixties, with a gruff manner but a heart of gold, came out of the house to see if she could be of any assistance.

She had the steps clear of snow and the porch nice and dry, so Jackson had no trouble getting into the house unaided. He'd become quite adept with his crutches by then, and his movements were so invigorated, that he seemed, at any moment, about to execute a dance step while perched upon them.

Mrs. Anderson closed the door after us, and laughed as Jackson spun around and regarded her. He had kissed her cheek as he'd passed her on the way into the house. Now he grinned and said, "Well, did you miss me?"

Mrs. Anderson laughed. *"Miss* you? I've been eating chocolates and watching my soap operas all day. *No,* I didn't miss you. I was hoping they'd keep you awhile longer."

And with that, she picked up his overnight bag and headed in the direction of the stairs as Jackson laughed heartily, rocking on his crutches. She looked back at him from the foot of the stairs.

"This is dirty laundry, I presume? Didn't they have a laundry service at that place? For what it costs for the privilege to stay there, they *should* have one."

She disappeared up the stairs.

"I believe she missed you," I told Jackson.

I went to him and kissed his cheek. "I have to be going, but I'll be back in a few hours."

His eyes raked over my face. "I don't think what you're planning is a good idea, Chey. I can manage on my own."

I pressed my cheek to his as we stood there in the foyer. "Don't argue with me, Jackson. Humor me this one time. . . ."

He turned his head until his lips were caressing my cheek. "I don't know how I'll be able to sleep knowing you're just down the hall."

I smiled into his eyes. "Who said anything about *sleeping?"*

I hastily kissed his mouth and walked swiftly to the front door, leaving him no time to respond to my comment. I blew him a kiss from the doorway. "Get off that leg."

When I arrived at the ranch, all members of my family were in the process of battening down the hatches.

When you've lived your whole life in a land where you run the risk of being buried under tons of snow every winter, there are certain rules you live by. One of them is: You take warnings of snowstorms seriously. We tend to keep the pantry well-stocked year-round; however, in winter we stock up on nonperishables; fill gallon jugs with water, in case the water in the well freezes, and lay in a good supply of dry wood for the fireplaces. If the electricity should go, which it has done quite often in winter months, we have a backup generator. If something happens to the generator, that's where the woodsupply comes in handy. Ranch houses are usually designed with at least one fireplace.

And they're not just for atmosphere. We use them to keep our houses warm *and* for cooking.

Clancy and Momma were in the kitchen filling plastic gallon jugs with water when I walked through the back door.

"So you and Jackson made it back," Momma said, stating the obvious. She handed Clancy two filled jugs. Clancy took them and went into the pantry to line them up next to the others on the floor in there. Momma looked at me. "How is he?"

I was hanging my coat and shoulder bag on the hall tree. "He's doing great. He's doing so great that he says I shouldn't spend the next few nights there with him."

"He's afraid of being alone with you," Momma said reasonably. She arched her brows. "How do *you* feel about it?"

"I think we'll be perfectly fine," I lied. The truth was: I was both excited and apprehensive about spending the night under the same roof with Jackson. And I was not at all sure I'd be able to resist him in a weak moment. But, he needed me, whether he was willing to admit it, or not.

Mrs. Anderson had a sickly husband, and she wouldn't be able to stay nights. Jackson's insurance company had covered the majority of his hospital bill, but he still had twenty percent of the bill to pay out of his own pocket. So he couldn't afford to hire a private-duty nurse. *I* was it. Logic dictated that I spend the night with him. For once, logic was on my side.

"You can't fool me," Momma said, smiling. "I can tell by that happy gleam in your eyes that you're looking forward to playing nurse."

"Okay," I admitted, "a part of me is delighted to be able to spend time alone with Jackson. Another part, the good little girl part of me, is worrying like crazy that she won't be a good little girl much longer."

"What *is* good, Chey? Is good defined by your chastity, or is it defined by the content of your character? You will still be a good person even if you decide to go ahead and sleep with Jackson. I hope you'll wait, because I'm your mother. And that won't change if you decide to do the opposite. I'm saying this because if you do weaken and something happens, I don't want you casting aspersions on your character."

* * *

The two weeks Jackson had been hospitalized, friends and neighbors, including Chad and Lucas, had been doing the chores around the ranch.

As it happened, my brothers were stacking cordwood in the bin on the back porch when I drove up.

I got out and ran onto the porch, greeting them: "Hey, you guys, thanks so much for bringing the wood. . . ."

"We wanted to make sure you and Jackson would be okay tonight in case the electricity went out," Lucas said, his dark-skinned face crinkling in a smile.

"They wouldn't freeze," Chad put in, grinning. "They have *love* to keep them warm."

"Oh you!" I cried, playfully punching him on the shoulder.

I turned and continued inside. There wasn't another soul in the kitchen. Mrs. Anderson had long since gone home for the night.

Jackson's kitchen was large and spotless. I believe Mrs. Anderson had a fetish for cleanliness. The floor didn't have a speck of dirt on it. The counters and the appliances gleamed. Jackson had built the house four years ago, and because of Mrs. Anderson's attentions, there'd been no noticeable depreciation.

If Jackson and I ever got married, I was going to lobby for her to stay on.

I walked through the kitchen to the back stairs. "Jackson!" I called as I ascended.

When I reached the landing, I heard a shower running in the direction of Jackson's bedroom.

His room door was open.

I went into the bedroom. I'd never been in his bedroom before. It was spacious, at least twenty feet by twenty-four.

The hardwood floor was highly polished and the huge, cherry-wood four-poster bed sat upon a rich royal blue carpet. The bedroom was as neat as the kitchen had been. Every item on the dresser, Jackson's comb and brush, a wooden jewelry box, several bottles of cologne and aftershave, were all arranged in an orderly fashion.

My eyes went to the French doors that opened out onto the balcony. I'd often wondered about the view from there.

My hand was on the doorknob when I heard the water in the shower go off.

"Jackson, it's me. Do you need any help?"

"No!" he answered immediately with a panicky edge to his voice. "Stay where you are. I'll be out in a few minutes."

I turned the doorknob and went out to stand on the balcony. The day was still gray, but it wasn't snowing any longer. I breathed in deeply, my hands on the railing. From my perch, I spied the King Cab pulling onto Highway 94. It was a Friday night. Having done their good deed, my brothers would probably go home, shower and change and then try to convince their girl-friends to go out with them in spite of the snowstorm warning. When their plan failed, either because Momma wouldn't allow them to risk life and limb just for a night out; or neither of the girls they were dating were that brain drained, they'd settle for a night at home watching ESPN and eating Doritos.

At any rate, I thought as I turned back around, *I'm alone with Jackson, finally.*

I tugged at the door's handle. I'd locked myself out. I peered inside the room. Jackson was nowhere in sight. He was probably still struggling to dry off and get into his bathrobe, the cumbersome broken leg getting in the way the whole while.

I still had my coat on, so I was not in danger of freezing anytime soon; so I stood there waiting for Jackson to put in an appearance.

About seven minutes later, he came limping out of the bathroom, covered in a white terry-cloth bathrobe, using only one of the crutches. He hobbled toward the bed. I rapped on the door and smiled sheepishly.

He looked up and saw me. His face broke into a grin and he shook his still-wet head.

"Couldn't wait to see the view, huh?" he said, as he opened the door. I stepped inside, rubbing my arms. "It's going to be chilly tonight."

"Chilly?" Jackson said, as he hopped on his good leg to maintain his balance. "Only a romantic would call below-freezing chilly."

I shut the door and grasped him about the waist, allowing him to use me for an extra crutch. "Better?"

He looked down into my upturned face. "So you came."

"I told you I would."

"I was hoping you'd change your mind and stay home."

"Why?"

"Because it's difficult to get in and out of that shower."

I laughed at his allusion that he'd require plenty of cold showers due to my presence. "I promise you, Jackson. I won't do anything to tempt you. I left the sexy lingerie at home and packed the flannel gown."

He sat on the bed and leaned his crutch against one of the posts.

I remained standing, and impulsively ran my hand over his damp curls. He caught the offending hand by the wrist and squinted up at me. "Don't do that, Chey."

I let my arm fall to my side. I glanced down and his bathrobe had come open, revealing his long, brown muscular legs. I quickly raised my eyes and took a step backward. "All right. I'm going downstairs to get my things from the truck; then I'll come back in and see about getting us some supper."

"That's a plan," he said, smiling at me.

I left. In the hallway, I paused to momentarily lean against the wall. My years of celibacy had left me entirely vulnerable to the beauty of the male body. This wasn't exactly an auspicious beginning. If I was going to be spending several nights only a few feet from Jackson and his overpowering sensuality, then I would have to mind my p's and q's.

Supper consisted of a chicken potpie Mrs. Anderson had left warming in the oven and a tossed salad.

Since it was easier for Jackson to maneuver in the kitchen rather than the dining room, we ate in the kitchen.

I'd also showered and changed after I'd moved my things into the bedroom adjacent to Jackson's.

I was wearing a University of Chicago sweatshirt and a pair of powder-blue Levi's. Jackson had opted for a crew-neck T-shirt in maroon and a pair of Wrangler's, one leg cut off to accommodate the cast. We were both wearing white athletic shoes. In Jackson's case: one shoe and one clean white sock on his right foot.

I was mindful of my movements as I served him. I stood to his left and spooned some of the chicken potpie onto his plate, not allowing any part of my body to come in contact with his.

"Cheyenne, sit down. My hands aren't broken. I can serve myself," he said, his voice tense.

I placed the serving spoon in the casserole dish and went and sat down. Our eyes met.

Jackson didn't say anything as he helped himself to the chicken potpie and then pushed the casserole closer to my side of the table. We continued watching each other as we began to eat the savory dish.

The chicken was tender, in a sauce that tasted buttery, and in every bite, a sweet pea burst between my teeth creating a crisp, sweet explosion in my mouth.

And the crust . . . the crust was a golden-brown and so tender and flaky that it disintegrated under your fork immediately upon touching it.

Jackson's eyes lowered to my mouth, and I licked a bit of sauce from my lips.

I continued eating, a faint smile working its way from my eyes to my lips. Jackson chewed slowly, his gaze never leaving my face. We didn't speak; we simply consumed the food on our plates and enjoyed the view.

Toward the end of the meal, I was smiling outright, and Jackson's eyes were caressing the curve of my breasts, in spite of the manly sweatshirt that adorned them.

He dropped his fork onto his nearly empty plate. The sudden cessation of silence surprised me and I jumped in my chair.

Frowning, Jackson said, "Look here, Chey. I'm only a man. This isn't working. You can sleep here tonight; but tomorrow, you have to go."

In his frustration, he knocked over his coffee mug. Black liquid spread onto the polished tabletop. I got up to get a dish towel from the rack over the sink. Going to his side of the table, I reached around him to wipe up the spill.

"I'm sorry," he said, his voice low and husky.

"Forget about it," I said absently. The enticing scent of him assailed my nostrils. I breathed deeply. It was then that I felt his hands on my waist. I let go of the towel and turned. His face was pressed to my midsection and I put my arms around him. Then I lowered my body until his nose was buried between my breasts.

The position was awkward because the broken leg was propped up on a chair; so I had to be careful not to bump into it as we clung together. However, he didn't seem to be in any discomfort as he murmured my name over and over.

"Chey, Chey, Chey . . . I need you so much. I'm afraid that when we finally make love, I won't be able to control myself and I might harm you in some way. Oh, God, help me," he said in anguished tones. "What if I turn out to be my father's son, after all?"

I took his face between my hands and we peered into each other's eyes. "I'm sure of one thing, Jackson, and that is: You'd never hurt me."

I put my arms around him and we remained that way a long while. Then he raised his eyes to mine, and said, "I was going to Billings that day to pick up your engagement ring, Chey. I was going to ask you to marry me on Christmas Eve."

My heart was so full, it was difficult to speak. He brushed the tears from my face. "I'm not going to wait any longer. I don't have the ring. It's paid for, but it's still at the jewelry store."

He gently touched my cheek, his eyes lovingly looking into my own. "Will you marry this broken down old cowboy, Chey?"

I nodded in the affirmative and kissed his lips. "Yes."

He removed his college class ring and put it on my thumb. It was way too big for any of my other fingers. "This'll have to do until I can get to Billings on my own two feet and get your ring."

I wiggled my thumb, peering at the huge gold University of Montana ring with the ruby setting. I returned my gaze to his. "I'm yours now."

Then, we kissed.

SEVENTEEN

That night, I lay in bed, unable to sleep. Twice, I heard Jackson walking about in his bedroom, the now familiar thump of his crutches a reassurance that he wasn't trying to get around without them, as Dave Carey had warned him against doing.

I'd set the thermostat at sixty-five degrees, so the temperature wasn't too warm for comfortable sleeping. Still, I didn't fall asleep until after two A.M.

I was fully in Morpheus' grip when I was awakened by the sound of Jackson shouting.

We'd agreed to leave our bedroom doors open so that if he should need something, I'd be able to hear him.

Therefore, I could make out every word he said. "I hate you! I hope you die. I can't wait until you're rotting in the grave. Rot in hell. I should have killed you myself years ago!"

Before I'd made a conscious decision to go to him, my feet were on the floor.

Running down the darkened hallway, I realized I'd forgotten to put on the robe that lay at the foot of my bed.

In his semidarkened bedroom, Jackson writhed in the throes of a nightmare, his arms up protecting his face as though he was trying to fend off the blows of an unseen assailant.

Risking getting slugged, I climbed onto the bed and grasped his arms, holding them down. "Jackson, wake up! You're dreaming."

I felt his muscles flex, and his eyes came open; he abruptly sat up, grabbed my arms with both hands and pushed me off him. I fell backward on the bed and promptly rolled onto the floor with a thud.

The sound of my body hitting the floor must have brought Jackson to his senses because he swung his broken leg off the bed, switched on the lamp on his nightstand, then lowered himself to the floor.

"God, Chey, are you hurt?"

My bottom was too well-padded to have sustained damage from the fall; besides, his pajama top was open and I was fairly preoccupied with his chest, scar and all.

"I'm fine."

He looked me over, as if he was unconvinced. His eyes lingered on my bare legs and thighs. "Where's the flannel nightgown?"

I tugged at the hem of my white nightie. It didn't help. "To put your mind at rest, I fudged the facts a little. I can't sleep in those things. I get hot during the night."

Jackson smiled. "Well, you might catch your death of cold in that," he said, admiring my long, brown, muscular limbs.

I got up on my knees, put my arm around his waist, and we slowly rose to our feet. Jackson sat down and I helped him swing his leg back up onto the bed. This done, I sat on the side of the bed and regarded him. "You want to tell me what you were dreaming about?"

I'd placed my hand on his chest, over his scar. The skin there was ridged and the scar itself was pink. But it had healed nicely and he wasn't experiencing pain when he breathed any longer.

"I suppose you need to know what kind of man you've promised to marry," he said, his voice low and controlled, and his warm brown eyes on my face. "The night my mother was killed, she came to me and told me she had something important to tell me. She was nervous and agitated. I couldn't imagine what she was going to say. Anyway, as you know, I'd recently graduated from college and I had plans to get on with another outfit and work and raise enough money to eventually buy my own place . . ."

"But as your parents' only child, didn't you stand to inherit this property?"

"I didn't *want* anything of his." The anger in his voice was raw and painful to hear.

I moved my hip against his. "Move over."

Giving me a confused look, he did. I snuggled against him and rested my head on his shoulder. "Go on."

He cleared his throat. "Anyway, the big secret Ma had to tell me was this: She'd been married before, to a man who drowned while fishing on the Yellowstone River. That man, Noah Hawk, was my father. Ma was three months pregnant when Noah drowned and she felt defenseless against certain men who'd made threats of taking her land, and doing things to her as well. So when she met Joseph Kincaid and he said he loved her, she married him for protection and to give me a father. This land, she said, belonged to me, and she wanted me to know it, should anything happen to her."

"What did she mean by, should anything happen to her?"

Jackson sighed, and it was a while before he spoke again.

"Apparently Joseph had threatened her. He despised me. He was incapable of having children. And all the years I thought he resented my mother because she couldn't give him more children, well that was just a cover for his deeper hatred of himself. Anyway, he didn't want to see me get my hands on this land. So he told Ma that if she ever told me the truth of my birth, he'd kill her."

It dawned on me then, the horror of what he was relating to me.

"The night they died, Joseph had been drinking. He came downstairs and announced he was going to the store to get more beer. You have to understand the dynamics of living with a man like Joseph. My mother didn't discourage his drinking. I think she felt when he was in his cups, at least he was out of *her* hair. Anyway, they had a routine: whenever he was drinking and wanted to go anywhere, she'd drive him. Therefore, when they got into the car, with my mother driving, I had seen it happen so many times before, I thought nothing of it."

"In the paper, it said *Joseph* was driving . . ." I began.

Jackson held me closer. "I know what the paper said, Chey. But I'm telling you: My mother was driving when they left the house. Don't you see? He made her give up the wheel; then he got into the driver's seat and purposely ran into that tree. He *meant* to kill her. He just killed himself, too, in the process."

"Oh my God," I cried as I sat up to look down into his face. "And you've blamed yourself for your mother's death all these years, haven't you?"

He looked away. "If I'd been thinking, instead of being stunned by what she'd just told me, I never would have let her get in that car. I should have known Joseph had eavesdropped on our conversation. I should have known that in his drunken state, he was capable of anything . . ."

I grabbed him by the lapels of his pajama top and made him face me. "How could you have known?" I exclaimed plaintively. My heart was breaking for him. Tears formed, blurring my vision.

To have spent the last thirteen years castigating himself for not being intuitive enough to sense Joseph's intentions, and thereby saving his mother from a horrible death . . . it was too much for one man to bear alone.

Jackson's arms went around me. "Baby, don't cry now. I couldn't take it . . ."

"She was so brave," I blubbered. I was remembering the story Momma had told me about Ginny. I'd thought of her as a timid, mousy woman with no backbone. Well, she'd loved her son more than life itself. She'd been willing to suffer the wrath of her brutal husband in order that Jackson would have his rightful inheritance.

I believe Jackson kissed me to silence my weeping; however, when his mouth touched mine, it incited another emotion that had been just below the surface anyway: passion.

My desire was to take away his pain. His was to comfort me. Our love for each other got in the way of good intentions.

Jackson found the strength to pull away, and his eyes were eloquent with longing when he looked up into my face. During the course of that long kiss, I'd straddled him and now I could feel his erection, through his pajama bottoms, on my thigh.

"I'm weak for you, Chey. Please, go back to your room now," he breathed, his eyes pleading with me.

"I don't think I can do that, Jackson," I told him honestly.

"I've got a broken leg. You're going to have to be the one to leave, Chey. Be reasonable. We decided we'd wait until marriage."

"*You* decided we'd wait until marriage," I corrected him as I ran my hands over his chest. I felt his body quiver. "I, on the other hand, consider us already married. I'm as much a part of you now, as I will be when we make it legal."

"You're going to have to marry me soon," Jackson said between clenched teeth as he reached up, grabbed me, and pulled me down for a soul-stirring kiss.

I moaned as the kiss deepened. I felt my body lose all tenseness and slide into a comfort zone that I'd never known before. My hands were on his torso, massaging his chest. When our lips came apart, I bent my head and kissed his scar. Jackson's hands were on my hips, gently squeezing.

His hand moved down to my thigh where he paused at the scar there. "I guess we've both been bruised and beaten the last few months," he said, his eyes looking intensely into my own. "I don't know how good I'm going to be tonight, Chey. Movement is cut down to a minimum with this leg . . ."

I placed a finger on his lips, silencing him. I then removed my nightie. He inhaled sharply and let out his breath slowly. I sat on his hips wearing only my bikini underwear. My breasts were full and firm, the nipples pointing north. To me, they were quite average, but the expression on his face told me I was mistaken. "I always knew you'd be beautiful, Chey, but you're absolutely exquisite."

My arousal quotient shot up even more when he said that. I felt an urgency to rush out of my clothes and tear his off so that nothing would be between us. Nothing to quell the sensations.

His work-roughened hands were tenderly caressing my breasts, awakening the buds, teasing them, causing my center to throb with the want of him. I arched my back, relishing the feel of his hands on them.

My eyes were closed when he bent his head and took a nipple into his mouth, his tongue manipulating it until I moaned with pleasure.

Then he moved on to the other one, taking his time, thoroughly immersed in the moment. My hands were on either side of his waist, holding on as he whipped me into a sexual frenzy.

"You're going to have to help me here, Chey," he murmured.

I opened my eyes and climbed off him. Then I unbuttoned his pajama bottoms and pulled them down and over the cast, tossing them onto a nearby chair. He got rid of the top, which had been hanging off him the whole while anyway.

Now, he was totally nude, his tumescent member, magnificent to behold. I smiled slowly. I'd been right, he was perfect from his well-shaped head to his toes.

He was watching me closely. I suppose he was waiting for the virgin to run the other way after seeing his male beauty. I was shivering slightly; but it wasn't from fear, it was from anticipation.

Still smiling at him, I slowly removed my bikini briefs and stood before him in all my glory. In his eyes, I saw my future. In his smile, resided his love for me. He held his hand out to me and I took it; whereupon, he pulled me on top of him. "It's too late to back out now, little girl."

"I've been riding all my life. There can't be that much of a difference," I joked.

Jackson laughed and pulled me down for a kiss. As I rained kisses on his neck and chest, he reached down to open the top drawer on his nightstand. Withdrawing a package of condoms, he handed it to me. "You do the honors."

I took the small box and got one foil-wrapped condom out and threw the box back into the open drawer. He closed it.

Tearing open the wrapper, I pulled the latex condom out and held it between my fingers. Then I held him in my hand and placed the condom on the tip.

"Turn it over," he instructed, smiling at my ignorance.

I rolled my eyes and did as I was told.

He moved in my hand as I rolled the condom onto him.

"Now what?"

"Now you get on and ride. Then you tell me if it was anything like riding a horse."

His hands were on my hips as I straddled him. I moved down further until I was directly on top of his manhood, which was fully erect by then. I felt the tip at the opening, and I panicked for a second. What if it hurt, and I cried out? Knowing Jackson, he would call the whole thing off and not come near me for a very long time.

Jackson pulled me down to kiss me softly. "Don't worry, it won't hurt. Like you said, you've been riding all your life. Your hymen was probably broken in your teens. But, take it slowly. Slow is good."

I tried again, and this time, a warmth pervaded my center, spreading until I felt as if I'd explode unless I had him inside of me. He was at the mouth, and then I pushed. It felt as though he was too big for me, but, soon, all of him was inside of me and I sighed with satisfaction.

Jackson smiled as he met my gaze. "That wasn't too bad, was it?"

Grinning dreamily, I said, "No . . ."

Then he thrust his body upward and a dazzling array of sensual responses shot through me. I thrust back and, then, we were pushing and pulling, his body going in and out of mine. I clung to him, and he groaned as if in pain. I cried out, still we continued. There was pleasurable sensation on top of pleasurable sensation.

It was at once too much for me, yet not enough. I rose and dipped, my body growing tense and peaking to a crescendo of kinetic energy. Then, the dam burst and every pleasure point on my body experienced nirvana. Spent, I collapsed on top of Jackson, my face on his chest. I felt his body spasm. Mine shivered delightfully.

He held me. "I promise, it'll be better when the cast comes off," he said a bit breathlessly.

"If it gets any better, I'll be a dead woman," I said, smiling into his eyes.

Jackson grinned. "So you like riding this horse?"

"Giddyup!"

Six weeks later, Jackson presented me with the engagement ring he'd chosen: a two-carat diamond solitaire in a white-gold setting. I'd been wearing his college class ring on a chain around my neck since he'd given it to me, and I'd been subjected to some cheap jokes from Chad about it, the worst being, "I hope he springs for a real wedding band, and doesn't give you the ring off a Coke can to wear."

Jackson had come out to the ranch to have dinner with the family that night, and we were all sitting around the table after dessert and coffee had been served.

Jackson got down on one knee beside my chair, and before all of my family, asked for my hand in marriage. Slim immediately responded with, "It's about time!" And Momma had tears in her eyes.

The wedding date was set for April 29, 2000, a little more than two months following the formal proposal.

The opening of the lodge was soon upon us. Dotty, Pete and the kids came out in March and stayed several days, met everyone, including Jackson of whom Dotty declared, "He's a walking dream, girl. No wonder you were saving yourself for him."

By the end of March, we were totally booked for the season, which would last from April until July.

The advertisement in the state of Montana's tourism brochure read like this: 3,600–ACRE WORKING RANCH WHERE NATURE'S BEAUTY ABOUNDS. FANTASTIC MEADOWS, PINE FORESTS, MEANDERING STREAMS. CLOSE TO THE YELLOWSTONE RIVER, WHERE YOU CAN GO TROUT FISHING. DAILY HORSEBACK RIDING. TASTEFULLY FURNISHED CABINS, EACH WITH ITS OWN FIREPLACE. HOME-COOKED MEALS. WE EAT BEEF HERE, BUT VEGETARIANS ARE WELCOME! ROBERTS RANCH AND LODGE (406) 555–2368.

The advertisement in national magazines, which had been targeted to African-American readers, read like this: 3,600–ACRE WORKING RANCH, OWNED AND OPERATED BY AFRICAN-AMERICAN FAMILY WHO HAS BEEN ON THE LAND FOR FIVE GENERATIONS. COME EXPERIENCE THE REAL WEST! FANTASTIC MEADOWS, PINE FORESTS, MEANDERING STREAMS. ON THE YELLOWSTONE RIVER WHERE YOU CAN GO TROUT FISHING. DAILY HORSEBACK RIDING. TASTEFULLY FURNISHED CABINS, EACH WITH ITS OWN FIREPLACE. SOUL FOOD. WE EAT BEEF HERE! BUT VEGETARIANS ARE WELCOME. PLEASE PHONE THE ROBERTS RANCH AND LODGE AT (406) 555–2368.

By mid-March we'd received so many calls, those whom we

couldn't talk into booking a reservation for the next season were reluctantly told we couldn't accommodate them.

On Saturday, April 1, Clancy and I were at the airport in Billings to pick up a family from Washington, DC, the Townsends. I'd spoken with the father, Spencer, a civil rights attorney, over the phone. He'd been quite explicit about what he was looking for in a vacation. A widower, his wife, Jeanne, had been killed by a carjacker less than a year ago, and since then, he said, he felt as if his children, a seventeen-year-old boy and an eleven-year-old girl, were drawing away from him. He wanted time alone with them in order to reconnect.

I'd explained to him about the solitude, and the genuine beauty of our property, and he'd said it sounded like heaven.

"I hope his son's cute," Clancy said. We were sitting in the waiting area. The Townsends' plane was due to arrive in less than ten minutes.

"What seventeen-year-old boy *isn't* cute?"

"Well then I hope he has a brain in his head," Clancy amended with a grin.

She and Chad were both preparing to graduate in June. She had matured quite a bit since I'd been back home. In the past, she had been preoccupied with leaving Montana forever; now she was more interested in college and what field to go into. She was diligent about school and all through her senior year, had maintained a 3.9, or better, grade point average. I was very proud of her.

The Townsends' plane arrived a few minutes late. I smiled when I saw the three of them. It was unlikely I'd mistake someone else for the small family, because they were exactly as Spencer Townsend had described over the phone: he was thirty-eight, six feet tall and lean. He wore his natural black hair in a short, conservative style. He had brown eyes, a broad nose, and a full-lipped mouth in his dark-brown face. He looked like a brother who was studious and hardworking.

His son, Kent, was an inch or so taller than his dad. He had the same rich, dark skin, but the shape of his mouth and nose were dissimilar to his father's. His light-brown eyes were almond-shaped; his mouth, full and heart-shaped.

The little girl, Sheryl, was lovely. I suppose she took after her mother. She had clear medium-brown skin that was the color of roasted almonds, and her doe eyes were dark, like her father's.

I walked up to Spencer Townsend and offered him my hand. "Hello, I'm Cheyenne Roberts."

His dark eyes rested on my face a few moments before he cleared his throat and smiled at me. "The voice on the phone."

"That's right," I said, my smile broadening. "Welcome to Montana."

Clancy was introducing herself to Kent and Sheryl as I spoke with Spencer. She had an easy rapport with children, and although I couldn't hear what she was saying to the brother and sister, I saw smiles on their faces where there had been looks of boredom.

"Thank you," Spencer said as he shook my hand. "We're looking forward to this vacation."

"Well we aim to make certain you enjoy yourselves," I assured him brightly. Reaching for his suit bag, I said, "Let me help you with that."

Clancy sat in the back with Kent and Sheryl on the return trip to the ranch and Spencer sat up front with me as I drove.

"This is beautiful country," Spencer said, admiring the scenery as we sped along at fifty-five miles per hour. "It must have been wonderful to grow up around here."

"It was never dull," I returned. "We grew up working the ranch. Going on cattle drives, roping, branding, salting, doctoring, calving in spring and winter. It could be a hard life. But very satisfying."

He was observing me closely. "I believe you," he said, his voice low. He was quiet for a while, then he said, "I noticed you're wearing a diamond solitaire. Did you recently become engaged?"

Jackson's image came to mind, and I smiled. "Yes. We're getting married at the end of the month."

"Congratulations. He's a lucky man."

"I'm the lucky one," I said softly.

The other guests, all African-American, had arrived the day before. They were: Angela and Terrance Hinsdale, a middle-aged couple on a their yearly quest to put more spice into their marriage. Then there were the honeymooners, Fraser and Veronica Mosby, from Des Moines, Iowa. And, finally, the occupant of Cabin D was Miss Amanda Wise, a woman in her seventies who'd always wanted to learn to ride. She was from Queens, NY, and was a successful mystery writer. When I'd shown her to her cabin, she'd told me that learning to ride was number twenty-seven on her list of things to do before she departed this world. I found her fascinating.

We'd hired two local boys, Lance Welch, nineteen, and Tommy Davis, twenty, to help with the trail rides and fishing excursions. Clancy, Chad and Lucas still had to attend school during the week, but they all had weekend duties. Momma and I were the only full-time staff members. Momma did the cooking, and I had various tasks, which included taking the guests on trail rides, cleaning the cabins and doing the books. After the first season, we were going to hire a full-time maid to come in and do the cleaning.

As for meals, the guests had the option of preparing their own meals in the fully equipped kitchens in their cabins, or joining the family in the main house for breakfast, dinner and supper.

That first week, we had meals with the Hinsdales, the Townsends and Miss Wise on a regular basis, but we rarely saw the Mosbys.

Clancy had taken them grocery shopping, but she said she didn't know how they subsisted on that amount of food for an entire week.

The Spring Roundup Dance was scheduled for the end of the week, the seventh, a Friday. A family-oriented event, we invited all of the guests to attend, explaining that the dress was semi-casual. Cowboy boots optional.

The guests were given a schedule of activities, and if they so desired, they could join in the fun. If not, they were free to simply remain in their cabins or, after telling someone where they were going, take a stroll in the woods.

The Hinsdales loved long walks in the woods, and Terrance went fishing a couple of times, bringing back a mess of catfish, which I had to show him how to clean and prepare for the pan.

Miss Wise was given personal riding lessons by Clancy who not only had a penchant for reaching children, but also loved the elderly. And Kent Townsend started showing up wherever Clancy happened to be. One day, I spotted him leaning against the corral, watching as Clancy put Miss Wise through her paces as the city woman sat upon Susie, who was being especially patient with her rider.

For some reason, Sheryl, Spencer's daughter, formed an attachment to me. When I was scheduled to take the guests on a trail ride, she would be in the group. Often, she'd persuade her father, who appeared to be more fond of fishing, to go with us.

On Thursday afternoon, Sheryl, her father, the Hinsdales and I were riding in the western section of the property. I was leading them through a pine forest to Slim's favorite spot, where we'd dismount and enjoy a packed lunch near the stream.

Sheryl rode next to me. I sensed she wanted to say something to me and I turned to smile at her. "How are you and Susie getting along?"

She grinned and ran her hand over Susie's flaxen mane. "She's so pretty. I wish I had a horse just like her back home."

"Do you live in the suburbs?"

"No, we live in an apartment in the city," she said wistfully. "I wish we lived someplace like this all the time."

I was pleased she was enjoying her stay with us, but I'd also detected a note of sadness and longing in her voice. She'd lost her mother less than a year ago. She was understandably melancholy.

I pointed ahead of us. "See that? It's called Tucker's Creek. Many years ago, my grandfather's two-year-old brother, Tucker, fell into the water and the current took him downstream to the Yellowstone River where some fishermen pulled him out, safe and sound. It was a miracle. Ever since then, it's been known as Tucker's Creek."

Later, Spencer, Sheryl and I sat together on a blanket near the bank of the stream. The Hinsdales sat a few feet away, their heads together, engrossed in intimate conversation.

"I want you to know how much we've enjoyed ourselves these last few days," Spencer said to me, his dark eyes on my face. He smiled and reached over to gently follow his daughter's jawline with a finger. "Isn't that right, honey?"

Sheryl's light-brown eyes met mine. "I love it here," she said with a sweet smile. Then, she asked her father cajolingly, "Daddy, may I follow the stream and see where it leads?"

"Okay," Spencer said, "but don't go far and be careful you don't fall in. It's a cool day and you might catch cold."

"Oh, Daddy!" Sheryl exclaimed with a grin as she got to her feet and left us.

"She misses her mother terribly," Spencer said in her absence.

"I can see it in her eyes and hear it in her voice," I said before thinking. My heart went out to Sheryl. I knew what it was like to lose a parent. "My father was killed while on a cattle drive nearly eight years ago. So I can sympathize with what she's going through. It was so sudden. Violent. Senseless."

"But you seem to have gotten it together," Spencer said, cocking his head in a bid to get me to meet his eyes.

I looked up at him. "It's taken me years to come to terms with it. And I don't think I'll ever be that carefree girl again. But, I *am* happy."

He glanced at my engagement ring. "And the fellow who gave you that is largely responsible, I gather?"

I smiled. "A hundred years with him wouldn't be long enough."

"Now that's something *I* know about," Spencer said, stretching his legs out and getting more comfortable. "Jeanne was the best thing that ever happened to me. . . ."

We sat for several minutes while he told me all about Jeanne, who had been an English literature professor at Howard University. And when he'd finished, I knew the depth of his loss.

Sheryl returned and plopped down between her father and me. "Cheyenne, your grandpa told me that this area was near where Custer bought it . . ."

"Sheryl, where do you get that sort of language from?" her father reprimanded her.

"All the kids talk that way, Daddy," Sheryl said as though her father was so behind the times, he'd never catch up.

"As a matter of fact," I said, hoping to curtail an argument, "in 1876, around 260 soldiers were killed by an underestimated force of Sioux and Cheyenne warriors. I can take you to the Little Bighorn Battlefield National Monument, it's near Hardin, if you care to go."

"Can we, Daddy?" Sheryl asked excitedly, her eyes sparkling.

Spencer looked at me. "The dance is tomorrow night, isn't it Cheyenne? You must have a long list of things to do, without having to take us on a field trip."

"We can go in the morning, at around ten, and be back in plenty of time to get ready for the dance," I assured him.

The night of the dance, the whole Roberts family had dates, except for yours truly. Momma was going with Harry, who was picking her up. Clancy and Kent were a couple. Slim had been talked into going by Miss Wise who found the cantankerous old cowboy to be a fount of information on the Old West, where she was setting her next mystery. And Slim thought she was a handsome woman.

Both Chad and Lucas were bringing dates. It was the first time we'd actually get to meet the women they were dating, so that was something to look forward to.

When I'd reminded Jackson about the dance, he'd come up with the excuse of having to stay close to the ranch because he had a mare about to foal. I knew the real reason though. He didn't dance. I was willing to overlook it. He did so many things well. I was not one to harp on the things he didn't do as competently.

I just wanted him by my side.

At the dance, which was held in the local Veterans of Foreign Wars hall, Spencer was gracious enough to serve as my date for the night. Between me and Sheryl, he was constantly on the dance floor.

The Hinsdales, who seemed to have rekindled the romantic fires of their marriage, danced all the slow dances with their cheeks pressed together, and contented smiles on their faces.

Even the Mosbys left their cabin long enough to join us. They were equally inseparable that night.

The whole town was represented. There was a mixture of African-Americans, Native Americans and European Americans, all enjoying the music of a seven-member band that played standards, country-western and the occasional rhythm and blues piece.

When Momma and Harry took the dance floor, I looked around to see if there would be a reaction from the other couples. No one blinked an eye. I relaxed in Spencer's arms as we gyrated to the band's rendition of Garth Brooks' "The Dance."

I knew the song well; it spoke of missed chances, and what a person gives up when they choose wealth over the things that really matter in life, such as family and true love.

Halfway through the song, a man walked up behind Spencer and tapped him on the shoulder. "Mind if I cut in?" he asked in a deep, resonant voice.

Spencer kindly stepped aside as Jackson, dressed in a crisp white shirt, bolo tie and Wrangler's, pulled me into this arms.

He smiled down at me. "This isn't so bad."

"What did you think it would be like, torture?" I inquired, totally delighted to see him.

"To tell the truth, I was just always a little afraid of looking stupid."

"Mmm huh. So what changed your mind?"

He pulled me closer. "Well, I came to the conclusion that if you were willing to give up your life in Chicago for love, then the least I could do is learn to dance."

With that, he spun me around and dipped me. When I came back up, safe and secure in the crook of his arm, I knew that everything I'd done to be there at that moment had been well worth it.

"Wait a minute," I said suddenly, my jealous streak raising its ugly head. "Who gave you lessons?"

Jackson laughed. "Your mother."

"So that's where she'd been disappearing to the last few evenings," I said, laughing along with him.

"Yeah," Jackson explained. "She told me no daughter of hers was getting married to a man with two left feet. So she whipped me into shape." He pressed his cheek to mine. "Happy?"

"Nearly as happy as *you're* going to be later," I said, smiling.

About the Author

Janice Sims, a native Floridian, is the author of four full-length Arabesque novels and one novella.

A writer the majority of her life, she's written countless poems and short stories. And, recently, has set out to learn the art of writing for the silver screen.

She lives in Central Florida with her family.

Janice enjoys hearing from her readers. For a prompt reply, enclose a self-addressed, stamped envelope.

Janice Sims
P.O. Box 811
Mascotte, FL 34753–0811

CAPTIVATING ROMANCE BY *MARGIE WALKER*

BREATHLESS   0-7860-126-7 $4.99US/$6.50CAN
When Monique Robbins's classy Houston nightclub is plagued by mysterious thefts, she hires Solomon Thomas to help her. He's so arrogant . . . and so handsome that he takes her breath away. Now, together, Solomon and Monique fight a growing threat and find a way to be equals—in business and in love.

CONSPIRACY   0-7860-0385-5 $4.99US/$6.50CAN
Pauline Sinclair and Marcellus Cavanaugh had the love of a life-time—until she left. When she returns, so does their romance. But when the President of Marcellus's company turns up dead and Pauline is the prime suspect, they must risk all to save the love that none are willing to lose again.

INDISCRETIONS   0-7860-0279-4 $4.99US/$6.50CAN
Sydney Webster returns home to Texas only to find that her sister's fiancé is dead and Sydney herself is the prime suspect! To clear her name, she needs the help of defense attorney Perry MacDonald. For Perry, cases like this don't come along every day . . . and neither do women as lovely as Sydney.

PUBLIC AFFAIR   0-7860-0501-7 $4.99US/$6.50CAN
After Marlena Lord decides to run for her father's former congressional seat, she becomes involved in both politics and danger. When she meets real estate developer Miles Chases, she finds herself in a different kind of danger—heartbreak.

A SWEET REFRAIN   0-7860-0041-4 $4.99US/$6.50CAN
Teacher Jenine Jones once had a brief taste of love . . . until jazz musician Nathaniel Padell left Texas to seek fame and fortune in New York City. Now he's back, with a baby girl. When an unexpected danger threatens his child, Jenine must fight for Nate and their new-found love, before someone stops the music forever.

USE COUPON ON NEXT PAGE TO ORDER THESE BOOKS

OWN THESE NEW ARABESQUE ROMANCES!

__*ONE LOVE* by Lynn Emery
1-58314-046-8   **$4.99US/$6.99CAN**

When recovering alcoholic Lanessa Thomas is reunited with the only man she ever loved, and the man she hurt the most, Alex St. Romain, she is determined to ignore her temptations. But when Lanessa's hard-won stability is threatened, both she and Alex must battle unresolved pain and anger in order to salvage their second chance at love.

__*DESTINED* by Adrienne Ellis Reeves
1-58314-047-6   **$4.99US/$6.99CAN**

Teenage newlywed Leah Givens was shocked when her father tore her away from bridal bliss and accused her husband Bill Johnson of statutory rape. His schemes kept them apart for thirteen years, but now Bill's long search for his lost love is over. Now the couple must struggle to heal the scars of their past and surrender to their shared destiny.

__*IMPETUOUS* by Dianne Mayhew
1-58314-043-3   **$4.99US/$6.50CAN**

Four years ago, Liberty Sutton made the worst mistake of her life when she gave up her newborn. But just as handsome Jarrett Irving enters her life, she's given the chance to reclaim a life with her child. Trying to reconcile her past with her promising future will take luck and love.

__*UNDER A BLUE MOON* by Shirley Harrison
1-58314-049-2   **$4.99US/$6.99CAN**

After being attacked at sea, Angie Manchester awakens on an exotic island with amnesia—and Dr. Matthew Sinclair at her side. Thrown together by chance, but drawn by desire, the puzzle of Angie's identity and Matt's own haunted past keeps a wall between the two until the thugs return. Forced to hide in the lush forest, their uncontrollable passion finally ignites.

Call toll free **1-888-345-BOOK** to order by phone or use this coupon to order by mail.

Name _____

Address _____

City _____ State _____ Zip _____

Please send me the books I have checked above.

I am enclosing $_____
Plus postage and handling* $_____
Sales tax (in NY, TN, and DC) $_____
Total amount enclosed $_____

*Add $2.50 for the first book and $.50 for each additional book.

Send check or money order (no cash or CODs) to: **Arabesque Books c/o Kensington Publishing Corp., 850 Third Avenue, New York, NY 10022**

Prices and Numbers subject to change without notice.

All orders subject to availability.

Check out our website at **www.arabesquebooks.com**

WARM YOUR SOUL WITH ARABESQUE . . .
THESE ROMANCES ARE NOW ALSO MOVIES ON BET!

INCOGNITO
by Francis Ray   (0-7860-0364-2, $4.99/$6.50)
Erin Cortland, owner of a successful advertising firm, witnessed a horrifying crime and lived to tell about it. Frightened, she runs into the arms of Jake Hunter, the man hired to protect her. He doesn't want the job. He left the police force because a similar assignment ended in tragedy. But when he learns that more than one man is after her and that he is falling in love, he will risk anything—even his life—to protect her.

INTIMATE BETRAYAL
by Donna Hill   (0-7860-0396-0, $4.99/$6.50)
Investigative reporter, Reese Delaware, and millionaire computer wizard, Maxwell Knight are both running from their pasts. When Reese is assigned to profile Maxwell, they enter a steamy love affair. But when Reese begins to piece her memory, she stumbles upon secrets that link her and Maxwell, and threaten to destroy their newfound love.

RENDEZVOUS
by Bridget Anderson   (0-7860-0485-1, $4.99/$6.50)
Left penniless after her no-good husband turned up murdered, Jade Bassett was running from the murderer whom she knows was intent on killing her as well. On the streets of Atlanta she had nowhere to turn to until she encountered successful graphic designer, Jeff Nelson. Can she trust the handsome stranger promising to give her back her life?